B...
Sh...
liv...
at...

Pr...

'T... ...ve affairs . . .
un...able' Adriana Trigiani

'A sweeping saga' *Glamour*

'Secrets, mystery and passion run through the book and you feel you are actually in the Tuscan and Devonshire countrysides . . . a great read and perfect to take on holiday – I loved it and couldn't put it down' *New Books Magazine*

Praise for Santa Montefiore:

'Santa Montefiore is the new Rosamunde Pilcher' *Daily Mail*

'A superb storyteller of love and death in romantic places in fascinating times – her passionate novels are already bestsellers across Europe and I can see why. Her plots are sensual, sensitive and complex, her characters are unforgettable life forces, her love stories are desperate yet uplifting – and one laughs as much as one cries' Plum Sykes, *Vogue*

'A gripping romance . . . it is as believable as the writing is beautiful' *Daily Telegraph*

'Anyone who likes Joanne Harris or Mary Wesley will love Montefiore' *Mail on Sunday*

'One of our personal favourites and bestselling authors, sweeping stories of love and families spanning continents and decades' *The Times*

'The novel displays all Mo... ...memorable characters, an... ...yearning love and surging ...passion' Wendy Holden, *Sunday Express*

'Engaging and charming' Penny Vincenzi

Santa Montefiore

The House By The Sea

**SIMON &
SCHUSTER**

London · New York · Sydney · Toronto · New Delhi

A CBS COMPANY

First published in Great Britain by Simon & Schuster UK Ltd, 2011
A CBS COMPANY

This paperback edition first published 2012

20

Simon & Schuster UK Ltd
1st Floor
222 Gray's Inn Road
London WC1X 8HB

www.simonandschuster.co.uk

Simon & Schuster Australia, Sydney
Simon & Schuster India, New Delhi

A CIP catalogue record for this book
is available from the British Library

Paperback ISBN 978-1-84983-106-2
Ebook ISBN 978-1-84737-932-0

This book is a work of fiction. Names, characters, places and incidents
are either a product of the author's imagination or are used fictitiously.
Any resemblance to actual people, living or dead,
events or locales, is entirely coincidental.

Typeset by M Rules
Printed and bound by CPI Group (UK) Ltd, Croydon, CR0 4YY

To my darling Sebag, with love

Acknowledgments

I couldn't have written this book without the help of two very special people. Firstly, my husband, Sebag. I knew my story, but I couldn't work out how to fit all the pieces of my plot together. Sebag paced up and down the kitchen floor of our cottage while I hugged a mug of tea and wrote notes. We tossed about ideas as the day melted into evening ... and then the plot began to take shape. Finally, as the moon settled high in the sky and the owls began to hoot, we put it to bed — exhausted! However, there was one problem — good though we thought it was, we couldn't work out how to pull off the central twist.

For such a technical problem I needed an expert. I called upon the experience of my old university friend, Charlie Carr — an investigator. Thank you, Charlie, for slicing through the Gordian knot — it seems so simple in retrospect, but all the best plots do! I couldn't have done it without you.

And thank you, Sebag, for once again being my Sherlock Holmes.

A large part of this story takes place in Tuscany. I lived in Italy in my early twenties but that doesn't prevent me from making terrible errors. So, I sought the help of my trusty Italian friends. I thank them all: Eduardo Teodorani Fabbri, Stefano Bonfiglio and Sofia Barattieri di san Pietro.

When I was considering where to set my story, I went to stay with Olga Polizzi at her enchanting country house hotel, Endsleigh. There is something magical about Endsleigh. Snuggled deep in the Devon countryside it is built above a winding river and sheltered by ancient trees. Olga has great flair and warmth so Endsleigh feels more like a home than a hotel – and I felt right at home there! It was autumn. Giant log fires filled the rooms with the cosy smell of wood-smoke and clusters of tea lights in purple glass tumblers glowed on every surface. The atmosphere was soft and embracing and I didn't want to leave.

So, I have based my hotel, the Polzanze, on Endsleigh, and hope that I have channelled some of its spirit. I thank Olga for inspiring me because with two small children it's hard for me to travel, so inspiration is in short supply – I have to rely on memories. But there is nothing as invigorating as discovering new and wonderful places.

Everything I write comes out of the great big cauldron that contains all my life's experiences. If it is rich it is thanks to my parents, Charles and Patty Palmer-Tomkinson. I couldn't have written a single word without their wisdom, guidance and love.

I want to give special thanks to my agent, Sheila Crowley. Tireless in her support and always positive, she's a valuable ally and a good friend. The team at Curtis Brown are buzzing with energy and enthusiasm and I thank them all for the work they do on my behalf.

I am fortunate enough to be published by Simon & Schuster both sides of the Atlantic. I have two dynamic editors, Suzanne Baboneau in the UK and Trish Todd in the USA. Both steer me in the right direction and bring out the best that I can give. I'm so grateful for their belief in my writing and their astute and sensitive editing.

I would also like to thank Libby Yevtushenko for working so hard on the manuscript and improving it with intelligence and tact.

The House
By The Sea

Prologue

Tuscany 1966

The little girl stood outside the imposing black gates of Villa La Magdalena and peered up the drive. A long avenue of cypresses cut straight through the grounds, climaxing at the end in a tantalizing glimpse of a primrose-yellow palazzo. La Magdalena sat with the dignity and poise of a grand empress. Her tall, shuttered windows were an elegant teal green, her crown a decorative balustrade built along the top of the façade, her walls as resplendent as silk; she belonged to a world as enchanting and inaccessible as fairy tales.

The bright Tuscan sun threw inky shadows across the drive and the little girl could smell the sweet scents of the garden that rose in the heat and saturated the air. She stood in her sandals and grubby sundress, her long brown hair matted with dust and sea water, hanging down her back and over her eyes, which were dark and troubled and full of craving. Around her neck she wore a Virgin Mary pendant her mother had given her before running off with a man she had met over the tomato stall in Piazza Laconda, taking her younger brother with them.

The little girl came to La Magdalena often. She liked to climb the wall where a part of it had crumbled, leaving it low enough for her to scale. She'd sit on the top and survey the beautiful gardens of stone fountains, graceful umbrella pines and marble statues of elegant ladies and semi-naked men twisted into theatrical poses of love and longing. She liked to imagine that *she* lived there surrounded by such heavenly splendour – a young lady with expensive dresses and sparkly shoes, cherished by a mother who threaded her hair with ribbons, and a father who indulged her with presents and tossed her into the air before catching her in his strong, protective arms; she came to La Magdalena to forget her own drunken father and the little apartment on Via Roma that she struggled to keep clean.

Her small hands gripped the bars and she squeezed her face between them to get a better look at the boy who was now walking towards her, accompanied by a mongrel dog. She knew he was going to tell her to go away, so she wanted to get a good look first, before running back down the path that snaked its way to the beach.

The boy was handsome, much older than she, with fair hair brushed off his forehead and a kind face. He appraised her with pale, smiling eyes and on closer inspection she could see that they were green. She stood her ground, daring herself to remain until the very last moment. Her fingers curled around the bars and she clenched her jaw in determination, but his grin disarmed her; it didn't look like the expression of a person about to shoo her away. He put his hands in his pockets and examined her through the gate.

'Hello there.'

She said nothing. Her head told her to flee, but her legs wouldn't listen. She remained staring at him, unable to tear her eyes away.

'Do you want to come in?' His invitation caught her off guard and she straightened up suspiciously. 'You're obviously curious.'

'I was just passing,' she replied.

'So you *can* speak.'

'Of course I can speak.'

'I wasn't sure at first. You looked so frightened.'

'I'm not frightened of you, if that's what you mean.'

'Good.'

'I was just on my way somewhere.'

'That's funny, we're rather isolated here.'

'I know that. I was on the beach.' Which was true, at least.

'So you just wandered up to have a look?'

'It's so pretty. It caught my attention.' Her face brightened at the mention of the villa and her eyes strayed longingly up the drive.

'Then come in and I'll show you around the gardens. My family isn't here so I'm alone. It'll be nice to have someone to talk to.'

'I don't know . . .' Her eyes darkened again, but he opened the gate.

'Don't be afraid. I'm not going to hurt you.'

'I'm not afraid,' she retorted. 'I can look after myself, you know.'

'I'm sure you can.'

She stepped in and he closed the gate behind her. She watched him lock it and her heart lurched a moment with anxiety, but then her gaze was drawn back to the villa and she forgot her fear. 'Do you live here?'

'Not all the time. I live in Milan mostly, but we summer here every year.'

'Then I will have seen you.'

'Really?'

Her excitement at being in the grounds gave her courage. 'Yes, I spy from the wall.'

'You little devil.'

'I like to look at the gardens. The people don't interest me so much.'

'Then I'll give you a better look so you won't have to spy any more.'

She walked beside him, her heart now swelling with pleasure. 'Is all this really yours?'

'Well, my father's.'

'If this is your summer house, your house in Milan must be built for a king.'

He laughed, tossing back his head. 'It's big, but not big enough for a king. This is bigger. There's more space in the countryside.'

'It's old, isn't it?'

'Fifteenth century. It was built by the Medici family, designed by Leon Battista Alberti in 1452. Do you know who he was?'

'Of course I do.'

'How old are you?'

'Ten and ten months. My birthday's in August. I suppose I'll have a big party.'

'I'm sure you will.'

She looked down at her feet. She had never had a party. Now her mother had gone, no one would even remember her birthday. 'What's your dog called?'

'Good-Night.'

'That's a funny name.'

'He was a stray I found on the road in the middle of the night. We bonded immediately, so I called him Good-Night, because it was a good night, finding him.'

She bent down to stroke him. 'What is he?'

'I don't know. A mixture of lots of different breeds.'

'He's sweet.' She giggled as the dog licked her face. 'Whoa, steady there, doggie!'

'He likes you.'

'I know. Stray animals always like me.'

Because you look like a stray yourself, he thought, watching her wrap her arms around Good-Night's neck and rest her head against his fur.

'I've made a friend,' she said with a triumphant smile.

He laughed at her exuberance. 'No, you've made two. Come on.'

They walked the full length of the drive side by side, her confidence growing with each step. He explained the architecture, showing off his knowledge, and she listened enraptured by every detail, trying to remember in order to later tell her friend, Costanza. The villa was even bigger than she had thought. She had seen only the central part between the trees at the end of the avenue. It had two other wings not quite as tall as the bit in the middle but just as wide. Classically proportioned and unfussy, it had an understated grandeur, the yellow paint giving it a happy, complacent look as if it knew it didn't have to try at being beautiful. She longed to go inside, to walk through the rooms and gaze at the paintings that hung on the walls. She was sure it was even more wonderful than the outside. But he took her round to the back where a sweeping stone staircase descended from the villa into a formal garden of statues, terracotta pots of topiary and lofty pines. It was as though she had died and now walked through paradise, for surely only Heaven could be as beautiful as this?

He directed her through a small gate in the wall, into a pretty ornamental garden settled within a circular stone colonnade. The centrepiece was a glorious fountain of mermaids throwing water into the air. Around the fountain a path was planted haphazardly with thyme, and pretty iron benches were set on all four sides against low hedges that boxed four neatly trimmed lawns and flowerbeds. She took a while to take it all in, standing there in her sandals, clutching her heart because she had never before seen so much splendour.

'This is my mother's garden,' he told her. 'She wanted a place where she could read in private without being spied on.' He winked at her and laughed again. 'You'd have to be a very accomplished spy to get in here.'

'I bet your mother's pretty,' she said, thinking of her own mother and trying to remember what she looked like.

'She is, I suppose. One doesn't really think of one's mother in that way.'

'Where does she read?'

'I think she probably sits on one of these benches, by the fountain. I don't know. I've never bothered to notice.' He ambled over, suddenly infected with the little girl's wonder. 'It *is* rather lovely, isn't it?'

'Imagine sitting here in the sunshine, listening to the trickling water and watching the birds washing themselves in it.'

'It's very peaceful.'

'I love birds. I bet you have many birds here. Different ones, probably, from those we have in town.'

He laughed incredulously. 'I think you'll find the same old birds as the ones you have in Herba.'

'No, you'll have special ones in here.' She was so certain, he looked around, half expecting to see parrots in the pine trees. 'Do you ever sit here?'

'No.'

'Why not?'

He shrugged. 'What would I do?'

'Oh, there's plenty to look at. I could sit in here for hours – days even. I could sit in here for ever and never want to leave.' She carefully lowered herself onto the bench as if it were a sacred thing she was afraid might break. Once sitting, she watched the water and imagined having a garden of her own where she could enjoy the changing light from dawn till dusk. 'God is in here,' she said softly, feeling a strange sense of awe creep over her skin, like the warm breath of an angel.

He sat beside her and stretched out his legs, putting his hands behind his head. 'Do you think?'

'Oh, I know. I can feel Him.'

They sat there a long time, listening to the breeze in the

cypress trees and the doves contentedly cooing on the roof of the villa. Good–Night sniffed the borders, cocking his leg against the hedge.

'This is the best day of my life,' she said after a while. 'I don't think I've ever been so happy.'

He looked at her curiously, a tender smile curling his lips. 'What's your name, *piccolina*?'

She looked back at him, her eyes full of gratitude and trust. 'Floriana,' she replied. 'And you?'

Somehow, they both knew that exchanging names *meant* something. He hesitated, staring into her gaze, that was now open and no longer afraid. He held out his hand. Tentatively she took it. Hers looked small and dark in his big pale one.

'Dante Alberto Massimo,' he said softly. 'But you can call me Dante.'

Chapter 1

Devon 2009

ARTIST WANTED

TO SPEND THE SUMMER

TEACHING RESIDENTS TO PAINT

AT THE HOTEL POLZANZE, DEVON

FREE BOARD & LODGING

TELEPHONE: 07972 859 301

The Morris Minor rattled down the narrow lane towards the village of Shelton. The hedgerows were high and luxuriant, laced with pretty white cow parsley and forget-me-nots. A spray of sparrows took to the sky where feathery clouds floated inland on a salty wind. The car moved cautiously, swerving into a lay-by to avoid an oncoming lorry, then continued through the quaint hamlet of whitewashed cottages whose grey-tiled roofs shone like gold in the enthusiastic glare of dawn.

In the heart of Shelton a grey stone church huddled among a cluster of magnificent plane trees, and below, a sleek black cat trotted lithely along the wall, returning home from a success-ful night's hunting. At the end of the village, as the lane turned sharply to the left before descending to the sea, a pair of imposing iron gates opened onto a narrow drive that swept in a graceful curve through banks of rhododendron bushes, already in bloom. The car turned in and made its way past fat pink flowers to the grey stone mansion at the end, positioned in splendid seclusion overlooking the sea.

The Polzanze was a harmoniously proportioned mansion built in 1814 by the Duke of Somerland for his whimsical wife, Alice, whose asthma benefited from the sea air. He demolished the old building, an unsightly pile of bricks dating back to the sixteenth century, and designed the present house with the help of his talented wife who had strong ideas of what she wanted. The result was a mansion that felt like a large cottage on the inside, with wood panelled walls, floral wallpapers, log fires and big latticed windows that looked onto the lawn and the ocean beyond.

The duchess adored her garden and spent her summers cultivating roses, planting exotic trees and designing an intricate maze of walkways through the lush woodland. She constructed a small garden for her children outside her study, where they could grow vegetables and flowers, and edged it with a miniature aqueduct so that they could float their boats in the water while she wrote her letters. Enamoured of Italy, she decorated her terrace with heavy terracotta pots of rosemary and lavender, and planted vines in the conservatory, training them to climb the trellises so that the grapes hung from the ceiling in dusty clusters.

Little had changed and much had been enhanced by her descendants, who added to the beauty of the place with their own flair and extravagance until they fell on hard times and were forced to sell in the early 1990s. The Polzanze had been converted into a hotel, which would have broken Alice's heart had she lived to see it. But her legacy remained, as did much of the original hand-painted wallpaper of birds and butterflies.

The cedar tree that sheltered the east side was reputed to be over five hundred years old, and the grounds boasted an ancient walled vegetable garden, built long before the duchess arrived to cultivate rhubarb and raspberries – as well as an ancient gardener who had been there longer than anyone could remember.

Marina heard a car draw up on the gravel outside and hurried to the first-floor window. She peered through the glass to see a dirty old Morris Minor, stuffed with canvases and paint-stained dustsheets, stall in front of the hotel like an exhausted mule. Her heart accelerated with anticipation and she hastily checked herself in the mirror on the landing. A little over fifty, she was at the height of her beauty, as if time had danced lightly across her face, barely leaving a footprint. Her luscious honey-brown hair tumbled over her shoulders in waves and her eyes were deep set and engaging, the colour of smoky quartz. Petite, with small bones and a narrow waist, she was none the less curvaceous, with wide hips and a generous bosom. She smoothed down her dress and fluffed up her hair, and hoped that she'd make a good impression.

'Marina darling, it looks like your first potential artist-in-residence has arrived,' exclaimed her husband, Grey Turner, peering through the glass and chuckling as an elderly man stepped onto the gravel in a long brocaded coat and black breeches, his scuffed shoes decorated with large brass buckles that glinted weakly in the spring sunshine.

'Good Lord, it's Captain Hook!' remarked Clementine, Grey's twenty-three-year-old daughter, who joined him at the window. She screwed up her nose in disdain. 'Why Submarine wants to invite a painter to sponge off us every summer is beyond me. It's very pretentious to have an artist-in-residence.'

Grey ignored the disrespectful nickname his children had coined for their stepmother. 'Marina has a good nose for business,' he said mildly. 'Paul Lockwood was a great success last year, our guests loved him. It's only natural that she should want to repeat it.'

'She might change her mind when she sees this old sea-dog!'

'Do you think he has a parrot tucked away with all that luggage?' Grey continued, watching the old man walk stiffly round to the boot and pull out a shabby portfolio.

'I think most certainly, Dad – and a ship moored down at the quay. At least he doesn't have a hook for a hand.'

'Marina will think he's delightful. She loves eccentrics.'

'Do you think that's why she married *you*?'

Grey straightened up and put his hands in his pockets. He was very tall with curly, greying hair and a long, sensitive face. He looked down at his daughter and shook his head. 'Don't forget you carry my genes, Clemmie. If I'm eccentric, there's a good chance that you have inherited the same flaw.'

'I wouldn't consider it a flaw, Dad. There's nothing more boring than regular people. Mind you,' she added, as the artist closed the boot. 'You can have too much of a good thing.'

'He's here! How exciting!' Marina joined her husband and stepdaughter at the window. Clementine watched her joy deflate as she laid eyes on her first candidate, staggering towards the entrance with his artwork tucked under his moth-eaten sleeve, and felt a small swell of pleasure.

'My God!' Marina exclaimed, throwing up her hands. 'What am I going to do?'

'Too late now, darling. You'd better show him in or he might draw his sword.' Marina implored her husband with a desperate look, but he shook his head and laughed at her affectionately, digging his hands deeper into the pockets of his corduroy trousers. 'This is your project. I know how you hate me to interfere.'

'Why don't you interview him with me?' She tried to seduce him with a grin.

'Oh, no, darling, he's all yours.'

'You're a wicked, wicked man, Grey Turner,' she retorted, but her lips curled at the corners as she took her place in the middle of the hall by the round table and extravagant flower display, while Shane Black, the porter, helped the old man in with his portfolio.

Ignoring the amused faces congregated at the window – for by now Jennifer, one of the receptionists, and Heather, a waitress, had found an excuse to come into the hall – Marina smiled at her first candidate warmly, extending her hand. His was rough and calloused, his fingernails ingrained with old paint. He seized hers with a firm grip. His eyes devoured her with the relish of a man who has been at sea for many months, and he seemed lost for words. 'It's so good of you to come, Mr Bascobalena. Let's go into my office where we can have some coffee and a little chat. Perhaps you would prefer tea?'

'Or a barrel of rum,' Clementine hissed to her father.

Mr Bascobalena cleared his throat and swallowed. 'Black coffee, no sugar – and please call me Balthazar.'

His deep baritone startled Marina and she flinched, withdrawing her hand. She could see her stepdaughter sniggering out of the corner of her eye and she lifted her chin defiantly.

'Shane, see to it that Heather brings Mr Bascobalena a pot of black coffee right away and a cappuccino for me.'

'Will do, Mrs Turner,' said Shane, suppressing his mirth.

Picking up the portfolio, Shane followed them across the hall, through the drawing room, where a few clusters of guests sat reading the newspapers, and into the pretty green sitting room beyond which Marina's office overlooked the Children's Garden, redundant aqueduct, and the sea. She gestured that he place the portfolio on the coffee table, then watched him leave the room, closing the door behind him.

Marina invited Balthazar to sit on the sofa and winced as his dirty clothes made contact with the pale green chenille. She sank into the armchair and turned her face to the open window, where the sea breeze carried on its breath the sweet scent of cut grass and ozone. She could hear the distant roar of the ocean and the plaintive cry of gulls wheeling on the wind, and felt her heart ache with yearning to be down on the beach, her feet in the water, her hair tossed about by the breeze. Reluctantly, she wrenched her thoughts back. She already knew that Balthazar Bascobalena would not be spending the summer at the Polzanze, but she had to do him the courtesy of going through the motions.

'You have a wonderful name – Bascobalena. Sounds Spanish.' She was aware that he was staring at her, his jaw a little slack, as if he had never seen a woman before. In spite of the open window, his unwashed smell was beginning to fill the room. She wished Heather would hurry with the coffees, but guessed Shane was hanging around in the hall discussing their visitor with the rest of her staff. She hoped none of her guests had seen him come in.

'Perhaps, somewhere in my family history, there's a Spaniard. But we're Devon folk through and through, and proud of it.'

Marina raised her eyebrows doubtfully. He had the dark skin and eyes of a Spaniard. When he bared his teeth, they were brown and rotten like those of a sailor with scurvy. 'And Balthazar. You have the name of a hero in a book.'

'My mother was fanciful.'

'Was she an artist, too?'

'No, but she was a dreamer, God rest her soul.'

'So, tell me, Balthazar, what do you paint?'

'Boats,' he replied, leaning forward to open his portfolio.

'Boats,' Marina repeated, trying to inject some enthusiasm into her voice. 'How interesting. But not surprising,' she added humorously.

Mr Bascobalena missed her reference to his pirate outfit. 'Oh, I've been fascinated by boats since I was a nipper.'

'Raised on the sea?'

'Oh, yes, as was my father and grandfather before him.' He was distracted by a couple of paintings hanging on the wall. 'Those are good landscapes. Are you a collector, Mrs Turner?'

'Sadly not. I don't paint, either. I just admire people like you who do. So, let's see some of your work.'

He pulled out a sketch of a fishing boat in a tempestuous sea. For a moment Marina forgot his smell and his extraordinary clothes and stared incredulously at the picture before her.

'It's beautiful,' she gasped, shuffling to the edge of her chair. 'You have a gift.'

'Look at this one, then.' He pulled out another, his enthusiasm rising. Marina was stunned by the wistful charm of his work. He had sketched boats of all kinds: from fleets of Elizabethan ships to modern yachts and barges. Some drawn in calm waters at dawn, others on the high seas by moonlight, all with the same stirring sense of melancholy. 'I paint in oils, too, but they're too big to bring. You can come and see them if you like? I live near Salcombe.'

'Thank you. I'm sure they're as lovely as your sketches.' She looked at him with sincerity. 'You have an extraordinary talent.'

'If I could paint people, I'd paint you.' Marina ignored the lecherous look in his eyes.

'You don't paint people?' She feigned disappointment.

'Not a chance.' He ran a hand through thinning grey hair that reached the gilded epaulettes on his shoulders. 'Never have done. Can't get them right. Whatever I do they always look like monkeys.'

'What a shame. You see, Balthazar, I need my artist-in-residence to teach my guests how to paint everything. Not just boats and monkeys. I'm sorry.'

As Balthazar's shoulders hunched in defeat, Heather appeared with the tray carrying a silver coffee pot and a cappuccino. Marina shot her a furious look for having taken so long and Heather flushed a little as she placed it on the desk. Marina hoped he'd leave right away, but his greedy eyes settled on the gingernut biscuits and his spirits lifted. Reluctantly she poured him a cup of coffee, handed him the biscuits and watched him sink back into her sofa.

Clementine climbed into her red Mini Cooper and drove down the winding narrow lanes towards the town of Dawcomb-Devlish. Woolly fields undulated in a patchwork of assorted greens beneath a clear cerulean sky. Swallows dived and seagulls wheeled, and every now and then she glimpsed the sparkling blue ocean gently rippling into the hazy mists on the horizon. And yet, in spite of the beauty, Clementine's heart was a nugget of resentment.

She stared miserably at the grey tarmac and considered her lot. She wished she was travelling around India again, enjoying the freedom that three years and a respectable degree at university merited, instead of schlepping into Dawcomb-Devlish every morning to slog away as secretary to the desperately bland Mr Atwood and his sleepy estate agency on the high street.

It had come as something of a shock when her father had declared that he no longer had the money to fund her self-indulgence. She had hoped to defer work for another year at least. He had offered her a job at the hotel, like Jake, who had worked his way up to manager, but she'd rather die than call her stepmother boss. So he had found her a position for six months while Mr Atwood's secretary, Polly, was on maternity leave. If she lasted six weeks it would be a miracle, not only was she barely able to type, but she was very disorganized, relying on Sylvia, Mr Atwood's partner's secretary, to do most of the work for her. She was aware that Mr Atwood's patience was being sorely tested, but as he was indebted to her father for sending him clients there was little he could do.

It was a bore to be in Devon at all. If her mother hadn't had to sell her house in London and move up to Scotland she'd have found a far more glamorous job in Chelsea and would be spending every night with her friends in Boujis. As it was, she found herself in Devon, which she loathed on account of the many summer holidays she had spent being dragged onto cold beaches and shivering on rocks while her brother and father went crabbing. Marina used to make lavish picnics and would take her up and down the beach looking for shells, but Clementine always refused to take her hand. It was a small act of defiance. But she had always felt inadequate beside this beautiful creature who had stolen her father's heart. She was well aware of the light in his eyes when he looked at her, as if he were gazing on an angel, and the way the light dimmed when he looked at *her*, as if she were an interruption. She didn't doubt his love; he just loved Marina more.

Approaching the town, Clementine noticed a black object lying in the middle of the road. At first she thought it was an old boot, and slowed down. But on closer inspection she saw that it was a hedgehog, crawling leisurely across the tarmac. She glanced in her rear-view mirror to see a couple of cars behind her and knew that if she didn't stop, the hedgehog would surely be crushed. The animal's plight drew her out of herself and she braked suddenly, threw open the door and hurried to his aid. The man in the car behind tooted angrily. Clementine ignored him and bent down to move the hedgehog along. The trouble was, he was very prickly and riddled with fleas. She thought quickly, noticing a couple of cars coming towards her, and took off her shoes. Carefully, she scooped the hedgehog off the ground in one and put him down on the grassy verge. It gave her pleasure to watch him shuffle into the bush and disappear. By the time she climbed back into her car there was a small queue behind and in front. She waved her thanks as she passed, beaming a smile at the drivers who scowled back at her.

When she burst into the office, mumbling apologies, it was well past ten. Sylvia Helvin, a feisty redhead divorcee with big breasts barely restrained by her tight green V-neck sweater and silk scarf, placed her hand over the telephone receiver and grinned broadly. 'Don't panic, lovely, they're both out at a meeting this morning. We have the office to ourselves. Be a darling and get me a latte.' She lifted her scarlet talons and laughed throatily into the telephone. 'Now, Freddie, you're a naughty, naughty boy. You'd better behave or I'll have to smack you again.' Clementine wandered off to the Black Bean Coffee Shop. When she returned, Sylvia was still talking, the receiver clamped between her chin and shoulder, busy filing her nails. Clementine plonked the coffee carton in front of her and threw her bag onto the floor. 'Bad morning?' Sylvia asked, hanging up.

'Submarine is interviewing artists.'

'Ah, the artist-in-residence. Very posh.'

'But that's just it. It's not posh at all. It's pretentious.'

'Does it matter, if he's handsome?'

'Handsome? Some chance. You should have seen the pirate that rocked up at dawn. Old, smelly and clearly mad. All that was missing was his ship.'

Sylvia sipped her latte cautiously so as not to ruin her lipstick. 'You know, she's either brave or foolish inviting a total stranger into her home.'

'It's not a home, it's a hotel. Anyway, that's the business for you — total strangers traipsing in and out all day, every day. Ghastly!'

'No, I mean with the robberies. They've started calling him Baffles, the gentleman thief. He targets hotels like your father's, as well as big houses. Haven't you read the paper this morning?'

'I don't read the *Dawcomb-Devlish Gazette*.'

'You're missing out. It's a veritable mine of local information. It's all getting rather bizarre. He descended on a big house just outside Thurlestone, crept in while they were all asleep, and left with loads of cash and a serious work of art. The weird thing is he seemed to know where everything was, as if he'd been there and checked it out first.'

'How do they know he's a he?'

Sylvia shrugged. 'Well, he signs his name Raffles, after the fictional character, and *he* was a man. That's why they've nicknamed him Baffles.' She laughed through her nose. 'Typical journalists, they're loving it! Get this, though: he didn't leave a single clue except for a little note saying "thank you" in neat and tidy writing.'

'You're joking!'

'Would I make light of such a serious matter?' She sucked in her cheeks. 'I tease you not, Clemmie dear. The robber has good manners. To think, only a week ago he targeted the Palace Hotel in Thurlestone. Hope he doesn't come down here.'

Clementine laughed and flopped into her chair. 'Well, I don't really care if he targets the Polzanze and steals all Submarine's precious paintings. He'd be doing me a favour if he managed to carry *her* off with his loot.'

'I think you're being unfair. I like her. She's glamorous.'

'Cheap glamour.'

'Don't be such a snob.'

'I'm not a snob. I don't care where people come from if they're nice.'

'She's a local girl, like me.'

'Not that you'd know. She tries so hard to sound posh

there's barely any trace of her original country accent.' Clementine chuckled. 'The trouble is she's ended up with a very strange accent that's neither one thing nor the other – at times she even sounds foreign!'

'You're very hard on her, Clemmie. So, she has the odd character flaw. You should be more forgiving.'

'She's pretentious. I don't like people who pretend to be what they're not. She should stop trying to sound grand.'

Sylvia rounded on her crossly. 'You say you're not a snob, Clementine, but you're sounding just like one. What's your posh education done for you? Given you a plum to carry in your mouth and a sense of superiority. You're working in the same office as me, earning a lot less. Your father would have done better to have saved his pennies.'

'I didn't mean to offend you, Sylvia. She's my stepmother. I don't think she's good for my father, that's all. He could have done better for himself. You know he was a highly successful barrister in London. What on earth inspired him to come down here and run a hotel?'

'His wife.'

'My point exactly. He'd be a judge by now if he'd hung in there.'

'Maybe he didn't want to be a judge. Perhaps he's happy with the choice he made. Anyway, you're not meant to love your stepmother. Had she been born the daughter of a king you still wouldn't think her good enough.'

'I think she wanted the house because it was owned by the Duke of Somerland. She sits in her study, which used to be the duchess's, and feels important. Dad was so far above her on the food chain I'm surprised she managed to get him in her sights.'

'I think she's beautiful. There's something deep and sad in her eyes.'

'Trust me, she has nothing to be sad about. She's got every-thing she ever wanted by sheer manipulation.'

'Then you should take a leaf out of her book and use your beauty cleverly.'

'I'm not beautiful.'

Sylvia shook her head and grinned at her kindly. 'You are when you smile.'

Marina watched with relief as Balthazar's car finally spluttered its way out of the driveway. She found Grey up a ladder in the library next door, looking for a book to lend the Brigadier, who had breakfasted on eggs and fried bread at the Polzanze ever since his wife died five years ago.

'Oh dear,' he said. 'So that didn't go well.'

She raised her hands to heaven and inhaled theatrically. 'I couldn't get rid of him. My office now smells like a hostel for the homeless and I'm about to interview another one.'

'Why don't you sit outside? It's a beautiful day.'

'If Elizabeth Pembridge-Hughes is presentable, I will. However, if she's crazy, I'll have to hide her away for fear of scaring our guests. I've lit a scented candle but I fear it will take more than that.'

'I thought you'd like him. You love eccentrics.'

She smiled grudgingly. 'Not eccentrics with blackened teeth and bad breath, long greasy hair and ridiculous clothes!'

'You surprise me.' He came down the ladder.

'I like *presentable* eccentrics. Ones that smell of lime, wear clean shirts and brush their teeth.'

'Ah,' he raised an eyebrow.

He kissed her forehead. 'This is meant to be fun, Marina. It's your idea, after all. Enjoy it.'

'But what if I don't find someone suitable?'

'You don't have to have an artist-in-residence.'

'Oh, but I do. We need something to make us different, to draw people in. I don't have to remind you of the trouble we're in. We have to think of new ways of attracting business or we'll be another credit-crunch tragedy. We're not making money,

Grey. In fact, we're haemorrhaging money. Think about it, half the guests who come here in the summer, come to paint. My London ladies have booked in for their week in June simply because they want to repeat the fun of last year. I'm building a reputation that will bring people back year after year.'

'Then if the right person doesn't appear we'll hunt him down.'

She knitted her fingers. 'Clementine thinks it's in poor taste.'

'She's young.'

'She's rude.'

'Ignore her. She wants to get a rise out of you.'

'Then I am not going to be a soufflé. She should show me some respect. I'm her stepmother.' She turned away sharply, the word 'mother' lingering on her lips like an affront.

'Do you want me to talk to her?'

'No. Leave her alone. Perhaps I'm just not very good at it.'

'You have tried, darling. I know how hard you've tried and I'm very grateful. It's an impossible situation.' The air was suddenly heavy with words too painful to articulate.

When she spoke, Marina's voice was quiet. 'Let's not talk about it, Grey. Elizabeth whatever-she's-called will be here any minute and I don't want to look strained.'

'You look beautiful.'

'Only to you.'

'Who else matters?'

Her expression softened. 'You're my champion, Grey.'

'Always, my darling.'

Shane shuffled awkwardly by the door, pretending not to hear. He wiped his large nose with the back of his hand, then stood to attention as he heard a car draw up on the gravel outside. Jennifer left Rose at the reception desk and pressed her nose to the window to see what *this* candidate was like.

Chapter 2

Elizabeth Pembridge-Hughes was extremely presentable. Tall and willowy, with fine, aristocratic features, porcelain skin and sensitive blue eyes, she was the epitome of what an artist of refinement *should* look like. Marina shook her hand and noticed at once how cold it was.

She led her through the hotel to the terrace, stopping in the conservatory on the way to admire the lemon trees in urns and the grapevines that climbed the trellising, spreading their tentacles across the glass ceiling like pretty octopuses. Elizabeth was highly complimentary, missing nothing, and Marina's heart swelled with relief that she had found her artist-in-residence at last.

They sat outside at one of the small round tables, surrounded by big terracotta pots of rosemary and lavender yet to flower. Elizabeth crossed her legs, wrapping her pale lilac pashmina around her shoulders, for there was a cold edge to the wind. Her naturally blonde hair was streaked with grey and the wisps that had escaped her ponytail were caught by the breeze and blew about playfully. She was not blessed with beauty, but her face possessed a certain haughtiness that was arresting.

'Do you mind if I smoke?'

Marina hated cigarettes and was a little disappointed. But Elizabeth had asked so politely, her educated accent clipping the words so efficiently, that Marina decided not to hold it against her. No one was perfect.

Elizabeth reached into her bag and burrowed about in search of cigarettes and lighter. This took a while, during which time Marina ordered herbal tea for her guest and a fruit juice for herself. At last Elizabeth's long fingers appeared with a packet of Marlboro Lights and she popped one between her thin lips and lit it, turning her back to the wind.

'You have a beautiful place, Marina,' she said, blowing smoke out of the corner of her mouth. 'It's jolly inspiring to see the sea.'

'I have to be near the sea,' Marina replied, resting her heavy gaze on the glittering water. 'It has always been the most consistent thing in my life.'

'I agree with you. It's good for the soul. I once travelled with a famous actor – who discretion prevents me from naming – who meditates by the sea. I suppose I was his artist-on-tour. He was an inspiration to me. I've tried to meditate but my mind is too busy. I can't shut it up.'

'Do you travel a lot with your work?'

'All the time. I've accompanied kings, queens and princes all over the world. Jolly lucky, really.'

Marina felt uneasy. Even she was realistic enough to appreciate that the position of artist-in-residence at the Polzanze was not a highly covetable one. Surely, if Elizabeth Pembridge-Hughes was used to painting for kings, she would not consider spending the summer in Dawcomb-Devlish, teaching old ladies for her board and lodging. 'How fascinating, Elizabeth. Tell me, which kings and queens and princes? I would love to hear your stories.'

Elizabeth pursed her lips. 'Well, that's the thing. You see, if one is privileged enough to be invited on their foreign tours, one has to keep shtoom. I'm sure you understand.' She laughed a smoky little snort through her nostrils.

'Perhaps when we know each other better I'll share some gems.'

'Of course.' But Marina doubted she had any gems to share.

Just as Marina's spirit began to plummet, Grey walked out onto the terrace. 'Ah, my husband,' she said, smiling at him gratefully.

Elizabeth took in his stature, his broad shoulders, his thick, curly hair and genial face, and thought how incredibly attractive he was. An intellectual, clearly, and noble, too, one could always tell. 'It's a pleasure to meet you,' she gushed, giving him her hand.

'I thought I'd come and join you,' he replied, shaking it. He noticed her weak grip and the cold, thin feel of her fingers. 'Are you warm enough out here?'

'Perfectly,' she replied. He pulled out a chair and sat down. A waiter hurried to the kitchens to fetch him some coffee. 'We were just saying how lovely it is to see the sea.'

'I agree, the view is spectacular.'

'I'd love to paint it.'

'Well, perhaps you shall,' he said. Then he caught his wife's eye and deduced from her expression that Elizabeth Pembridge-Hughes would not be coming back to paint anything.

'So, this position of artist-in-residence, what does it involve, exactly?'

Marina felt the familiar tug in her stomach, an internal warning system that never failed. She didn't want Elizabeth Pembridge-Hughes in her hotel, name-dropping all summer. Once again, she found herself having to go through the motions in order not to be impolite. 'Last year we had a charming man who resided with us for three months, teaching the hotel guests painting. It's something different I like to offer our residents.'

'What a brilliant idea — and such lovely surroundings to paint.'

'I think so. Last summer Paul taught us all how to paint.'

'You as well?' She directed her question at Grey.

'Not me, I'm no artist. Marina had a go, didn't you, darling?'

'Yes, though I'm no good at it, either. It was fun to experiment and he was such a nice man. It was a pleasure to have him to stay all summer and we missed him when he left. He'd become part of the family.'

'As shall I. One loves nothing more than to roll up one's sleeves and get stuck in. All hands on deck.'

'Absolutely,' said Grey, finding her heartiness comical. The waiter placed his coffee on the table along with herbal tea and a glass of grapefruit juice.

Elizabeth rested her cigarette on the ashtray. 'Now let me show you what I do.' She delved into her bag and pulled out a black photo album. 'I'm afraid my art is too big to carry around. Some of my paintings are hanging in royal households, so you can imagine, one can hardly go asking to borrow them, can one? This will give you a good idea.' She handed Grey the book. Marina pulled her chair closer to her husband and nudged him with her elbow. 'I'm jolly good with people,' Elizabeth continued. 'You see, it's one thing knowing how to paint, but quite another knowing how to teach. I'm fortunate enough to be adept at both.' Grey nudged his wife back.

They leafed through photographs of horses sketched in charcoal, to still lifes in oil. There was no doubt that Elizabeth had talent. However, her work had nothing of the heart of Balthazar Bascobalena's melancholy boats, nor his flair. She was extremely good, but she had no soul. 'You're very talented, Elizabeth,' Marina said, trying to sound enthusiastic.

'Thank you. One loves what one does and I think it shows, don't you?'

'Oh, it really does,' said Grey, but Marina could see no traces of pleasure in her work at all.

Elizabeth finished one cigarette and lit another. As she sipped her tea, Marina noticed her face fall in repose. She suddenly looked old and sad, like an actress weary of playing her role. Marina felt a twinge of compassion but she couldn't wait to be rid of her.

'She was dreadful,' she exclaimed to her husband once Elizabeth's car had disappeared up the drive.

'You have to kiss many frogs before you find your prince. Perhaps the same applies to your artist.'

'Oh really, Grey. I suppose you think this is all very funny.'

'I'm amused.'

'Well, at least one of us is.'

He put his arm around her and squeezed her affectionately. 'Darling, you have to keep your sense of humour. The world is full of wonderful people – wonderfully ghastly and wonderfully pleasant. Elizabeth Pembridge-Hughes was certainly entertaining.'

'I'd enjoy it like you if I didn't feel so anxious.'

'There's nothing to be anxious about. It'll all work out in the end. Consider this a study in human nature.'

She grinned up at him. 'From which I deduce that God has a sense of humour, too.'

'Yes, but I think He was very serious when He created you.' He laughed and Marina couldn't help but laugh with him.

At midday Harvey Dovecote strode into the hall. A determined bachelor, Harvey had worked for Grey and Marina from the very beginning, having been estate manager for the last and least fortunate Duke and Duchess of Somerland. Now, at seventy-five, he did little more than odd jobs for Marina, clad in his habitual tweed cap and sky-blue boiler suit. The regular guests delighted in his familiar presence as he went about his work with irrepressible optimism and charm. He was a beloved character, as much a part of the hotel as the bricks and mortar, and Marina had grown entirely dependent on his down-to-earth good sense. He swept leaves, filled the log baskets, mended broken pipes and fused light switches. He repaired roof tiles, leaking ceilings, and plastered and painted when the decoration needed touching up. There was nothing he couldn't do and he had the energy of a man twenty years his junior.

Fit and wiry, Harvey had thinning grey hair and a long, genial face that always smiled. His skin was scratched with deep laughter lines but his eyes sparkled with the reflection of an agile mind that missed nothing and saw the humour in everything. He arrived as Elizabeth Pembridge-Hughes sped off in her Range Rover.

'Another one bites the dust!'

'Oh, Harvey, I'm so pleased you're back!' Marina exclaimed, feeling a pleasant calm wash away her doubts. 'You wouldn't believe the people I've had to interview today. A pirate and a name-dropper. If the third interview isn't a success I don't know what I shall do.'

'You shall wait for the right person to appear.'

'You think he will?'

'Oh, he will.' Harvey's certainty was comforting.

'How's your mother? I'm sorry. I'm so wound up in my project I forgot to ask.' She placed her hand on his arm for his mother's health had declined recently and she'd been put in a home. She was ninety-eight and Harvey was devoted to her, visiting her up to three times a week.

'She's bearing up. Sun Valley Nursing Home is dreary, but me and my nephew, Steve, keep her entertained, as much as we can. She's very excited because Steve's gone and bought a second-hand Jaguar. Beautiful car. Purrs like a big cat. He drove it to the nursing home and they wheeled her out so she could get a good look at it.'

'You haven't told me about Steve before. I never even knew you had a nephew. He sounds very successful.'

'He is. He lives in a big house just outside Salisbury, full of beautiful things. He's a collector, you know. You'd be amazed by the things he has. My brother, Tony, never amounted to much, but his boy Steve's broken the mould. He'll lend me the Jag if I ask him, he's that generous. Might have to bring it down here and show it off.'

Marina laughed. 'You at the wheel of a swish car? Now *that* I'd like to see.'

'And I'd like to see the look on your face when I take you out in it!' He opened his wide mouth and laughed heartily.

'Oh, I'd love that, Harvey. It's many years since I've been in a beautiful sports car.'

She suddenly grew serious. 'You heard the news this morning?'

'I did indeed. He's like Macavity the Mystery Cat.'

'Really, Harvey . . .'

'He's called the Hidden Paw –
For he's the master criminal who can defy the Law.'

He grinned as he managed, yet again, to make her smile.

'It's no laughing matter, Harvey.'

'I don't like to see you worried.'

'But it *is* a worry, Harvey. We have to be vigilant and hope he doesn't target us. We're small compared to the places he's robbed so far, so I hope he'll overlook us.'

'I expect he will. There's not much to steal here, is there.'

'Nothing really valuable, no.'

'So put it out of your mind.'

'Only once the police have caught him.'

'He's the bafflement of Scotland Yard, the Flying Squad's despair:
For when they reach the scene of crime – Macavity's not there!'

'You don't seem at all anxious about it.'
'Being anxious isn't going to stop him targeting the Polzanze.'
'Then what is?'
'I'll stand outside with a shotgun.'
'I don't think I'd feel any safer with you wielding a gun, Harvey. We need something else.'
He scratched his chin. 'A dog?'
'You know I don't allow dogs on the premises.'
'You'd feel a lot safer if you had one. Cats like Macavity don't like to rob places with dogs.'
She turned away and folded her arms. 'I couldn't bear a dog. I just couldn't . . .'
'Dogs are very friendly animals.'
'I know . . . but I really couldn't . . .'
'Then we'll think of something else,' he said soothingly.
She smiled with relief. 'Yes, please. Anything but a dog.'

Marina's third and final candidate arrived late. A bumbling university graduate in jeans and beige corduroy jacket, he was foppish with long blond hair and a baby face that barely looked old enough to be out of school. They had tea in the conservatory for the wind had picked up, and he told her about himself while she tried to concentrate and look interested. Harvey caught her eye as he wandered out to the terrace to fix a wobbling table, and pulled a face. She didn't need his confirmation, but it was nice to know that he agreed; George Quigley would not be staying the summer, either.

It was hard to get rid of him. He drank endless cups of tea and ate four slices of cake and whole handfuls of little egg sandwiches. Marina listened patiently while he chatted on about Exeter University, his girlfriend and his somewhat optimistic plans for his future, exhibiting all over the world. His work was abstract, as she expected it would be. She laughed away her disappointment, imagining what her old ladies would make of it.

Marina explained that his work was simply too modern for her guests and cut him off briskly when he tried to tell her that he could paint anything she wanted. He could have painted like David Hockney for all she cared; she simply did not like him. Just as he was on the point of leaving, Clementine strode into the hall. She took one look at him and her face flowered into a smile. They exchanged glances and he returned her smile, looking her up and down appreciatively. Clementine watched him leave then turned to her stepmother excitedly.

'Is *he* coming to stay the summer?'

'I'm afraid not. He's highly unsuitable.'

Clementine's face snapped shut. 'What's unsuitable about him? If you ask me, he's just what you want.'

'Which is why I'm not asking you.'

'You're very hard to please. Anyway, your fusty old ladies would love a handsome young man like him.'

'His paintings are much too modern.'

'If he's talented he can probably paint boring landscapes to your heart's content.'

'I didn't warm to him.'

'I did.'

'Then go out and talk to him. Look, he's hanging around his car. He clearly fancies you.'

'No,' she retorted sharply.

'Not interested?'

Clementine clicked her tongue crossly and stalked off. 'You wouldn't understand.'

Marina sighed. 'I'm going out,' she said to Jennifer. 'I need some air. This has been a very trying day. Have you seen Jake?'

'Not back yet.'

'How long does it take to see a dentist? Well, I'm off. Grey is around, should you need him.'

Marina walked purposefully along the cliff top, arms folded, shoulders hunched against the blustering wind. She could never gaze upon the ocean without her heart aching with longing, especially on a clear day such as this, when the setting sun pulled at her soul until it hurt.

She hurried down the well-trodden path to the beach where the last rays of sun were gradually being swallowed into shadow, and kicked off her shoes to tread barefoot over the sand. The fresh air filled her lungs and her chest expanded with the beauty of the dying day. She had held it together for so long, burying her sorrow down deep where she believed she wouldn't find it. But now, as she approached her mid-fifties, it had found her, bubbling up through the cracks in her ageing body, and she could no longer ignore it.

The disappointment of the day and her worries about their business overwhelmed her, and she began to sob. Why hadn't one of those artists been suitable? Why had they all been so totally inappropriate? Why did she feel her life was suddenly without purpose or direction? Why now, after nearly forty years, did her past suddenly open behind her like a dam and flood her with painful memories? She was overcome and sank to her knees. Hugging her belly she rocked back and forth in an effort to assuage the ache inside.

It was there that Grey found her. He ran down the beach and gathered her into his arms. She yielded without resistance, burying her face in his chest and blocking out the sea. Neither said a word. For what was there to say? No amount of carefully chosen words could soothe the agony of childlessness.

They clung to each other. Marina unburdened her sadness and stopped crying. She closed her eyes, soothed by his hand gently stroking her hair and his lips tenderly kissing her temple, and inhaled deeply until she felt a calm wash over her, like warm honey poured onto the wounds in her heart. The sorrow was slowly replaced with gratitude that she had found in Grey a man who loved her unconditionally, in spite of all her faults.

'I came down to tell you that you have another candidate for your artist-in-residence. A man called Rafael Santoro just called and asked whether the position has been filled. He sounded very pleased when I told him it hadn't.'

'I don't think I have the energy to see anyone else,' she sniffed.

'You will tomorrow. You're exhausted right now so don't think about it.'

'Where's he from? Italy?'

'Argentina.'

'Did he sound . . . normal?'

Grey laughed into her hairline. 'What's normal?'

'He's not a mad tango dancer, or a fancy polo player?' She lifted her head and wiped her eyes, smiling tentatively.

'I don't know. But as far as I can tell he sounded normal enough.'

'What time is he coming?'

'Ten.'

She sighed heavily, regaining her strength. 'OK. So all is not lost.'

'It's not lost until you say it's lost, darling.'

'I wish Paul would come back.'

'We'll find another Paul. This Rafa, as he likes to be called, might even be better than Paul.'

'You're as optimistic as Harvey.' She laughed, the sparkle restored in her eyes. 'If you ask me, Rafa Santoro sounds like a brand of dog biscuits.'

*

Clementine met Sylvia, her lover, Freddie, and Freddie's friend Joe in the Dizzy Mariner pub in Shelton, surrounded by model boats and what looked like rusted relics of the *Mary Rose*.

'Shelton must be the sleepiest village in Devon,' said Clementine, looking around at the empty tables. A couple of old people sat in the corner, tucking into steak and kidney pie, without saying a word to each other. An elderly man, in a tatty tweed suit and cap was perched on a stool chatting up the barmaid, who leaned on the counter, grateful for the company.

'Most people go to the Wayfarer in Dawcomb, but I like it here. It's cosy and less noisy,' said Sylvia.

'I like it quiet,' said Freddie, putting his arm around Sylvia's waist. 'I don't have to share you.'

'Or risk bumping into your wife,' Sylvia added, raising a plucked eyebrow.

'I bet it's a culture shock coming down here from London,' said Joe, gazing on Clementine admiringly.

'It is. I didn't want to come. I don't get on with my father's wife.'

'So, why did you?'

'Because I have to earn some money.'

'I thought the likes of you would have a trust fund or something.'

Clementine laughed bitterly. 'There was a time when Dad threw money at us. You know, the classic father trying to win his children's affection with treats to make up for the divorce. But he's not so rich any more. Submarine — that's his wife — is *very* high maintenance and I know they've been hit by the financial crisis as I pick up fag ends when they don't know I'm listening. Then there's Mum, married again to Michael, hopeless with money. They've had to sell their house in London and move up to Edinburgh so that he can join the family business. He's lost loads in the credit crunch. I think I'd rather be poor, living in London, than rich, living in Edinburgh.'

'Edinburgh's more happening than Dawcomb and Shelton put together!' said Sylvia.

'Perhaps, but it's cold. At least it's sunny down here.'

'Sometimes. You've just had it lucky.' Sylvia arranged her dress, pulling the neckline lower to expose her cleavage. Freddie lost himself there a moment. 'I couldn't live in a city for all the world. Much too noisy, and the people, oh, I couldn't bear having to fight for space on the pavement. It's bad enough in Dawcomb during the summer when all the tourists come down and fill the place to bursting. I like it now, when it's quiet. Just us, the locals, empty beaches, empty sea, long, empty days.' She giggled as Freddie put his hand on her upper thigh. 'And you, dear Freddie, with your empty head!'

'Not empty. Full of you, Sylvia.'

She wriggled with pleasure. 'Fancy coming out for a ciggie?'

Sylvia wandered slowly through the pub, her hourglass figure squeezed into a tight blue dress, causing the man in tweed to spill his beer as he swivelled around to follow her with lusty eyes. 'Close your mouth, dear, you're much too old,' said the barmaid with a cackle, reaching for the cloth to wipe the counter.

'She's quite something,' said Joe, shaking his head. 'A real vixen.'

'How long have they been together?'

'Together isn't a word I'd use. They're lovers, plain and simple. He's married with kids. She's divorced. It's going to get messy. About six months, to answer your question. Snatched moments and I'm the beard.'

'You're very good to put up with it.'

'He's my mate. I'd do anything for Freddie. Trouble is, he's in love. A man don't use his head when he's in love.'

'I was very little when my parents divorced, but I know it's damaged me. I mean, how could it not? Anyone who thinks children escape unscathed when their parents divorce is kidding himself. All through my childhood I dreamed of them getting back together. Even when Dad had married Submarine and moved down here, I still wished.' She leaned across the table and lowered her voice. 'I wished Submarine would meet with an accident.'

'Naughty girl.'

'Very.'

'Sounds like she's still alive and kicking.'

'Unfortunately. At least she hasn't given Dad any children. There's some justice, after all.' She knocked back her vodka tonic. 'I'm still Dad's only daughter. There's consolation in that.'

Joe laughed. 'You're funny.'

'Gallows humour.'

'Can I get you another drink?'

'You most certainly can, Joe. Thank you.'

He walked over to the bar. Clementine sat back on the bench and watched him sleepily. He was easy on the eye. A little coarse, perhaps, but she liked the way he laughed at her jokes and looked at her so appreciatively. When he returned with her vodka he was grinning.

'What are you smiling about?'

'Us.'

'How do you mean?'

'Well, Sylvia and Freddie, they've set us up.'

'Really?'

'Of course.'

'I thought they'd just gone out for a cigarette.'

'No. They've gone out for a shag. But they've left us together on purpose.'

'She wouldn't set me up without warning me.'

'Of course she would. That's Sylvia. She has a big heart. She wants everyone to be as happy as she is.'

'So, Joe, if you're my date, we might as well order something to eat. I'm ravenous.'

He stared at her eagerly, mouth twisting at one corner with anticipation. 'There are less stars in the sky tonight.'

'There are?'

'Yes, because the brightest star is sitting here at this table with me.'

Perhaps it was the alcohol, or her lonely heart, which was ready to open for the first man with a key, but she laughed heartily at his lame line and took another gulp of vodka.

When Sylvia and Freddie came back, Sylvia smoothing down her dress and patting her up-do, Clementine and Joe were enjoying cottage pie and laughing inanely at everything they said.

'So, looks like you two have hit it off,' said Sylvia, shuffling onto the bench and filling the air with the overpowering smell of tuberose.

'Where have you been?' Clementine demanded.

'For a ciggie, lovely.'

'Long ciggie.'

'Yes, we made it last.' She laughed huskily.

'Let's order,' Freddie suggested. 'Smells good.'

'It *is* good,' enthused Joe, his mouth full.

'Sylvia, are you setting us up?'

'I'd never do such a thing without telling you, Clemmie,' she replied, looking appalled.

'Just that Joe said—'

'Don't listen to a word Joe says. He's a terrible old rogue. Why, have you really hit it off?' She didn't wait for a reply. 'If you have I'll happily take the credit.'

'You won't find a better man than Joe.'

'Freddie's right. Thirty-two, unmarried, no kids, good job – and that's saying something these days.'

'What do you do, Joe?' Clementine asked.

'Anything you want.' He laughed at his own joke.

'No, really.'

'Yes, really. I'm a handyman.'

'Like Harvey,' she muttered, giggling at the thought of him in a blue boiler suit and cap.

'I can do anything.' He raised his eyebrows and grinned. 'Anything at all.'

Chapter 3

The following morning Marina sat at the breakfast table with Grey in the private house they had converted from the old stables across from the hotel.

'I'm glad to see that Jake is back this morning,' she said tightly. 'Long dentist appointment. What was the man doing? Taking out all his teeth and putting them back in again?'

'He went to Thurlestone.'

'Why? He's the manager here, not in Thurlestone.'

'He's interested in that robber.'

'So he went to do a little detective work?'

'Exactly.'

'Good. Now we can all sleep better at night.' She sipped her coffee.

'I don't think Jake's presence there is going to be of much help in finding the burglar.'

'He obviously thinks he can make a difference.'

'Amateur detective.'

'He should put his energy into his job here or I'll give it to someone else.'

Grey glanced at the clock on the wall. 'I think you should wake Clementine or she might find herself begging you for a job as well.'

'That girl needs to learn to be responsible.'

'Necessity is the mother of invention.'

'A bit late to teach her to stand on her own two feet. She knows you'll always bail her out.'

'If she wants to go back to India she has to earn the money herself.'

'Grey darling, she shouldn't be going back to India. She should be getting a proper job. India is simply a way of avoiding the rest of her life.'

'She loves travel.'

'I had to fend for myself when I was her age. I didn't have rich parents to support me.'

'So, isn't it lucky that Clementine does?'

'*Did*. We don't have any more beans to share.'

'I don't see anything wrong in travelling and seeing the world while she's young and free.'

'Of course, there's nothing wrong in that. But she's doing it for the wrong reasons. She won't grow up until she takes responsibility for her life. You're too soft. You always have been.'

'I'm a guilty father.'

'You have no reason to feel guilty. You've given those children everything they've ever wanted. Jake lives and works here, Clementine has spent every holiday travelling the world. She didn't even have to work to pay for her university fees. They've both had it good and as a result are highly spoiled. But they are not my children so . . .' she shrugged, '. . . I shouldn't criticize.'

'But you do.' He looked at her indulgently.

'Because I care.'

He smiled. 'I know.'

'*They* don't. They think I'm the enemy.'

'That's not true. Deep down they like you.'

'Then they don't show it.'

'Neither do you.'

She sighed. 'Stalemate.'

'Have a croissant.'

'You're changing the subject.'

He grinned. 'Yes, I am.'

'Very well, I'll have a croissant. Soon it will be time to meet "the Dog Biscuit".'

'And wake my daughter.'

'I won't be thanked.'

'But you'll have done good.'

Marina drained her coffee cup. 'I suppose you're out fishing this morning.'

'It's a good day for it.'

'Beautiful. Sometimes I wish I could come with you.'

'I wish you would. It would do you good to get away and think about something else.'

'I wouldn't know what to think about. This place is all-consuming.'

'That's what I mean.' He got up. 'I'll be back for lunch. Good luck with the Biscuit.'

She pulled an anxious face and sighed helplessly. As he passed her chair, Grey bent down to kiss her head. He lingered there a moment, absorbing her apprehension, aching to carry her burden for her. He closed his eyes and inhaled her warm vanilla scent. 'No matter what, darling, we're in this together.'

She placed a hand on his as he squeezed her shoulder. His touch was loaded with so many unspoken words she didn't have the courage to reply, so she squeezed him back instead. They remained still, allowing their love to console them where syllables could not. Then he kissed her again and left the room.

Clementine awoke with a head full of warring rhinoceroses. She put her hand to her brow and rubbed it ineffectively. As she slowly came to her senses, fragments of the night before surfaced one by one, until an unsavoury picture began to form in her mind. She groaned at her own folly. Not only had she allowed Joe to kiss her, which had been quite nice at the time, but she had allowed him to do all sorts of *other* things, of which she had only jumbled recollections and a lingering sense of shame. She rolled over and pulled a pillow onto her head. Had they gone the whole way? She was mortified to discover that she couldn't remember.

The door opened and Marina crept in. 'Clementine, you have to get up. It's eight-fifteen.' Clementine lay inert, pretending not to hear. Marina walked over to the window and opened the curtains. Sunlight tumbled in. 'It's a beautiful day again. Not a cloud in the sky.' She approached the bed and lifted the pillow. 'I know you're awake. Heavy evening?'

'Too much vodka at the Dizzy Mariner,' Clementine mumbled.

'I'll make you a strong coffee. Take a cold shower, you'll feel better.'

'I want to sleep.'

'I'm not going to phone and pretend you're sick.'

'Please.'

'No. That's beyond the call of duty. Now hurry, or you'll be late.'

Clementine dragged herself into the bathroom and peered at her reflection in the mirror above the basin. Her face was grey, the circles beneath her eyes as dark as purple storm clouds, and she had an unsightly spot on her chin. Her shoulder-length hair was tangled and knotted as if a bird had spent the night in it, trying to scratch its way out. Her lips were swollen from too much kissing. No amount of eye drops would restore her bloodshot eyes, and as for her self-respect – she fumbled for the paracetamol – nothing could restore that.

At last she made her way down to the kitchen. The smell of fresh coffee and hot croissants revived her flagging spirit. Marina was at the table, reading *Vogue*. She looked poised and polished in a pair of beige trousers and bright floral blouse, her

small feet tucked into a pair of high wedge heels. She raised
her eyes over the magazine and smiled sympathetically. 'That's
better.' But only marginally. Clementine had tried to cover up
with too much foundation and kohl.

'I should never have drunk so much.'

'We all do silly things.'

'Oh, I don't know, Marina. You don't look like you've done
a single silly thing in your entire life.'

'You'd be surprised.'

'Yes I would.' Clementine didn't imagine her stepmother
had ever got drunk and allowed a coarse odd-job man to have
his wicked way with her. She poured herself a cup of coffee
and gingerly nibbled the corner of a croissant. Shame clawed
at her stomach. She would have liked to share her worries, but
knew that Marina was the last person on the planet who
would understand. As she chewed, her fears mounted. What
if he hadn't worn a condom? What if she was pregnant? What
if he had a disease? Should she go to the doctor? She felt the
blood drain into her feet.

Marina glanced at her, sensing her misery. 'Are you all right?
You look sick.'

'I'm fine. Just hung-over.'

Marina wasn't convinced. 'If you really are unwell, you
shouldn't go into work and you certainly shouldn't drive. I'll
call Mr Atwood and let him know.'

'Stop fussing. I said I'm fine.' Clementine hadn't meant her
voice to sound so sharp, but she was too frail to apologize. She
looked at her watch. 'I'd better go.'

'You've barely eaten.'

'I'm not hungry.' She stood up.

'Take the croissant to eat in the car.'

'I'll get something in town.'

Keen not to fuss, Marina did not insist. She looked at the
barely eaten croissant discarded on the table and felt a rush of

maternal angst. It wasn't healthy to start the day on an empty stomach.

'See you later, then. Have a good day.'

Clementine didn't reply. She left the room, taking her darkness with her. A little later the front door closed with a loud bang. A gust of wind swept into the kitchen, but then the air settled and the place felt light again.

Marina turned her thoughts to Rafa Santoro. She was not looking forward to meeting him. Her spirits felt heavy with dread and anticipated disappointment. If only Paul Lockwood would come back, everything would be all right. She drained her coffee cup and cleared the table. As she stacked the plates she heard the door open again and the loud, habitual sigh that always accompanied Bertha's arrival.

'Morning,' Bertha groaned. 'Another lovely day at the Polzanze.' She bustled into the kitchen, heaving her heavy body across the room. A porcine woman with mottled pink skin and pale blonde hair tied into a ponytail, Bertha worked at the hotel, doing a couple of hours every morning for Marina at the stable block.

'Morning, Bertha. How are you today?'

'Well, my cold's definitely on the way out, but my back. Well . . .' She handed Marina a postcard then sank into a chair and helped herself to Clementine's half-nibbled croissant that still sat on the table. 'Come all the way from Canada. Pretty writing.'

'Katherine Bridges,' Marina replied with a smile. 'My old teacher.'

'Funny to still keep in touch with your teacher.'

'She was more than a teacher. She was special.'

Bertha pulled a face. 'The doctor has suggested I try those needle things. What are they called?'

'Acupuncture,' Marina replied absentmindedly, scanning her eyes down the postcard.

'Sounds painful, all them little needles. Don't think I could bear it. I have a very low pain threshold. Giving birth nearly did me in. If I hadn't been given epidurals for all my children I would have died.'

Marina stiffened. 'I had better wander over now. Would you give Clementine's room a good clean this morning?'

'I saw her driving down the lane. Doesn't look very well this morning. I didn't even get a smile.'

'Neither did I, Bertha.'

'Doesn't cost much to smile.'

'It does if you're as hung-over as she is. Don't forget her room, will you?'

'I'll do my best.' She got up slowly, one hand in the small of her back, and lumbered over to the dishwasher where she began to load the plates half-heartedly.

Marina put the postcard in her pocket and made her way across the gravel to the hotel. Bertha checked that she was well and truly gone before switching on the kettle and sitting down again, extracting the *Daily Mail* from her handbag and settling into a gripping article about a kitten that was flushed down the lavatory and survived.

Jennifer and Rose were at the reception desk talking to Jake when Marina entered. Unlike his sister, Jake was a sunny young man with a ready smile and easy charm. Tall like his father, he was classically good-looking, with clear blue eyes and a long, straight nose. What undermined his appeal was the lack of character in his face. There was little to distinguish it from other generically handsome Englishmen who had experienced nothing in their lives but pleasure.

He greeted his stepmother jovially and she couldn't help but smile back at him. 'I should be angry with you.'

'I know. I'm sorry. I should have told you I was going to take a detour to Thurlestone. But I never expected to stay so long.'

'So, what did you discover about the robber?'

'Besides the fact that he leaves a thank-you note?'

'That's his signature, is it?'

'I think he's rather relishing being called Baffles, the Gentleman Thief. I suppose he's got a fixation with Raffles, the character from that old movie. You know, the one David Niven starred in.'

'It was originally a novel by E. W. Hornung, brother-in-law to Arthur Conan Doyle, the creator of Sherlock Holmes. Grey told me. He's good with books. Well, Baffles had better watch out. It'll be his downfall. They always get too pleased with themselves.'

'You're probably right. At the moment, though, they're baffled.' He laughed at his pun. 'He clearly knows the hotels and stately homes intimately, but no one can work out how.'

'I'm not a detective, but even I can see that he must pose as a guest.'

'Perhaps. But how do guests have access to all the other rooms?'

'He climbs out of the window and jumps from sill to sill, like a cat.' She smiled at the thought of Harvey reciting 'Macavity'.

'Or he's a serviceman who works for hotels – a gas man or carpet cleaner.'

'They'll catch him sooner or later,' she added hopefully. 'These people never get away with it.'

'He should quit while he's ahead.'

'If he's leaving little notes it's because he's enjoying himself. He's on a roll.'

Jake shook his head. 'He'll trip up, mark my words. He'll get too cocky and do something stupid.'

'Let's hope so, sooner rather than later.'

Jake followed her into the hall. 'So, I hear your interviews didn't go so well yesterday.'

'I'm very demoralized.' She dropped her shoulders and smiled pathetically.

'Dad tells me you have an Argentine coming this morning.'

'Rafa Santoro. Sounds like a fancy brand of dog biscuits.'

'Let's hope he's less flaky than a biscuit.'

'I just hope he's a normal painter. I'm not asking for anyone special. I don't want eccentric; there are enough of those around here already!'

'Speaking of which, Mr Potter needs to speak to you. Something about sweet peas.'

'Later.' She looked at her watch. 'I'll just go and chat up the old Brigadier before the Biscuit gets here. I'll be in the dining room, if he's early. Show him into my study and don't tell me if he's odd. I can't cope with odd this morning.'

The Brigadier sat at his usual table at the end of the dining room, beside the window. He was dressed in a three-piece tweed suit and pale yellow tie, drinking tea and reading *The Times*, chuckling loudly at the absurdity of the world. The room was blessed with tall ceilings and giant windows that gave onto the magnificent cedar tree so that the morning sun flooded the room with brilliance and lit up his head like a halo. When he saw Marina he staggered to his feet, in spite of her repeatedly telling him not to, and greeted her cheerfully in a stentorian tone.

'What a delightful sight first thing in the morning.' His face was a fleshy mass of ruddy skin and broken veins, with neatly clipped sideburns and moustache, and a full head of thick white hair. His eyes may have been as small as raisins, but his sight was perfect and he swept them over her as if appraising a pretty mare. 'You're a picture of loveliness, Marina.'

'Thank you,' she said, sitting down.

'Grey lent me a very interesting book yesterday. I started reading it last night and couldn't put it down.'

'Which one is it?'

'Andrew Roberts's *Masters and Commanders*. Great read. Beautifully written. Pure pleasure. Sometimes I wish I could turn the clock back. Best days of my life.'

'I'm very glad we can't do that.'

'Call me an old fool, but my life had purpose then. I had a cause to fight for and nothing has been as good in my life since. I'm like an old train in the junkyard, remembering happier times.'

'You have purpose, Brigadier. You have children, grandchildren and your great-grandson, Albert. You are certainly not in the junkyard.'

He chuckled. 'Ah, yes. Children are a blessing. One doesn't really feel one's left one's imprint on the world if one doesn't produce offspring. I'll die knowing my blood line continues. We didn't fight for nothing, although most young people don't appreciate what we did for them. If it wasn't for us they'd be speaking German and kowtowing to a load of Huns! God damn it!' He choked on his laughter, coughed loudly, then cleared his throat of phlegm. 'Speaking of children, how are yours? That Jake gets taller every time I see him.' Marina didn't have the heart to remind him that they weren't hers.

Talking to the Brigadier had distracted her from the imminent arrival of her ten o'clock interview. When Jake strode across the room, she had almost forgotten about it altogether. 'Ah, speak of the devil,' said the Brigadier.

Marina noticed the strange expression on Jake's face. It was a mixture of amusement and delight.

'Morning, Brigadier. Marina, the Biscuit has arrived,' he said.

'Why the funny look?' she asked, her stomach churning with anxiety.

'What funny look? He's in your office.'

'And? Is he ... normal?'

'I'd say he's not normal at all.'

'You're teasing me.'

'Just go and meet him.'

'What's this about a biscuit?' interrupted the Brigadier. 'Sounds good to me, especially if it has a little milk chocolate on the top.'

Marina reached the hall to find Shane, Jennifer, Rose, Heather and Bertha standing in a huddle by the reception desk, giggling like a group of silly schoolchildren. When they saw Marina they sprung apart guiltily. The air was charged with excitement, as if Father Christmas had come seven months early and was waiting in her study.

'Would you like me to bring you some coffee?' asked Heather, her cheeks aflame.

Marina narrowed her eyes. 'Well, let's see what he wants.'

'Looks like a coffee drinker to me,' said Bertha.

'And what brings *you* into the hotel, Bertha?' asked Marina.

'Run out of Cif,' she replied with a snigger. 'Timing couldn't be better.'

'Then why don't you go and get some from the cupboard? Heather, come with me, and the rest of you can get back to work.'

It was with some optimism that Marina walked into her office. By the blushes glowing on the faces of her staff it was obvious that the artist was attractive. That didn't surprise her; Argentine men were notoriously good-looking. However, she was not prepared for the quiet magnetism of Rafael Santoro.

He stood by the window, looking out over the sea, hands in pockets, lost in thought. In a pale suede jacket, blue shirt and faded denim jeans, he was of average height, broad-shouldered and athletic. From his profile she guessed he was in his thirties. His skin was weathered, his chin bristly, his light brown hair falling slightly over a forehead that was broad and creased with frown lines. When he heard her at the door, he seemed to hesitate a moment before turning, as if collecting himself. She took

in his patrician nose and the strength of his jaw-line, and felt her
spirits swell with admiration. He was undoubtedly handsome. He
turned and looked at her and she was immediately struck by his
eyes. They were brown like fudge, and deep set, but it was the
expression in them that made her catch her breath. It was almost
familiar, and she stumbled on her words.

'It's . . . it's nice to meet you.'

'It's very nice to meet you, too,' he said, extending his hand.
His accent was as soft and warm as caramelized milk. She took
his hand and felt the heat of his skin travel all the way up her
arm.

'I think you're the first Argentine to set foot in the
Polzanze,' she said for lack of anything better to say.

'That surprises me. South Americans love to travel.'

'Well, it's a pleasure to welcome you,' she said, averting her
eyes a moment. His gaze was too heavy to carry. 'It's nice to
hear a foreign accent for a change.'

'I would imagine a place of great beauty like this would
attract people from all over the world.'

'You flatter me.'

'I mean to flatter you.' His comment was delivered with
such casualness that she did not take it for flirtation.

She smiled politely. 'Thank you.' She liked him already. He
didn't have Jake's shallow good looks, but the lines and imper-
fections of a man who had experienced life in all its shades and
textures.

'I hope you weren't hoping for an *English* artist.'

'Not at all. I have no preferences so long as the person is
right for the position.' She noticed the silver buckle on his belt,
engraved with his initials: R.D.S.

He grinned, his skin creasing into deeply carved laughter-
lines around his mouth and eyes. 'A present from my father.'

'It's lovely. Let's sit down.'

He sat on the sofa and Marina sank dreamily into the

armchair. She had quite forgotten Heather, who remained in the doorway, transfixed, a blush soaked into her skin.

'Would you like tea or coffee?' Marina asked, remembering herself.

'I'd love a fruit juice.'

'I'll have one, too. Orange juice, freshly squeezed,' said Marina.

Heather looked surprised. 'Shall I bring some nice biscuits?'

'Good idea, Heather.'

'A little ice in your juice?'

'No, thank you,' he replied.

Her blush deepened. 'Anything else?' She made not the slightest movement to leave.

'Just the door, Heather,' said Marina deliberately. 'Close it behind you. So, what's an Argentine doing in Devon?'

'You might well ask. I'm a long way from home.'

'Very.'

'I work for an advertising agency in Buenos Aires, on the creative side. I do all the artwork. My father died, so I decided to take a sabbatical.'

'I'm sorry to hear that.'

'He was very old. I am the youngest child of five, by twenty years.'

'Quite an after-thought.'

'Something like that. Anyway, I decided to travel. So, I have passed the last couple of months travelling around Europe.'

'Painting?'

'Yes. It's a good way to take time to see the places properly.'

'You must have a wonderful collection by now.'

'I do. But I'm afraid I don't keep them all. I can't travel around with suitcases full of pictures.'

'Of course not. So, what do you do with them? Don't tell me you throw them away?'

'No. That would be too painful. I'm attached to each one,

in a way. So, I leave them in hotels, restaurants ... or I give them away.'

'That's generous of you.'

'It's easy to be generous. They cost me nothing.' He shrugged. 'And anyway, they aren't worth much. I'm not famous. I'm not even well known.'

'If you were, you wouldn't be here.'

'You're probably right. I came to Devon by chance and found it so beautiful I decided I would stay. As I was trying to work out how that would be possible, I saw your advertisement in the local paper. I would like to remain here for the summer.'

'Then return to Argentina?'

'Yes. Back to Buenos Aires.'

'I have never been to Argentina.'

'It is beautiful, too. Judging from your good taste here at the hotel, I would say you could not fail to love it.'

'They say it is full of Italians who speak Spanish and want to be English.' She laughed, relaxing into her chair. He had such an appealing face she wanted the interview to go on and on. She knew already that Rafa Santoro would be spending the summer at the Polzanze, whether he could paint or not.

'I suppose that is quite accurate, where I am concerned, at least. Although, I don't think I'd want to be English. I'm happy being who I am.'

At that moment the door opened and Heather entered with a tray of juice and biscuits, followed by Harvey, keen to see what all the fuss was about. He had ordered the quartet in the hall back to work, knowing that Marina would hate them to be standing idle, especially Bertha, who was as lazy as a sow in sunshine.

'Meet Harvey,' said Marina, eyes brightening at the sight of him. He shook Rafa's hand and grinned down at him. Marina recognized his approval at once and felt her spirits soar.

'Harvey has been with us since we bought this place eighteen years ago. He's my Man Friday. I couldn't have made a success of this without him.'

'Don't listen to her,' Harvey protested, a twinkle in his eye. 'There's just no one else on the premises who can change light bulbs like I can. Even at seventy-five.'

'You don't look seventy-five, Harvey.'

He winked at Rafa. 'It's that kind of flattery that keeps me climbing ladders and clearing drains.'

'Did you bring any of your work to show us?' Marina asked.

'Of course.' Rafa pulled a brown leather bag onto his knee and unzipped it. He withdrew a sketchpad and placed it on the coffee table.

Marina leaned forward eagerly. 'May I?'

'Please.'

She opened the first page. 'Perfect,' she breathed, gazing on a watercolour of a river, painted with flair and warmth. A flock of birds was taking to the air, some still in the water, others already reaching for the skies, and she could almost feel the spray as they agitated the water with their feet. The next was a sketch of old women gossiping in a market, their faces full of expression, from bitterness to pride. 'You are very versatile.'

'I have to be, in my business. I might draw a cola bottle one day, a landscape the following day, a caricature the next. It is never the same.'

'Where did you learn to draw?'

'Nowhere special.'

'You were born with the gift.'

'Perhaps.'

'You're lucky.'

He grinned at Harvey. 'But I'm not good at clearing drains.'

Marina flicked through the whole book, her admiration

growing with each new picture. 'We would love you to spend the summer with us,' she said, sitting back in her chair.

Rafa looked pleased. 'I'd like that very much.'

She looked a little embarrassed. 'We can't pay you, I'm afraid. But you'll have your board and lodging for free. All we ask is that you are available to teach the guests to paint. We'll provide all your materials, of course.'

'When would you like me to start?'

She clapped her hands in delight. 'Next month. Shall we say, the first of June?'

'First of June.'

'Come the day before to give yourself time to settle in.'

'I look forward to it.'

'So do I,' she replied, pleased that he looked happy with the arrangement. 'You don't know how hard it has been to find you.' Then her thoughts turned to Clementine. At last, the girl would have something to thank her for.

Chapter 4

Clementine staggered into work in a pair of skinny jeans and pumps, a thick grey sweater hanging almost down to her knees. It was spring but she felt cold to her bones. She didn't know what hurt more, her morale or her head. Sylvia sat at her desk in a tight dress and stilettos, painting her nails red. Mr Atwood's partner, Mr Fisher, was already in his office talking on the telephone. She was relieved she had got there before her boss, though she didn't imagine she was going to be of much use.

'Oh, deary dear,' said Sylvia, shaking her head. 'You don't look well.'

'I feel terrible.'

'Go and get a coffee.'

'I've already had one at home.'

'Then get another. Mr Atwood will be in shortly and he'll be wanting a skinny latte and a blueberry muffin. If you have them waiting for him on his desk he'll forgive your sickly pallor.'

'Do I look that bad?'

'Yes, lovely, you do. You shouldn't wear foundation at your age. When you're pushing thirty like me you can pile it on with a shovel.'

Clementine flopped onto her chair and switched on her computer. 'I can't remember much about last night.'

'What *do* you remember?'

'Joe.' She closed her eyes, hoping he might go away.

'Isn't he lovely? So handsome. You two really hit it off, which puts a smile on my face this morning as I was the one to set you up. I think he's smitten. I've never seen him behave like that before.'

'Behave like what?'

'He was all over you.'

'Was he?'

'Oh, yes.' Sylvia grinned. 'It's usually the other way round, and he's having to fend them off.'

'That's encouraging.'

'You don't sound very happy about it. He's quite a catch, you know.'

'I'm sure he is. A big fish in a small pond.'

'Nothing wrong with a small pond. Better than a small fish in a big pond.'

'I don't know. Regardless of the pond, I'm not sure about the fish.'

Sylvia knitted her eyebrows. 'Now you've lost me.'

'I remember going to his place. I remember you and Freddie dancing.'

'Freddie loves to dance.'

'Then I remember his sofa.'

Sylvia laughed throatily. 'I bet you do. That sofa's seen a lot of action in its time.'

'That makes me feel so much better. Thank you.'

'You know what I mean. He's no monk.' Sylvia held her nails up and waved them in the air to dry. 'And you're no angel.'

'I don't want to think about it.'

'You don't regret it, do you? The secret of life is not to regret anything. Waste of time. You had fun, didn't you?'

'I can't remember.'

'You looked like you were having fun when we left.'

Clementine felt her spirits dive. 'I feared you'd left.'

'I'm no voyeur, Clemmie. Besides, me and Freddie had business of our own to see to. Mmm, now there's a man who knows how to pleasure a woman without having to use satellite navigation.'

The door swung open and Mr Atwood walked in. 'Morning, girls,' he said cheerfully. Then he saw Clementine hunched on her chair, with her handbag on her knee. 'You leaving us already, Clementine?'

'Just going to get you a skinny latte and a muffin,' she replied, getting up.

'Good girl. Will you get me the *Gazette* and *Telegraph*? Oh, and while you're there, it's my wife's birthday tomorrow, see if you can find something appropriate.'

'Appropriate?'

'A scented candle or something. You're a woman, you know what women like. I haven't a clue and I always get it wrong.'

'I don't know what your wife likes.'

'I do,' said Sylvia, screwing the top onto the varnish. 'Go into Kitchen Delights and get her something in there. It's her favourite shop.'

'What if she has it already?'

'It's the thought that counts,' said Mr Atwood. 'The thought will be enough to keep the little lady happy.'

'I'll do my best.' Clementine rather relished the idea of spending time outside the office.

'Be a love and bring me a chocolate brownie and a cup of tea, milk no sugar,' Sylvia added. 'And a black coffee for Mr Fisher.' The telephone rang. She picked it up, careful to avoid ruining her nails, and answered in a singsong voice. 'Atwood and Fisher, Sylvia speaking. How can I help you?'

Mr Atwood strode into his office, straightening the magazines on the coffee table in the reception area on the way, and closed the door behind him. Clementine squinted in the sun as she stepped into the street. She wanted to keep walking until she lost herself.

She went to Kitchen Delights first, deliberately spending as much time as possible browsing for a suitable present. She envisaged poor Mrs Atwood in an apron, slaving away at the oven for a man who couldn't even be bothered to choose her birthday present himself. What sort of husband was that? She couldn't imagine the woman being happy with a few cooking bowls. What was wrong with a pretty necklace or handbag? Mr Atwood had no idea, and nor, for that matter, had Sylvia. Provincial people, she sniffed disdainfully, picking up a set of jelly moulds. After a good fifteen minutes, she settled on a shiny pink food mixer.

Very fetching, she thought, pleased with her choice. She looked at the price tag and winced. *Expensive, but it costs to be lazy*.

She wandered around to the Black Bean Coffee Shop with her bag, buying the newspapers, a birthday card and wrapping paper on the way – she lingered a good ten minutes over the cards, finding the most *in*appropriate card possible to cheer herself up.

By the time she reached the coffee shop she was feeling a lot better. She flopped into one of the velvet sofas with a latte and a bun, and read the latest on the robberies in the *Gazette*. Another twenty minutes was wasted in the most satisfactory fashion. She took a luxurious deep breath and watched the other customers: a couple of mothers with toddlers, a trio of businessmen having a meeting, schoolgirls playing truant. But she couldn't stay away all morning. Reluctantly, she drained her cup and joined the queue to buy the long list of requests to take back to the office. She thought of Joe and her fears returned to churn her stomach to butter. The door swung open and a man in a suede jacket and denim jeans walked in.

She glanced at him. But instead of turning back, she remained agog, unable to tear her eyes away. He looked around the coffee shop, then took his place in the queue behind her.

Clementine wrenched her eyes off him with some effort, though not before she had extracted a smile. She felt a blush creep up her chest and flourish on her face, and she forgot all about Joe and her sense of inadequacy. She could smell the sandalwood of the stranger's cologne. She breathed it in, savouring the scent of foreign places. He was obviously not English. Englishmen didn't wear jeans so well and they never bothered with such elaborately buckled belts. She looked down at his feet: brown suede loafers. She hadn't seen a pair of those since she'd left London. The queue moved quickly and soon she was at the counter, giving her order. She stood aside to make room for the stranger as the girl placed the muffin and brownie into a bag and went off to make her tea and coffee.

'Are both those cakes for you?' he asked.

Clementine was startled. She hadn't imagined he would talk to her. She tried to act coolly but her heart danced noisily in her chest. 'Are you suggesting I shouldn't?'

'Of course not. It's important for a girl to eat well.' He was now grinning at her.

'Are *you* going to have something naughty?'

'If you put it like that, I think I'd better.'

'Rude not to. Where are you from?'

'Argentina.'

'Argentina? The land of polo.'

'How well you know it.'

She laughed, feeling foolish. 'I don't know it at all. I've been to the Cartier Polo Match, watched the Argentines slaughter the Brits, and seen *Evita* at the theatre. That's as much as I know.'

'It's a good start.'

'You've come a long way.'

'Not really. The world is getting smaller all the time.'

The girl at the counter stood poised by the till. 'Can I help you?' Clementine noticed how she perked up at the sight of him, too.

'A chocolate brownie and an espresso.' He turned to Clementine. 'As you say, it would be rude not to.'

She laughed. 'It really would. If you're from Argentina you should go to Devil's and taste our scones with clotted cream and jam. They're out of this world.'

'Next time we meet, you can take me.'

'Deal.' She sincerely wished for a next time.

She paid for her order. He didn't invite her to join him. Perhaps he wasn't staying, either. 'Well, so long, stranger.'

'So long. Enjoy your naughty muffin.'

'Not for me, actually. For my boss.'

'Lucky boss.'

'Lucky boss indeed. He certainly doesn't deserve it.' She was left no alternative but to leave. The queue behind them looked on impatiently. She tossed him a casual smile, as casual as she could muster when her mouth wanted to swallow her entire face with happiness, and left.

Clementine hurried back to the office in a state of excitement. Throwing herself against the door with her bags, she fell in. 'Oh my God!' she exclaimed to Sylvia, who was now rubbing oil into her cuticles.

'You look better. What have you done? Got the present?'

'A pink food mixer.'

'Fabulous!'

'I think so. I've got wrapping paper and a card.'

'Let's see?' Clementine placed the bag on Sylvia's desk. 'You'll have to get them out, lovely, my nails are still tacky.'

'I've just bumped into the most delicious man I've ever seen!'

'More delicious than Joe?' Sylvia looked disappointed.

'Forget Joe, Sylvia. Joe's not a runner.'

'Shame, he's just sent you round a bouquet of roses.' She nodded at Clementine's desk.

Clementine's heart sank at the sight of ten plump roses in transparent paper, tied with ribbon. 'Oh Lord!'

'He can't help you.'

'I can but ask.'

'So, go on. Amuse me.'

'This divine stranger from Argentina just sashayed into the Black Bean Coffee Shop and chatted me up.'

'Are you serious? With all that make-up caked onto your face?'

'Yes.'

'Foreigner. And?'

'Well, that's it.'

'Did you give him your number?'

'Of course not.'

'Did he give you his?'

'No.'

'Does he know where you work?'

'Sylvia, he knows nothing about me. We had a little chat. That's all.'

'I'm not even mildly amused. So you're turning Joe down because of a man you've talked to for five minutes and will never see again.'

'I feel on cloud nine.'

Sylvia looked perplexed. 'You're a very strange girl, Clemmie. What sign are you?'

'Aries.'

'Must have Aquarius rising.'

'Whatever. My hangover is cured.' She smiled broadly.

'Well, thank the Lord for that.'

Clemmie handed her the card. Sylvia looked at the black and white 1950s photograph of a woman in an apron, smiling serenely while wielding a wooden spoon. The caption read, 'Bet you can't imagine where I'd like to stick this?' 'Do you think this is appropriate?'

'He won't know until she opens it. I think it's funny.'

'*He* won't.'

'But Mrs will.'

Sylvia laughed, handing it back. 'I think she will, too. Now give me the gift and the paper and once my nails are dry I'll wrap it for you. If your wrapping is anything like your dressing, Mr Atwood will throw it back at you.'

Clementine spent most of the morning stuffing documents into the nearest files without any consideration for the person who might later need to find them. She dreamed of the handsome Argentine. She wondered what he was doing here in Dawcomb, if he was staying, or whether he was on a train bound for London, gone for ever. She didn't expect to see him again, yet she couldn't help fantasizing about taking him to Devil's for scones and clotted cream. Perhaps, when she'd earned enough money, she'd go to Argentina instead of India. She wished he'd call to rent a property for the summer, and kicked herself for having not found a way to get Atwood and Fisher into the conversation. It would have been easy to have just slipped it in somewhere and she was only round the corner. He could have wandered along after his coffee and invited her out for lunch.

Unfortunately, it wasn't the Argentine who strode into the office at twelve thirty, but Joe, suggesting they have a quick bite at the brasserie on the sea front. Clementine feigned delight, clutching her stomach to stop it churning with regret, and thanked him for the flowers. She barely dared look into his eyes in case they triggered more memories of the night before. She decided she was better off not knowing, at least that way there still remained the possibility of having *not* done it.

Joe was very coarse compared with the stranger, his features blunt and regular, void of character. In a pair of badly cut jeans and V-neck sweater he was easily outshone by the man she would never see again. She could still smell the sandalwood on his skin and picture his raffish grin and deep-set eyes. There was nothing deep about Joe, just the hole she was now unintentionally digging herself into by agreeing to lunch.

Mr Atwood granted her an hour, as long as Sylvia was in to man the office. He was pleased with the gift for his wife, neatly wrapped and tied with a ribbon. It looked like he had gone to great trouble to find the perfect gift. She'd be thrilled with the mixer; pink was her favourite colour. He signed the card without looking at it and placed it in the bag with the present, then reached for the telephone to call his mistress.

Back at the hotel the dining room was almost empty, but for a few resident guests eating quietly by the window and an elderly couple who had come from town to celebrate their golden wedding anniversary with an expensive lunch. Heather waited on the tables sleepily, while Arnaud, the sommelier, heaved his enormous frame around the room importantly, waving the silver *tasse de dégustation* that dangled around his neck on an elaborate chain.

Marina was too happy to lament the empty tables. She had found her artist-in-residence. He was charming, talented and warm. Above all, Harvey liked him and Harvey had a good nose for people. She sat at her desk and began to write a list of things to buy in spite of the little money she had available. She was sure Rafa would draw people to the hotel once she posted it up on their website. Shelton was famous for its beauty and birds. If she could somehow reach people all over the world who liked to paint she was sure she could save the hotel from bankruptcy.

The sound of the sea and crying gulls swept in through the

open window, drawing her thoughts onto the water where her secret pain lay scattered on the waves and in the wind. For a moment she felt an overwhelming sense of bereavement. She paused her pencil above the paper and almost gave in. But then she remembered her beloved Polzanze, the house she had built into a beautiful hotel with all the resolve and purpose of a woman determined to create with her hands where her body could not. The Polzanze had sustained her when her grief had threatened to break her. She had poured all her love into its conception and birth. Without it, she would be lost. She began to scribble until the roar of the ocean and the squawking of gulls faded into a dull lament.

She was interrupted by a light tapping at the window. She looked up. There, with his woolly face pressed against the glass, was Mr Potter, the gardener. When he saw that she had noticed him, he pulled off his cap and grinned toothlessly, signalling with his hand that she come out and talk to him. With a sigh she got up.

'I'm so sorry, I completely forgot,' she said, leaning out. 'The sweet peas.'

'That's right, Mrs Turner.'

'Give me a minute to put on my boots and I'll come out.'

'Sorry to bother you. You looked busy in there.'

'It's OK. The gardens are as important as the house.'

His grey eyes twinkled beneath white candyfloss eyebrows. 'They most certainly are.'

'I'll meet you at the greenhouse.' She withdrew from the window and watched with a surge of affection as the old man replaced his cap and plodded off, his stiff hip causing him to limp slightly.

Just as she was about to go out, Marina remembered the postcard from Katherine Bridges and pulled it out of her pocket. She read it again, smiling fondly to herself as she remembered her old friend, now in her late sixties and living on the edge of

Lake Windermere in British Columbia. Love had taken her to the other side of the world and she couldn't blame her for that, but she missed the only woman she had ever truly depended on. She pulled a floral box file down from the shelf and opened it. Inside were dozens of items of correspondence from Katherine, which she had kept over the years. She placed the postcard inside and put the box back. Then she went out into the garden to find Mr Potter.

'Well, she's found her artist,' said Bertha, sitting at the kitchen table with Heather. Lunch was over, the few guests had left, the three chefs taken off their aprons and retired for the afternoon.

'He's lovely,' sighed Heather, her broad Devon accent curling around the words like the steam swirling up from her hot chocolate.

'Do you think it's true what they say about foreigners?'

'What do they say, then?'

'That they make good lovers.'

Heather giggled. 'I wouldn't know.'

'Why would they be better? What do they do that Englishmen don't do?'

'Last longer?'

Bertha grunted. 'Nothing good about that.'

Heather hugged her mug of hot chocolate. 'Do you think she'll calm down now she's found her artist?'

'Hope so. She's very tense. I think she's having a midlife crisis.'

'Really?'

'Oh, yes. She's over fifty and she's got no kids. I bet that hurts.'

'Poor love. Every woman deserves to have kids.'

'It can drive you mad, you know, not having kids. Something to do with the womb drying up.'

'Really?'

'Oh, yes. It dries up, and that drying-up does something to the brain.'

'So, what will happen?'

'Don't know.' Bertha shook her head, her face full of doom. 'Perhaps her artist will cheer her up.' Her bosoms jiggled with laughter. 'Sure as hell will cheer me up!'

Clementine insisted on paying half the lunch bill. It wasn't very much and Joe was determined to treat her, but she placed twelve quid on the plate and refused to take it back. 'You've bought me a bunch of roses. I can't allow you to pay for lunch as well.'

'I'm glad you liked them.'

'I do. They brighten up the office.'

'You've brightened up my day.'

'Good.' She felt the tightness in her voice and smiled stiffly.

'Last night was fantastic.'

'Great. Good.' She frantically searched for the waiter.

'You don't sound very convinced. Wasn't it good for you?'

She tossed her gaze at the little fishing boats that bobbed about on the sea and wished she could just sail away in one. 'I don't remember much,' she mumbled. 'I drank too much vodka. Felt terrible this morning. So, no, it wasn't so great for me.'

Joe shrank in disappointment. 'I'm sorry.'

'So am I.'

'I shouldn't have let you drink so much.'

'I'm not used to it,' she lied.

'You were fun, though.'

'I'm sure I was.' She glared at him. 'I don't usually sleep with someone on the first date.'

Joe looked astonished. 'You think you slept with me?'

'Didn't I?' It was her turn to shrink.

'What sort of man do you take me for? You think I'd ply you with drink and take advantage of you?'

'You didn't?'

'Of course not.'

'So, we just fooled around?'

'I wouldn't put it quite like that. You didn't mind at the time. In fact, you mewed with enjoyment.'

'Steady with the details.'

He grinned. 'Feel better now?'

'Yes, much. I awoke feeling ashamed. I'm not that sort of girl.'

'I know that. That's why I like you.'

It wasn't going to be so easy to extricate herself while she felt this grateful. 'Thank you.'

'You're quirky. I like that.'

'Am I?'

'I like your overbite, it's sexy.'

'My overbite?'

'Yes, the way your top teeth—'

'You make me sound like Goofy.'

'When can I see you again? Tonight?'

'Not tonight, Joe.'

'Tomorrow then?'

'Maybe.'

He grinned at her. 'I like a woman who's hard to get.'

Clementine returned to the office deflated in spite of discovering that she had remained chaste after all. She had hoped to finish it with Joe, but it seemed to be starting all on its own, without any regard for her.

Chapter 5

Grey anchored his fishing boat in Captain's Cove and cast his line. The sea gently swelled beneath him and gulls dropped out of the sky to swim about his boat, greedy for the bread he tossed them. With the sun on his back and the breeze sweeping across his face he took pleasure from the peace. Green velvet meadows plunged sharply into precipitous cliffs, where birds nested in the rocks and only one or two white houses stood to brave the winds that whipped off the water. A yellow beach nestled secretively in the bay. He'd never seen anyone walk there, in spite of a narrow path leading down through the rocks. It looked enticing and he imagined setting down the picnic rug and lying there with Marina, enjoying the tranquillity undisturbed.

His thoughts turned to his wife as they always did, for she was growing increasingly anxious. He understood her concern. No one loved the Polzanze more than she. When they had first met, it was her dream to create a beautiful home. Had he had the money he would have bought her one without hesitation, but his barrister's pay wouldn't have afforded so much as a wing of the kind of house he'd have liked to give her. So he had bought a run-down mansion instead and watched with pleasure as she had slowly and laboriously created the palace of her fantasy. At first he had left it to her, returning at weekends on the train from London to see what she had done during the week. She'd had Harvey to help and together they had painted and decorated while Mr Potter had toiled in the gardens with his sons, Ted and Daniel. It had been a labour of love for all of them – Marina with her vision, and Harvey and Mr Potter with their memories of the glory days when the house had been a magnificent family home.

Grey left London when they opened the Polzanze. Being an hotelier was a full-time job and Marina was keen to give it a family feel, as if she were opening her own home to paying guests, welcoming every one at the door as a hostess would. They were soon written up in prestigious magazines and people poured in to admire her flamboyant decoration and splendid gardens. There was plenty to do. A golf course was conveniently situated near the hotel and a six-court tennis club boasted the Shelton Tournament for the young every summer. Grey organized fishing expeditions, supplying the hotel with fresh mussels, lobster and crab as well as a large variety of fish. A narrow path took guests along the cliff tops into Dawcomb-Devlish, where they were entertained with classy boutiques and restaurants. Children queued beneath the plane trees in the square for hair braids and spray-on tattoos, while their mothers shopped and their fathers arranged speed boating and day trips to Salcombe.

Marina wanted children from the moment she married. At thirty-three she was so much younger than Grey, who was forty-two with a broken marriage and two small children of three and five, who came to stay at odd weekends and during the holidays. As much as she adored Clementine and Jake, she longed for a baby of her own. Grey was happy to oblige, not that he desperately wanted more offspring, but he desperately wanted to make her happy. He was aware of the age gap and compensated by indulging her every whim as a father might indulge a beloved daughter. She began going to church, praying to God to bless her with a child, but none came. He either didn't hear her, or did not consider her deserving. Marina agonized over which it might be.

Now Marina did not go to church. She no longer prayed and her eyes would water at the smallest mention of children. God had deserted her and she felt the chill of His rejection with an overwhelming sense of shame. The Polzanze had sustained her for so many years, but now a curtain had come down on her dreams of motherhood. She spent more time on the beach, gazing out to sea as if she was expecting a child to come across the water. Grey knew she saw her future as a bleak, empty void, when it should be bright with the laughter of children and eventually grandchildren. They were in dire financial trouble, having borrowed heavily to build their business. She knew she was on the verge of losing the Polzanze, although she couldn't bear to articulate it. In those soul-searching hours on the beach Grey knew she must ask herself what she had besides him and her precious hotel; and he knew she believed she had nothing.

He felt a tug on the line and wrenched his thoughts back to the task at hand. Slowly, with great patience and skill, he drew it in. He sensed the fish was a big one. Shame they didn't have a full dining room to enjoy it. He was proud of supplying the kitchen with fresh catch every day. Sometimes he'd go out with Dan Boyle and Bill Hedley, two local fishermen who'd been fishing these waters for over fifty years. Then he'd bring in enough fruits of the ocean to last a week.

Finally, the fish rose above the water. It was a large, slippery Cornish bass, wriggling to free itself. Grey forgot about Marina and her grief for the child they couldn't have, and dropped the fish into the boat. He opened its tender mouth and released the hook. A wave of excitement washed over him as he admired it – must be at least four pounds.

He replaced the bait and cast his line again. He'd spend all morning out there, detached from the world and its worries. While he was in his boat, the Polzanze seemed a very long way away. He didn't dare wonder how Marina had got on with Rafa Santoro – if he'd believed in the power of prayer he'd have shot one up on her behalf. He knew how much this mattered to her – and if it mattered to her, it mattered even more to him.

Rafa Santoro returned to his hotel and took a table outside, against the wall. The sun was warm and he was sheltered from the wind. An audacious seagull landed on his table but he had nothing to give it so the bird turned up its beak and flew off to harass someone else for treats. He noticed a couple of girls at another table, giggling into their lunch, and averted his eyes. He didn't want to encourage them. The waiter took his order – cola, steak and chips – and he settled into the *Gazette*, the surest way to find out the local gossip.

So, he had arrived. He wasn't sure how he was meant to feel. Part of him felt elated, another saddened – saddened perhaps because the most vital part of him felt nothing at all. He tried not to think about it. The waiter brought his food and he took a sip of cola, feeling the girls' eyes boring into him with the cumbersome weight of their admiration. Any other day he would have invited them to join him. He might even have taken them up to his hotel room and made love to them. Any other day that thought alone would have been enough to raise his spirits and put a spring in his step for the rest of the afternoon, but not today. He buried his face in the *Gazette* and finished his lunch alone.

The girls left, not before deliberately passing his table and flashing their prettiest smiles. He nodded politely but let them go without a second glance. The seagull dropped onto their abandoned table and stole a half-eaten bread roll. He looked at his watch. It would be early morning in Argentina, but he needed to talk. He pulled out his BlackBerry and pressed speed dial. He didn't have to wait long.

'Rafa?'

'*Hola, Mamá*.'

'Thank God. You haven't called for a week. I've been worried sick. Are you OK?'

'I've arrived.'

'I see.' Her voice was tight. He sensed her sitting down. She sighed heavily, anticipating the worst. 'And?'

'It's a beautiful mansion overlooking the sea. I'm going to spend the summer there, teaching residents how to paint.' He laughed cynically. 'I don't know what I was expecting.'

'You shouldn't be there at all.'

'Calm down, Mamá.'

'What would your father think? *Dios mío*, what would he say?'

'He would understand.'

'I don't think he would.'

'Well, he'll never know.'

'Don't think he's not up there watching you. After all he did for you, Rafa. You should be ashamed.'

'Don't make me feel any worse. I'm wrestling with my conscience, too. You said you understood. You said you'd help me.'

'Because I love you, son.'

He felt a sudden surge of emotion rise through his chest and put his head in his hand. 'I love you, too, Mamá.'

There was a long silence. He could hear her breathing down the line, the familiar sound of his childhood that had once wrapped him in a warm blanket of security and unconditional love, but was now laboured and old and full of fear. Finally, she spoke and her voice wavered. 'Come home, *hijo*. Forget this silly idea.'

'I can't.'

'Then don't forget me.'

'I'll call you in a couple of days, I promise.'

'Do you have everything you need?'

'Everything.'

'Be careful.'

'I am.'

'Spare a thought for *them*.'

'But of course, Mamá. I won't hurt anyone.'

But you're hurting me, she thought as she put down the receiver and wiped her eyes with a clean white *pañuelo*. Maria Carmela Santoro heaved herself up from the armchair and wandered down the tiled corridor to Rafa's bedroom. The house was quiet now. Her husband was with Jesus and her four older children had flown the nest long ago. Rafa was her youngest, a gift from God when she was really too old to have more children. Her others were dark-skinned and dark-haired like their father, but Rafa had been a very blond child. With his light hair and natural charm he was special.

She stood in the doorway and looked round the room that held so many memories, warmed by her constant, tender caressing. When her other children were little they had had to share two to a room, for the farmhouse in the middle of the pampa was only small. But Rafa, being the last, had had a room of his own.

Now, of course, he lived in Buenos Aires in an elegant apartment just off Avenida del Libertador. But he came home often, more than the others. He was a good son. Now his father was no longer alive to take care of her, she knew she was safe in his capable hands. He had invited her to come and live with him, but she hated the noise and pollution of the city. She had spent all her life on the farm, worked hard as a maid for Señora Luisa and then, after she died, for her daughter-in-law, Marcela, for over fifty years, burying her roots deep in the fertile soil where now the remains of her dear husband lay, marked by a simple headstone and the flowers she took weekly to honour him.

She walked over to the window and threw open the green shutters. The smell of autumn blew in and she inhaled with pleasure. The sun was already warm and a few leaves lay on the grass, curled and dry and brown like wistful epistles to be tossed about by the wind. Plane trees stood tall and magnificent, lining the long drive that cut through the estancia and led up to the main house where her employers spent their weekends and holidays in languid splendour. Dappled light fell onto the dusty track and a dog barked loudly only to be berated by Angelina, the cook, in a round of furious Spanish.

Maria Carmela remembered little Rafa learning to ride with his father. She smiled affectionately at the mental picture. Big, black-haired Lorenzo in his beret, his red scarf tied loosely around his neck, the glittering coined belt and baggy *bombachas* tucked into worn leather boots. The little blond boy in white espadrilles, his brown ankles bare beneath olive-green *bombachas* and embroidered red sash, with a small beret of his own, nestled against his father's body, galloping up and down the plain to whoops of laughter. What a contrast the old, weathered skin of her husband against the smooth, new skin of their son. What joy he had brought, to everyone.

It was that angelic charm that had caught the attention of Señora Luisa. His father had let him bring round her pony one morning when he was just six years old. Proud to be given such an important role, he walked the animal to the front of the house and waited in the shade of the eucalyptus tree, his back straight, his chin high. When she had addressed him he had looked at her with an unwavering gaze and smiled broadly, and she had laughed at his audacity; so bold for such a little boy. She had engaged him in a long conversation, intrigued by the wisdom on so young a face, and he had made her laugh, answering so earnestly. It was clear he had an intelligence beyond that of his parents.

From then on she had sponsored him personally, taking an interest in his schoolwork and hobbies. When she had learned of his love of art she had seen to it that he had all the materials he needed and even helped him herself, with the little knowledge she had, until that became too limited and she had employed a young man from Buenos Aires to spend the summer tutoring him. Lorenzo and Maria Carmela were both proud and grateful, but Maria Carmela suffered terribly from the fear that Rafa would be taken away from her; that somehow, this gift of a child would not be hers for ever.

She went outside to feed the parrot, Panchito. He sat on his perch, basking in the sunlight, preening his green feathers in preparation for the day. She held out a handful of nuts, which he took one by one, using his beak and claw – he didn't like his breakfast to be rushed. Señora Luisa had enabled Rafa to rise above the low expectations thrust upon him by virtue of his birth. He had a good job, he earned well, he had a nice life . . . why was he now on the brink of throwing it all away?

Clementine left work early. Sylvia had convinced Mr Atwood to take his wife out for dinner and Clementine had booked the famous Incoming Tide restaurant and nipped out to buy a bouquet of roses for him to give her along with the present she had bought. She would have given him *her* bouquet if she could have been sure no one would notice, but Sylvia had put the flowers in water and placed them on her desk.

So Clementine departed at five with the roses tucked under her arm, dripping water down her coat. She looked forward to an early night, watching TV, forgetting about Joe and the prospect of seeing him the following night. At least she wasn't pregnant. She was overwhelmed with gratitude for that. He might be a little coarse, but he hadn't taken advantage of her

when he so easily could have. Perhaps he was a rough diamond – a gentleman beneath his workman's overalls. She
smiled at the thought of her mother and what she would make
of him. Her mother was a terrific snob, boxing everyone in
one of four compartments – proper, trade, common and foreign, proper being the only acceptable box.

She found her father and Marina in the kitchen, having tea.
Her father was ruddy-cheeked, having been out fishing for
most of the day, while Marina was glowing with happiness.

'Clementine,' she said, smiling up from the table, 'come and
join us.'

'How was your day?' asked her father.

'Dull.' Clementine unhooked a mug and helped herself to
a teabag.

'You're earning money and gaining experience, which is
very important.'

'Great, Dad. Thanks.'

'We've found our artist,' Marina announced.

'Hurrah!'

She ignored her stepdaughter's sarcasm. 'I think you'll like
him. He's very handsome.'

'I'm not interested. Look, he's *your* project. He's got nothing to do with me. After all, I can't paint and have no interest
in art.' She poured water into her mug and added a dash of
milk.

'Do you want to join us for dinner?'

'I'll eat it in front of the telly.'

'We're having bass. Your father caught it this morning.'

'Well, if there's enough, I'll have some.'

'Of course there's enough,' said Grey proudly. 'It's a four-
pounder, at least.'

'Wow, well done, Dad.'

'Fancy coming out with me this weekend?'

Clementine pulled a face. 'Why?'

'Just thought you might like to come out in the boat. How are those sea legs of yours?'

'I've never had sea legs, Dad. I hate boats and the sea makes me sick, if you remember.'

'That was years ago.'

'I don't think growing up changes either of those things.'

'It does change attitude,' interjected Marina coolly. 'Why don't you spend some time with your father?'

'OK, so you're bristling for another lecture. Is that it? I can't run off in the middle of the sea.'

'No lecture, just haven't seen much of you.'

'That's because I'm working, Dad. Welcome to the real world.'

Marina's good mood evaporated as Clementine sucked the air out of the room, replacing it with her dark presence. She glanced at her husband and felt nothing but contempt for her stepdaughter, who constantly rebuffed him.

'Another day, then,' said Grey, trying not to look disappointed.

Chapter 6

The following morning Mr Atwood strode into the office, his natural good humour overshadowed by a thunderous look. Clementine, who felt a great deal better after a good night's sleep, was already at her desk, looking at pictures of Buenos Aires on the Internet. Sylvia was late.

'If my wife hadn't been so delighted with her pink mixer I would sack you for the card you chose.'

Clementine hastily clicked out and pulled her most innocent face. 'I don't know what you mean, Mr Atwood.'

'Don't try that with me. You know exactly what I mean. The card was inappropriate, not to mention insulting.'

'Not to your wife, surely.'

'Of course not, you silly girl.'

'I thought it was funny.'

'So did she – at my expense.'

'Well, at least she had a laugh on her birthday.'

He narrowed his eyes. 'You're lippy this morning.'

'I had porridge for breakfast. It tends to make me a little feisty.'

'Well, have an egg tomorrow, instead. I don't expect my secretary to answer back.'

'You could have read the card when you signed it.'

'I pay you to do that.'

She shrugged. 'Did you have a nice dinner?'

'Yes.'

'That's good.'

He huffed irritably and strode across the reception area to his office, straightening the magazines on the way. Clementine wondered whether he was the sort of man who folded his clothes before making love. She suspected he was.

Sylvia arrived looking uncharacteristically tousled.

'You look like you've got out of bed backwards,' Clementine remarked.

'I did,' she replied, grinning mischievously. 'Freddie stopped by for breakfast, that's why I'm late.'

'That's the best excuse I've ever heard.' Clementine clicked into Buenos Aires again. 'I think I'm going to go to South America instead of India.'

'You're not still thinking of that Argentine, are you?'

'Dreams are cheap.'

'You get what you pay for.' Sylvia shot into the loos to tidy up. When she came out, her hair was neatly brushed into her usual up-do, her make-up flawlessly applied, her floral dress without a crease. Clementine wondered how it was possible to do all that in the lavatory.

'I'm meeting some friends for dinner tonight. D'you want to come?' Sylvia asked her.

'Sure.'

'Why don't you bring Joe?'

Clementine's shoulders slumped. 'Well, I kind of gave him the idea that I'd hook up with him tonight, so I suppose I should.'

'Give him a chance. I don't know what you want – heart flutters and stomach cramps, I expect – but life isn't like that. The point is, does he make you laugh and is he a good lover? Anything more than that is a bonus, or restricted to romantic novels. You wait around for that sort of hero and you'll grow old alone.'

'What a happy soliloquy first thing in the morning.'

'Sorry, lovely, but I'm just giving you a dose of realism.'

'I've had far too much realism recently. I'm going to go to Buenos Aires, to while away my days dreaming.'

'Now Argentines, apparently they're the worst.'

'How do *you* know?'

'Everyone knows. They're notorious for being irresistibly charming and compulsively unfaithful.'

'You're thinking of polo players, but go on, repeat the old cliché.'

'They make good lovers but bad husbands.'

'I'm not planning on marrying one. I don't intend to marry at all, ever.'

Sylvia looked bewildered. 'Why not?'

'I come from a broken home. I never want to do that to a child.'

'That's silly. You can break the cycle.'

'Don't want to.'

'I'm divorced, and yet I'd give it another go. I'd marry Freddie if he ever left his wife. They rarely do, though.'

'My father left my mother,' said Clementine bitterly. 'I'd never want to be the wedge that drives a family apart like Submarine.'

Sylvia shrugged. 'Maybe their love was so strong ...'

'Weren't you just saying that kind of love is reserved for romantic novels?'

'And the very lucky few.'

'Ah, so you do believe in love?'

'Yes, I do. But I don't believe it happens to each and every one of us. That's all. You might grow to love Joe if you give him a chance.'

'Do you love Freddie?'

'I love the way he touches me, the way he kisses me, the way he makes me laugh. I love who I am when I'm with him.

But do I love him? Like, would I die without him? I'd be sad, of course, but I wouldn't be broken-hearted.'

'Don't you want something more?'

'Of course. Every little girl wants to find her prince. But there's no point hankering after something you can't have. I'm realistic enough to know that I'm not one of the lucky ones.' Sylvia grabbed her handbag. 'I think I'll go out for a ciggie. Will you man the phone?'

Clementine watched her leave. She didn't imagine she was one of the lucky ones either, but deep down inside, she hoped there was more to love than Joe.

'I think we'll put Rafa in the suite at the top,' said Marina, sitting at her desk, sipping her espresso thoughtfully. 'No one's booked it for months and it's a shame to let such a beautiful set of rooms go unused.'

Harvey was up a ladder in his blue boiler suit and cap, screwdriver in hand to mend the curtain pole that had come away from the wall at one end. 'That's the nicest bedroom in the house,' he said, pausing his screwdriver. 'Used to be young William's room when he was a boy.'

Harvey remembered the Duke of Somerland's children fondly, three rambunctious boys with big blue eyes and smiles that held within them the promise of a whole heap of mischief. He had been just a lad himself, employed to help the estate manager, Mr Phelps, chopping logs and sweeping leaves. He still felt nostalgic when Mr Potter burned the leaves in autumn. It took him back to an innocent time in his life when things had been less complicated.

Ted and Daniel did the heavy work these days as Mr Potter was too old – older than he was, and *he* was as old as the hills – so he delegated and his sons dug and planted and cut back. Harvey suspected that Marina kept him on out of compassion, because she knew how much the place meant to him and understood the need to deny the years for as long as possible. After all, retirement for Mr Potter would be as good as putting him in his coffin and placing it in the ground.

Now the gardens looked as good as they had when the duke had owned the property, better, even, because Marina had such a clear vision of what she wanted and the determination to see it done. He watched her fondly from the window. She was always neatly dressed with crisp white shirts and slacks, or pretty dresses in summer, never jeans. Being short, she always wore heels to give her height. He felt paternal towards her, a feeling he relished, having never married or fathered children. The funny thing was, she blossomed beneath his praise and that made him feel good. This glamorous woman, who seemed to have the world at her feet, needed *him*.

'Is that a new watch, Harvey?' Marina asked, noticing the silver glinting on his wrist.

He shook his arm out of his sleeve. 'Isn't it a beauty?'

'It's very big.'

'That's why I like it.'

'It looks very expensive.'

'It's an Omega.'

'Sounds fancy.'

He was distracted by a damp patch in the corner of the room. 'Looks like there's a leak,' he said, frowning.

'A leak?'

'Might be a blocked gutter. Nothing I can't fix.'

She grinned at him affectionately. 'You always have just the right thing in that shed of yours. It's better stocked than any hardware shop.'

'That's because I don't throw anything away. You know, I have a wireless from the nineteen-fifties and the first black-and-white television I bought in the sixties.'

'And a healthy supply of Agritape and baler twine,' she added humorously, for it was a running joke that the Polzanze was held together by agricultural tape and string.

'So, where *are* you going to put Mr Santoro?' he asked, leaning on his screwdriver again.

'Paul had the blue room last year, but it's a bit run down; needs to be redecorated. The suite, however, has the original wallpaper, which is so pretty, and a little sitting room for him to paint in. It has a splendid view of the ocean and when the wind blows over the roof it whistles. It's got a special energy up there.'

'That's because William was a very happy boy. He and his brothers used to play up there all the time. It was the children's floor.'

Marina drained her coffee cup and stole a passing thought of her own children playing up there, had she been so blessed. 'He's come from Argentina; I want him to see the best England has to offer.'

'He'll see it here, there's no doubt about that.' Harvey gave the pole a good pull to make sure it was firmly fixed to the wall.

'I think he'll be perfect, don't you? My old ladies won't know what's hit them when they arrive for their week. I just hope the word spreads and people come.'

'They'll come,' Harvey reassured her. 'Life has its ups and downs, but mark my words, it always goes up after a down.'

Marina dropped her gaze into her empty cup. 'Am I a fool pinning all my hopes on Rafa Santoro? I know nothing about him. He could be an axe murderer, for all I know.'

'You have to trust your instincts. I sense he's a good man.'

'Do you?' She looked up at him.

'Yes, though I can't say whether he'll help put this place back on its feet again.'

'We're on our knees, Harvey.'

Harvey stopped working on the pole and looked down at her. 'I know.'

'I don't like to talk about it. I hope that if I don't talk about it, it won't happen.'

'It's quiet, all right, but it's just temporary.'

'I hope so, Harvey. We need money, fast.'

He came down the ladder and stood at the bottom, screwdriver hanging at his side. 'Now listen to me, Marina. You have to keep going. It's like walking a tightrope: look ahead or you'll lose your balance. Things will work out, people will come. We'll weather the recession like everyone else, and it'll blow over just like a storm.'

'Do you really see blue sky ahead?'

'Not a doubt in my mind.'

'I like your mind, Harvey. I wish I could curl up in it until the storm's gone.'

He smiled at her. 'I think William's floor will be perfect for Mr Santoro. Why don't I give the blue room a lick of paint?'

'Good idea.'

'Shall we go and have a look at it now?'

'Yes.' She stood up eagerly.

'Let's have a look at William's floor, too, and see if there's anything that needs to be done in there.'

'Yes, let's.' Her voice brightened. 'You can fix the leak later.'

As Marina and Harvey passed reception to get to the stairs, Jennifer paused her telephone conversation and smiled at them guiltily. Harvey shot her a reproachful look, knowing she was indulging once again in a private call.

'I've got to go, Cowboy,' Jennifer hissed once they had gone. 'I shouldn't be talking to you during working hours. I'll get fired.'

The voice on the other end of the line chuckled in

THE HOUSE BY THE SEA

amusement. 'Any nonsense from them and I'll take it out on their daughter. She's a liability as it is.'

'Oh, Nigel, that's not fair.'

'She's a useless secretary, and scruffy to boot. At least Sylvia is well-dressed and properly groomed.'

'Clemmie's young.'

'So are you, Jen, and you take pride in your appearance.'

'That's because I never know when you might saunter in here like John Wayne with your hand on your gun.'

'I'd like you to put *your* hand on my gun.'

'Is it loaded?' she giggled.

'It's always loaded, ready to go off with the slightest touch.'

'Oh, you dirty boy. Back on your horse!'

'Can I see you tonight?'

'Yes.'

'Then I won't call you again.'

'Text me instead. I like receiving sexy texts.'

'Do they turn you on?' he whispered, mouth very close to the receiver.

'Yes,' she whispered back.

'How much?'

'So much, I grow hot.'

'And wet?'

'Shame on you, Mr Atwood!'

'You love it.'

'I'll see you later.'

'Same time, same place. I'll go and polish my gun.'

'Easy now, Cowboy. Don't over-polish it.'

'Fear not, my precious. I'll leave the best for you.'

Grey was in the library reading *The Times* when Jake found him. His face looked old and weary in repose, a sadness hanging over him like a cloud. It lifted when he saw his son.

'Ah, Jake,' he said, putting down the paper.

'Dad, I've been thinking about how to revive the business.'

'Have you?'

'Yes.' Jake sank into the big leather armchair opposite his father. 'We need to do events. Get people in through a shared interest.'

'What do you have in mind?'

'Literary dinners. Something like that, anyway. A club of sorts. People pay to be members and they get to come to lectures. It's so quiet here, it's off-putting. We need an air of activity.'

'Well, you're certainly right about that.'

'I know Submarine's got her artist-in-residence.' He grinned wickedly. 'Give him a week and he'll be seducing every woman in Dawcomb. That'll teach her!'

'Don't be unkind, Jake. She's having a tough time at the moment. Be a little sympathetic.'

'Sorry. He's just so obviously a playboy.'

'I don't think he'd be coming here for the summer if he was a playboy.'

'OK, so not a playboy, a player.'

'Your idea's a good one,' said his father, decisively. 'I propose we begin with a lecture. Let's think of an author we'd like to invite to speak and I'll contact the publisher.' Grey was genuinely excited by the idea. He loved books and there were many authors he would like to meet. 'Well done, Jake. You're on the right lines.'

'I want to help, Dad.'

'Thanks, I appreciate it.' He watched his son leave the room, feeling a surge of gratitude. He wished his daughter could follow her brother's example and think about someone else for a change.

Clementine believed herself ill-treated and wronged, when she had so much to be grateful for. Grey knew it was his fault: he had spoiled her. If only she could see beyond herself she might come to understand a little more about the people who loved her. Not everything was displayed above the surface. He hadn't left her mother and run off with a temptress, as she believed, but taken the hand that reached out to him in the black pit of despair. So great was his unhappiness that he had decided to walk away from it. That meant leaving his small children – but what good would he have been to them anyway, cowed and broken? Marina had rescued him and breathed life into him again. Of course, Clementine would never know these things unless she asked him for his side of the story. Until that improbable moment all he could do was present his hand and wait patiently for her to take it.

That night Clementine sat in the Dizzy Mariner with Joe, Sylvia, Freddie, and Sylvia's dreary friends Stewart and Margaret. Sylvia dominated the conversation, telling funny stories in her strident way, wriggling her breasts in front of Freddie and leaving no one in any doubt that his hand was high on her thigh beneath the table, and climbing ever higher. Clementine knocked back her wine and made no effort to refuse when Joe filled her glass for the third time.

She watched the people around her as if through a pane of glass. Sylvia was brash, Freddie drooling, Margaret as dull as a dead mouse. Perhaps she was dead – Clementine couldn't tell – the woman sat there unblinking, without uttering a word. Were she in London she would be surrounded by like-minded people, but here, in the very depths of obscurity, she might as well have wound up in a farmyard full of animals.

By dessert Clementine was well and truly sloshed. She had allowed the alcohol to dull her senses. She joined in, telling stories of her own, making everyone laugh more heartily than they had laughed at Sylvia's, but Sylvia didn't notice, she was far more interested in Freddie's hand. As Freddie's hand reached as high as it was possible to go, Sylvia sprang up and

suggested they go out for a cigarette. Clementine did not want
to be left with Joe, Stewart and Margaret so she got up to leave
as well, placing a twenty-pound note on the table.

Once outside, the cool air revived her a little. Joe was not
far behind. He handed back the note.

'Why are you giving me this?' she asked.

'Dinner is on me.'

'You shouldn't.'

'I want to.'

Clementine sighed. She didn't want to feel any more
indebted to him than she already did. 'Thank you,' she replied
grudgingly.

He pulled her into his arms and kissed her mouth. His was
nicer than she remembered. 'You know you said you weren't
that sort of girl?'

'Yes.'

He kissed her again. 'Do you think you could be now?'

She laughed. 'I don't know, Joe . . .'

'Come home with me.'

'I don't love you, you know.'

'I know.'

'Do you love me?'

'I really fancy you.'

'Well, that's a start. I might never love you, though. I don't
want to break your heart.'

'Let me worry about my heart.'

'All right. I'll come home with you.'

'You'll let me do what you thought I did, but didn't do?'

She laughed sleepily. 'Maybe.'

Back at Joe's house they made love. Clementine wasn't too
drunk to enjoy the experience. The earth didn't move, but it
was pleasant enough. She left him asleep and drove home in
the early hours, having sobered up enough to make it up the
narrow lanes without crashing. The sight of the stable block

did not fill her with joy, so she took the path Marina so often trod and walked down to the beach. The sand looked golden in the eerie light, the sea swelling and glittering as far as the eye could see, until the twinkling lights on the water blended with the stars in the sky. She walked up the beach, her feet just missing the waves as they rushed up to catch her.

The beauty of the night made Clementine melancholy. She wanted to weep at the sight of so many stars. Something pulled on her heart, a gentle tug. She put her hand there. It wasn't a physical pain, but a feeling deep down that she couldn't explain.

She thought of Joe. Perhaps this was as good as it got. Perhaps Sylvia was right and she shouldn't wait around for Big Love, because there was no such thing, at least not for her. And yet, tonight, her heart felt as if it was opening up and willing something, or somebody, to slip inside. She sat down and let her mind still in the peaceful seclusion of the little bay. Soon, she forgot about Joe as the sea lulled her to sleep.

Chapter 7

Tuscany 1966

Floriana was in love for the first time in her young life. She knew it was love because it lifted her so very high she could almost touch the clouds. She was sure that if she extended her arms she would leave the ground altogether and fly like a bird, right out over the ocean, soaring carelessly on the wind. Oh, if only she *could* fly, she'd build a nest in one of those umbrella pines in the gardens of La Magdalena and make it her home for ever.

What a day she'd had. She couldn't wait to tell Costanza. It no longer mattered that her mother had run off with her little brother and left her with her hopeless father, Elio. It no longer mattered that he was most often drunk and that she had to look after him as a grown-up would. It didn't matter either that she was poor, because today she had been given riches beyond her most extravagant dreams. She had sneaked a peek at paradise and now she knew that however precarious her life, one thing was certain: she would marry Dante and live at La Magdalena.

She skipped all the way up the path that sliced through the meadows, taking pleasure from the crimson poppies that gently swayed to let her pass. The sea was calm and as blue as the sky that dazzled above it. Little crickets chirruped merrily, invisible in the long grasses, and she smiled because they, too, filled her heart with joy. At last she reached the Etruscan town of Herba, where she lived with her father. The familiar sounds rose on the heat: the barking of a dog, the high-pitched squeaking of children playing, the staccato cries of a mother berating her child, the musty smell of ancient walls and fried onions.

Soon she was hurrying over paving stones, past yellow houses with dark green shutters, wide arches and red-tiled roofs, towards the centre of town. Widows in black dresses sat in doorways like fat crows, sewing, gossiping or fingering their rosaries, eyes squeezed shut, muttering inaudible prayers. Skinny dogs trotted in shadow along the wall, stopping every now and then to sniff something of interest, lingering outside the butcher's in the hope of being tossed the odd scrap.

She took a narrow street that climbed steeply up the hill and hurried beneath row upon row of washing lines. A woman leaned out of the window to hang her dripping petticoat and called to her, but Floriana was too busy to wave back and scampered on until she reached Piazza Laconda, which opened in the heart of town like a giant sunflower. There, dominating the square, was God's own house, the most beautiful building of all, la Chiesa di Santo Spirito.

She was now quite out of breath and slowed to a hasty walk. The sun bathed the square in a bright golden light and flocks of pigeons pecked the ground in search of crumbs or washed their dusty feathers in the fountain. A restaurant spilled onto the cobbles, infusing the air with the smell of olive oil and basil. Tourists sat at the little tables beneath stripy parasols, smoking cigarettes and drinking coffee, while local codgers sat in their waistcoats and caps playing *briscola*.

Floriana didn't stop to talk to anyone on the way, although she was well known in the town on account of her infamous mother, and cherished like a stray dog. She went directly to the church to talk to the only Father who loved her unconditionally and was always there, no matter what. She had to thank Him for her good fortune, because if she didn't, she feared it might be taken away like her mother.

She stepped quietly over the shiny stone floor, inhaling the incense that saturated the air and mingled with the sticky smell of melting wax. A few people prayed in the pews, their shadowy figures kneeling in the gloom. Tourists wandered around in T-shirts, muttering to each other as they admired the frescoes and iconography. Gold leaf shone in the candlelight, giving the haloes around the heads of the Virgin, Christ and the saints an otherworldly glow. Floriana felt at home there because she had been coming for as long as she could remember. Her mother had been very religious, until she had sinned and turned her back on God out of shame. Didn't she realize that Jesus welcomed the sinner with open arms? Floriana sinned all the time, like spying at La Magdalena, and she was full of pride and vanity, yet she knew God loved her in spite of this, perhaps even *because* of this, for it was well known that, like His son, He loved sinners best of all. So did Father Ascanio, otherwise he wouldn't have a job.

Floriana padded down the aisle to the table of candles, which stood against the wall to the right of the nave. She lit one every day to pray that her father might find someone to run off with as well, because she was weary of looking after him. So far, God hadn't listened. She would have thought the Virgin would be more sympathetic, being a mother, but she seemed not to listen, either. Perhaps they didn't realize that he was utterly useless and a great burden. She'd be better off without him, then she could go and live with her aunt Zita. Aunt Zita was her mother's sister. She was married to Vincente and they had five children already so they could easily accommodate one more. In fact, they'd barely notice another mouth to feed, because she was only small and didn't eat a lot.

With that thought in mind she lit her candle to thank God for Dante and La Magdalena. She prayed that he'd wait for her to grow up so that she could marry him. Then she sidled into a pew and kneeled on the cushion to pray. She glanced around at the other people in prayer and wished they would all leave now so that God could hear what *she* had to say. It must be awfully distracting to have so many people talking all at the same time. But they didn't leave, so she was left with no alternative but to think as loudly and clearly as she could.

She remained there for a long while, thanking God for every tree, flower, bird and cricket she had seen that morning. She was sure that if she buttered Him up a little He might be better disposed towards her when she got round to putting in her requests. Finally, she read out her mental list. She did not ask for her mother back, which was usually her most ardent desire, because she felt she couldn't ask for too much and today she wanted to marry Dante more than she wanted her mother. She hoped her mother would never find out.

When she had finished, she crossed herself in front of the altar, smiling sympathetically at the statue of Christ on the cross, for the poor man must be so tired of hanging there all the time, and left.

She found Costanza in the courtyard of her home, reading in the shade on a swing chair. Costanza lived in a big villa on the hillside just outside the town, but it was run down, like the fortunes of her once illustrious family. Her parents were aristocrats, carrying the titles *conte* and *contessa*, which greatly impressed Floriana, whose father was their chauffeur. They had once owned a grand palazzo on Via del Corso in Rome, and a villa by the sea on the fashionable Amalfi coast. But Costanza's father had suffered big losses that Floriana didn't understand, and they had come to live in Herba when Costanza was three years old, in the holiday house they had once used only for a few weeks each summer. There they shut themselves in, barely socializing with anyone. But Costanza was lonely and isolated in her hilltop palace and even her snobby mother could see that she needed the company of children her own age. So the countess finally relented and sent her to the local school when she was six.

Her friend might have had the grand house and title but Floriana easily led by virtue of her charisma. Not only was she pretty, with a gamine little face and wide eyes, but she was confident of her appeal and instinctively clever. She had all the best ideas for games and seemed totally fearless when the games got a little dangerous, involving the sea or cliffs.

Costanza was not so physically blessed, with heavy features and a stout body. She was afraid of heights and of drowning, and admired her friend's courage, looking on as she showed off in front of all the other children, causing them to catch their breaths as she performed heroic acts for which their mothers would most surely beat them. But she was jealous, too, that Floriana's life was so carefree. Costanza's mother made her study, tidy her room and mind her manners, while Floriana had no one to tell her what to do and did as she pleased. Costanza had felt sorry for her when her mother had run off, but Floriana had thrown her pity right back in her face, puffed out her six-year-old chest and said, 'Who needs a mother anyway?' So, Costanza envied her instead; she was too young to see the broken heart behind the little girl's defences.

'*Ciao*,' said Floriana cheerfully, stepping into the courtyard where lemon trees grew in pots and tomatoes flourished on the south-facing wall.

Costanza looked up from her book. '*Ciao.*' Then, registering her smug expression, she asked, 'What have you been up to?'

'I'm in love,' Floriana replied carelessly.

'Who with?'

Floriana sat down next to her and pushed off with her toes to make the chair swing. 'He's called Dante.'

'You mean, Dante Bonfanti, who lives at Villa La Magdalena?'

'You know him?' Floriana was a little put out.

'Sort of.' Costanza screwed up her nose. The truth was she had never met him, but her parents knew his parents, so that almost counted.

'He's just showed me around the gardens. Oh, Costanza, they're the most beautiful gardens I've ever seen. They truly are.'

'They would be. They have an army of gardeners. Mamma used to have a big garden in Rome.'

'You have a lovely garden here.'

'But it's not well looked after. We no longer have the money for such extravagances.' She didn't quite know what that meant but she heard her mother say it all the time, usually accompanied by a sorry sigh.

'The gardens there are very well looked after.'

'You know they're one of the richest families in Italy?'

'Really?'

'Dante's father, Beppe, is one of the most powerful men in the country.'

Floriana did not know how to respond to that, so she remained silent, waiting for Costanza to continue.

Costanza relished knowing more about him than her friend. 'Dante is the eldest son,' she continued. Then she allowed her envy to get the better of her and added maliciously, 'He's like a prince, so he will have to marry a princess. There's no point you falling in love with him.'

Her words were a dagger to Floriana's heart. She put her hand there and pressed hard to stop it bleeding. Then she remembered God and the candle she had lit, and a small spark of hope ignited to transmute the pain.

'I'm not expecting to marry him,' she said breezily, adding a little chuckle to sound more convincing. She was a master at dissembling. 'He says I can come as often as I like. His parents are away travelling.'

'How old is he?'

'Nearly eighteen.'

'So what does he want with a little girl of ten?'

'Nearly eleven and he doesn't want anything. I think he felt sorry for me.'

'Like everyone else. They don't know how strong you are.' Costanza nudged her playfully, suddenly feeling bad for having squashed her enthusiasm. 'Can I come next time? I'd love to see the gardens.'

'We'll go tomorrow. I showed him the broken wall I climb when I spy.'

'Can I spy, too?'

'Sure, if you can keep quiet.'

'I can keep quiet.'

'And not hiss at me when I jump down and snoop around?'

'I can, honestly.'

'I don't think I'll have to snoop. He says he'll look out for me.'

'Shouldn't we just ring the bell?'

'Much more fun stealing in over the wall.'

'If I say my father's name, they'll let us in.'

'We don't need to do that. We'll climb over the wall and find Dante. We'll surprise him. He won't mind, he's my friend now. We'll go tomorrow morning.'

So, that settled, Floriana grabbed some fruit from the kitchen and made her way back down the hill into town. The sun was now slowly sinking in the western sky, turning the light a melancholy amber colour, throwing long shadows across her path for her to jump over. She chewed on a juicy fig and thought of Dante. It didn't matter that he was supposed to marry a princess, because love was more important than titles. After all, Cinderella married a prince and she was just a scullery maid. Floriana loved La Magdalena more than anything else. She belonged there, in that little mermaid garden, reading a book on the bench by the fountain. It didn't matter that she couldn't read very well, because she'd learn. She was clever, she could learn anything.

She skipped up the streets to the big archway in the yellow wall that had once meant home, but since her mother had gone it was now only a door that indicated the place where she lived. She gave it a firm push. It was heavy and large and opened into a courtyard. The ground was covered in cobbles, between which weeds grew and flourished until they were unceremoniously cut by Signora Bruno, whose late husband had left her the ramshackle building of small apartments to rent. Pretty iron balconies overlooked the courtyard, decorating the disintegrating walls with the occasional pot of flowers and more commonly, lines of washing, drying in the sun.

Signora Bruno stopped sweeping when she saw the little girl come in, and leaned on her broom. Any excuse to stop working. 'Your father's at Luigi's, propping up the bar, no doubt.' She watched Floriana with suspicion as the little girl skipped over to the steps and sat down. 'What are you up to? You look like a mouse that's eaten all the cheese.'

'I'm in love, Signora Bruno.'

The woman looked at the child's misty eyes and laughed, the mole on her cheek protruding. 'Who's been putting ideas in your head? Fancy a child of your age even thinking such a thing. Love!' She clicked her tongue. 'You love when you're young and know no better. Until your heart breaks and you realize you're safer living without it.'

'That's sad, Signora Bruno.' Floriana looked genuinely sympathetic.

'Who is this lucky man?'

'He's called Dante Bonfanti.'

Signora Bruno looked at her in astonishment. 'Dante Bonfanti? Where did you meet *him*?'

'I was peeping into his house from the gate, so he invited me in. Villa La Magdalena is the most beautiful palace in the whole wide world.'

'I'd stay well away from them, if I were you,' Signora Bruno said darkly. 'They're not good people.'

'Dante is,' Floriana protested.

'That may be so, but his father is a very dangerous man. You leave them well alone and stay down here where you belong.'

'But I love him.'

The old woman smiled at her indulgently. 'You're too young for love – not that you don't deserve it, mind you. Out of all the children in Herba, you deserve to be loved most of all.'

Floriana looked at Signora Bruno's thick ankles and skin-coloured stockings that gathered in rings down her calves, and wondered what had become of Signor Bruno. 'Where's your husband?'

'Dead.'

'I'm sorry.'

'I'm not. He was hard work.'

'Like my father.'

Signora Bruno chuckled like a hen. 'Your father.' She shook her head. 'A burden to you, he is. It's not right. He should take some responsibility.'

'Do you think he'll die soon?'

Signora Bruno's face turned grey with pity. 'No, *cara*, he won't die soon.'

'Shame,' Floriana said with a shrug.

'You don't want him to die, do you?'

Signora Bruno looked shocked and a little confused. She put down her broom and came to sit beside Floriana on the step, squeezing her soft body into the small space between the child and the banister. 'I know he's not what you'd want for a father. He's been in prison twice and drinks too much. It's not really a surprise that your mother left him. But you? I don't know why she left you – a little defenceless thing – and took your baby brother. I suppose he was too young to be left with a father who couldn't take care of him.' She put her arm around Floriana, who winced. 'She should have taken you with her as well, but she always was selfish, probably thought that Zita would look after you for her. But her sister's as useless as she is. Where's Zita when you need her, eh? She can't even control her own children. A child is a blessing from God, your mother should know that.'

'Do you have children?'

'Grown up now, living in Rome.'

'Do you miss them?'

'Yes, *cara*, I do.'

'Do you think Mamma misses me?'

Signora Bruno's heart buckled and she didn't know what to say. 'I should think she does, dear.'

'It doesn't really matter any more.'

'What doesn't?'

'If she doesn't come back, because I'm in love. I don't need a mother, you know.'

'You talk a lot of nonsense, you do.' Signora Bruno dabbed her eye with her apron. 'I tell you what, you go and fetch your father and I'll help you put him to bed.'

'Thank you.'

Signora Bruno pulled herself up slowly, her knees creaking and clicking as she straightened them. 'Every child needs a mother. You shouldn't have to be doing this at your age,' she sighed.

Floriana followed Signora Bruno across the courtyard. Nothing mattered because tomorrow she was going to see Dante.

*

Floriana found her father in Luigi's just round the corner from where they lived on Via Roma. He was hunched over the bar with an empty glass in his hand. Luigi was denying him another drink and he was getting angry. Floriana approached him and the huddle of men trying to persuade him to go home parted to let her through.

'Papà,' she said, prodding his arm. 'It's time to go home.'

Her father looked down at her irritably, his rheumy eyes cold and strange. 'Go home yourself, scamp,' he retorted.

Luigi and the other men defended her angrily. 'You can't treat your daughter like that, Elio. You go home now and be a good father.' Floriana had heard it all before and wasn't in the least bit ashamed of him. If she felt anything at all, she felt weary of this tiresome routine night after night. It astonished her that Costanza's father still employed him. She wondered whether he, too, felt sorry for her and employed him out of charity. She didn't imagine her father drove very well with his shaking hands and blurred vision.

Finally, they cajoled him into going home and watched, anxiously, as the little girl helped him out into the street, although she barely reached his waist. He leaned on her as if she were a walking stick, grunting and mumbling incomprehensibly. When she reached the door of her home, Signora Bruno was there as promised. She threw his arm over her broad shoulder and heaved him up the narrow staircase to their apartment. Once inside, she let him fall onto his bed. Floriana removed his shoes while Signora Bruno drew the curtains, noticing the hole in one and the stain on the other. No one could expect a ten-year-old child to wash and mend curtains. It was enough that she washed their clothes, as Signora Bruno had taught her to do after her mother left. 'You're going to have to be mother now,' she had said and the little girl had listened bravely, trying not to cry. She had a way of puffing out her chest and holding her chin up in order to appear strong.

Signora Bruno watched Floriana cover her father with a quilt. He grabbed her hand and his face crumpled into a sob like a soggy dishcloth. 'Forgive me,' he mumbled.

'Go to sleep, Papà.'

'I should be a better father to you. Tomorrow I will stop drinking, I promise.'

'You say that every night. It's boring.'

'Your mother's to blame for leaving us. If she hadn't left us, everything would be all right.'

'You started drinking long before she left.'

'You're wrong.'

'Maybe she left because you drank.'

'You don't know what you're talking about. I love her and I love our son. Where are they now? Will I ever see them again? What sort of boy has he grown up to be? He probably doesn't even remember me. But I love them and I love you. I drink to drown the pain of my pitiful life. I drink to forget my guilt, because I haven't been a good father to you. Forgive me, Floriana. My little Floriana.' He reached out a hand to touch her face.

'Go to sleep, Papà.' He closed his eyes and his hand dropped onto the bed beside him. She gazed down at him a moment, searching in vain for the father she longed for him to be.

'Have you enough to eat?' Signora Bruno asked as they left the room and closed the door.

'Yes.'

'Are you going to be OK?'

'Sure.' She shrugged. 'Sometimes I think he'll be dead in the morning.'

'Then what would you do?'

'Go and live with Aunt Zita.'

'She has enough children to feed.'

'I don't eat much.'

'But you'll grow and then you'll eat plenty.'

'When I grow, I'll get married and live in a palace.'

'We all dreamed of living in palaces when we were little. Look where I live now. Not quite the palace of my dreams.'

'But I've requested it.'

'God doesn't always deliver, Floriana.'

'I know. But He owes me.'

Signora Bruno smiled at the child's spirit. 'In that case, He will turn you into a princess, for sure.'

'You'll see,' Floriana replied brightly. 'If you're good, you can come and work for me.'

'Well, thank you, *signorina*!' The old woman laughed all the way down the stairs into the courtyard. 'It had better be soon or I'll be dead.'

Floriana ate a chunk of bread and cheese and drank a glass of milk. She could hear her father snoring through the wall and grimaced. He sounded like a pig. After eating, she ran a bath. If she was going to see Dante in the morning she had to look her very best. She scrubbed herself from top to toe in the warm water and washed her hair, spending a long time laboriously combing it through until all the knots had gone. She cut her toenails and filed the ones on her hands as her mother used to do. She brushed her teeth until they shone. It was hard to find a dress that wasn't dirty or too small, but she pulled out a white one imprinted with red flowers that she never wore because it marked so easily. She'd be careful not to climb trees. One day she'd have a wardrobe full of pretty dresses – day dresses and evening dresses – all clean and ironed and hanging on silk hangers in a room especially designed for her clothes. She'd have a maid to look after her and keep everything in order.

She sat on the windowsill in her bedroom and lost her gaze among the glittering stars. If she married Dante perhaps her mother would come back because she'd be proud that her daughter had married so well. She would sit in that little mermaid garden and tell her how very sorry she was that she had run away, and Floriana would forgive her because she would understand.

The snores grew louder in the room next door. It must have been intolerable to share her bed with a man who snored like a pig.

Chapter 8

The following morning the two girls walked through the poppy field towards Villa La Magdalena. Costanza had immediately noticed her friend's pretty dress and shiny hair, and was choked with jealousy. In reality Floriana had so little, and yet, striding confidently through the field that morning, she appeared to have everything. Costanza followed grudgingly, dragging her feet.

'If you don't want to come, you don't have to,' said Floriana, stopping a moment so that she could catch up.

'I *do* want to.'

'Then hurry up.'

'Why the rush? La Magdalena's not going to go away.'

'But Dante might.'

'You needn't have dressed up for him, you know. He'll look on you as a child whether you're in your best dress or your usual grubby one.'

'I haven't dressed up for him,' Floriana retorted.

'Then who have you dressed up for?'

'For me, silly. Signora Bruno told me that now I'm almost grown up I should take better care of myself.'

'Mamma won't let me out of the house unless she's brushed my hair and washed my face. She's *so* annoying.'

Floriana glanced at Costanza. In her immaculately pressed blue dress and clean sandals she looked infinitely more groomed than she did. Her long fair hair was scraped off her face and tied with blue ribbons. It really did make all the difference having a mother who cared. Floriana strode on, pushing the thought of her absent mother to the back of her mind.

'What if he's not there?' asked Costanza anxiously.

'We'll snoop around the garden all the same. I know where everything is now that he's shown me.'

'What if we bump into someone? There's bound to be loads of staff.'

'I was seen with him yesterday. They all know me now.'

'They might call the police.'

'Of course they won't. What can two girls possibly do to threaten them? We hardly look like gypsies, do we?'

'We could get into trouble. Beppe is a very powerful man.'

'So what? He's still a human being like the rest of us. Don't be such a scaredy-cat.'

'I'm just being sensible.'

'Well, don't. Sensible isn't fun.'

At last, they stood at the big black iron gates and gazed inside. The yellow villa peeped out coquettishly from between the avenue of cypress trees.

'It's certainly a fine-looking *palazzo*,' said Costanza admiringly.

'It's more than that. It's magical.'

'I've seen plenty of houses like this, you know.'

'I bet you have.'

'In fact, our home in Portofino was very similar.'

'Shame your father lost it.'

'It's not really a shame at all. It's hard work looking after a house that size.'

'Not if you have people to look after it for you.'

'Well, of course we had staff. Lots of staff.'

'This is where I met Dante yesterday,' said Floriana dreamily.

'He's clearly not coming.'

'Oh, he'll come.'

'I think we should go home now.'

'You're scared.'

'I'm not. I just don't think it's very cool hanging onto these gates like a couple of stray dogs.'

'If he doesn't come, we'll scale the wall.'

'In our dresses?'

'Not a problem. We can take them off.'

Costanza was horrified. 'Take them off!'

'Yes, take them off and throw them over the wall, climb up and put them on when we get to the other side. Simple.'

'You're joking.'

'No, I'm not. Come on, I'll show you.'

Floriana skipped off carelessly, leading Costanza along the boundary she knew so well, following the line of the wall until they reached the part where it had crumbled, making it low enough to climb. 'If we sit on top we can see into the gardens. They're really beautiful.'

'I don't want to climb it. If I get a hole in my dress, Mamma will kill me.'

'Take it off, then.' Costanza watched, appalled, as Floriana stepped out of hers and stood naked but for a pair of white panties, worn to a grim shade of grey. She still had the body of an eight-year-old. Costanza, on the other hand, was more voluptuous and already had the beginnings of breasts.

'I'm not doing that,' she protested as Floriana did a little dance to torment her.

'I feel liberated not wearing any clothes. Come on, it's fun!'

'You're too old to be dancing around without anything on.'

'Fine. Don't then.' Floriana stopped dancing and tossed the dress over the wall with a whoop of laughter. 'There it goes! Hope there's not a dog on the other side!' She proceeded to climb up like a little monkey. Once she was on the top she sat there proudly, smiling down at her friend. 'I'll give you a hand. Come on!' Costanza reached up and took it. 'Put your foot in that hole to lever yourself up.'

She did as she was told, and slowly, with great care and anxiety, she joined her friend.

'I can't believe you did that,' said Costanza hotly, smoothing down her dress. 'If anyone sees you!'

'Who's going to see me?'

'I am,' came a deep voice from the other side of the wall. Floriana looked down to see Dante holding her dress up for her. 'I'm not looking,' he said, shielding his eyes with his other hand. With a hoot of laughter, and not a bit embarrassed, she took the dress and stepped into it, pulling it up over her shoulders. 'Can I look yet?'

'Of course you can,' she replied, buttoning it up. 'There's nothing to see anyway.'

Costanza was blushing to the roots of her hair, imagining the horror, had she been foolish enough to copy her friend and toss *her* dress over the wall. It was bad enough being caught climbing into his property uninvited.

'Who's your friend?' he asked, settling his lofty gaze on Costanza.

'Costanza Aldorisio,' Floriana informed him.

'Don't I know your parents?'

'Yes,' Costanza replied.

'Conte Carlo Aldorisio?'

'Yes.' Her voice was little more than a whisper.

'Well, don't stand up there all morning. Let's get you both down.' He reached up his hands, which Floriana took without hesitation, and helped her jump onto the grass.

Costanza was shy and took his hands with a rush of mortification. He was so handsome, she didn't blame Floriana at all
for having fallen in love with him. She had never seen anyone
as good-looking in her entire life. She jumped down, aware for
the first time of how heavy she must be in comparison to
Floriana.

'So *you're* little Costanza Aldorisio,' he mused, grinning at
her. 'We've met before, but you wouldn't remember, you were
too small.'

'Really?'

'You came here with your parents.' She nodded dumbly.
'Do you spy on us as well?'

Costanza's blush intensified. 'No. Not me. Just Floriana.'

'So, you're the Lone Spy, are you?' he turned to Floriana.

'I don't think anyone loves your garden more than I do.'

'I think you're right about that.'

'Can we go into the colonnaded garden again? I'd love to
show Costanza.'

'Sure we can.'

At that moment Good-Night trotted out of the trees.
Costanza squealed with fear as the dog came rushing excitedly
towards them.

'Good-Night!' exclaimed Floriana, bending down to greet
her friend with open arms.

'Don't be frightened, Costanza,' said Dante, placing a protective hand on her shoulder. 'He's very friendly.' Costanza
watched as the dog fell into Floriana's embrace, nearly knocking her over.

'Isn't he adorable! Look, he's licking me again!'

'Don't you like animals?' Dante asked Costanza.

'No,' she replied.

'I love them,' Floriana gushed. 'I wish I had a dog. A companion who is always by my side and loves me without
question. I'd like that.'

'You can borrow Good-Night whenever you like,' said Dante, finding her delight infectious. 'Come on, let's go and sit in Mother's garden.'

He put his hands in his pockets and strode off in the direction of the house. Good-Night sensed something moving in the bushes, pricked up his ears and stiffened his tail, then bounded over to have a look. Floriana smiled at her friend, as if to say, 'Didn't I tell you he was handsome?' and Costanza smiled back nervously, feeling better now they had been properly introduced.

They walked through the gardens, marvelling at the marble statues and hedges cut into perfect spheres. A few gardeners worked in the borders, watering before the sun got too hot, and weeding, tossing the offending plants into wheelbarrows. When they saw Dante they stopped what they were doing and took off their hats, nodding respectfully. Floriana noticed and felt proud to be walking beside such an important man.

Dante smiled indulgently as the two girls chatted away excitedly. Costanza forgot her nervousness and let Floriana show her everything, as if the place already belonged to her. When they reached the mermaid garden she sat down and announced that this was her favourite spot because she could hear the birds in the trees and the water trickling in the fountain and feel the sun on her face.

'This is Heaven,' she stated simply, leaning back and closing her eyes. 'A place as beautiful as this must be where God lives, mustn't it? When He's not in church.'

Dante laughed and joined her on the bench. 'Perhaps church is where He works, like going into the office, and here is where He comes to get away from all those people making impossible requests.'

'*My* requests aren't impossible,' Floriana said. 'I would never put Him under pressure.'

'What do *you* ask for, *piccolina*?'

She smiled secretively. 'I can't tell you. If I do, I'll have to kill you.'

'Well, you had better not tell me, then.'

'She asks for her mother to come back,' volunteered Costanza, feeling more confident now and a little jealous that he had just called Floriana 'little one', as if he had known her a long time and was fond of her. She sat on one of the other benches.

'Where's your mother?'

'She ran off with a man she met at the market,' said Floriana carelessly. Seeing as she was going to marry Dante, he might as well know everything about her.

'I'm sorry.'

'So am I. I used to wish she had taken me with her, but I wouldn't be sitting here now in this lovely place if she had.'

He looked at her curiously. 'You'd rather be here than with your mother?'

'Of course. I don't imagine my mother has a garden like this. She might have a vine – after all, the man she ran off with sold tomatoes.' She laughed as if nothing mattered.

'So, you live with your father?'

'He's my father's driver,' Costanza added grandly.

'He's useless,' said Floriana.

Dante frowned as she suddenly looked disheartened. 'Come, I've got something I want to show you.' He stood up. 'A surprise.'

Floriana shrugged off the thought of her father, and smiled again. 'I love surprises,' she beamed.

The girls followed him through the gate in the wall, out into the ornamental garden where stone steps swept up to the house in a graceful curve. A man in a green overall was raking the gravel, his head shielded from the sun by a white hat.

Another watered the formal borders with a hose. A grey cat lay asleep on the balustrade and Floriana skipped over to stroke it. 'Is this yours?'

'Doesn't really belong to anyone,' Dante replied. 'Another stray.'

'You are lucky. I wish I could adopt a stray.'

'I'd say you could adopt him, but he'll only come back here where he knows he'll be fed.'

'I wouldn't dream of taking him away from here. Look, he's a little prince asleep at the foot of the palace. He'd be very unhappy in my little apartment.'

'Your father would probably skin him,' said Costanza.

'No, he wouldn't,' Floriana retorted defensively. 'But he wouldn't like him.'

Dante watched Floriana, intrigued. She was like a stray cat herself – a bold, independent little cat who really wanted someone to take care of her. He led on, to the other side of the garden where an olive grove was planted behind an ancient stone wall. Among the olive trees were fig and apple trees, cherry and orange trees and giant terracotta pots with their lids in place, once used for storage. The ground was scattered with hundreds of little yellow flowers peeping out from the long grass, and lining the wall were twisted eucalyptus trees, standing guard like decrepit old men.

'This is a wonderful surprise,' enthused Floriana, enjoying yet another stunning garden.

'You haven't seen the surprise, yet,' Dante laughed, hands in pockets, searching the area for something. 'Ah, there he is.'

Floriana and Costanza followed the line of his gaze to see a magnificent peacock pecking the ground, his blue feathers glistening on his chest like oil.

'I told you there were rare birds in this garden,' said Floriana. 'He's beautiful. Does he have a name?'

'No. He's just Peacock.'

'How lazy of you not to think of a name. I shall think of one, then.' She narrowed her eyes and then grinned jubilantly. 'Michelangelo.'

'A bit grand, isn't it?'

'Yes, grand for a grand peacock. He has to hold his head up in this place, so let's give him a famous name.'

'Does he bite?' Costanza asked a little nervously.

'I don't think he'll like you to get too close,' Dante replied cautiously.

Floriana ignored them both and edged quietly towards the peacock, hand outstretched, offering friendship.

'Careful, *piccolina*.'

Dante and Costanza watched as Floriana approached him. Michelangelo lifted his head and eyed her warily. As she advanced he took a step towards her, curious to see what she held in her hand. With jerky movements he observed her and she whispered encouragingly, creeping closer.

Finally, she reached him. He stiffened but didn't peck her as she gently ran her fingers over his proud chest, smoothing down the little feathers that felt like fur.

'I think he likes you,' said Dante. Costanza wished she wasn't so afraid. At that moment the bird opened his glorious feathers in a bright, shimmering fan. 'Now I *know* he likes you,' Dante laughed.

'You're a very special bird, aren't you, Michelangelo?' Floriana whispered. 'I think he likes his new name.'

'It's very dignified.'

'Better than Peacock. How would you like to be called Man?'

'Not very much.'

'He likes Michelangelo.' She kneeled on the grass and placed her hand on his back. The bird enjoyed her caress for a moment, then moved away. 'He's had enough,' she announced. 'How does he get on with the cat?'

'Cordial,' Dante replied. 'He doesn't like the cat half as much as he likes you.'

They walked around the orchard, followed at a distance by Michelangelo, who was as curious about Floriana as Dante was.

'My sister's coming for a week, with some friends. You should come and use the pool,' he said.

'Oh, I don't think we should,' said Costanza quickly.

'Why not?' Floriana asked. 'I'd like to meet your sister. How old is she?'

'Sixteen. I have another one of thirteen, Giovanna, who's in Mexico with my parents.'

'She's only a little older than us,' said Floriana to Costanza.

'I don't think we should impose. Especially if Giovanna isn't here.'

'Damiana will enjoy having you about the place. She likes younger children she can boss around.'

'I don't know . . .' Costanza mumbled anxiously.

'You can't sit on the wall and spy all the time.' He winked at Floriana. 'Would you be happier if I called your mother and invited you formally?'

Costanza was relieved. Her shoulders dropped and she smiled. 'Yes, please.'

'As for you, *piccolina*, who do I call?'

'No one,' she said breezily.

'No one?' He raised an eyebrow.

'No.' She shrugged as if it couldn't matter less. 'No one cares.' At that moment, looking at her impish face gazing up at him defiantly, he realized that, in a brotherly kind of way, *he* did.

Dante honoured his word and telephoned Costanza's mother that evening. She was delighted that her daughter was invited up to La Magdalena to swim with his sister, Damiana, and

Dante suggested that she take her friend, Floriana, with her for company.

'She's the daughter of Carlo's chauffeur,' the countess explained grandly, as if making excuses for the child's inadequate pedigree. 'She's a sweet girl and Costanza likes having her around. I tolerate her for my daughter's sake, although I would much prefer her to befriend someone of her own class.'

'She's very welcome to come,' said Dante, smiling to himself at the woman's grandiosity.

'I'll send our maid with them.'

'Of course.'

'Please thank Damiana for the invitation.'

'I will.'

'I hope they won't be any trouble.'

'Of course not. It will be a pleasure to have them. I hope they will come as often as they like.'

'How very kind. Lovely to think of Costanza mixing with the right sort of people. Send my regards to your parents. It's been so long since we last saw them. Will they be spending time down here this summer?'

'I doubt it. They're taking Giovanna on a tour of South America.'

'What a shame they're missing the summer.'

'Mother hates the sun. It ages her skin.'

'Well, she *is* very fair.'

'So, we'll expect the girls tomorrow.'

'Thank you. I know Costanza is very much looking forward to it.'

The following morning the girls arrived at the big gates of Villa La Magdalena accompanied by Graziella, the maid, a dark little woman as round as a teapot, dressed formally in a pastel-pink uniform and clean white shoes. They were met by one of the gardeners, who unlocked the gates and accompanied them up the cypress avenue to the house. Floriana skipped happily across the shadows, her thoughts full of Dante and the day ahead that promised to be so thrilling.

Costanza was nervous; anxious about the strangers she was going to meet, so much older than her, and about having to put on a bathing suit. She wished she were as fearless as her friend. But she needn't have worried. They were taken straight down to the swimming pool, which was built at the end of a long path, high up on the rocks overlooking the sea. Four girls in little bikinis lay in a colonnaded alcove at one end on sun loungers, sipping drinks and reading magazines, tanning their skin golden in the sun. Bob Dylan sang out from the little hut at the other end, where there was a bar, tall stools, and changing rooms.

Dante was in the water at the edge of the pool, chatting to the girls. When he saw the children descending the steps he waved and called out to them. Damiana sat up and waved too, her beautiful face flowering into a smile. Her blonde hair was tied into a ponytail beneath a wide sunhat and her wrists were adorned with gold bangles. She stood up in her skimpy white bikini and walked around the pool to greet them.

'Dante has told me so much about you,' she said to Floriana. 'And I believe *we*'ve met before,' she added to Costanza.

Costanza felt very important, being singled out, and replied firmly that their parents knew each other. 'Why don't you change into your swimsuits and join us out here? Would you like anything to drink?'

'I'm fine, thank you,' said Costanza, too embarrassed to ask for anything.

'I'd love something,' said Floriana boldly.

'What will you have?'

'What is there?'

Damiana smiled indulgently. 'Come and have a look. We

have a whole bar at your disposal.' They followed her into the hut, where Graziella was already sitting, fanning herself. An attendant stood behind the bar in a formal black suit and white shirt. Costanza thought he looked very hot. 'Why don't you let Primo make you a fruit juice?'

'You can choose your fruit,' Primo said to Floriana.

'That sounds fun,' she replied, climbing onto the stool. 'Why don't you have one, too, Costanza?'

'Well, all right,' she replied, grateful to her friend for having persuaded her. She really was very thirsty.

The changing room was very smart, with two lavatories, and marble basins with all sorts of lotions and perfume flasks lined up on shelves beneath big, elaborate mirrors. The girls hung their dresses on hooks and put their shoes neatly on the wooden bench beneath. They wriggled excitedly into their swimsuits.

'Isn't she glamorous?' Costanza hissed. 'Did you see how skinny she is? And her bikini is tiny. She shows everything!'

'She's like an angel,' Floriana replied, hooking her straps over her shoulders.

'She's nice.'

'I don't think a person could be anything but nice, living in a place like this.'

'You're right. You couldn't be unhappy here, could you?'

'Never.'

'Are you going to swim straight away?'

'Of course,' Floriana enthused. 'I'm boiling.'

Costanza shivered nervously. 'OK, I will if you will.'

As they came out of the hut with their drinks, Damiana was waiting for them with a drink of her own. She had been chatting to Graziella, who was very surprised that the young woman had deigned to speak to her at all, and was blushing with pleasure beneath her brown skin. 'Right, girls, let me introduce you to my friends. You already know my silly brother, so I won't introduce you to *him*.' They followed her around to the sun loungers where an attendant in white shorts and polo shirt was putting out two more, draping towels over the mattresses and extra ones for swimming neatly folded on the ends. Floriana noticed everything and her spirit swelled with happiness.

The other three girls looked up from their magazines and smiled. Damiana introduced them as Maria, Rosaria and Allegra. They were all pretty, with slim figures and flawless skin, but none was as lovely as their hostess, who, together with her brother, seemed to shine with a superior gloss.

'Well, are you going to come in?' said Dante from the water. 'It's lovely in here.' Floriana didn't need to be persuaded. She placed her drink on the little white table next to her lounger and tossed her towel onto the ground. With a big leap she jumped straight into the water. Costanza held back timidly.

'That's the little stray, *l'orfanella*,' she heard Damiana say to her friends as Floriana swam over to Dante.

'*Poverina!*' Allegra sighed compassionately.

'Terrible not to have a mother,' said Maria.

'Better to have a dead mother than a mother who doesn't want you,' added Rosaria, lighting a cigarette.

'Dante's rescued her,' said Damiana. 'He's like that. If there's a wounded dog within a ten-kilometre radius, he'll find it, bring it home and look after it. He can sense a bird with a broken wing at a hundred paces!'

'And *this* one?' whispered Allegra, nodding at Costanza who was pretending not to listen.

'She's the daughter of Contessa Aldorisio.'

'Very aristocratic,' said Rosaria, impressed.

'The count employs the little stray's father as chauffeur.'

'How sweet of Costanza to gather her up,' said Allegra approvingly. 'That's beyond the call of duty.'

At this, Costanza felt very proud. She held her nose and jumped into the water, pleased that they all knew she was not a simple working-class girl like Floriana, but one of them. As she swam over to her friend she smiled happily to herself; it was right that she was there. As for Floriana, she was *very* lucky.

Chapter 9

The day was such a success that Damiana invited the girls back the following day. She telephoned the countess, who nearly wept with joy at the thought of her daughter being embraced by one of the wealthiest families in Italy, and sent Graziella again to accompany them. Without her parents around Damiana enjoyed playing hostess. They ate lunch on the terrace, cooked by the chef according to *her* instructions, drank fine wine from her father's cellar, and smoked.

Floriana was full of stories and made them laugh until their bellies ached. She made fun of her father and Signora Bruno, standing up and imitating them in a brutal satire. Humour was the only way she could deal with the misery her father caused, and the fact that everyone laughed made him somehow more acceptable.

Costanza sat quietly, seemingly content to give her friend centre stage. Good-Night lay at Floriana's feet, quietly eating the scraps she secretly fed him under the table. Dante noticed but said nothing. After lunch the two young guests disappeared into the olive grove to play with Michelangelo. Once they were out of earshot, the group discussed them, agreeing that it cost them nothing to allow the children to play in the grounds and swim in the pool. They wondered what sort of mother could run off and leave a daughter as adorable as

Floriana. They couldn't understand why she hadn't taken her with her. Damiana had grown fond of her in such a short time. She had stolen her heart in the same way that she had stolen Dante's, and she was eager to take the little stray under her wing.

The following day the girls arrived with Graziella, but the day after that they came alone. By now the countess felt they were familiar enough with the lady of the house to go unaccompanied. From then on they came most days, sometimes in the morning, sometimes in the afternoon, but they were never a burden to Dante and Damiana, who liked having them around, like a couple more strays to add to the menagerie that had already taken up residence at La Magdalena. They wandered around without needing to be entertained. They played in the gardens and never tired of their games. They explored, spied on the others when they were lying by the pool unaware, and asked the gardeners to tell them the names of all the flowers and trees. Floriana played with Good-Night and draped the cat over her arms as she carried him with her everywhere. Michelangelo was too arrogant to show his growing affection for the little girl who stroked his tummy, and followed them at a distance, pretending not to care.

The days rolled on in a blissful haze. Floriana stopped minding about her father's drunken evenings at Luigi's, and when she wasn't at La Magdalena she played with Costanza at her house, beneath the disapproving gaze of the countess.

'Do you have to take Floriana with you every time you go to the Bonfantis'?' she asked her daughter one evening after Floriana had gone home.

'Why?'

'Because, my love, she's not of your class. It's inappropriate. It's very kind of them to tolerate her but ...'

'If I don't take her, I'll have no one to play with.'

'What about the younger daughter? What's she called?'

'Giovanna. But she's in Mexico. I don't think she's coming at all this summer.'

'All right, then. You may take Floriana, if they really don't mind, until Giovanna returns. Then you must leave her behind and make friends with Giovanna. Do you understand?'

'Yes, Mamma.'

'It's for your own good, my love. It's all very well you having a little friend from the town to play with, but now you're getting bigger you should mix with your own class. It's your father's fault, I know, that you had to be brought up here and go to the local school. If he hadn't made such stupid business decisions we'd be living in Rome and you'd have friends like yourself.'

'I *like* Floriana.'

'She's very sweet, I agree, and it's unfortunate to say the least that her mother ran off and left her with that hopeless Elio. But you mustn't forget who you are, my dear. One day you'll marry and live in a place like La Magdalena, I promise you. I'll see that it happens, mark my words. If you constantly hang around girls like Floriana you'll end up like her and you wouldn't want that, would you?'

'Floriana wants to marry Dante,' Constanza said disloyally.

The countess laughed at the absurdity of such a notion. 'It costs nothing to dream, I suppose,' she said, wiping her eye. 'She thinks she is like you, Costanza. You see, your friendship is damaging for both of you, in different ways. That sort of dream can only end in disappointment. Poor child.' She sighed and wandered off to sit in the shade and read a magazine. But she didn't read the words, she was too busy thinking about Dante and whether it wasn't completely improbable that when her daughter was a little older, *she* might catch his eye. After all, they were the perfect match: *she* had the pedigree, *he* had the money.

*

Floriana wished the summer holidays would never end. She loved spending her days at La Magdalena, breathing the same rarefied air as Dante. He treated her like a younger sister, pulling her onto his knee and hugging her, chasing her in the swimming pool, throwing her into the water like a rag doll, grinning at her across the table as if they had a special secret. She sat on the bench beside the tennis court and watched him play in white shorts and shirt, whacking the ball at his sister, who complained all the time that he was hitting it too hard. Sometimes he asked Floriana to be ball girl, and she and Costanza would scurry around picking up the balls. She always threw hers to Dante, while Costanza was left to retrieve for his sister.

Damiana looked effortlessly glamorous in a little white skirt with pleats around the back, and white socks with bobbles at the ankles to match her white tennis shoes, and Floriana longed to be like her. Damiana was a gracious loser, but sometimes, when she played with Dante against her friends, she won. Then she was a gracious winner, laughing carelessly as if winning didn't matter, and Floriana thought her the most beautifully mannered woman she had ever seen.

Then one day another visitor arrived and the air changed around the pool. Gioia Favelli was tall with short brown hair and long tanned legs, a slim waist and wide, curvaceous hips. Her breasts were large and round, and somehow very provocative in the little black bikini she wore.

Costanza and Floriana whispered to each other in the water, giggling into their hands, until Dante put his arm around Gioia and caressed her back absentmindedly, as if they belonged to each other. Suddenly Floriana didn't feel like laughing any more. Sickened in her heart, she watched furtively from the water. It became obvious that Dante and Gioia were more than just friends; they were a couple.

Floriana sulked. She couldn't help herself. When Dante came to play with her in the pool, she swam off. When he tried to draw her into his arms at lunch she wriggled away.

Damiana laughed at the girl's sudden shyness, but she was perceptive enough to know the real reason. 'She's jealous,' she explained, when the girls had disappeared into the garden.

'How darling,' gushed Gioia, lighting a cigarette. 'I don't blame her; Dante is very handsome.'

'She's little,' said Dante, feeling bad. 'And she's alone in the world.'

Damiana rolled her eyes. 'There you go again! Feeling sorry for the bird with the broken wing or the unwanted dog. It's now the unwanted child.'

'Don't pretend *you* don't want to mother her. You go all mushy when you look at her.'

'I know, she's a special little girl. But she adores you, Dante. Don't break her heart.'

'What can I do?' He reached across the table and took Gioia's hand.

'Be kind,' said his sister. 'And aware.'

That afternoon Dante made a special effort to give Floriana his undivided attention, and after much endeavour, she yielded and allowed him to play with her.

Costanza watched from the other side of the pool where she sat dangling her legs in the water. She remembered her mother's words about 'above her station' and thought it was probably just as well that Gioia had turned up to burst the bubbles Floriana had been creating in the whimsical well of her imagination.

Floriana forgot about Gioia, or perhaps she believed Dante's affection for her outweighed his affection for the stranger who had suddenly appeared in their midst. Gioia lay on her sun lounger reading a magazine, not at all interested in the activity in the water. Damiana was happy the child had been coaxed out of her sulk, but she sensed the end of the summer would bring her only unhappiness. When they returned to Milan she would become a stray once again without anyone to take care of her.

After a while Dante tired of his game and retreated to his sun lounger to sunbathe.

'I wish the summer could go on for ever,' said Floriana, following him out of the pool.

'But it can't, *piccolina*. I will have to return to Milan.'

'And then to America, and goodness knows what else your father has planned for you,' added Gioia thoughtlessly. 'And I shall be very sad.'

Damiana glanced at Floriana and registered her stricken face. 'You'll be back soon, though, won't you, Dante?'

'He'd better be back. I'm not hanging around while he goes gallivanting around the world.'

'Dante,' Damiana warned, but it was too late. Floriana now understood that she wouldn't see him again for many years and by then, who knew . . .?

'Why does your father have to send you so far away? Aren't there any good universities closer to home?' Gioia continued.

Floriana walked up to the edge of the rocks and stared down at the sea below. It gently lapped the rocks, calling to her, goading her to jump. She turned to see Costanza's face blanch, which encouraged her all the more, and she recalled those times when she had dived into the sea from great heights to scare the other schoolchildren. This was higher than anything she had ever jumped from before, but her heart was breaking so what did it matter if she hurt herself?

Damiana managed to catch Floriana's attention and pulled a face, but the little girl edged closer to the verge. Then, without a thought for her own safety, she leaped off in a graceful dive. One moment she was there, the next she was gone.

Dante jumped to his feet in panic. '*Che cazzo fa!*' he shouted, and dived in after her.

'Oh my God!' Gioia cried, rushing to the edge. 'He's going to kill himself.'

Damiana and the girls joined Gioia to stare helplessly into the water below. For a while there was nothing, just the waves and a little wisp of foam where the divers had penetrated the surface.

Costanza's heart froze. She was too afraid to get out of the pool. Floriana was courageous but also reckless. What if she had gone too far this time and killed them both? She squeezed her eyes shut and wished she were at home with her mother.

Floriana let the water wrap her in its cool, silent embrace. For a second the pain in her heart was quelled by the surge of adrenalin that set it racing. She could hear it thumping behind her ribcage and felt relief that she was no longer beside the pool, having it stabbed with unkind words. Then she felt a hand grab her arm and wrench her out of her watery refuge.

With a loud whoosh they both exploded through the surface, taking in great gulps of air.

'You stupid child!' Dante yelled when he had caught his breath. 'Don't you have any sense of self-preservation?'

Floriana stared back at him in horror. His entire face was contorted with fright.

'My God, you could have died, you silly girl! Don't you realize there are rocks beneath the surface that you can't see? If you had hit your head you'd have been killed instantly. Is that what you want?'

She shook her head, big eyes gazing at him in astonishment. She had expected his admiration, not his fury. He swam angrily to a place in the rocks where it was safe to climb out and she followed slowly, wishing she could disappear to the bottom of the sea and never come up again.

'She's OK,' he shouted up to his sister, who retreated from the edge with relief.

'What an idiotic child, showing off like that,' said Gioia furiously. 'She could have led Dante to his death.'

'I don't think she meant to do it,' Damiana defended her. 'She didn't know.'

Dante and Floriana dragged themselves onto the rocks and sat side by side.

'I'm sorry,' Floriana said in a small voice. 'I didn't mean to frighten you.'

'You frightened me more than I've ever been frightened in my entire life.' He shook off his rage with a brisk toss of his head and put his arm around her. His face softened into a forgiving smile. 'Promise me you'll never do anything like that again.'

'I promise,' Floriana replied. Her chin began to tremble. She felt her heart revive, like a punctured tyre filling again with air, and she began to cry.

'Don't cry, *piccolina*.' But her shoulders shuddered and she let out a violent sob. 'Come on, my little friend, I'm sorry I shouted at you. I was scared, that's all. I thought you were dead.'

Floriana couldn't stop herself. She rarely let herself cry, but now her usual tools of defence failed to work. She stuck out her chest and raised her chin, but her emotion was too strong for such clumsy fortification. It wasn't his fury that made her cry, but his concern. She had forgotten what it felt like to be valued.

After that, the summer no longer felt like it was going to last for ever. Every moment of pleasure with Dante was paid for with a sharp sense of loss, as if a little less sand remained in the hourglass to warn Floriana that time was running out. She no longer existed in a limbo of endless summer, for a cloud of gloom hung over the horizon to remind her of its transience, edging its way a little further inland each day, eating up those blissful summer days until the rain came at last to sweep him back to Milan.

'You'll look after Good-Night for me, won't you?' he asked of her as he said goodbye.

'I shan't come into your garden if you're not here,' she replied, struggling to control her sorrow.

He swept her into his arms and squeezed her. 'But you'll spy from the wall, won't you?'

'I don't know.'

'Of course you will.'

'When will you come back?'

'Soon,' he replied, but he couldn't be sure.

'I'll miss you every day.'

'No you won't. You'll forget about me as soon as I've gone.' He put her down. 'Be good now. No more diving off rocks. Promise?'

'Promise.' He grinned and Floriana smiled back weakly. Inside, she felt as if her heart were filling with cold concrete.

Damiana tried to reassure her by promising that she would be back soon with Giovanna, who was very keen to meet them. Then she hugged the little *orfanella* and found a lump had formed in her throat, preventing her from saying anything else.

Costanza felt the warmth of their goodbyes but knew it wasn't meant for her. She was just Floriana's companion – and Floriana had become a sister to them.

The two girls walked slowly back to the town in the rain. They barely said a word to each other, so heavy was Floriana's heart and so full of envy was Costanza's. Finally, as they reached the fork in the road, Costanza asked Floriana if she wanted to come back to her house to play, but Floriana shook her head. She wanted to run down to the beach and cry her sorrow into the sea. So, Costanza hurried home, to the warmth of her hearth and her mother's embrace, while Floriana wandered down the path to the lonely, cold beach.

The wind had picked up. It was gusty on the shore. The waves pounded the rocks and raced up the sand to snap at her feet. Her hair flew about her head and whipped against her cheeks. She stood broken and alone, and allowed the rain to wash away her tears. Now she understood love, in all its pain and glory. She understood that it never came alone, that it was always accompanied by its inseparable companion, sorrow.

She knew instinctively that it couldn't be any other way, as a coin is bound to its duality, but she didn't mind. The agony was worth the exquisite feeling of love, for even though Dante had gone she loved him in her heart and that feeling would never go away. She'd carry it always and for ever. And she'd wait for him. She'd stand at those big black gates come rain or shine and, like a faithful dog, she'd wait. And there would be pleasure in her waiting, for it would be tempered with hope. Hope that he would come back. Hope that he would remember her.

Chapter 10

Devon 2009

On the last day of May Rafa Santoro arrived at the Polzanze. A bright sun welcomed him as he stepped out of his hired Audi, and a cool sea breeze raked careless fingers through his hair. He took a deep, satisfied breath and ran his eyes over the house with an air of fondness, as if to say, 'Home at last.'

His arrival had been much anticipated at the hotel, and the small wood-panelled hall was crowded with staff. Jennifer and Rose had left their desk, Bertha her duties, and Heather was hovering by the door to the dining room, her lips an unusually provocative shade of crimson. Jake stood in the middle of the hall in front of the round table, which laboured beneath the weight of a lavish display of lilies, while his father positioned himself beside the open fireplace, hands in pockets, a bemused look on his face. Tom, a young Cornish lad who worked with Shane, was already outside offering to carry bags.

This being Sunday, Clementine was not at work, but she felt it was beneath her dignity to hang around the hall like a desperate groupie so she remained alone in her bedroom, challenging herself not to sneak a peek at the new artist from behind the curtain. Having not seen him she couldn't understand what all the fuss was about.

Marina had joined the Brigadier for breakfast, concealing her excitement behind a large cup of coffee, but now Shane hurried across the dining room to tell her that Mr Santoro had arrived.

'Thank you, Shane,' she said, getting up. 'Is Jake in the hall?'

'Along with everyone else,' he replied with a snigger.

'Who else?'

'Jennifer, Rose, Bertha ...'

A shadow of irritation darkened Marina's face. It was Jake's duty to make sure everyone was doing his or her job. She smiled despairingly at the Brigadier. 'I'd better go and set the cat among the pigeons.'

'I'm rather curious myself,' he replied. 'Would rather like to be a pigeon.'

'I don't imagine there's a spare inch in the hall – even for a very discreet pigeon such as yourself.'

'Then I shall wait here and you can introduce me later. I think I'll go and read the papers in the library.'

'You'd have thought they'd never seen a handsome man before.'

'They're all too young to remember me,' he added with a chuckle. 'In my day I was what they called "a dish".'

When Marina stalked into the hall she found only Jake and Grey, and guessed correctly that Shane had warned them all to return to their jobs. Tom was coming through the doors with a couple of bags, followed by Rafa, casual in his brown suede jacket and jeans, his silver-buckled belt glinting on his hips. Marina greeted him warmly and he settled his brown eyes onto her with the familiarity of an old friend. She could see Jennifer and Rose in her peripheral vision, craning their necks round the corner like a couple of geese. But her smile did not falter, nor did her gaze. There was a brightness about him that seemed to light up the whole room and reduce all her fears to superfluous particles of dust. It had been so long since she had been able to breathe without tension in her chest. She couldn't wait for Clementine to meet him; she knew her stepdaughter would approve her choice and that thought made her smile even broader.

'Let me introduce you to Jake, our manager, and my husband, Grey.'

'Father and son?'

'Yes,' said Grey.

'You look very alike.'

'I'm not sure that's a compliment,' said Jake with a grin.

His father rolled his eyes. 'No respect from the young these days! Welcome.' He extended his hand.

Rafa's handshake was firm and confident. 'It's lovely to be here,' he said happily. 'I hadn't forgotten how beautiful the house is.'

Marina beamed with pride. 'I'm so pleased you like it.'

'I will paint it, for sure.'

'And we will hang it up somewhere prominent,' said Grey.

'I can see we're going to have a whole gallery,' Jake added, not without an edge of sarcasm.

'We'd be so lucky,' added Marina. 'Would you like coffee, or to see your room first?'

'I'd like to see my room,' Rafa replied. 'Any excuse to see more of this fantastic house.'

He smiled at her and she couldn't help but smile back with girlish enthusiasm. She noticed how his mouth turned up at the corners, causing the skin on his cheeks to fold into leonine creases, and wondered why Clementine hadn't surfaced to meet him.

'Come, let me show you.'

They walked past reception, where Rose and Jennifer stood in suspended animation, their mouths frozen into inane grins. Rafa broke the spell by shaking their hands and introducing himself. They were caught off guard by his confidence and good manners – most people only talked to them when they wanted something.

'He's gorgeous,' sighed Rose as he disappeared upstairs with Marina, Grey and Jake.

'They don't make them like that in this country,' said Jennifer. 'I don't know a single Englishman who has his easy charm.'

'And his accent. I'd like to listen to *that* on my pillow.'

'Oh Lordie, so would I.'

Their dreaming was interrupted by the loud ringing of the telephone. Jennifer was quick to pick it up. When she heard the familiar voice she looked mildly irritated. 'Oh, hello there, Cowboy. You know you shouldn't call me at work . . .'

Marina led Rafa to the top floor, where a bathroom, bedroom and sitting room made up a cosy suite. 'Is this all for me?' he asked, surprised.

'Well, you're going to be here all summer and you need space to paint.'

'*Qué bárbaro!*' He wandered into the bedroom where Tom had placed one bag on a rack and the other on the floor beside it. There was a dark wood-framed superking-size bed and elegant lamps on the bedside tables where piles of books were neatly stacked.

'Grey chooses the reading material,' she said, noticing him glancing over the spines.

'Edith Wharton, Nancy Mitford, P. G. Wodehouse, Jane Austen, Dumas, Maupassant, Antonia Fraser, William Shawcross.'

'Do you think you'll have any time to paint?' Grey asked, smiling proudly as Rafa read out his favourite authors.

Rafa rubbed his chin. 'I'm not sure. I might never leave my room.'

'How lucky then that you have the whole summer.'

'I think I'm going to like it here,' he mused, grinning at Marina. 'You have very good taste, señora.'

'Thank you. I had great fun doing it. It was a challenge to keep the best of the old and bring in the best of the new without changing the feel of the place. This used to be the children's floor when it was a private house. There's a heavenly view of the sea from here.' She walked over to the bedroom window, kneeled on the window seat and peered through the little square panes of glass set in lead. 'You wouldn't believe the number of glass panes we had to replace.'

Rafa put a hand on the wall beside her and leaned over. 'I love the sea. Having been brought up on the pampa, I find the sea is a great novelty for me.'

'It's nice to drift off to sleep listening to it crashing on the rocks.'

'Have you always lived here?'

'No, we bought the house eighteen years ago, but I love it like a person.'

'It has so much character. I felt that the minute I first walked in. It must be very demanding, like another child.'

Marina didn't bother to correct him. Most people assumed that Grey's children were hers. 'It's somehow more helpless,' she said softly. Once again she felt the weight of foreboding fall upon her heart as she was reminded of why Rafa was here and how much depended on him.

'Let me show you your sitting room,' interrupted Grey, and Rafa followed him down the corridor, leaving Jake and Marina in the bedroom.

'I'm still not sure why you've given him the best set of rooms in the house,' said Jake quietly.

'They're not the best. The first-floor rooms are prettier.' She stood up and faced him.

'Yes, but this is a whole floor.'

'It's an attic.'

'But what if we get honeymooners who want to book it?'

'Then they have the rooms downstairs. We have twenty

rooms, Jake, of which under half are booked so far this summer.'

'We're going to get busier.'

'It's all relative, Jake.'

'He's charismatic, but I'm not sure how he's going to suddenly fill the hotel with wannabe painters.'

'Don't be so negative. You haven't come up with any better ideas.'

'Actually, Dad and I are going to start a literary club.'

'Really?'

'Didn't he tell you?'

'No, he didn't.'

'We're going to invite famous authors to come down and give talks.'

She nodded thoughtfully. 'It's a good idea.'

He looked surprised. 'Yes, it is.'

'Have you approached anyone yet?'

'No. But we will soon. Dad and I have to work it all out. It's only an idea at the moment.'

'Well, you'd better do it quickly or you won't have a hotel to invite them to speak in.'

'It's not that bad, is it?'

Marina closed her eyes and sighed painfully. 'It's bad. I wish it wasn't true, but it is. We're sinking into the mud.'

'God, I didn't know it was that desperate.'

'I don't suppose your father wanted to worry you.'

'Perhaps you're overreacting.'

'I wish I was, but I'm not. I'll do whatever it takes to keep this place. I don't care how low I have to stoop.'

The men returned to the bedroom as Jake was just stepping out into the corridor.

'Do you like your sitting room?'

'It's charming,' Rafa replied. 'And I like the way you have retained all the old bathroom fittings. It's so English.'

'Sometimes the old things are better made than their modern equivalents. These fittings have lasted nearly two hundred years; some of the modern fittings last only two before they begin to crack or leak,' Grey explained.

'For sure,' Rafa agreed emphatically.

'We'll leave you to freshen up and sort yourself out, and wait for you outside on the terrace. Can I get you something to drink?' Marina asked.

'Coffee, thank you.'

'It will be waiting when you're ready.'

The trio walked downstairs, careful not to talk about the artist while they were in the stairwell, the acoustics being such that the entire hotel could hear conversations there. Rose and Jennifer were still giggling to each other behind the reception desk while Tom and Shane were loitering in the hall, waiting for new arrivals to summon them outside or for the existing residents to appear in the hall and ask directions to the gumboot room or some other part of the hotel, for it was a confusing layout of rooms and guests often lost their bearings.

Marina instructed Tom to tell Heather to bring coffee for all of them. As they walked through the drawing room they greeted a couple of Americans who had come for the weekend, sitting on the comfy sofa by the redundant fireplace, drinking Earl Grey tea. Grey hung back to answer their questions on the history of the house, leaving Jake and his stepmother to walk on through to the terrace.

It was an unusually clear day with not even the most delicate wisp of a cloud in the sky. The ocean was calm and looked almost as blue as the Mediterranean Sea. Marina sat down and lost her gaze there a while, her thoughts drifting aimlessly on the gently undulating water. Jake stopped to talk to the waiters, quietly discussing the business of the day, and Marina was left alone to contemplate her predicament.

She was sidetracked a moment by the sight of a grand-mother with her grandson, sitting quietly at the end of the terrace, playing Old Maid. Her expression softened as she took in the tender sight. The grandmother let the child win and feigned annoyance at losing. The little boy grinned up at her, his cheeks as rosy as crab apples, and demanded to play again. The grandmother shuffled the cards patiently, as if she had no desire to do anything else but spend the morning entertaining him. Marina envied them with a painful yearning and had to look away.

Jake joined her at last and Grey appeared with Rafa. She swept the little boy and his grandmother from her vision and settled her attention onto Rafa, grateful for the distraction.

'I see you have supplied paints and paper,' he said, sitting down.

'I didn't know what you needed, but took the liberty of guessing, based on what Paul Lockwood worked with last year. Our guests will need materials, although some will bring their own.'

'I have brought supplies too, but thank you.'

Heather stepped out with a tray of silver pots and pretty cups. One of the waiters helped to unload it, placing a plate of biscuits in the centre of the table.

'I suggest you take some time to look around,' said Grey. 'There are beautiful places here to paint, and Harvey knows all the private houses and hotels nearby if you need to take your students off to paint elsewhere. Last year Paul spent a lot of time in neighbouring homes where the gardens are quite spec-tacular. He relished the diversity and I'm sure they'd be very happy to have you.'

'Yes, you must take the opportunity to see as much of England as you can. This part of the country is so beautiful and we know lots of people who have really pretty houses.'

'I will take your advice and see all that I can.'

'Harvey will be your guide,' said Marina decisively. 'There's no one better than Harvey.'

At that moment Clementine appeared in a turquoise kaftan hanging loosely over skinny white jeans. Her hair was scrunched messily onto the top of her head and she wore no make-up, as if determined not to look like she'd made an effort for the artist who seemed to have already whipped the female members of staff into a froth of excitement.

'Ah, Clementine darling, come and meet Rafa Santoro,' said Grey, giving his daughter an enthusiastic welcome in a sub-conscious attempt to lift her mood.

Rafa turned round to see the girl he had met a few weeks before in the Black Bean Coffee Shop. Clementine recognized him at once and blushed. Suddenly she wished she had put on mascara, brushed her hair, sprayed herself with perfume, not worn white trousers or the kaftan, for that matter, and she imploded with anxiety. She didn't know where to put herself for embarrassment.

Rafa stood up, ignored her outstretched hand and kissed her coolly on the cheek, as was the custom in his own country. 'Hello again.'

'You've met before?' Marina asked in surprise.

'Yes, after I came here to meet you I went into the town to have a look around. I met your daughter in the Black Bean Coffee Shop.'

'You never told us,' said Grey.

'I didn't know who he was, Dad,' Clementine explained, her embarrassment translating into defensiveness. She didn't mean to sound so unfriendly. She wanted to smile but felt gauche. How could she not have bothered to ask more about the artist who was coming to spend the summer? Why had she wilfully shown no interest? Now she just looked foolish.

'You made me buy a brownie,' he said. 'A *naughty* brownie.'

'Sounds good,' said Jake.

'It was good.'

'Come and join us,' said Marina as the waiter brought over another chair. Clementine wanted to rewind the scene and start again, but she was left no option but to sit down and continue as she had begun, awkward and self-conscious. She folded her arms and wished everyone would talk among themselves.

'I don't believe you already know each other,' Marina continued.

'We hardly *know* each other,' said Clementine. 'I told him to buy a brownie and that was it.' She shrugged carelessly, but she hadn't forgotten her dash back to the office to tell Sylvia she was in love and her certainty that she would never see him again. Well, here he was and all she could do was scowl at him.

Marina was confounded by her stepdaughter's sulkiness in the face of possibly the most attractive man ever to set foot in their corner of Devon, and she tried to cajole her out of herself.

'Clemmie loves to travel, don't you, Clemmie? She's been all over India. That's why she's down here, working to earn the money she needs to go back.'

'I think the best education is travelling the world,' said Rafa. 'I admit, though, that I have never been to India.'

That should have been Clementine's cue to engage in conversation, but she sat back, leaving her stepmother to fill the silence for her.

'Neither have I, though the way Clementine talks about it, *when* she talks about it, fills me with the desire to go.' She smiled at Clementine kindly but all the girl could muster was a mumble.

She watched her stepmother chat on effusively, and sighed. Yet another man caught in her silky web.

'I admire people who speak languages,' said Grey. 'I tried to encourage Jake and Clementine to learn French, but neither has a particularly good ear for it.'

'That's because French is a useless language,' interjected Jake. 'Only spoken in France and a few small islands far away.'

'I bet you speak French,' said Marina to Rafa.

'Once you know one Latin-based language the others come very easily. I grew up speaking Italian to my parents, Spanish to my friends and we learned English in school. I've picked up a little French along the way but it's not very good. I'm an excellent bluffer.'

'Your parents are Italian?' Marina asked.

'So many Argentines are Italian,' he replied. 'My father left Italy for Argentina after the war. My mother's family have lived in Argentina for generations.'

'They say it's a wonderful melting pot of cultures,' said Grey.

'It is,' Rafa agreed. 'But we don't have the culture you have in Europe. It's fascinating to walk through the streets of London and imagine what it was like in the days of the infamous Tudors. I confess I went to the Tower and just stood and soaked it up, this rich history of yours, for most of a morning. It was time well spent.'

They talked on. Clementine joined in, slowly warming up as Rafa seemed deliberately to include her, though he seemed more interested in Marina. She wondered whether her father ever noticed his wife's flirting, or whether he was so used to it as not to be bothered. She suspected he was just happy that *she* was happy, at any cost. Marina's contentment was of paramount importance to him.

'Clemmie, why don't you show Rafa around?' Marina suggested. 'You're not doing anything today, are you?' She turned to Rafa. 'You've already seen the Black Bean Coffee Shop, which is clearly one of the highlights of Dawcomb, so it might be nice to explore a little of the countryside with a guide who knows her way around.'

'One who has no interest in Devon,' Jake added mischievously. 'Clemmie makes no secret of the fact that she hates everything about Devon.'

'That's not fair,' interjected Marina. 'Clemmie doesn't *hate* Devon. She's just got her mind on India.'

'Perhaps my enthusiasm will be infectious,' said Rafa and his eyes twinkled at Clementine as they had done in the Black Bean Coffee Shop. She felt her chest inflate with happiness. 'What do you say? Will you be my guide?'

Clementine smiled in spite of herself. It was impossible not to respond positively to Rafa's uninhibited geniality. 'Sure, if you like.'

Marina watched her face open like a sunflower and wished she would smile more often; she was really very pretty when she did.

Chapter 11

After they had finished their coffees Grey suggested Clementine begin her tour in order to be back in time for lunch. 'Take him on a drive, that way he can get his bearings.'

'Do show him the beach,' said Marina. 'It's such a lovely day, you can walk up and down with your feet in the sea.'

'Make sure you take him to the Wayfarer,' Jake added.

Clementine huffed irritably. 'I'll make my own arrangements, thank you very much.'

'You can borrow my car,' said Grey.

'What's wrong with my Mini?'

'Well, it's a little small.'

Clementine turned to Rafa. 'Do you think a Mini is too small?'

He shrugged. 'You're the boss. If you were all cooks you'd have spoiled the cake.'

Marina laughed. 'You're so right. Come on, let's leave them to it. We'll see you back at one.'

'Whatever. I'm going to change, Rafa. I'll meet you in the hall in five.'

Clementine left them on the terrace and found that once she was alone in her bedroom she was able to breathe again.

'Oh my God!' she exclaimed into the bathroom mirror. 'He's delicious. He's even more delicious than I recall. And he remembered me.' She painted her lashes with mascara and covered up the dark circles beneath her eyes with concealer. 'I don't know why I bother, really. I mean, he'll never look at me. Why would he? And he probably has a girlfriend already. Men like that are usually taken.' She squirted herself with Penhaligon's Bluebell eau de toilette. Sighing melodramatically she watched the excitement stain her cheeks pink.

What will Sylvia say when I tell her that the Argentine I never thought I'd see again has come to spend the summer with us? Is it Fate? Am I destined to fall in love and live happily ever after?

She exchanged her white jeans for a pair in blue denim and chose a blue Jack Wills check shirt which she wore over a white T-shirt. She hadn't yet painted her toenails for flip-flops, so she wore blue Nike trainers instead, which were very casual. She didn't want to look like she was trying too hard, so she left her hair as it was. However, when she appeared in the hall, Marina wasn't fooled and she smiled at her knowingly. Clementine noticed that her stepmother's cheeks were also glowing with the same brand of pink and she pitied her for her delusion. If Rafa was a little higher than Clementine on the food chain, he was on a totally *different* food chain from Marina, being so much younger. She didn't mean to feel smug, but smugness crept upon her all the same.

Both Jennifer and Rose were also in the hall, trying to look like they had something official to do there, but deceiving no one. They resembled a pair of curious cows with their long eyelashes and dumb expressions, jostling each other as they moved slowly around the display of lilies.

'Right, ready. Let's go,' Clementine announced, holding up the car keys.

'I'm looking forward to this,' said Rafa, following her outside.

She stood in front of her red Mini Cooper, excited that it was just the two of them. 'Are you sure you don't mind my car?' she asked, unlocking it with the remote.

'It's a charming little car. Why would I mind?'

'Dad's too long-legged for it.'

'Your father is very tall. I am not.'

'Well, isn't that lucky, then?'

'For today, yes.'

Clementine climbed in, hastily gathering up the empty coffee cartons, Cadbury's Flake wrappers and magazines that had collected on the passenger seat. She tossed them into the back and adjusted Rafa's seat to give him more leg room. He sat down and she felt a sudden prickle of electricity for their arms almost touched across the hand brake.

'Now for the fun part,' she said, turning the key and pressing a button on the dashboard. Slowly the roof folded away, leaving them drenched in sunshine, the breeze gently sweeping through the car to carry away the smell of warm leather and any residue of Clementine's irritation. Without her family to hamper her, she felt her confidence grow. 'Isn't this a joy?'

'It certainly is. So, where to first?'

'I'm going to take you on a magical mystery tour.'

'That sounds exciting.'

'It is. Marina can take you to the beach and Dad can drive you around so you get your bearings. Jake can take you to the Wayfarer. But I'm not going to take you there. No, I'm going to take you to a secret little place of mine that holds no interest to anyone else in the county but me.'

'They said you didn't like Devon.'

'They're right,' she replied, driving up the avenue of pink rhododendrons. 'I don't like *their* brand of Devon, but I have my own secret Devon that I like very much and I'm going to show it to you if you promise not to tell anyone.'

'I promise.'

She glanced at him and he grinned back. 'You might even like to paint it sometime.'

They drove up the windy lanes lined with phosphorescent

green leaves and delicate white cow parsley. The air was rich with the scent of regeneration and the hedgerows alive with young blue tits and goldfinches. With the wind in their hair and a sense of elation from the sight and smell of the sea, they chatted away with the ease of old friends. He told her of his love of horses and the rides he enjoyed across the Argentine pampa; of the vast, flat horizon that glows like amber in the dying light at the end of the day, and the dawn in early spring, when the land is veiled with mist. He told her of the prairie hares that play in the long grasses, and the smell of gardenia that would always remind him of home. And he told her of his mother, who worried about him constantly, even though he was in his thirties, and his dead father, who he still mourned, and his siblings, who were so very much older than he that he barely knew them at all.

By the time they reached their destination Clementine felt like a different person. Her usual defensiveness had been carried off by his enthusiasm and in its place there remained a growing sense of confidence. Rafa had lifted her out of herself with stories of his life in Argentina and she had listened intently, her heart swelling with compassion – and surprise that he had chosen to confide in her.

She parked the car by the gate at the top of a field and got out. Below them, on the top of the cliff, stood a pretty little church with a turreted tower and grey slate roof.

'Here we are,' she announced. 'It doesn't look like much . . .'

'Oh, but it does. It's the house that God forgot.'

She smiled, pleased he liked it. 'You're so right. That's exactly what it is, the house that God forgot, and doesn't it look sad and forlorn?'

They climbed over the gate and walked down the hill. The grass was long and lush, scattered with bright yellow buttercups that gleamed in the sun. Fat bees buzzed around the flowers and a pair of butterflies fluttered about them in a flirtatious dance. As they got closer Rafa could see that the windows were boarded up. The church did indeed look sad and forlorn.

'No one comes here. Everyone's forgotten it. You can't even see it from the lane. I spotted it from the sea when I went out fishing with Dad as a child, and it pulled at me somehow. As soon as I could drive I found it. I'll show you inside.'

'You can get inside?'

'Where there's a will, there's a way, as they say. Come on.'

She hurried round to the back of the church where a few steps led down to a little wooden door carved into the stone. 'Must have been a back entrance for dwarfs,' she said with a chuckle. 'Or maybe people were very small all those hundreds of years ago.'

'How old do you think it is?'

'Well, inside, there are tombs of people who died in the thirteenth century.'

'*Increíble!*' he exclaimed under his breath.

She pushed and the door opened with a deep groan. Inside, the air was cold and dank. They left the door wide open to let in the light and proceeded up a windy stone staircase into the main body of the church. It would have been dark were it not for the holes in the roof and where some of the boards blocking the windows had rotted in the damp and come away from their frames. They stood in silence and looked around.

In spite of the cold the place felt strangely warm, as if the air itself were made of something soft. The altar was draped in the habitual white cloth with a mildewed vase sitting empty on the top. The pews were in their neat rows, made of oak, blackened over the years, and on the stone beneath them remained a few cross-stitched hassocks for prayer. On a table by the front door was a pile of green hymn books and opposite, a crimson velvet curtain separated the nave from a little annex where the stone font was dry.

'It's as if they finished a service and left, locking the door behind them for ever,' said Clementine.

Rafa sat on the organ stool and began to play a few notes. The inharmonious sound echoed off the walls, unsettling a couple of pigeons that had made their nest underneath the eaves.

'Good Lord, that organ's out of tune!' Clementine exclaimed, putting her hands over her ears. She stood in the choir stall that consisted of two rows of pews facing each other in front of the altar. 'Do you play?' she asked.

'No. Can't you tell?'

'I thought it was organ that sounded dreadful, not you.'

He got up. 'So what do you do when you come here on your own?'

'Nothing.' She shrugged. 'I wander around and read the inscriptions on the tombstones. The names are wonderful. I stand above them and wonder whether all that remains of them is beneath my feet, or whether their spirits are in some other dimension beyond our senses. I'd like to believe there's a Heaven.'

Rafa wandered over to a large slab that stood out from the rest by virtue of its size and the clarity of the words engraved onto it. 'Archibald Henry Treelock,' he read.

'Great name, Archibald.'

'What do you think Archibald might be doing now?'

'My head tells me that dear old Archie is nothing but dust. But my heart tells me he's in Heaven dancing a branle with his wife, Gunilda.'

'I think your heart is right. At least, that's what my heart tells me, too. I don't believe my father is dust and earth. I believe his old body is buried in the pampa but his spirit is somewhere else.' He ran his eyes around the church and lowered his voice. 'Perhaps he is here with us now, in the house that God forgot.'

'I haven't yet encountered death. Both sets of grandparents

are alive, unfortunately. My mother's parents are very tiresome, but thankfully they live far away so I never see them.'

'Where do they live?'

'In Scotland with my mother.'

He stared at her for a long moment, frowning. 'Sorry, I don't understand. Your mother lives here with you, no?'

'No, Marina's not my mother. God forbid! No, my mother lives in Edinburgh with her second husband, Martin, who's a fool. Marina is my stepmother.'

'I thought she was . . .'

'Most people do. But I don't know why. We don't look at all alike.'

'No, you don't.'

'I look like my mother, which is a pity as she's no beauty. I was taught that beauty comes from within and I choose to believe it.' She gave a hollow laugh.

Rafa wandered up the steps to the pulpit. 'Does Marina have any children of her own?'

'No. She's unable to have children. It's a very sore point so don't ever bring it up.'

'I see.' He put his hands on the edge of the pulpit as if he were a vicar about to give a sermon. His face looked grave.

'Jake and I are the closest to children she's ever going to get.'

'You don't seem very sympathetic.'

'Am I so transparent?' She gave a little sniff. 'We're very different, she and I.'

'How old were you when she became your stepmother?'

'Three – and I believed she came to steal my father away.'

Rafa descended the little stair and stood before her. His expression was so full of compassion she felt a gentle tug somewhere in the middle of her chest. She hadn't meant to disclose so much about herself.

'I understand,' he said, and touched her arm. The way that

he touched her and the dark shadow that made his face look so serious convinced her that he did, indeed, understand.

'Thank you,' was all she could think of to say.

He smiled gently. 'Come, let us go back out into the sunshine. Is there a beach below? I'd love to see the sea.'

He put his hand in the small of her back and led her past the altar to the narrow stone staircase by which they had entered. The church was *her* secret place and she was *his* tour guide and yet, in that brief moment, she felt as if *he* was looking after *her*. She basked in the new sensation, feeling feminine in a way she had never felt before. Why she had opened up to a total stranger, she didn't know. Perhaps *because* he was a stranger with no preconceptions about her or her family. Or perhaps because there was something intimate in his soft brown eyes that drew her out of herself and won her trust.

They emerged into the sunshine like a pair of vampires, blinking in the glare. The buttercups shone brightly like small sparks of fire and the air smelled thick with life after the stale smell of decay inside the church. They inhaled with satisfaction and let the warm sun caress their faces. Below, the sea was calm, lapping the rocks in a lazy rhythm as if its mind were lost in daydreams. They walked down to the beach. Once there had been a path but now it was overgrown with ferns and brambles. Clementine was relieved she had worn jeans as the thorns tore the material instead of her flesh.

They laughed and chatted all the way down. Rafa helped her untangle herself once or twice when the brambles became too greedy and wrapped their thorny tentacles around her ankles.

'All this for a beach,' he exclaimed, setting her free.

'But it's not just any beach. It's really lovely.'

'It doesn't look like anyone's been here for a long time.'

'They haven't – *I* haven't. I saw it from the boat but I've never attempted to reach it by foot.'

'Then we shall make a path so we can come here whenever we like and not get eaten by plants.'

The thought of coming here often with Rafa caused her spirits to rise even higher. They had the whole summer ahead, and she would enjoy showing him every corner of Devon.

Finally, the path opened onto a sandy bank that expanded into a secluded yellow beach. It had looked beautiful from the sea, but now she was there, Clementine saw to her delight that it was even lovelier than she had imagined. The fact that neither Marina nor her father had claimed it for themselves gave her a heightened sense of joy. This would be *her* beach, beneath *her* church, and she wouldn't share it with anyone but Rafa.

'You won't tell the others about our find, will you? We don't want the whole county joining us here.'

He put his hands on his hips and gazed out across the ocean. 'I won't tell anyone. It's spectacular.' He breathed deeply, flaring his nostrils. 'I'm finally here,' he added, and the way he said it made Clementine suspect he was talking to himself.

They walked down to the sea. Rafa took off his shoes and rolled up his jeans. Inspired by his enthusiasm, she did the same. The water was cold but he insisted they walk the entire length of the cove. Small waves rolled in, each wrapping their ankles in white foam before retreating to make way for the next. Rafa's denim grew dark where it was wet until finally he was soaked up to his knees. He laughed it off with a genial shrug.

'If I had swimming shorts I'd dive in.'

'Let's do that,' she suggested. He looked at her in surprise. 'Let's dive into the sea.'

'If you do, I will, too.'

She giggled nervously. 'OK.' With her heart beating wildly she ran a little up the beach and wriggled out of her jeans and shirt, standing before him in only her T-shirt and pink floral knickers.

He threw his head back and laughed at her daring. '*Qué coraje, nena!*'

'I hope that's a compliment.'

'It is. You have courage!'

'Well, don't leave me standing here like this. Come on!'

He joined her on dry sand and gamely stepped out of his jeans, jacket and shirt, tossing them beside hers. 'You ready?'

She barely had time to admire his athletic body, clothed in nothing but a pair of Calvin Klein undershorts, before he was running into the water making loud huffing noises at the cold. She followed him happily, marvelling at the incredible twist of Fate that had brought them together in this extraordinary way.

They frolicked about, laughing and splashing each other. Once they got used to the water it ceased to feel so cold. They swam out a little so that the waves lifted them up and down like buoys.

'You're very brave,' he said admiringly.

'Only because you put the idea into my head.'

'But you didn't hesitate. You thought nothing of leaping into the water.'

'Well, what can I say? That's just the sort of girl I am,' she grinned at him playfully.

'I like that sort of girl.'

'We haven't got any towels but it's sunny. We can dry on the beach. I bet you've never been in such a cold sea.'

'There you are wrong. The sea in Chile is much colder than this. It's impossible to stay in for very long, that is, if you're willing to go in at all.'

'I'd like to see South America.'

'Marina said you are planning on going back to India.'

'I love India, but it doesn't have to be India. I just want to get away from *here.*'

'Why?'

'I don't know what I want to do. I'm afraid of starting the rest of my life. If I travel I can avoid it.'

'Travelling *is* life.'

'But it's not responsibility. I'm supposed to be starting a career and becoming "grown up". The trouble is I don't want to.'

'Then you mustn't.'

'That's not what my father says.'

'You have to do what *you* want to do. If travelling is what you love, then you should see the world. I don't think it is so important to conform to other people's expectations. It's your life, after all, and you don't know how long you've got to enjoy it.'

'Now, that's a morbid thought.'

'Perhaps, but it focuses the mind. You have to find your way, Clementine, even if it doesn't happen to be the way your family have envisaged for you.'

'I'm working in Dawcomb to save up so I can go off somewhere, anywhere.'

'Anywhere but here.' He grinned at her.

'I know, I sound so ungrateful.'

'I don't know you well enough to know if you're being ungrateful. But I know human nature enough to know that you will never be happy living your life for other people. You have to go your own way and work it all out for yourself.'

'You're very wise, Rafa.'

'Thank you, Clementine. Now I think we should get out because I can no longer feel my toes.'

They sat on the sand to dry and Clementine was able to appreciate how fit he was and how handsome, with his wet hair falling over his forehead. It seemed unbelievable that she was there beside him, as wet as a fish, laughing as if they had always been friends. Finally, even though they were not yet dry, they dressed and walked back up to the car. Clementine felt uncomfortable with her wet bra and knickers beneath her clothes but she wouldn't have missed that swim for anything in the world.

They drove back to the Polzanze, discussing the reactions they were going to get when they told everyone that they had been swimming.

'I'll be sacked as your guide,' said Clementine.

'I'll be sacked as the artist.'

'No, you won't.'

'You don't think?'

'So long as you don't lead the old ladies astray.'

'Old ladies?'

'Your pupils.'

'Ah, *por supuesto*, my pupils.' He rubbed his chin. 'How old are they?'

'Very old.' Clementine laughed. 'But apparently very entertaining. They're wildly eccentric. They were here last year and Marina's still talking about them.'

'You weren't here last year?'

'Of course not!'

He shook his head. 'No, silly me. You were somewhere, anywhere, but not here.'

Chapter 12

Clementine and Rafa burst into the hotel like a pair of wet dogs. Rose and Jennifer watched them run upstairs, their laughter filling the stairwell and bouncing off the walls like sparks.

Rose looked at Jennifer and raised her eyebrows. 'What do you think they've been doing?'

'Whatever it is, I wish I had done it, too,' Jennifer replied longingly.

'Do you think they've been swimming in the sea?'

'Well, unless they've fallen into a giant puddle I'd say the sea is a strong possibility.'

'To think he's going to be here all summer.'

'Hearts are going to be broken.'

'I wouldn't care,' Rose sighed. 'I'd happily have him break my heart.'

Lunch was in the dining room at a long table by the window. Marina placed Rafa between herself and Clementine. She noticed their wet hair and that both of them had changed their clothes. They were exhilarated, exchanging banter like intimate friends. Clementine's face was lit up like a Chinese lantern, her habitual dark presence infused with light. Marina marvelled at the sudden change in her. Her stepdaughter even smiled at her and Marina was ashamed that she felt so pathetically grateful for such a small crumb of kindness.

'What have you two been up to?' asked Grey.

'We went for a swim in the sea,' Clementine replied nonchalantly, as if it were something she was in the habit of doing every Sunday morning.

Rafa grinned mischievously. 'I take the blame.'

'That's very gallant of you,' Jake commented.

'I find the allure of the sea irresistible.'

'No, it was my suggestion,' Clementine admitted, the breadth of her smile leaving no one in any doubt that she had not the slightest regret.

'Wasn't it very cold?' asked Marina.

'Freezing,' Rafa replied. 'But it made us very hungry.' He looked down at the plate of seared tuna, cucumber nori rolls in toasted sesame, honey and chilli dressing and his mouth watered. 'This looks delicious.'

'We have an excellent French chef,' said Marina.

'Fresh tuna,' Grey added, picking up his knife and fork. 'I would like to say that I caught it myself but I had work to do in the office this morning.'

'What have you been doing?' asked Marina.

'Jake and I are putting together our plan for the first literary dinner.'

'We're going to ask William Shawcross to come and talk,' Jake added.

'I've met him once or twice in London and heard him speak at the Royal Geographic Society,' Grey explained. 'I think we could get him to come. After all, his wife owns a hotel on the edge of Dartmoor.'

'I think that's a wonderful idea,' Marina enthused. Sitting there in the sunlight, which flooded the dining room, with her new artist at her side and the prospect of a literary dinner with William Shawcross, she felt optimistic about the future. There were only a few other tables of guests, but once word got around that an artist had set up residence for the summer, she had no doubt that the place would fill up and feel busy again.

'Darling, where's Harvey? I need him to do one or two things this afternoon,' said Grey.

'He's gone to visit his mother again,' Marina replied.

'He's the most devoted son.'

'His mother must be ancient,' said Jake. 'He's already on borrowed time.'

'That's not kind, Jake,' Marina chided. 'He's young in spirit.'

'Longevity is all about how you think,' said Rafa, tapping his temple. 'I think most illness is in the mind.'

'That's ridiculous,' Jake retorted. 'Are you saying that people who are dying of cancer are only sick because of the way they think?'

Marina was embarrassed that Jake had spoken out in such an aggressive manner but Rafa had not taken offence.

'I think our emotions affect our bodies in ways we are still learning about. Doctors who prescribe drugs are treating the symptoms, not the cause. I believe there is a direct relationship between our heads and our health. We'd all feel better if we thought positively.' Jake pulled a face. Rafa smiled. 'Imagine lying in bed at night. You are warm and safe and you are drifting off to sleep. Then, a thought pops into your head that frightens you. Perhaps you imagine that someone is prowling about outside. Your heart begins to race, your breathing grows shallow, your skin grows cold and damp. The stress that fear induces disrupts the energy flow through your body. But it is just a thought, nothing more.'

'You're right, of course, Rafa. Most illness is psychosomatic,' said Grey.

'I agree,' Clementine added.

Jake frowned at his sister and took a swig of wine. 'You would, Clemmie. You know, Rafa, Clemmie hasn't swum in the sea for what? Twenty years?'

'What's that got to do with the mind's impact on health?' Clementine snapped.

'Just illustrating the link between your mind and your mood.' He raised his eyebrows suggestively as Clementine scowled back at him.

'Well, thank you for stating the obvious.'

'My old ladies arrive tomorrow,' interjected Marina, sensing her civilized lunch was unravelling.

'Clementine tells me they are wildly eccentric,' said Rafa. 'I can't wait to meet them.'

'They're very English. Oh, except for Mrs Delennor, who is American.'

'I love Americans,' Rafa enthused. 'I spent three years in New York working for an advertising firm.'

'That's why you speak such good English,' said Grey.

'With a slight American twang,' Jake added, unable to resist a little jibe. 'If I had such an accent I'd have a lot more success with the girls.'

'You'd need a lot more than a foreign accent, Jake,' said Clementine.

'Tell me, Rafa, have you left a girlfriend back in Buenos Aires?' Clementine looked down at her plate, hoping Rafa wasn't about to declare that he was already married with children.

'No,' he said with a smile. 'I am not attached.'

'We'd better not advertise that fact,' said Grey. 'Or we'll have all the girls from Dawcomb suddenly wanting to learn how to paint.'

'So long as they fill my rooms, I don't care,' said Marina.

'Did you take Rafa into Dawcomb?' asked Grey.

'No,' Clementine replied. 'Anyway, he already knows Dawcomb.'

'I suggest you give him a tour this afternoon. It's important he gets his bearings.'

'Oh, really, Dad. What's so important about bearings?'

'Trust me, darling, a man needs to know where he is.'

Rafa laughed and turned to Clementine. 'You owe me a scone with clotted cream,' he said. 'You haven't forgotten, have you?'

Clementine beamed with pleasure that he had remembered. 'Devil's for scones and jam it is, then, so you can get your bearings.' She grinned at her father and Grey felt his heart inflate with gratitude.

After lunch Clementine and Rafa disappeared into Dawcomb. Grey went down to the quay to tinker with his boat and Marina went back to the stable block. She was surprised at Jake's behaviour at lunch. He had been uncharacteristically aggressive. Did he feel threatened by Rafa? Was he jealous of all the attention the new artist was receiving? After all, no one in the hotel could talk of anything else. He hadn't been very enthusiastic about having an artist in the first place, perhaps he was put out that the man was obviously going to be a great success. What Jake didn't realize was that they *all* depended on Rafa, regardless of whose idea it had been to invite him. This was no time for petty jealousies. This *had* to work.

Marina was in her kitchen reading the papers when Jake burst in, his face pink with excitement.

'Baffles has struck again!' he declared. Marina stared at him in shock. 'The Greville-Joneses were robbed in the early hours of the morning.'

'Good God, are you sure?' It frightened her that the thief was targeting people she knew personally. It brought him closer to *her*.

'My mole on the police force called me just now. He says they're trying to contain it so that people don't get scared.'

'We'll all be reading about it tomorrow, then.'

'They won't hear about it from me.'

Marina sighed anxiously. 'Poor John and Caroline. It's just

horrendous.' Jake grinned, clearly enjoying the drama. 'You shouldn't look so pleased, Jake. We could be next.'

'I doubt it. It's not as if we have any goodies to steal.'

'He doesn't know that.'

'Of course he does. It's clear he knows the houses very well before he robs them. He goes straight for the loot and leaves everything else untouched.'

'Was anyone hurt?'

'John Greville-Jones heard a noise in the hall and crept down with his rifle. Apparently, he keeps it under his bed.'

'He should be careful Caroline doesn't use it on him.'

Jake chuckled. 'I don't think she'd know how to unlock it.'

'Did he see him?'

'No. He was very quick. In and out like a mouse.'

'What did he take?'

'All the silver from the dining room.'

'Nothing else?'

'My mole says he must have known it was there because he went straight for it. He didn't bother going into any of the other rooms, and you know the Greville-Joneses have a draw-ing room full of valuable paintings.'

'Any clues?'

'Just a note saying "Thank you."'

'Really, that's absurd.'

'Signed Raffles.'

'He's loving the attention, obviously. Whoever heard of a polite robber? It's a contradiction in terms.'

'Robbers always like to leave their mark.'

'Poor John and Caroline. I was going to suggest that Rafa take my ladies to paint their folly. Last year Caroline put on a picnic for them and Harvey sat in the kitchen all afternoon, flirting with their cook.' She sighed. 'They might be less keen to invite strangers into their property now.'

*

Rafa and Clementine sat in Devil's, staring at a three-tiered silver tray of scones, a big bowl of clotted cream and a dish of jam. Penny and Tamara, two pretty young waitresses, hovered around the table hoping the handsome foreigner would toss them another dashing smile.

'So these are scones,' said Rafa, helping himself to the biggest one.

'I'll show you how it's done.' Clementine cut open his scone and spread a large dollop of cream onto each half, placing a spoonful of strawberry jam on top. 'Now tuck in! It's more than a taste, it's an experience.'

Knowing he had an audience, for by now not only the waitresses but the table of middle-aged women beside them had suspended their conversation to listen in, he lifted one half and took a somewhat theatrical bite. There was so much cream and jam he couldn't help but catch some on his lips. Instead of using his napkin, he licked it off with relish, his crow's-feet deepening as he grinned with comical delight. Penny and Tamara giggled and the middle-aged women smiled at his readiness to laugh at himself. It wasn't long before Sugar Wilcox, christened the less tasty name of Susan, came out of her office at the back of the café to see what all the commotion was about.

Sugar's heart was as soft as her scones and as ready to be devoured as the jam and cream. When she laid eyes on the charismatic stranger sitting with Clementine Turner by the window she adjusted her sherbet-pink dress and took full advantage of her position as proprietor to sweep across the room and introduce herself.

'Clemmie, who is your charming guest?'

Rafa wiped his mouth with the napkin, jumped politely to his feet and extended his hand to the petite blonde woman who now stood before him. 'Rafa Santoro,' he said. The strength of his handshake startled her and she withdrew hers hastily, nursing her fragile fingers with her other hand.

'Italian,' Sugar gushed. 'I love Italy.'

'Argentine,' he replied. 'You'd love Argentina.'

'Goodness me, you are funny. Please, enjoy your scones.'

Rafa sat down again. 'I am enjoying them. They're delicious. If I lived here I'd grow fat on them, happily.'

'You know, I'm a little familiar with Argentina. I had my Eva Peron moment, scraping my hair back into a chignon, wearing nineteen-forties dresses and painting my lips crimson.'

'Are you sure it wasn't more of a Madonna moment?'

'Well, I suppose it was really. I liked the way she looked in the movie. So, how long are you staying?'

'The summer,' interrupted Clementine, just to remind Sugar that she was still there. 'He's my stepmother's artist-in-residence.'

'Really? How delightful. I'd love to learn how to paint.'

'You have to be a hotel guest, I'm afraid,' said Clementine.

'Does lunch count?'

'No.'

Sugar sighed and opened her blue eyes as wide as they would go. 'Will you be giving lessons after hours?'

'I've only just arrived so I don't know what I'll be doing.'

'I warn you, Marina will keep you very busy at the hotel.'

Rafa shrugged, feigning helplessness. 'I have to earn my board and lodging.'

'The rent at my place is less demanding,' Sugar breathed suggestively. 'Come and have a scone or two any time you like. On the house. You'll be good for business.' She smiled sweetly and wafted away.

Clementine laughed quietly. 'Is it your aftershave?'

'What do you mean?' But he knew what she meant, for the corners of his mouth twitched mischievously. 'I don't suppose they're used to foreigners down here.'

'Rubbish, of course they are. They're just not used to handsome ones.'

'They'll get over it. Looks can carry a person only so far.'

'At least you've got personality. Most beautiful people have never had to develop one.'

His brown eyes appraised her thoughtfully. 'I think that less obvious beauty is more attractive. When it's leaping out at you there's nothing to look for.'

Clementine began to feel hot. Was he referring to her? 'Everyone has something,' she said lamely.

'Your stepmother has a very beautiful face.'

'You don't think it leaps out at you?'

'No. She has mysterious eyes.'

'Then you're seeing something that I don't see.'

'Of course, because I am not blinded by prejudice. When a woman is her age, the face reflects the person she is, whether she likes it or not. She cannot hide her nature. Marina has a sensual, generous face, but there is something guarded and sad about her eyes.'

'Men!' Clementine rolled her eyes. 'You're no different from all the rest.'

'Why did you imagine I would be?'

'I don't know. I hoped . . .'

He shrugged and took a sip of tea. 'The problem you have with your stepmother is *your* problem, not hers. Don't let what happened in the past control who you are *now*.'

Clementine was taken aback by his comment. She had thought he understood. But when all was said and done he was a man like every other man, he just had a more beautiful face. In one morning, Marina had managed to wrap her tentacles around him like Medusa. Clementine had lost him as an ally.

That night, after dinner, Rafa went into the garden to call his mother. He sat on the ground beneath the cedar tree and pulled out his Blackberry.

Maria Carmela seemed to sense when it was her favourite son and hurried to pick up her phone before it had the chance to ring.

'*Hijo.*'

'Mamá. Are you well?'

'I am, Rafa. Thank the Lord, I am in good health. A little tired but what can one expect when you are as old as I am.'

'You're not old.'

'I feel old. I'm full of worry.'

'I've told you not to worry.'

'I wish your father were alive.'

'If he was, I wouldn't be here and I'm glad I'm here.'

'So tell me. What do you do with yourself all day?'

Rafa told her about his excursion to the forgotten church with Clementine and their swim in the sea. 'I had a proper English tea this afternoon in a place called Devil's. I had scones.'

'What are they?'

'Like *alfajores de maizena*, more or less. I'll bring you some when I come home.'

'Have you said anything?'

'Not yet. The time isn't right.'

'If you leave it too long you might miss the moment.'

'I have to be sure, though I'm pretty certain this is the right place. All the clues lead to here.'

'If you're not sure, come home and forget the whole silly venture.'

'I've come this far, I'm not giving up now.'

'No one can say you're not a man of courage. For that I'm proud of you.'

'So be proud and stop worrying.' There was a long pause and a crackle over the airwaves. 'Mamá, are you still there?'

'I feel guilty, Rafa.' Her voice was quieter now.

'Why?'

'If I hadn't told you, you'd never have set off on this mad

quest. It's all my fault. Your father and I promised we'd keep it all secret. While he was alive he gave me the strength to hold my tongue. He took it to the grave, as he always said he would. But I . . . it is because I love you that I couldn't hold it in any longer. You had a right to know the truth. But now I have told you, I'm frightened of what you might dig up. I'm afraid I have given you the key to Pandora's box.'

'Nothing's going to happen.'

'You don't know the people you are dealing with. They are dangerous.'

'That was many years ago. Times have changed.'

'I worry that I have put you in danger again.'

'Let me worry about that.'

'Oh, Rafa, you give me such strength. I will try not to worry.'

'I'm going to come home at the end of the summer and everything is going to be just the same as it always has been. Trust me.'

'I trust you, *hijo*. I just don't trust . . . *them*.'

Rafa distracted her with questions about the farm, his siblings and their children. Little by little her voice grew less strained and she sounded more herself. When he hung up he felt a little better. He hated to think of her sitting alone in the middle of the pampa, worrying about him. He knew how precious he was to her, and that since the death of his father he had become even more so. He stood up and put his hands on his hips, staring out into the eternal blackness of the night, lost in thought. He wasn't ready to go back inside, there were so many knots to unravel in his head. So he took a walk.

The scents of the garden were intensified by the dew and he was reminded of the midnight walks he used to take as a younger man across the pampa. As his mind delved deeper into his past he felt the sharp pain of longing pull at his heart.

When Rafa was a small boy, Lorenzo was already an old man in his sixties. His other children were all grown up and his wife worried that he no longer had the patience or the energy to endure the constant demands of a small child. But little by little Rafa had won him over with his enthusiasm and curiosity, following him around the farm like a worshipful dog. When his older children were small Lorenzo had been too busy to indulge them, but in his old age he had found to his delight that he had all the time in the world to indulge his youngest. He taught him how to ride and took him on long excursions across the pampa, telling him about the history of the land and his own childhood in Italy. He taught him to play cards and to smile when he lost, and at night, by the warm light of the fire, they'd sit on the grass with the other gauchos and sing songs while Lorenzo strummed his guitar. The old man relished having one child to dote on instead of four, and he spoiled him with the indulgence of a man who has little else in his life to afford him pleasure.

Rafa had loved those times, alone with his father, a gruff bear of a man with the quiet, gentle nature of a hound. How he missed him.

Chapter 13

Marina hadn't suffered nightmares for many years, not since she first settled into married life. But that night she awoke in a sweat, her heart throbbing frantically against her ribcage, her throat choked with sobs. She sat up and clutched her bosom, slowly returning to the present and her bed, where Grey lay sleeping peacefully beside her. She reached over to her bedside table and picked up the glass of water. With a trembling hand she brought it to her lips. Gradually, her pulse slowed down and her heart stopped pounding. She took a deep breath and wiped her face. Yet the sadness that dream provoked hung over her like a shroud.

She climbed out of bed and walked unsteadily to the closet where she kept her clothes. Taking care not to make a sound, she opened the door and reached into the very back of the top shelf, where a shoe box lay hidden against the wall, behind her sweaters. She hadn't taken it out for years, even though it emanated a strange kind of magnetism whenever she opened her cupboard, to remind her of its presence.

With the box safely tucked against her chest she tiptoed into the bathroom and locked the door. She switched on the light and winced at the brightness. Slowly she went over to the lavatory, replaced the lid and sat down. She remained still, staring at the box with its simple white lid until her eyes stung. It looked like a little coffin, so pure and unblemished. She ran her fingers over the smooth surface and her tears fell heavy and fast. Her heart contracted with dread until it was a little nugget, like a cold stone.

She dreaded what the box contained, although she was as familiar with its contents as she was with her own pain. Her breathing grew laboured and she cried out, muffling her sob against her hand. She closed her eyes and quietly wept. It didn't matter whether or not she opened it, for it would always be there to remind her of her error. And if she threw the box away? The memories would still be there, indelibly marked upon her soul, to resurface in night terrors to remind her of her guilt. Only God knew how much she suffered.

She remained in the bathroom until her heartbeat slowed again and her grief subsided. Then she replaced the box in the far corner of her wardrobe and went back to bed.

Grey rolled over and pulled her close. 'Are you all right, darling?' he whispered sleepily.

'I am now,' she replied, snuggling into his embrace.

'Not that dream again?'

'Yes, but it's gone now.' It had been years since that recurring nightmare had stalked her sleep. He kissed her head and she closed her eyes, knowing she could drift off safe in the knowledge that it wouldn't come back tonight.

The following morning Harvey appeared in her kitchen with a big smile and Marina had to restrain herself from throwing her arms around him like a child.

'Oh, Harvey, I'm so pleased you're back. We missed you.'

Harvey looked at her, concerned. 'Are you all right?'

'Yes. But Rafa arrived yesterday and my old ladies arrive today, and Grey wanted you to help him with something. He left early to go fishing so I can't ask him what it was. Anyway, it doesn't matter now. Why don't you have a cup of tea and talk to me while I have breakfast? Bertha will be arriving soon and then I'll have to leave.'

Harvey rolled his eyes. 'You mean the Workaholic?'

Marina laughed. 'Wonderful name for her.'

'Never seen anyone move so fast from room to room.'

'If only.'

'I think the minute you're gone, she settles down, makes herself a cup of tea and reads the papers.'

'I'm sure she wouldn't dare.'

'That's what she wants you to think.' He pulled out a chair and Marina poured boiling water from the kettle into a mug. She knew how he liked it: Earl Grey with a large spoonful of honey. As she handed it to him her battered heart recovered a little. She watched him take it, his big hand rough and lined like the bark of an old oak tree.

She sat down opposite and poured herself another cup of coffee. He looked at her with kind eyes. 'So, what's up, then?'

'Besides the robbery?'

'I know, I heard. He's running rings around the police.'

'No leads. Nothing. It seems unbelievable in this day and age, with forensics and all the technology at their disposal, that they can't find something.'

'They must have had a lot of silver in their dining room to make it worth the robber's while to break in and steal it.'

'At least he didn't explore further. Think of all those paintings.'

'I imagine he knew what he wanted. Silver is easy to sell.'

'Has it come out in the papers?'

'Haven't read them yet. I have my mole in the police force.'

'Same one as Jake's mole, I suspect. He doesn't waste any time in telling everyone, does he? Probably tells the local paper, too.'

'I think he enjoys being in the know.'

'And showing off to anyone who'll listen. No wonder they can't catch him, they're too busy gossiping.'

'So, how's the artist settling in?'

Marina's face lit up at the mention of Rafa. 'He's charming. A positive, happy presence to have around the hotel, just like you.' Harvey grinned over his tea cup. 'He's nice to everyone, you know. Jennifer and Rose are on cloud nine because he takes trouble with them and everyone seems happier. It's as if he has sprinkled fairy dust over the place. I sense he's going to make a real difference here.'

'I'm sure you're right.'

'I don't think Jake likes him, though.'

'Really?'

'The green-eyed monster.'

'Ah,' said Harvey, knowingly.

'Sometimes Jake's very immature. But Clemmie thinks Rafa is wonderful.'

'That's good.'

'The trouble is, she's rather obvious about it.'

'He probably doesn't notice. Men notice less than you think.'

'I don't know. But he's a grown-up. I'm sure he'll take it in his stride.' She looked uneasy.

'You don't want her to get hurt.'

'She's never really been in love before. She's had boyfriends.' Marina pulled a face. 'Lots of boyfriends. But she's never loved.'

'You think she's going to fall in love with Rafa?'

'Almost certainly. I fear she's going to get hurt.'

'It might be a perfect match.'

'I don't think so. He lives on the other side of the world and he's almost too handsome for his own good. He must be used to girls falling in love with him.' She lowered her eyes and frowned. 'I don't trust beautiful men when it comes to love.'

'But you like Rafa.'

'Yes, I like him very much. I'm just being silly.'

'No, you're not. You're being a good stepmother.' She looked at him, now smiling at her with such affection, and felt her throat tighten for no reason at all.

'Thank you, Harvey. You know I only want what's best for her.'

'I know you do.'

The front door opened, bringing in a gust of wind and Bertha. 'Goodness me, it's blustery this morning.'

'Time to go over to the hotel,' said Marina to Harvey as Bertha made her way across the hall towards the kitchen. They both drained their cups. A cloud of Anaïs Anaïs wafted in on the draught, then Bertha filled the doorway, her large body squeezed into a yellow floral tent dress. Marina put down her coffee cup and stared in horror, while Harvey was unable to take his eyes off her. The yellow fabric fell straight from the neck edge to her ankles, which stuck out of the hem like two uncooked sausages. Her feet were squeezed into gold pumps. Marina blinked at her, lost for words.

'Don't say you don't like it,' said Bertha, unfazed. 'I've spent all morning trying to zip it up.'

'You look very bright,' said Harvey. He stood up and replaced his cap. 'I need my sunglasses to look at you.'

'I felt positive this morning.'

'That's good,' said Harvey. 'Perhaps you'll put some of that positivity into your work.'

'You know me, forever the perfectionist.' She dropped her handbag onto one of the kitchen chairs. 'I think I'll make myself a cuppa.' Harvey caught Marina's eye and raised an eyebrow. 'Anything special you need me to do today?' She directed her question at Marina.

'Um, no. I mean, no, nothing special.'

'Who's going to clean the artist's room, then?'

'I don't know. It's up to Jake.'

'Well, if you want it done properly, you know you can count on me.'

'Thank you, Bertha.' Marina made for the door.

'Have a word with Jake. Perhaps he can assign me to that room for the summer.' She bustled over to the kettle and thrust it under the tap. 'I wouldn't necessarily trust those silly house-maids to do a good job. He's a handsome lad and they might get into trouble.' She gave Marina a meaningful look. 'You know what young girls are like. Much too free with their loins.'

Harvey and Marina crossed the gravel to the hotel, laughing together at the absurdity of the woman.

'I didn't know they made dresses that size,' said Marina. 'Or that shape. I dread to think what the rest of my staff are wearing. Has everyone gone mad?'

They entered the hotel to find Rose and Jennifer on reception. There was nothing unusual about their clothes, but they had certainly applied their make-up with more care than usual.

'He's in the dining room,' said Jennifer, as Marina swept in.

'Good.'

'He's sitting with the Brigadier.'

Marina looked worried. 'Oh, OK.'

'He'll love the old Brigadier,' said Harvey as they walked on through the hall. 'They don't make them like that in Argentina.'

'What do you know of Argentina, Harvey?' Marina laughed.

'That they don't make men like the Brigadier.'

Rafa was indeed sitting at the Brigadier's usual table by the window. They were deep in conversation. When the two men saw Marina approach, they got to their feet to greet her.

'Please don't get up,' she said, watching the Brigadier, who had only just managed to lift his bottom off the chair, drop back into it. 'So, you two have met.'

'Fascinating young man,' enthused the Brigadier. 'His father fought in the war, for the *other* side.'

'Then he migrated to Argentina to forget about it,' Rafa added.

'I don't want to forget about it. The day I forget about it they might as well bury me in the ground. Best days of my life.'

'No, your life is good now,' said Rafa.

'Not as good as the past, young man,' chuckled the Brigadier a little sadly.

'But the past is just memory, the future just anticipation, the only reality is now.' Rafa looked around the room. 'And here you are in a beautiful place, eating a delicious breakfast. There's not a lot wrong about that.'

'Is it bad to dream?' Marina asked.

'Of course not, as long as your desires don't make you unhappy.'

'I gave up all my pipe dreams when I was no longer young enough to smoke them. Now I just smoke conventional tobacco,' said the Brigadier.

'You're young in your heart,' said Rafa kindly.

'This old heart. Nothing made it beat more surely than the sound of gunfire and the smell of battle.' He raised his rheumy eyes and gave a little sniff. 'Or the pretty face of my girl.'

Rafa sensed that his girl was up there with his father and looked on the Brigadier's wistful face with empathy. 'You know, she's still here,' he said softly.

'Oh, I know she is. It's been five years – five *long* years. I can feel her sometimes, but then is it just my mind playing cruel tricks on a sad old man who wants to believe?'

'Most certainly not,' interrupted Marina. 'You have to believe what you feel.' She turned to Rafa. 'What are your plans for today?'

'He's going to teach me how to paint,' said the Brigadier.

'Really?'

'Oh, yes. He thinks it'll make me feel young again.'

'Then he should teach us all how to paint,' said Marina with a laugh.

'You're all welcome.'

'Any other takers?'

'No, just the Brigadier. We're going to paint in the garden.'

'Good.'

'We're going to paint a tree.'

'A tree?'

'Yes,' Rafa confirmed decisively. 'A tree.'

Clementine had slept better than she had in a long time. Last night she had ignored a call from Joe at ten o'clock and switched off her mobile. Rafa had come in from the garden at about eleven and they had sat in the conservatory until midnight, talking in the candlelight until the wax had all but melted. He had told her more about his father, whom he missed dreadfully, and about his childhood. She felt flattered that he had opened up to her, as if she were his confidante. They already shared the secret church, the house that God forgot, and the hidden cove. When they stood up to go to bed she had almost expected him to kiss her. But he hadn't. He had smiled and said good night, leaving her in the hall with Bill, the night porter.

She had floated across to the stable block, her head swimming with wonderful fantasies and her chest full of something light and fizzy. She had hummed as she enjoyed a bath, danced as she had dried herself and laughed as she had smoothed her body with some lotion she had bought but never used. She had snuggled beneath the duvet with a contented sigh and for the first time in as long as she could remember, she had actually looked forward to waking up in the morning.

She had seen Rafa before dashing off to work in her Mini.

They had bumped into each other in the hall (not that she had any business to be there), and he had suggested they go out in a boat after work. The promise of an excursion together fuelled her all the way into Dawcomb. She drove down the narrow lanes, past frothy green hedges and white-flowered blackthorn that lay heaped on the branches like snow. She observed the little birds that dived in and out, and the gulls that circled above in a glittering sky. Her heart filled with happiness at the sudden glimpses of the ocean as she weaved down the coast towards the town. She took in the beauty around her and wondered why she had never noticed it before.

Sylvia was standing by her desk in a tight red skirt and satin blouse tied at the throat in an extravagant bow. She was fussing over a bunch of lilies, cutting out the pollen-laden anthers with a pair of scissors. When she saw Clementine she did a double take and paused her cutting.

'Oh my Lord, what's up with you?'

'Nothing's up,' Clementine replied, shrugging out of her jacket.

Sylvia narrowed her eyes. 'Now let me see. You've made an effort today so something must be up. You usually look like a sack of potatoes.'

'Thank you for the compliment.'

'So, are you going to tell me, or am I going to have to torture you?' She put her hand on her rounded hip. 'The flowers are from Freddie, by the way. In case you were curious.'

'I'm not.'

'I'd like to think it's Joe, but it isn't, is it?'

'No,' said Clementine, sitting down and switching on her computer. 'Do you remember that Argentine I met in the Black Bean Coffee Shop?'

'Yes. Don't tell me he's come back?'

'He's the artist-in-residence.'

'Get out of here!' Sylvia put down her scissors and came closer to perch on the edge of her desk. She crossed her legs and folded her arms. 'Go on.'

'He arrived yesterday.'

'And you've already slept with him.'

'No,' Clementine waved her hand dismissively. 'Of course not.'

'Poor Joe. He'll be devastated. Have you told him?'

'There's nothing to tell.'

'Joe thinks you're The One.' She sniffed disapprovingly. 'God bless him, the fool!'

'Well, I'm not. I never have been.'

'Freddie's not The One, either.' She glanced at her red nails and clicked her tongue. 'Though he won't be convinced.'

'Is that why he's sent you flowers?'

'He senses he's losing me. Proof that if you treat them mean, you keep them keen. My mother would say that a woman has to play hard to get all her life.'

'How tiring.'

'The curse of womanhood.'

'One of them,' Clementine added.

'The others being?'

'Childbirth.'

'But think of the dear little thing you get at the end of it.'

'Do you want children, Sylvia?'

'Oh, yes, but I'm getting on, you know. That's why I'm keeping Freddie on the spit, basting him every now and then like a nice chicken.'

'I don't mean with Freddie. He's already got children.'

'He might be my only option.'

'You can't give up yet.'

'On finding love? You know I don't believe in it.'

Clementine grinned and turned to her screen. 'Well, I do.'

*

Rafa set up two chairs and easels on the lawn in front of the house, facing the cedar tree. The Brigadier had gone home to change into something more suitable and now took his seat in a pale blue linen jacket his wife had bought him years before but which he had never worn. He didn't like the way it hung; a good jacket had to follow the line of the waist. He had placed a Panama on his head to shade him from the sun and now looked in bewilderment at the blank sheet of paper.

'So, I'm to draw that tree, am I?'

Rafa nodded. 'Yes, but I want more than a picture of a tree.'

'Oh, yes, the birds in it, too, I suppose.'

'Perhaps. I don't want you to just *see* the tree. I want you to *feel* it.'

'Now that's jolly difficult. Seeing is one thing, feeling is quite another.'

'Not really, Brigadier. If I wanted an exact copy of the tree I would take a photograph.' He rubbed his chin a moment in thought. 'Tell me, how does this tree make you feel?'

'Nervous,' said the Brigadier with a chortle.

'Really, how so?'

'Because I don't know where to begin.'

'Look at the tree.'

'I'm looking at it.'

'Don't say anything. Just look at it. Take as long as you want.' The Brigadier did as he was told and looked at the tree. He looked at it long and hard until his eyes stung and he had to blink. 'Now how does it make you feel?'

The Brigadier was about to say 'nervous' again when he felt a strange sensation in the middle of his chest. He looked at the tree and thought of his wife. It reminded him of the day they had taken their eight-year-old daughter to boarding school for the first time. There had been a big cedar tree beside the chapel and it was full of children climbing the branches like monkeys. 'It makes me feel sad,' the Brigadier said gruffly.

'So, you see, the tree is more than a tree. It inspires you to feel things. I want to feel those things, too, when I look at your picture.'

'Oh dear, that's a tough order.' He cleared the unfamiliar emotion away with a cough.

'I don't care whether your painting is accurate or not, I care that you are moved by what you see and that you try to translate that feeling into the paint on your paper. Give it a go. Don't worry about it. Don't think too hard. Just dip your brush in the paint and let your feelings carry it onto the page.'

So, with his thoughts drawn back to his wife, the Brigadier began to paint.

Chapter 14

'Ah, isn't it delightful to be back in this charming place?' said Veronica Leppley, sweeping into the hall with the enthusiasm of an actress returning to the stage after a long absence. She raised her angular face and closed her eyes, inhaling through dilated nostrils. 'It smells just the same.'

'Lilies,' said Grace Delennor in her Southern Virginia drawl, running her string of pearls through long fingers. 'Hotels always have lilies.' It took a lot to impress Grace Delennor, who had stayed in the finest hotels in the world.

'Careful you don't get the pollen on your cashmere. It's a damn nuisance to get out,' warned Pat Pitman. 'Sue McCain swears by baking soda but I'm not convinced.' No one else in the group had ever met Sue McCain but Pat brought her into every conversation as if she were an old friend they all had in common.

Grace moved away from the lilies and ran her eyes over the room. 'I remember the wood panelling. It's so British.'

'I can smell that, too,' said Veronica excitedly. 'That and the lingering smoke from a winter of log fires. Isn't it lovely, don't you think?'

Grace shook her head and a single blonde curl escaped her coiffure and bounced onto her forehead. 'You must have a very acute sense of smell, Veronica. I can't smell anything at all. Not even lilies.'

Jane Meister hadn't said a word. She was quietly taking it all in, like a pigeon on a rooftop, watching everything going on about her. So much had changed since the last time she had been there, her world turned upside down by the shocking death of her husband, Henrik, at the age of eighty-six from a heart attack at the bridge table. She watched the two porters come in with their luggage and thought how young they were, with their whole lives ahead of them. She wondered what joys and sorrows lay in store.

At that moment, Marina walked into the hall to greet them. All four ladies recognized her at once.

'Well, hello there,' said Grace, extending her hand where a large diamond ring glittered on her bony finger.

'Welcome back,' Marina said, smiling broadly. 'I'm so excited you're here. Our artist-in-residence is already on the lawn giving a lesson.'

'Paul?' said Veronica. 'He was lovely, wasn't he? Such a gentleman. Didn't you think so, Pat?'

'I'm afraid Paul wasn't able to return this year. We have a new one,' Marina explained.

'I hope he's young and handsome,' said Grace, narrowing her eyes. Pale blue, like topaz, they were all that remained of a once beautiful face, Botox and surgical lifts having destroyed what nature had so generously bestowed.

'Oh, he's very handsome,' said Marina. 'He's from Argentina.'

'Oh, down *there*,' said Grace disparagingly.

'How glamorous,' enthused Veronica. 'The Argentines are a beautiful people, don't you think so, Pat?'

'Sue McCain once had a roaring affair with a polo player. We're talking back in the fifties. She's never got over it.'

'Hello, Mrs Meister,' Marina said, remembering how easy she was to overlook, being so quiet and shy. Marina noticed how much she had aged in the last year. Out of all of them, she had had the most youthful skin. Now she looked like she had been rinsed in grey.

'It's so nice to be back, dear. I have such happy memories of our stay last year.'

'I've chosen to put you in the same rooms.'

'Now *they* are very pretty,' said Grace. 'Especially the hand-painted wallpaper. I tried looking for something like it for the house at Cape Cod, but nothing came close.'

'How sweet of you to take such trouble,' said Jane, smiling at Marina.

Marina accompanied them upstairs to their rooms. As they climbed the stairs, Grace sidled up to her and hissed under her breath, 'Poor Jane's husband died last autumn. She wasn't going to come but we persuaded her it would be good for her to get out. It's hit her very hard, poor darling.'

'How sad,' said Marina, now understanding why she was even shyer and quieter than before.

'My husband, on the other hand, goes on and on and on. He was old when I married him, but now he's ancient, and still he hangs in there with steely determination. It's that pioneer spirit he's inherited from his ancestors. I haven't got that spirit. My ancestors were spoiled British aristocrats with no drive at all. I hope the Good Lord will bump me off the minute my face starts to show my age.'

Marina opened the door to number 10. 'This is Mrs Leppley's room,' she said, taking pleasure from their admiration. Veronica swept across the floor with light, happy steps, her gypsy skirt floating around her slender body and delicate ankles as if it had a life of its own. Having been a ballet dancer for most of her youth she was unable to wear flat shoes, so her small feet were clad in tailor-made wedge espadrilles, which gave her a little more height and a great deal more comfort. 'It's beautiful,' she exclaimed, gesticulating with all the grace of her art at the pictures of birds and butterflies on the walls.

'Even more beautiful than I remember. And the bed.' She gasped. 'Oh, the bed. So high I have to take a running leap.' She jumped lithely onto the mattress and laughed with girlish delight.

'At least you *can* leap,' said Grace. 'If I leap, I'll break. My bones are so brittle.'

'It's a proper bed,' Pat interjected approvingly. 'Nothing worse than staying somewhere where they don't understand about beds.'

'I like high ones,' said Jane meekly. 'And these are very high.'

'Let me show you to yours,' said Marina, stepping back out into the narrow hall.

'I like to imagine what this place was like as a private house,' said Grace. 'I suspect my ancestors lived in a mansion like this.'

'This was not the duke and duchess's main home,' Marina reminded her as she walked down the corridor to the next room. 'This was their holiday house, where they came to spend the summer.'

'How very grand,' said Grace.

'The sea air was good for the duchess's asthma,' Marina continued, putting the key in the lock of number 11.

'The sea air is good for everything,' said Pat. 'Unless you're a piece of furniture, of course.'

Jane smiled at the sight of her room and took a deep breath, pleased that she had come. She went over to the French doors that gave onto a small stone balcony. She opened them wide and stepped out into the sunshine, gazing over the navy sea to the misty horizon beyond. Then she looked down to the front lawn below, where Rafa was busy painting with the Brigadier. She caught the Brigadier's eye as he took his attention off the cedar tree for a moment. He lifted his hat and nodded politely. Jane was a little surprised and waved her fingers shyly, retreating into the safety of her room.

'I see your artist is at work,' she said.

'Yes, he's teaching the Brigadier.'

'Is that who he is. I can't see with my bad eyesight.'

'You would have met him last year,' said Marina. 'He comes up every morning for breakfast. Rafa has managed to persuade him to do a little painting. I think he's rather enjoying himself.'

Once she was on her own, Jane opened her suitcase and pulled out a picture of her husband in a shiny silver frame. She placed it carefully on her bedside table, then sat on the bed to look at it.

Pat strode into number 12. 'Jolly nice,' she said heartily, tossing her sensible brown handbag onto the quilt. Pat would have been happy anywhere, for she was unspoiled and practical, and abhorred people who made a fuss. She only tolerated Grace because they had known each other for so long and because Grace was funny, though her humour ran out pretty quickly if she was uncomfortable.

English boarding schools had trained Pat to accept what she was given and never to complain, however uncomfortable she was. Hardship was character building, after all, and Pat rather relished challenge, and being the only one in the group who rose up like a rhinoceros in the face of adversity. In her youth she had climbed the south face of the Eiger and would have sailed the whole way around the world had her boat not appealed to a great white shark off the coast of Australia, forcing her to radio for help and abandon it altogether.

Now in her eighties, Pat's life ran on a more predictable track. She had handed her torch to her youngest grandson, who was now in his thirties and halfway up Kilimanjaro. She walked over to the window and admired the view. The sea always stirred in her a deep longing to set sail.

Marina had left the best for last and showed Mrs Delennor to the duchess's suite at the other end of the corridor. Grace was suitably enchanted to find herself upgraded. Now, not only did she have a view of the garden and the sea, but a hand-carved four-poster bed – the duchess's very own bed – crafted in 1814 and handed down the generations, until it was eventually sold along with the house and its memories. Marina knew how difficult Mrs Delennor could be and had made a special effort to please her. On reflection, Mrs Meister should have had it because of what she'd been through, but Mrs Delennor was the most likely to complain and Marina wanted to avoid that at all costs. '*Très jolie*,' said Grace without even trying to put on a French accent. 'I shall enjoy staying in here very much.'

'I'm so pleased you like it. It's very special.'

Grace draped her cashmere coat over the back of the chair. 'The others are going to be wildly jealous. Except Pat, of course, who doesn't have a jealous bone in her body – only the strong bones of a very sturdy animal.' She laughed at the mental picture. 'It's a mighty fine room. Thank you.'

It wasn't long before the women appeared on the lawn to meet the artist. The Brigadier had been enjoying the peace and the progress of his painting, and was unamused at the invasion. He watched the old women flap about the Argentine like moths, and grumbled as he was forced to stand and greet them out of politeness. He had a vague recollection of seeing them at breakfast the year before, which had been perfectly fine as they had kept their distance. Now they were mounting an assault he was none too pleased.

Rafa was charming, turning his smile and laughing eyes onto each woman as if she were young and beautiful. The women sparkled with pleasure, even Pat, who considered it very silly to be seduced by flattery.

'Sue McCain would appreciate *him*,' she hissed to Veronica.

'He's very attractive,' Veronica agreed. 'He makes me want

to be twenty again. Really, at times like this my old body feels very alien, as if I shouldn't have put it on. It doesn't go with how I feel inside. Do you know what I mean, Pat?'

'Oh, I do, Veronica. My head tells me I can still do all the things I used to do, but then I get out of breath climbing the stairs. Still, one mustn't complain. I've had a fair innings and there's still a lot I can do, like a good route march along the cliff. Yes, I shall enjoy that very much.'

'I can't wait to put my brush onto paper again. I haven't painted a stroke since last year.'

'And you're very talented.'

'There's always something else to do, don't you find? It's hard to get down to it.'

'One has to *make* time. It's all about prioritizing.'

'Well, we have seven whole glorious days here without any distractions.' She grinned at the artist. 'Apart from our teacher.'

Jane Meister always felt on the periphery of things. She hovered a little way from the rest of the group, listening to their conversations but not really taking part. She was happier like that, letting the other women take centre stage. Veronica was a born performer, used to being watched and applauded, and even though she was old she still retained the enthusiasm and light steps of her youth. Pat thought she was head girl and captain of the lacrosse team even now. She had the confidence of her class, years of Pony Club camp and debutante parties, which she professed to have found very silly. Nothing fazed her – neither a bucking horse nor a roomful of people. Pat took everything in her stride and confronted every challenge with a vigorous snort.

Grace expected everyone to admire her, and if they didn't she just brushed them aside with a dismissive wave of her elegant hand. She had grown up in the highest echelons of American East Coast society and what she hadn't been able to acquire by way of her charm, she had simply bought with her vast wealth. It was hard to tell by which means she had won her three husbands.

Jane was an officer's daughter. She had grown up in a close-knit army community in Germany, met Henrik and married at eighteen. If it hadn't been for a random painting class her daughter had encouraged her to join in Knightsbridge eight years before, their paths would never have crossed.

Jane observed the artist. He was indeed very handsome and pleasant. She watched him laugh at Grace's jokes and knew that they would all have an enjoyable time in his company. She wasn't so sure about the Brigadier. He looked rather gruff. It wasn't that he lacked politeness – on the contrary, he was the very epitome of politeness – it was just that behind his good manners he didn't look very happy to meet them. Unlike the artist, whose smile was broad and genuine, the Brigadier didn't smile at all. Jane decided she would make sure that she was sitting as far away from him as possible.

Grace wasted no time and invited Rafa to join them for lunch. The Brigadier went home, leaving his painting in order to continue the following day. He didn't like the idea of sharing his teacher, and would normally have put his paints away for good, but he was enjoying the tree and the memories it evoked. It was like sinking into another world when he painted. As if his past was there, submerged beneath the branches, just waiting to be rediscovered.

Grace, Pat, Veronica and Jane sat outside on the terrace, beneath a green umbrella. Grace was wrapped in a pale pink pashmina, although the sun was strong and the breeze light and warm. Rafa was pleased to join them.

Jake watched him sit down and noticed the ripple effect he had on the whole terrace. It was by no means full, but the guests who were there stopped whatever they were doing to look at him. It was as if he glowed brighter than everyone else, and even Jake's gaze was drawn to him, quite against his will.

The artist had to endure his stepmother and sister buzzing about him like a pair of dizzy bees. The attention would go to his head and he'd become unbearable. Jake was sure he wasn't so magnetic in his own country.

That afternoon more easels were set up on the lawn and the four women looked at the tree as they were instructed. Grace found it quite hard to concentrate on anything but Rafa. However, after a while, with a little encouragement, she lost herself in the thick green pine needles and branches. The tree made her feel insecure and a knot tightened in the pit of her belly. She feared poverty more than she feared anything else. The more she looked, the more the tree pulled her into a dark world where she had nothing but the skin on her body. And the skin was as old and wrinkled as the bark.

Pat stared at the tree. She had no difficulty concentrating on it. It reminded her of her childhood, for she had loved climbing the big copper beech in her garden in Hampshire where her father had built her a playhouse out of wood. It made her feel young again, as if she could jump off her chair with the agility of a child and scale the cedar right to the top.

Veronica gazed at the tree with delight. The colour green was so dark and alluring, the branches so magical and mysterious, she wondered where they led. She imagined she was a bird, perched high up, observing the world with merry detachment. She would spread her wings and fly a swooping dance, and the music in her head inspired her to hum a tune.

Jane saw the regeneration of life in the branches of the tree that had stood for hundreds of years, watching the generations come and go in the grand cycle of life. Having felt so lost without her dear Henrik, she began to feel a little more positive. Wasn't it true that nature was reborn, season after season? Why would it not be so for human beings? Perhaps Henrik had been reborn in Heaven and was now among those branches, watching her. The tree gave her hope. The way it grew up from the ground, its roots deep in the earth, the highest branch soaring towards God. It made her think of Henrik's body in the earth and his spirit up there beyond her senses. She smiled wistfully as the hope in her heart gave way to a sweet melancholy.

Rafa watched them watch the tree. He observed their expressions as they lost themselves in its branches. He saw the fear in Grace's eyes, and the hope in Jane's. He saw the joy in Pat's and the awe in Veronica's, and when he decided they had all been inspired to feel something, he told them to pick up their brushes and paint. For once, none of them said a word.

Bertha stood at the window of Rafa's bedroom. As Marina hadn't got round to talking to Jake she had decided to have a private word herself. Jake had been only too happy to put her in charge of the artist's bedroom.

'You're the right person for the job,' he had said with a smirk, patting her shoulder. 'I can't believe I didn't think of it myself.'

Now she stood looking out as Rafa taught the old ladies how to paint. She remembered painting at school, a class she had hated because she was so bad at it. She hadn't a creative bone in her body. Still, she would give it another go if he asked her to. She pulled away and began to tidy his room. It smelled of sandalwood. As she bustled about, she picked up his things and sniffed them one by one, savouring the scent of this exotic stranger from a distant land.

She wasn't even sure where Argentina was on the map, but she remembered Diego Maradona and 'the hand of God' goal that had sent everyone into a frenzy during the 1986 World Cup. There had been something rather sexy about him, too. She didn't need to make Mr Santoro's bed, as it had been done that morning by the housemaids. In fact, she had no business to be in there at all. But since she had been given the task of looking after him, she felt it was only right to come up and check that everything had been done properly. Which it had, she could see. But in future she would be the one to do it. Every morning. Every evening.

Mr Santoro was very untidy. She hooked his suede jacket on the back of the chair and folded the shirt he had worn the day before. It excited her to feel so close to him and she went hot with nerves at the thought that he might come in at any moment and discover her smelling his clothes. She noticed his suitcase still sat on the rack where Tom had undoubtedly placed it on arrival. It didn't look heavy. She'd store it under the bed where it would be out of the way. As she went to lift it off, she saw that it was unzipped. She pulled up the top to make sure that there was nothing inside. She peered in. The case lay empty but for an important-looking folder. She glanced about the room, as if checking that she was, indeed, alone. Then she picked it up.

It looked old and faded but official, like the files they brought out on those American television dramas like *Law & Order*. Now, trembling with curiosity, she lifted the flap. Inside were papers, lots of papers, all in a language that she didn't understand. What did they speak in Argentina? Italian? That was it, then. Italian. At the back was a big pile of letters written in a very tidy hand, tied with an elastic band.

She pulled it out, frustrated that she couldn't understand what they said, and ran her eyes over the first one. A name leaped out. She had just read the words '*ti amo*', which she knew meant 'I love you' from the Laura Branagan song she used to listen to in her teens, when she thought she heard footsteps on the stairs. Hastily, she put the letters back in the file and placed the file back in the case.

She shot to the bed and began to smooth the quilt so it would look like she was cleaning. Her heart raced and sweat gathered on her nose. When she was sure no one was there, she took a deep breath and relaxed a little. She was now anxious to leave the room as quickly as possible. As she tiptoed down the stairs the name somehow stuck in her head. It was a funny name, because surely there should have been another 'n' in there. But perhaps they didn't use the 'n' in Argentina.

Costanza. Surely it should be *Con*stanza?

Chapter 15

Clementine was not surprised when Joe walked into her office. She had been avoiding him by not returning his calls, but she knew it would only be a matter of time before he came in person to find her. As he stood before her she felt the sinking feeling of waking from a dream and facing the dull reality of true life. As much as she could fantasize about Rafa, the truth was that he was out of her league. She looked at Joe, coarse and regular, like so many other men found in bars and pubs across England, and wondered whether this was the best she could expect. Was it healthy to reach for the stars when she was never going to touch one?

'Hi, Joe,' she said, masking her guilt behind an artificial smile.

'Where have you been? Haven't you noticed I've been trying to call you?'

'I'm sorry. It's been really busy up at the hotel. The new artist has arrived and Submarine needed my help. It's been full on.'

Joe didn't look convinced. 'The least you could have done is called.'

'I know. I thought you'd understand.' She delved into her bag for her lip gloss. 'I obviously overestimated you. My mistake.'

He suddenly looked lost and scratched his head. How had

she managed to make *him* feel guilty in such a short exchange? 'Can I see you tonight?'

'I'm afraid not. We're going out on Dad's boat. I don't know what time we'll be back.'

'Come and stay over?'

'No, Joe. I told you, I'm needed up at the hotel at the moment.'

He looked exasperated. 'Then when? We're meant to be having a relationship.'

'All right, then. Tomorrow night.' But she regretted it just as soon as she had said it.

Sylvia sat at her desk listening to every word. Once Joe had gone she put down her nail file and turned on Clementine. 'He's a good lad, Joe is. I don't know what's got into you!'

Clementine put her elbows on the desk and sank her chin into her hands. 'He's so ordinary compared to Rafa.'

'When the scales fall from your eyes, Rafa will be just as ordinary. Men are men whichever way you look at them.'

'No, Rafa is different.'

'That's what I thought about Richard and Jeremy and Benjamin . . . and countless others. It always ends in disappointment because your superman is just a man in underpants after all. Just as needy, just as demanding, just as selfish as every other man in the world.'

'You're so cynical.'

'I've lived longer than you, lovely.'

'I'm holding onto the dream.'

'It's made of soap, silly.'

Clementine sighed. 'So what do I do? I don't love Joe.'

'Do you like him?'

'After a couple of vodkas in the Dizzy Mariner he's quite charming.'

'A bird in the hand is better than two in the bush.'

Clementine screwed up her nose. 'What's that got to do with Joe?'

'You don't want to end up alone. I've taken Freddie back, only because his whining was so boring.'

'But that's such a tragic compromise.'

'Look who's talking! If you don't love Joe, bin him.' She shrugged. 'You're the one holding onto him. Ask yourself why?'

The telephone rang and Sylvia picked it up. Clementine took her tray of correspondence to the filing cabinets. As she slipped each letter into the proper place she considered what Sylvia had said. She was right, of course. If she didn't love Joe, why was she still with him? Was she so insecure that she would rather be with a decidedly average man than alone? Yet her spirit aspired to greater heights. Her thoughts soared among the planets and her heart longed for the burning white fire of the greatest love.

When she had finished, she realized that for the first time she had filed each letter correctly. Fuelled by something she was unable to identify, she decided to tidy all the files, one by one, until everything was where it should be. It was a big job, for she had spent the last month shoving things wherever they fitted, without a single thought to ever finding them again.

Mr Atwood returned from a viewing to find the floor littered with paper. His jaw dropped at the mess. 'What on earth is going on?'

'I know,' Clementine replied coolly. 'I'm a little shocked myself. Ask Sylvia, I don't know what's got into me. But I'll admit I've been putting things in the wrong files for weeks.'

Mr Atwood didn't know whether to be cross or grateful. He cleared his throat. 'Well, I suppose I should be pleased you're putting it right now, before you leave your chaos for Polly to find.' He stepped carefully over the islands of documents. 'When you've finished I have an errand for you.'

'Another present for Mrs Atwood?'

He looked embarrassed. 'Come into my office and don't take all day about it.' He disappeared inside and closed the door behind him.

Clementine caught Sylvia's eye and grinned. 'Why doesn't he just come out with it and say it's for his lover?'

'A good secretary turns a blind eye.'

'Who is she?'

'Someone with very bad taste and no sense of smell.'

Clementine laughed. 'He doesn't smell, does he?'

'What do you think?' She pulled a face. 'That kind of skin always smells, well, eggy.'

'Yuck!'

'I've had my fair share of eggy and it's not pleasant. Still, he's rich and probably spoils her with presents. Some women will do anything for presents.' She pulled out her nail file and sighed heavily. 'Oh, the things I've done for presents.'

'Let's not go there, Sylvia.'

'You're right. Let's not.'

Once all the documents and letters were filed in their correct places, in order of date, and all the old, redundant ones shredded, Clementine stood back to admire her work. She felt an unfamiliar sense of pride. 'There, all done,' she announced, walking back to her desk with a bounce in her step.

'Good for you,' said Sylvia. 'I'm surprised. I didn't think you were capable of doing a proper day's work.'

'Neither did I.'

'Now you'd better go and find out what Casanova wants you to buy his mistress.'

'Can't wait to spend his money for him. Whatever budget he gives me, I'll spend double!'

Clementine was disappointed to find that her errand involved accompanying Mr Atwood to a jewellery shop to choose a bracelet. 'It's our wedding anniversary,' he explained a little awkwardly.

'How many years have you been married?' she asked as they entered the quiet enclosure of Nadia Goodman, situated on the high street.

'Too many to count,' he replied tightly. 'When you're my age, you stop counting.' A pretty salesgirl brought out a tray of gold bracelets and smiled at Clementine. 'Now, which one do you like?' Mr Atwood asked. Clementine picked up a gold chain with emerald cabochons.

'Let me help you,' said the salesgirl. 'There, such a pretty colour against your skin.'

'It is, isn't it?' Clementine agreed. 'Daddy's so generous.' She grinned at Mr Atwood.

'Not sure about green,' he said crossly.

'But I love it.'

He ignored her theatrical doe eyes. She was clearly enjoying herself at his expense. 'Take it off,' he snapped.

The salesgirl unclipped it, looking confused. 'What about blue?' she suggested cheerfully.

'I love blue,' Clementine gushed.

Mr Atwood asked to see another tray. When the salesgirl went to the back of the shop he rounded on Clementine. 'Quit the monkey business. I've got a reputation in this town, you know.'

'I'm only teasing!'

'Well, stop it.'

'Anyway, what colour suits your wife?'

He hesitated. 'Red.'

'So, let's have a look at rubies. You're very generous.'

'I know. Have to keep the little lady sweet.'

'Oh, she'll be sweet all right.'

Clementine managed to restrain herself while they looked at gold bracelets with ruby cabochons. They were very pretty.

Still, she didn't think she could sleep with an eggy-smelling man, however many gold bracelets he bought her. She thought of Joe and imagined him buying her jewellery, but the emptiness of that thought convinced her that no amount of jewellery could take the place of true love.

Finally, they chose the gift and waited while the salesgirl wrapped it in a red and gold box and tied it with ribbon.

'Lucky Mrs Atwood,' said Clementine, thinking how very *un*lucky she was.

'Indeed,' Mr Atwood agreed, shiftily.

'That will be fifteen hundred pounds, please, sir,' said the salesgirl, smiling again at Clementine. 'Is it your birthday?'

'No,' Clementine replied. 'He's just pleased with me.'

'Oh,' said the salesgirl. Mr Atwood handed her his credit card. 'Thank you.'

'And thank *you*, Daddy,' said Clementine, taking the bag off the counter. She gave her sweetest smile, which the sales girl mistook for genuine affection.

Mr Atwood inhaled through dilated nostrils, punched in his PIN, then tapped his fingers on the glass impatiently, eager to leave the shop as quickly as possible.

Clementine laughed all the way back to the office, which infuriated Mr Atwood even more. 'I'm teasing,' she repeated. 'If you weren't so serious I wouldn't find it all so funny.'

'If I didn't owe your father for all the clients he's sent my way, I'd fire you for insubordination.'

'You love me, really. I know you do. You just don't want to admit how funny you think I am.'

'I don't think you're at all funny, Clementine,' he huffed, which made Clementine laugh all the more.

That evening she returned to the Polzanze with a bounce in her step. Rafa was on the terrace having tea with Marina, Grey and four old ladies, who Clementine presumed were the four painters from the year before. The sight of Rafa caused her heart to expand with joy. They were all talking at once, isolated in their mirth. They didn't even notice her as she walked towards them.

When she reached the table her father looked up. 'Ah, Clementine. Come and join us.'

'You haven't met my ladies, have you?' Marina interjected.

Clementine swept her eyes over their expectant faces and smiled only because Rafa was watching her. If it hadn't been for him she would have avoided meeting them altogether. Marina introduced each one and Clementine shook their hands. She was grateful that her father squeezed a chair between him and Rafa so she didn't have to waste her time talking to them.

'So, how was your day?' Rafa asked, drawing her away from the general conversation, which had revved up again.

Clementine basked in the warmth of his eyes. He had a way of looking at her with such intensity, as if she was the only woman in the world he really wanted to talk to.

'My boss took me shopping to help him choose a bracelet for his wife. Though we all know she's never going to see it.'

'Ah, he has a mistress?' said Rafa.

'Yes, though I can't imagine anyone wanting him.'

'There is someone for everyone.'

'That's the miracle of life.' She smiled. 'Lucky, eh?'

'Are we going out in the boat this evening?'

'Of course,' Clementine enthused, although she knew it wasn't possible to go just the two of them, as she wasn't sure how to work her father's boat. 'I'll have to ask Dad,' she added, prodding Grey.

Her father turned round. 'Yes, darling?'

'Will you take me and Rafa out in your boat this evening?'

Grey's face lit up in surprise. 'What a good idea. Beautiful evening for it.' He looked out over the calm waters and clear sky. 'We can go to Smuggler's Cove and do a bit of crabbing. What do you say?'

Clementine only had unpleasant memories of crabbing in Smuggler's Cove, of sitting on the rocks, bored to her core, while Jake and her father had tossed bits of bacon on string into the sea. The bucket of crustaceans had repulsed her, all climbing on top of each other in their futile attempts to escape. But the thought of spending dusk in the quiet seclusion of the cove, just the three of them, was very appealing. 'Great idea,' she replied, sure that she could suffer a few crabs for the pleasure of spending time with Rafa.

Just as Clementine was enjoying the romance of their impending excursion, Marina leaned across the table. 'Did I hear the word crabbing?'

'Yes,' Grey replied. 'I thought I'd take Rafa out to sea. Show him Smuggler's Cove and a few crabs.'

'Why don't you take my ladies with you? There's room in the boat.'

Clementine was scarcely able to conceal her horror. Astonished, she watched her stepmother sabotage her plan. 'Mrs Leppley, would you like to go out in Grey's boat this evening?'

Veronica's eyes opened wide. 'I'd love to,' she said, clapping her small hands. 'How delightful.'

'Did I hear the mention of a boat?' Pat interjected.

'You certainly did,' said Grey. 'I'm taking Rafa crabbing.'

'Then count me in. Nothing like a bit of crabbing to work up an appetite for dinner. I was going to take a route march along the cliff, but this sounds much more fun.'

Clementine's heart sank. Rafa didn't seem at all put out. 'I've never caught a crab before,' he said, to which the ladies roared with laughter and Pat volunteered to show him how it was done. At least the other two bowed out. Grace declared that she would like to have a long, hot bath and read her book, while Jane said that she'd prefer to wander around the gardens, suffering as she did from seasickness. Clementine scowled at her stepmother, sure that she had kiboshed her evening on purpose. *She can't have him, so she doesn't want me to have him,* she thought crossly. *Well, I have all summer. One setback is not going to deter me.*

Marina offered to give Jane Meister a tour of the garden, which the old lady gratefully accepted, disappearing up to her bedroom to get a headscarf. Marina watched Rafa leave with Clementine, Grey, Mrs Leppley and Mrs Pitman, and knew that she had infuriated her stepdaughter – but what alternative did she have? If the girl hadn't learned by now that leaping into bed with a man was not the cleverest way to win him, she'd have to be forced to hold herself back. Marina knew men like Rafa – before meeting Grey she had had her fair share of love affairs. They were used to girls rolling over for them, sleeping with them, then they discarded them when they ceased to pose a challenge. But she couldn't talk to her; Clementine thought she knew better. Marina had to watch it all from the sidelines, powerless to help.

Clementine sat between the two old ladies as they drove down to the quay. Mrs Leppley smelled of roses and talcum powder. Mrs Pitman was extremely hearty, holding forth about her own adventures on the sea. Rafa sat in the front with Grey, listening to her stories with interest. Clementine wondered whether he really was interested, or whether he was just being polite. If it was the latter, he was a very good actor.

They reached the harbour and Grey parked the car. Shelton was a quiet village, but this evening it had spilled out onto the waterfront. There were children eating ice creams and young women chatting beside their pushchairs. A few old people sat on the benches enjoying the sunshine and the view of the ocean. Seagulls swooped down to scavenge for food, brawling over scraps left behind by careless grown-ups and mischievous children. Craggy-faced sailors fussed about their boats while fishermen returned with their small hauls. Clementine cheered up in spite of herself and led the way to her father's boat, tied securely to a bollard.

Mrs Pitman was overjoyed to see the boat, aptly named *Marina*. It wasn't anything special, but by the fruitiness of her voice and her ecstatic exclamations, one could have been mistaken for thinking she had just clapped eyes on the *Lady Moura*. 'Oh, I say. What a stunning boat!' She put her hands on her sturdy hips and smiled appreciatively. 'What luck with the weather and the sea's calm. We're in for a jolly ride.'

'It's lovely,' Veronica agreed, tying her silk scarf at her throat. 'I shall sit by the cabin, out of the wind.'

'If you want to stay out of the wind, Veronica, you'd better sit inside.'

'And miss all the fun? No, I'll huddle. I'm good at making myself small.'

'All aboard, then,' said Grey.

Rafa jumped down and turned to help the ladies. Clementine noticed the way he looked at them as they took his hand and stepped onto the deck. His smile was as seductive, his eyes as intense, as when he looked at *her*. She awaited her turn, then gave him her hand. She felt the warmth of his skin and the way his touch made her tingle all over. She laughed, embarrassed, as if the tingle showed through her clothing.

'Your brother told me that you don't like boats,' he said.

'I don't know what he's talking about,' she replied coolly, not wanting him to know that *he* was the only reason she was going anywhere near a boat. 'What's there not to like?'

He shrugged. 'Seasickness?'

'I find if I keep my eyes on the horizon I tend to be all right.' She took her place on the bench at the back, next to Pat. Veronica sat as near to the cabin as possible. Clementine hoped that Rafa would come and sit beside her, but he jumped back onto the quay to help untie the ropes. She watched him crouch down and pull them free, appreciating the vigorous energy of his movements. He looked accustomed to physical labour and Clementine imagined him working with his father on the pampa. Grey started the engine and Rafa pushed the boat away from the side, then leaped back in.

'You girls look comfortable,' he commented cheerfully as the boat chugged slowly out of the harbour.

'Haven't been called a girl for a very long time,' said Pat with a chuckle. 'Hurrah, off we go! Isn't this jolly!'

'He's very naughty,' said Veronica.

'Sue McCain would like him,' added Pat, watching him join Grey at the helm. 'Her Argentine was a terrifically good lover.'

'I don't doubt it,' Veronica agreed. 'The difference between Latin men and Englishmen is the way they feel about women. Latin men love women. Englishmen prefer to be with other men, which is why we have so many men-only clubs in this country.'

'Is that true?' Clementine cut in, suddenly interested.

'My husband prefers sport to women. That's not to say he doesn't *like* women, but if he had the choice he'd be on the golf course with his chums,' said Pat.

'Rafa's a terrible flirt,' said Clementine, longing to talk about him if she couldn't talk *to* him.

'They're all like that,' said Veronica.

'Oh, yes, Sue McCain told me that chatting up women is an Argentine national sport.'

Clementine felt her spirits sink. 'Do you think Rafa is like that?'

'No, I don't,' said Veronica, sensitive to the blush that had just expanded onto Clementine's cheeks. 'I think he's very kind. Why otherwise would he bother with silly old bags like us?'

'That's true,' Pat agreed. 'He takes trouble with everybody. I think he's just one of those rather unusual men who likes *people*.'

'Really? Do you think so?' Clementine cheered up again.

'You can see it in his eyes, he empathizes. He's an old soul, wouldn't you agree, Veronica?'

'Most certainly.'

Once the boat sailed out into open sea it picked up speed. Grey left Rafa at the helm and disappeared inside, returning with blankets. 'It can get pretty cold,' he said, handing them to the women. 'Right, do you want to see how fast this lady can go?' Pat whooped with joy while Veronica cowered against the cabin, holding her headscarf in place.

'Oh, yes, this is the way to go,' Pat shouted over the roar of the engine. 'I love the wind in my face. Reminds me of the time I crossed the Atlantic in my little *Angel*. Gosh, that was a rocky ride, I can tell you. No fooling around in those seas.' Her enthusiasm was infectious and Clementine laughed with her.

'Tell her about the time you nearly got eaten by a shark,' Veronica asked, and Pat needed no further encouragement.

At last they turned inland, motoring slowly into Smuggler's Cove. It was dark there, in shadow, and quiet out of the wind. The sun had sunk low, turning the sky a pale, flamingo pink.

'Isn't it beautiful?' sighed Veronica, emerging from her sheltered corner.

'You can just imagine the smugglers bringing their loot here to hide in those caves,' said Rafa, edging around to join them.

'Enough of loot, young man, you're going to catch a crab,' said Pat.

'What do we do after we've caught it?'

'Put it back,' said Clementine knowledgeably. 'Unless it's big and tasty, in which case, we'll eat it for supper.'

'Run away, crabs! Run away!' he pretended to shout into the water.

'That'll do no good. They're suckers for bacon,' said Grey.

'Undone by their own greed,' said Pat.

Grey sailed as near to the pebble beach as he was able, then turned off the engine and dropped anchor. Rafa wasted no time in taking off his shoes, rolling up his jeans and jumping in. The water reached mid-calf. 'You coming, Clementine?'

'What is it about you and water? You just can't resist, can you?'

He laughed. 'Perhaps it's got something to do with you.'

'I can't pretend I enjoy getting wet. But here goes.' She tossed the blanket aside and pulled off her trainers.

'I'll carry you,' he offered, holding out his arms.

'I'm much too heavy,' she protested.

'Trust me, I've carried calves far heavier than you.'

'Well, all right then. But if I *am* heavy, don't let it show on your face.' She fell into his arms. He pretended to stagger, his face twisted into a grimace. 'Oh, stop, you fool!' she laughed.

'I ... think ... I'm ... going ... to ... have ... to ... drop ... you.' He stumbled towards the beach where he put her down. 'Any other takers?' he asked, grinning at Pat and Veronica.

'I think I'll make my own way,' Pat replied. 'Bit of water won't hurt!'

'I'll stay on the boat and watch,' said Veronica.

Grey poured Veronica a glass of wine. 'I have smoked-salmon sandwiches,' he said. 'We'll celebrate once we've caught a few crabs. Now, Clemmie, are you going to show them how it's done?'

Clementine forgot her aversion to crabs and tied a piece of bacon to the string as if she had done it all her life. Rafa stood beside her as she tossed it into the water. 'It's a bit like fishing,' she told him. 'You wait until you feel a tug and then slowly pull it in.'

He got the bucket ready and sure enough, after only a minute or two, there was a tug on the line.

Clementine's heart leaped. 'Oh my God, we've got one. Dad, we've got one!'

'Well done, you!'

'I think it's a big one.' She pulled the line, lifting a large black crab out of the water. 'It's huge!'

'Wow! My first crab,' said Rafa.

Mine too, thought Clementine. 'Not so fast, pirate! This is *my* crab.' She dropped it into the bucket of water. 'Now, you take a piece of string and some bacon, and see if you can catch one as big as mine. It's a competition.'

'And the winner?' He raised his eyebrows suggestively.

'Gets to eat it,' said Clementine.

'I was thinking of something much more fun.'

'What?'

'Not telling you now.'

'Go on!'

'Let's see who wins. If I do, I might just take my prize without asking.'

Chapter 16

As the sun sank slowly towards the sea Rafa and Clementine stood side by side on the pebbles, tossing their bacon strings into the water. Their laughter ricocheted off the cliffs with the cries of gulls, who circled greedily in the hope of food. Pat was a crabbing veteran, having spent her childhood holidays in Cornwall. When the bacon didn't lure the crabs fast enough, she just thrust her hand into the sea and caught them with her fingers, holding them up triumphantly for everyone to see. Veronica watched from the boat, her glass of wine almost down to the last drop. Wrapped in a blanket, enjoying the rough beauty of the little cove and the merry banter of her companions, she applauded each catch with a whoop of delight.

Grey watched his daughter. It had been many years since he had been able to entice her onto his boat. She had always loathed crabbing and fishing, and had found the sea a dull place to be. But now, watching her with Rafa, one would have thought she had been raised on it. She was deft at handling the lines, confident at bringing them in and unruffled at disentangling the crabs from the string. He noticed that she was showing off to Rafa. So, it had taken the allure of a handsome foreigner to get her to come out in the boat, but that didn't matter. The fact was that she was out, enjoying the best of Devon, sharing the beach with her father.

Clementine sensed the pull of Grey's stare and turned.

When she caught his eye he smiled. Not his usual jolly smile, but a wistful one, tinged with pride. She grinned back, surprised by his affection. Then she averted her gaze and settled it on her line, which had just begun to quiver. However, she wasn't thinking of the crab she was about to catch, but her father's gentle face. She couldn't remember the last time he had looked at her like that.

When their buckets were full they drank wine and ate the smoked-salmon sandwiches in celebration. 'So, who wins?' asked Clementine, holding up her bucket.

'You do,' Rafa replied.

'Are you sure?'

'Why let her win so easily?' Pat asked, munching heartily on her sandwich.

'Because I'm a gentleman.'

'So, you won't be taking your prize without asking?' said Clementine, a little disappointed.

'Because I'm a gentleman,' he repeated with a grin that made her stomach lurch.

'So what is my prize?'

'Admiration.' He wound his arm around her waist, pulled her against him and kissed her cheek. Pat roared with laughter while Veronica watched with interest at the blossoming of young love.

Grey raised his glass in a toast. 'To a wonderful evening with friends,' he said. 'But now we must be getting back. It'll be dark soon.'

Rafa stood once more at the helm, but Clementine didn't mind. Veronica and Pat were a hilarious duo and the three of them laughed all the way back to the harbour.

'Oh dear, I think I'm a little tipsy,' said Veronica, taking Rafa's hand and stepping onto the quay.

'It's good for you, Veronica,' said Pat. 'That's why the French live so long. It's all the wine they drink.'

'It feels as if the ground is going up and down, don't you think?' Veronica added, grabbing hold of Rafa's arm to steady herself.

'Let me escort you back to the car,' he suggested, placing his hand on hers.

'You are a very dear man.'

'Thank you.'

'Not many young people would be so considerate. You know, when you're young you don't ever imagine you're going to be old. But it falls upon you quite unexpectedly and then, there you are: one of the old people you rather despised.'

'I've never despised old people,' he said, walking her gently along the quay. 'I love old people. They have lived many lives and experiences, and are full of wisdom.'

'You seem much older than you are, Rafa.'

'I know. I'm an old man in the body of a young man. One day the body will catch up with the mind and then I will feel complete.'

'Don't you feel complete?'

'I feel dislocated, actually,' he confided.

'That's got nothing to do with you being too old for your skin. So, why is it, do you think?'

'Because I am rootless, Mrs Leppley.'

'Please call me Veronica. We are all rootless, Rafa, until we find our soul mate. I don't imagine you have found yours yet?'

'No, I am still looking.'

She smiled tenderly. 'You will find her and when you do, the world will shift into place and you will no longer feel dislocated.'

'I'm sure you are right.'

'I'm an old bird who's seen a lot.'

'Did you find your soul mate?'

'Yes. My husband fell in love when he saw me dance.'

'I bet you were a beautiful dancer.'

'I was never Margot Fonteyn, but I was good. That's the sadness of growing old, one has to concede that there are things one can no longer do. But I love my husband and I have lots of grandchildren and those are the things that I value now. Not my ballet shoes.'

'Family is everything,' he agreed firmly.

'Oh, yes, it is.' She sighed. 'I am very blessed.'

They returned to the Polzanze in high spirits. Pat recited limericks while the car wound up the lane. It was nearly dark. The lights twinkled in the windows of passing houses and in the sky, which was studded with stars, but none was as welcoming as the lights of the Polzanze.

Tom and Shane marched out to open the doors.

'I'm still feeling a little light-headed,' said Veronica happily. 'It's been a lovely day.'

'I'm so pleased,' said Grey, letting her slip her hand around his arm.

'I'm feeling very old, but very happy.'

'I feel revitalized,' said Pat, striding past them. 'Nothing like the sea wind to sweep away the years.'

Clementine opened the boot and lifted out the bucket. Inside were five fat crabs. 'These will do for dinner,' she said.

'Here, let me help you.' Rafa took the bucket from her. 'Where do you want them?'

'In our kitchen. Come, I'll show you.'

'So, this is where you live,' he said, looking up at the pretty, grey stone building with its white clock tower and weathercock.

'It's the old stables. Submarine converted it for her private use.'

'Submarine?'

'Oh, I forgot. Sorry. Silly name I call my stepmother because she's so devious, like an enemy submarine.' She laughed, expecting him to do the same. But he didn't. He just looked uncomfortable. Clementine was embarrassed. She wished she hadn't said it.

She opened the front door and showed him through the hall to the kitchen. 'Why don't you put it on the kitchen table?' He did as she asked, but when she looked at him his whole face had changed. She knew she had to say something to justify her comment. She so needed him to laugh again. 'Look, I'm sorry I was rude about Marina. But you don't know her like I do.'

He shrugged stiffly. 'Your relationship is none of my business.'

'Then why are you offended by my nickname for her?'

'I'm not offended.'

'Yes, you are. Look, you've gone all strange.'

'I like your stepmother.'

'And it's OK to like her. You're a man, it's no surprise. But I have a complicated relationship with her.'

'Yes, I know. It's a problem because you're allowing it to be one. It doesn't have to be a problem at all.'

'How do you mean?'

He sighed and leaned against the sideboard. 'You have the power of choice, Clementine, and you are choosing to hold onto old grievances.'

'I can't help it.'

'Of course you can. The past no longer exists but in your mind. You can choose to let it go whenever you like.'

'I can't.'

'It is not who you are now.' She frowned crossly. 'Have you ever stood back and looked at the situation through *her* eyes?'

She lowered her voice. 'I don't think I have to understand her point of view at all. She's the one who stole my father and caused my parents to divorce.'

'Which was devastating for you at the time, of course. But

208   *Santa Montefiore*

nothing is ever quite that simple. Have you ever sat down and asked her what happened, woman to woman?'

'My mother told me the whole story.'

'How could she? She only knows her portion.'

Clementine felt her fury mount. 'She knows enough. She was there, for God's sake.'

'No, she wasn't.' He smiled at her sympathetically. 'I'm not suggesting you forget the past, just that you accept it and let it go so that it doesn't ruin your present. You cannot change what happened but you can change the way you view it. There is always more than one side to every story. You are not a child any more. You should try to understand it with compassion rather than cast blame and continue to feel wounded.'

'You know nothing about it, Rafa. You're way out of line here,' she snapped.

'I'm sorry. It's none of my business.'

'No, it isn't.' She folded her arms defensively. 'I think you should go.'

'Listen, Clementine, I can see that you are bitter. I'm only telling you that you don't have to be. It's your choice.'

'I don't want to talk about it.'

'OK, I'll go.' He made for the door. When he turned back, he smiled at her sadly. 'Enjoy the crabs.'

Clementine watched him leave, seething with rage and self-pity. How dare he come into her family and tell her how to behave? She had clearly misjudged him. From a few well-chosen words in the church she had believed he understood her. From the way he looked at her she had believed he was attracted to her. But now, on reflection, she realized he looked at everyone in the same way. Perhaps he was a typical Argentine man after all, out to seduce for the sheer pleasure of the sport. Shouldn't she know better? Looks were only skin deep.

She was distracted by the ringing of her mobile telephone.

Joe's number was displayed on the screen. She sighed with resignation. At least Joe was kind. He didn't glare at her when she
told him about her stepmother, or try to make her see Marina's
point of view. As if *that* was important, or of any interest to
her! Above all, Joe was in love with her.

'Hi, Joe,' she said. 'Fancy a crab for dinner?'

'Your place or mine?'

'Which do you think?' she asked sarcastically.

'OK. Come over as soon as you can. I'm hungry.'

As he wandered back to the hotel, Rafa realized he had acted
foolishly. His father had always told him not to try to put the
world to rights. As a young man he had always been drawn to
the lame duck, the wounded dog, the broken spirit, but a
person only accepted help if he reached out for it. Clementine
believed she was content where she was. She didn't want to be
rescued, and anyway, he had his own problems. He'd make it
up with her in the morning then never touch the subject
again.

After returning to his suite for a bath and change of clothes,
he went downstairs. There were a few guests chatting to Jake
in the hall and he could see through to the drawing room
where small clusters of people sat around coffee tables having
pre-dinner drinks. He found Marina in front of the fireplace
with her four ladies. Pat and Veronica were giving an account
of their excursion.

'You should come next time,' said Pat to Grace and Jane.
'What we all need at our age is a little adventure. After all, one
is only as old as one feels, and right now, I feel fifty.'

'It's OK for you, Pat, but Jane gets terribly seasick, and I'm
not that fond of the swell myself,' said Grace, lying back against
the cushions, sipping champagne. In her cream cashmere and
delicate shoes she didn't look like she suited the outdoors, let
alone the high seas.

'Perhaps if I took a pill . . .' said Jane meekly.

'Quite,' Pat agreed. 'They make wonderful things now. Pills for everything.'

'I think we should take a nice walk along the cliff tops tomorrow,' Veronica suggested. 'Then we can all enjoy an excursion together.'

'You can walk to Dawcomb-Devlish,' said Marina. 'There are a couple of new boutiques to check out. Oh, hello, Rafa.'

The artist stood before them in a blue shirt and chinos, smelling of the usual sandalwood, his hair damp and tousled.

'Good evening,' he said politely. The women smiled up at him appreciatively.

'Do sit down,' said Marina. He took a seat on the club fender.

'What have you done with those crabs?' Pat asked.

'Clementine said she's going to have them for dinner.'

'All of them?' Veronica exclaimed.

'She's got a boyfriend,' said Marina in a half-whisper.

Veronica raised her eyebrows in surprise. 'Really?'

'Yes, some boy from town called Joe. Of course, we haven't been allowed to meet him.' She glanced at Rafa. It was vital that Clementine seemed unavailable.

'Typical young people. When my daughter was her age she had a boyfriend for over a year before we were introduced,' said Pat.

'I bet once you'd met him you realized why she had kept him a secret,' laughed Grace.

'You're absolutely right, Grace. He was a shocker!'

'Not the right sort?'

'I've always been very open-minded when it comes to my children's choices,' Pat replied magnanimously. 'I've learned to accept that what makes them happy doesn't necessarily make me happy. That's true of Duncan. Perfectly nice fellow, just not my sort. He's a journalist.'

'Oh,' said Grace with emphasis.

'So long as they make each other happy,' said Veronica to Marina.

'Yes,' she replied thoughtfully. 'That's all I ever want for her.'

At that moment Jake appeared to take them through to the dining room. 'Will Mr Santoro be joining the ladies?' he asked.

'No,' said Marina before Rafa had time to think of an excuse. 'I'll cook him pasta at home. I make a very good tomato sauce.'

'Our loss, your gain,' said Grace, getting up stiffly.

'You can have him all day tomorrow,' said Marina.

'I suppose you're used to being fought over,' Pat grinned at Rafa, remembering Sue McCain and her Argentine lover.

'I'm flattered,' he replied.

'That's not an answer,' Grace cut in. 'But we'll take it as a yes.'

They all laughed as they followed Jake from the room. Veronica hung back to walk with Jane, who smiled at her gratefully.

Marina and Rafa walked across to the stable block. A fat pigeon sat on the clock tower cooing at the weathercock.

'They're a lively bunch, aren't they?' said Marina.

'They're all so different. I wonder what brought them together.'

'Art.'

'Really?'

'Yes. They joined the same art club in London and suffered at the hands of a monstrous teacher.'

'When are *you* going to paint?'

'I've got the whole summer,' she replied evasively.

'You don't like painting?'

'I'm not very good at it.'

'That doesn't matter. It's the enjoyment that counts.'

'And I don't have time.'

'Poor excuse.'

She smiled at him. 'We'll see. Right now, you have your hands full with the ladies and the Brigadier.'

'You're right about hands full. It will be either a disaster or a great success. The Brigadier did not like the intrusion this morning.'

'He'll warm up, you'll see. They're quite an attractive group of women.'

'To an eighty-year-old,' said Rafa.

Marina opened the door and led him through the hall to the kitchen. 'You have a beautiful home,' said Rafa. 'It smells delicious. What is it?'

'Fig,' she replied, pointing to a glass bottle positioned on the hall table. 'Every time I go past I give it a quick spray.'

'It smells very foreign.'

'I think so, too. I'm glad you like it.' She unhooked her cooking apron from the kitchen door. 'Now, where's my husband?' She called out his name. There was no reply. 'He's probably buried in the library, reading. There's nothing he enjoys more than a good book.'

'And his boat,' Rafa added.

'And his boat.' She sighed. 'It doesn't take much to make *him* happy.'

She opened the fridge and pulled out a bottle of wine. 'Why don't you sit down while I make dinner?'

'Can I do anything? I'm good at chopping onions.'

'All right. You chop the onions and I'll chop the tomatoes. It'll be a team effort.'

Rafa pulled out a chair and Marina poured two glasses of wine and laid the table for three. She placed a chopping board in front of him and gave him two onions. 'These are from the garden,' she said proudly, sitting opposite with her own chopping board. 'We have a beautiful walled vegetable garden. Mr Potter is a wizard with a magic touch. Look at these tomatoes.'

THE HOUSE BY THE SEA

She held them up. 'Aren't they lovely and plump? You wait, they taste so sweet. Tomorrow you must take time to look around. We have a fabulous greenhouse full of orchids, and the flowers are at their best this time of year, before everything gets overgrown and out of control.'

Rafa noticed how her eyes shone as she spoke about her garden.

'Tell me about *you*,' he said, peeling the first onion.

'There isn't much to tell,' Marina replied.

'Have you always lived in Devon?'

'Yes, I'm very sheltered, really. I haven't travelled much. We put all our energy and money into this place; there was no time to see the world.'

'Surely you've been to Europe?'

'Oh, yes, the usual places: Italy, France, Spain and Portugal. A week or two here or there. But I've never put on a rucksack and gone where my desire leads me. I'd love to do that. But I have too much commitment here and it's where I feel safe.'

'Do you feel unsafe when you leave it?'

She paused her knife over the last tomato. 'Yes.' The honesty of her reply surprised her. She had known Rafa no more than two days, hardly sufficient time to trust him enough to divulge her fears. Yet, there was an intimacy in his eyes, an understanding, that drew her out of herself.

'You're not content just to scratch the surface of people, are you?' she said with a smile.

'Human nature fascinates me.' He grinned bashfully. 'I'm unable to stop myself . . .'

'Doing what?'

'Searching.'

'Are you searching for something in me?'

'Yes. You've created this beautiful place, in such good taste. Where does it all come from?'

She placed her hand on her heart. 'Here,' she replied softly.

She stood up and filled a large saucepan with water. After sprinkling a little salt into it, she put it on the stove to bring to the boil.

'I'm afraid I upset Clementine this evening with my fascination,' he confided.

'Oh?'

'I think she's very cross with me.'

'Well, expect it to last a few days then. When Clementine shuts down, the door stays closed for a long time.' She poured olive oil into a frying pan and warmed it on the hob.

'I like her. I regret what I said.'

'What did you say?'

He hesitated, aware of making the same mistake again, with Marina. 'I simply told her not to let her past ruin her present. That nothing is ever black and white. The more experience she has, the more wisdom she has to judge her life and the people who have shaped it. The more tools she has to understand people's motivations.' He sighed. 'I was trying to encourage her to detach emotionally and see it from an adult's perspective.'

Marina grew serious. 'You're talking about the divorce.'

'Yes. It was none of my business. But I see a wounded creature and I want to make it better.'

Overwhelmed by a surge of gratitude and sympathy, Marina felt a sudden compulsion to touch his shoulder. She reached out and patted it. 'You're very sweet, Rafa. But it's such a sensitive subject. I wouldn't go there, if I were you.'

'I realize that now.'

'You know, Clemmie was three when her parents divorced. She doesn't remember what life was like when they were together, but she has an idealized image of what she *thinks* it was like. The truth is very different.' She poured Rafa's chopped onions into the olive oil. They sizzled noisily. 'I don't think that's the problem, Rafa. But it's easier to blame other people than to take responsibility for her own troubles.'

'Memories in themselves are not problems – we can all learn from the past. They only become a problem when we allow them to take us over completely and make us unhappy. Then our past becomes our prison.'

Marina turned around. 'How do we get out of our prison?'

'By focusing on the present.'

She turned back to stir the tomatoes into the onions. 'By focusing on the present,' she repeated broodingly. 'By focusing on my home.'

Just as she was straining the spaghetti, Grey strode into the hall. 'Something smells good,' he exclaimed, putting his book on the hall table.

'Spag,' Marina replied from the kitchen. 'I've invited Rafa to give him a break from the ladies.'

'Splendid.' He walked into the kitchen and gave Rafa a pat on the shoulder. 'I'm glad to see that Marina has given you a glass of wine. It's looking a little depleted, though.' He filled the young man's glass before pouring one for himself. 'Has Rafa told you about our crabbing expedition?'

'Pat and Veronica got there first.'

'I think they had a good time.'

'They did.'

'Where's Clemmie?'

'Gone to have dinner with Joe.'

'She proved quite an accomplished crabber,' he said, sitting down and stretching his long legs under the table. 'I was pleasantly surprised.'

'Oh, I think Clemmie can do anything she puts her mind to,' said Marina, placing the bowl of steaming spaghetti in the middle of the table. 'She just doesn't know it.'

'You were very sweet to her, Rafa,' said Grey. 'You made it fun.'

Rafa helped himself to some spaghetti. 'But you are wrong, Grey,' he replied with a shrug. '*She* made it fun for me.'

Chapter 17

Clementine lay in Joe's arms, dismayed to discover that her fury had accompanied her there. She recalled the conversation with Rafa word for word, and smarted with indignation. While Joe had been making love to her she had been distracted, content to give in to her longing, confusing the momentary high of orgasm for love. But now, as she lay against him, his arms wrapped around her body to anchor her to the present, she was pulled back into the familiar dark.

She considered his words: that her bitterness was *her* problem but that it didn't have to be. All she had to do was look at the divorce from Marina's point of view. Her anger mounted at the suggestion that Marina's love for her father justified the hell she had put them all through. As if love exempted her from any responsibility. The trouble was Rafa didn't know what he was talking about. He didn't know what sort of woman Marina had been before she set her sights on Grey and raised herself a few rungs higher on the social ladder. It was all very well standing on his pedestal, playing the philosopher, but down on the ground things weren't so neat and tidy.

'I should go,' she said to Joe, climbing out of bed.

He looked at his watch. 'Midnight. But you're not a pumpkin.'

'I will be if I don't get my sleep. I'll be a grumpy, inanimate vegetable.' She pulled on her clothes. 'The last thing I need at

THE HOUSE BY THE SEA

eight in the morning is Submarine marching in and opening my curtains.'

'That's the trouble with living at home. You should move in with me.'

She stopped dressing. 'Do you mean that?'

'Of course. It's not much but it's home.'

'That's a great idea. I won't have to face Submarine every day, nor that arrogant Argentine.'

'Who's the Argentine?'

'He's Submarine's artist-in-residence, come to teach old biddies how to paint for the summer.'

'You don't like him?'

'He's full of himself. Typical Latin man, thinks he can seduce anything in a skirt.'

Joe sat up. 'Has he tried to seduce you?'

'He wouldn't dare. He knows I don't like him.'

'Good.'

She laughed at his jealousy and rolled back onto the bed. 'Are you my knight in shining armour?'

He pulled her into his arms. 'Yes. I don't like the idea of anyone trying to seduce you but me.'

'Would you fight for me?'

'You know I would. Tooth and nail.'

'I like it when you're jealous,' she purred, curling up against him, her anger dissipating in the might of his devotion.

'That Argentine had better watch it. He's not flirting with *my* girl.'

Clementine drove home with a sense of empowerment. She'd move in with Joe and all her problems would be solved. She couldn't think why she hadn't thought of it before. It was the perfect solution to every problem. The CD player filled the car with the rousing music of Pixie Lott. She wound down the window and sang out into the night about what would her mama do.

She parked on the gravel and hurried across to the stable block. The light had been left on in the hall but the rest of the house was dark. She grinned as she climbed the stairs two steps at a time. There'd be no more creeping in like a thief in the night. No more annoying questions at the breakfast table. No more having to share the same living space as her stepmother. She'd be free.

The following morning she announced her plans to her family over coffee and croissants. Marina was stunned. 'Are you sure that's what you want, Clemmie?'

'It's absolutely what I want,' she replied emphatically.

'But do you love him?'

'I don't think that's any of your business.'

'It's just rather quick.'

'Clemmie *is* rather quick,' quipped Jake.

'Look, I'm telling you, not asking for your opinions.'

Grey was more pliant. 'Darling, if that's what you want, then you have my blessing. No one knows better than you what will make you happy.'

'Thank you, Daddy.'

'Grey, I don't think . . .'

'Darling, Clemmie is old enough to know what she's doing.'

Marina looked at her stepdaughter in desperation. She wondered whether her fight with Rafa had anything to do with her decision. 'Well, you can always come back if it doesn't work out.'

'Thanks for your faith in me,' Clementine snapped.

'It's a big deal, moving in with a man.'

'One step away from marriage,' Jake added helpfully.

'As if I'd get married after the fine example our parents set us.'

'That's unfair,' said Marina.

'Oh, I don't think it is. After the hell we went through, why on earth would I wish that on children I might have?'

Grey interjected. 'Now, Clemmie, this is no time to start a

row. I think it's a very good idea that you move in with Joe and gain some independence. You're a woman now and it's no business of ours what you do.'

'So that's settled then,' Clemmie replied, getting up.

Marina noticed that she hadn't eaten anything, but refrained from suggesting she take a croissant to eat in the office.

'So when are you planning to move out?' she asked.

'Tonight.'

'So soon?'

'What's the hurry?' Jake asked.

'I want to be with Joe,' she replied. 'I'm in love.' But her words sounded hollow even to her.

'Do you want any help packing?' Marina asked, knowing the answer before her stepdaughter turned on her angrily.

'For God's sake, I'm not a child. I'll do my own packing, thank you.'

They watched her march out of the room, slamming the front door behind her.

'They're going to love her in the office this morning,' said Jake, pouring himself another cup of coffee.

'What's got into her?' Grey asked.

'I think I know,' said Marina with a sigh.

'It's great she's moving out,' Jake added. 'We won't have to suffer her dark moods every morning.'

'She's unhappy, Jake,' chided Marina, one eye still on the door, hoping Clementine might return through it any minute to apologize.

'The divorce happened a long time ago,' said Jake carelessly. 'Shit happens, but hey, we've survived.'

'She's chewing on an old bone,' said Grey wisely. 'Try to take it away and she growls.'

The front door opened. However, it wasn't Clementine who stepped into the hall but Bertha. Her habitual sigh was replaced by an exuberant smile.

Marina got up. 'I feel sorry for her,' she said, taking her coffee cup to the sink.

'She'll find her way,' said Grey, giving his wife a sympathetic smile.

Bertha bustled in, filling the kitchen with Anaïs Anaïs. 'What's got into Clemmie this morning? She very nearly ran me over.'

'She's running away as fast as she can,' said Jake.

'She's moving out,' Marina added.

'Going to live with her boyfriend, is she?' said Bertha, tossing her handbag onto a chair.

'That's right,' said Grey. 'I'm off, darling. I'll be back for lunch.'

'No news from William Shawcross?' asked Jake.

'Nothing yet. I'll chase him up. I'm sure he's in high demand,' replied his father.

'There are others we can approach.'

'But Shawcross is the one I want,' said Grey.

Bertha began clearing away the breakfast. It was Grey who noticed first that she didn't lumber over to the counter and switch on the kettle, or sigh wearily, clutching her back and complaining about her aches. He made eyes at his wife. Marina hesitated in the doorway to see what he was grinning about. Sure enough, Bertha, clothed in a sky blue dress with a red bead necklace dangling merrily over her bosoms, was almost dancing around the table, stacking the plates and saucers, a hum hovering upon glossy lips.

'At least someone's in a good mood this morning,' said Grey.

'Oh, yes,' Bertha replied. 'It's a beautiful day.'

'But Clemmie nearly killed you,' said Jake.

'But she didn't.' She piled the plates on the sideboard and opened the dishwasher.

'You look very nice,' said Marina. 'Colour suits you.'

'I know. That's what Mr Santoro said, and he's a man who notices women.'

Marina didn't dare look at Grey in case she laughed. 'He certainly does,' she agreed.

'I'll do an hour here then go over to make up his room. Then I'll come back and finish off,' Bertha informed her.

Marina looked at Jake in surprise. 'You're in charge of Mr Santoro's room?'

'It's not a job for the young ones,' Bertha said importantly.

Jake got up. 'She's the right woman for the job,' he said, grabbing his jacket and slipping past his stepmother, who still stood in the door frame.

'Fine,' Marina said tightly. 'Just don't forget to come back and finish off here.'

Bertha smiled. 'Of course not. Clemmie's room will need a good going-over once she's moved out. Who knows what we'll find in there.'

Marina strode over to the hotel in search of Harvey. She found him in the garden, talking to Mr Potter. Harvey had his hands on his hips while Mr Potter leaned heavily on his spade. The two of them were laughing cheerfully as they shared a joke.

'Harvey,' said Marina as she approached, 'I need you.' She hadn't meant to sound so desperate. Both men turned to look at her in alarm.

Harvey immediately noticed the strained look on her face. 'Catch you later, Potter,' he said before striding across the lawn towards her. 'Is everything OK?'

'I need to talk to you.'

'Righty-oh.' He followed her through the Children's Garden where the little aqueduct remained barren, and through the French doors into her office. She collapsed onto the sofa with a moan.

'Clemmie's moving out,' she stated, shaking her head forlornly. 'I don't know what to do.'

Harvey sat beside her, his wise old face smiling at her kindly. 'When did she tell you?'

'This morning. She had a row with Rafa last night and now she's moving in with a man she doesn't even care about.'

'Marina, love, it's out of your control. She's a woman now.'

'But I see her making a terrible mistake.'

'Which you are powerless to do anything about.'

She swallowed back tears. 'Rafa said he had upset her, but it's not really about him. It's about *me*.' Harvey took her hand between his big rough ones and stroked it tenderly. She turned to him slowly, her dark eyes shiny and sad. Suddenly, she wasn't a woman in her fifties but a little girl, gazing up at him lost and alone. 'I can't have children, for the love of God, I can't have children of my own . . . and . . . and . . .' the words caught in her throat.

'It's OK.' He drew her into his arms and held her tightly as a father would hold a hurting daughter.

She rested her head on his shoulder and closed her eyes, tears squeezing through her lashes. 'I can't even win the love of my stepchildren.'

He embraced her with all his might, wanting more than anything to make her smile again. 'But that's normal, Marina. Stepchildren will always love their natural parents more and most often they see the step-parent as a usurper. It's the way it will always be.'

'I feel I'm being punished.'

'Whatever for?' He felt her hands grip his sweater.

'I'm frightened, Harvey.'

'What about?'

'I've done something terrible.' She drew away and looked into his eyes. His heart lurched to see the terror in hers.

'Tell me, love, what have you done?'

She thrust a trembling hand against her mouth as if fighting to contain an awful secret and shook her head. 'I can't . . .'

'Whatever it was, I'll understand. I know you so well, Marina. Nothing you could do would make me think less of you.'

'I've never told anyone, not even Grey.'

Harvey considered it a minute. There was something wild in her that he'd never seen before. A flash of someone he didn't recognize. 'If you want to confide in me, I won't tell a soul, I promise.' His words were like a rope to a drowning woman and she seized them with relief.

'I trust you, Harvey.'

'I know you do.'

She took a deep breath, about to share the burden of her secret at last.

Suddenly, there was a knock on the door. They stared at each other in alarm, like conspirators caught hatching a plot. There was nothing they could do. The moment was lost. As the door opened the air was sucked out of the room and with it all the tension that had been steadily building. Marina's resolve deflated like a soufflé. She raised her bloodshot eyes to her stepson, who now stood in the doorway.

'Sorry, have I interrupted something?' he asked. He was used to his stepmother's mercurial nature and wasn't in the least surprised to see her crying on Harvey's dependable shoulder.

'No, carry on,' she said, wiping her cheek with the back of her hand.

'We've just had a booking from Charles Roache.'

Marina paled. '*The* Charles Roache?'

'Yes, booked in for two nights with his wife, Celeste.'

'Really?'

'I thought you should know.'

'Have you told your father?'

'He's out.'

'When are they coming?'

'Friday the twelfth of June.'

She ran a hand through her hair. 'There's only one reason why he's booking in.'

'To take a look,' said Jake.

'With a view to buying it.'

Harvey's face darkened. 'Who is this man?'

'He's bought up some of the finest hotels in the world,' Marina replied.

'Good Lord,' Harvey sighed. 'Do you think he really wants ours?'

'Perhaps. Why else is he coming to stay?'

'Why doesn't he send a gofer?' Jake asked. 'I mean, why bother to come himself?'

'Oh, that doesn't surprise me. That's very Charles Roache. He's a famous micromanager. He probably just wants to check us out.'

'What shall we do?' said Jake, scratching his head.

'We shall entertain him in the same way that we entertain all our guests,' Marina told him and there was a steely edge to her voice.

'And if he makes an offer we can't refuse?' said Jake.

'Never say "can't", Jake.' She stood up. 'That is one lesson my life has taught me, which I had all but forgotten. I won't forget it again.'

Laughter bubbled across the lawn from beneath the cedar tree.

'Oh, you do have a good sense of humour, Brigadier,' said Pat, dipping her brush into green paint.

The Brigadier ran his eyes over the four women positioned in front of their easels and decided that they were rather good company for an old fellow tired of being on his own.

'You'd better behave, Pat,' said Grace. 'Teacher's coming.' Pat chuckled into her chins as Rafa wandered behind her to look at her progress.

'Not bad,' he said, scratching his bristles. 'I can feel the happiness and nostalgia in your tree.'

'Can you?' she asked, surprised.

'Yes, I can.'

'Reminds me of my girlhood,' Pat said wistfully. 'The only difference now that separates me from who I once was is my cranky old body. I still feel exactly the same inside.'

'I try not to look in the mirror,' said Veronica.

'You're very quiet, Jane,' said the Brigadier.

'I'm concentrating,' she replied.

'Can I have a look? I need to stretch my legs.'

'If you must. It's not very good.'

The Brigadier stood up and lumbered over. As he stood beside her he caught a warm whiff of roses. He dilated his nostrils to catch another but the breeze swept it away before he was able to savour it. He peered at her painting. 'It's more than good,' he murmured, recognizing something melancholy in the misty pinks and greys she had used. Unlike his painting, however, there was a hopeful feeling in the way she had painted the sky. 'I think it's *jolly* good, Jane.'

Jane flushed with pleasure. 'Do you mean it or are you just being polite?'

'I'm not frightfully good at being polite,' he reassured her.

'Then I'll thank you for the compliment.'

'You're a bit of a dark horse, aren't you, Jane?'

'Sue McCain always says it's the quiet ones you should look out for,' said Pat. 'And she should know because she was as quiet as a dormant volcano, just waiting for the right man to set her on fire.'

'That's rather good, Pat,' said Veronica. 'You should be a writer.'

'And I suppose that's just what the Argentine did?' said Grace. 'Never trust an Argentine.' She sucked in her cheeks as Rafa moved behind her to appraise her work.

'Are you flirting with me, Mrs Delennor?' he teased.

'Good Lord, no, I'm much too old.'

'I think your painting needs a little more depth,' he said. 'Here, let me show you.' He took her brush and dipped it in paint. She watched with admiration as he swept it over the paper.

'It's so terribly easy for you, isn't it?' she gushed.

'It's what I do.'

'Like shopping for me. That's what *I* do. What can I say? I'm terribly good at spending money.' Pat and Veronica laughed like a Greek chorus. Jane was too busy talking to the Brigadier to hear.

'You smell of roses,' he said, catching another whiff. 'Roses with a hint of something sweet . . . I know, it's honey.'

'You have a very keen sense of smell.'

'It's one of the few pleasures I have left,' he replied.

Jane paused her painting. 'That's not true, surely. There must be lots of things you enjoy. Like good company, good food, beautiful views.'

'I don't know.'

She lost her gaze in the branches of the tree. 'When my husband died I thought there'd be nothing left for me to love. He took such a big part of me with him, you see. But now I realize that I'm still *me*, continuing along the path of life but in a different way. It's up to me to make that way special, otherwise what's the point of going on?'

'My wife died, too. I can't pretend I'm not lonely.'

She looked at him, her expression softening as her heart filled with empathy. 'I know how you feel,' she said kindly. 'I'm lonely, too.'

Later that afternoon Sugar Wilcox came to the hotel for a drink with four girlfriends. She wore a baby-blue dress unbuttoned to her solar plexus and a coy smile intended to lure the mysterious artist-in-residence. They sat on the terrace in a cloud of perfume, revealing tanned legs and painted toenails, sipping cocktails out of pretty purple glasses. Rafa had finished giving lessons and was looking for Clementine. She had been very much on his mind all day and he was anxious to apologize and make friends again. As he strode onto the terrace, expecting her to be taking tea in the sunshine, he found Sugar grinning up at him invitingly.

'Well, hello there, stranger,' she gushed.

'Sugar,' he replied, taken aback.

'Do join us for a cocktail.'

'Well, I was just . . .'

'I won't accept any excuses. Let me introduce you to my friends: Jo, Becca, Hailey and Flo.' Rafa was left no means of escape. Sugar clicked her fingers to summon a waiter. 'What will you have?'

'A Martini,' he replied politely, sitting down.

'I've been telling my friends about you,' she continued. 'We all want to have painting lessons.'

'I'm sure that can be arranged.' He swept his eyes over the grinning, sun-baked girls and knew none of them had the slightest interest in art.

'Good. It's not every day that a handsome stranger saunters into our town. We'd be crazy not to take advantage of your services.' The girls giggled. Rafa couldn't help but laugh, too, at their silliness. He sat back as the waiter put his cocktail in front of him. He could play their game far better than they could.

'So, girls, how many of you have boyfriends who don't know you're here?' They glanced at each other guiltily.

'Flo, Becca and Hailey,' said Sugar, giggling into her glass.

Hailey pulled a face. 'Brian's not a boyfriend, he's a friend with privileges.'

'And you, Sugar?' He took a sip and watched her smoulder beneath his gaze.

'Me? I'm single and *very* lonesome.'

*

Clementine returned home after work and packed her suitcase. Marina wasn't there for her to torment. Her father and Jake must have been still over at the hotel. The house was empty. Suddenly, moving out didn't seem such a good idea. She slumped on the bed and bit her nails. As much as she resented her stepmother, the stable block had begun to feel like home. Her bedroom had always been a place she could escape to. Now where would she go when she wanted to be alone? Would Joe be constantly making demands? Would she get any peace?

She left some clothes in the wardrobe and a few winter sweaters in the chest of drawers. She wouldn't be needing them until autumn. With one final look she closed the door and pulled her case down the stairs. She hoped Marina would come back and beg her not to leave. Perhaps if both Marina *and* her father implored her to stay, she might be persuaded to change her mind. But no one came.

She dragged the case across to her car and heaved it onto the back seat. Still not a sign of anyone. Not even Rafa, who had bobbed about all day at the top of her mind like a stubborn cork. Curious to know where they all were, she wandered into the hotel and approached the reception desk where Jennifer was busy behind the computer.

'Hi, have you seen Marina and Dad?'

Jennifer looked up. 'Hi, Clementine. They're around. Rafa is in the conservatory.'

Clementine caught sight of the bracelet hanging on her wrist. It was very familiar. Jennifer noticed her drop her eyes, but she was too slow to hide it with her sleeve. 'Pretty,' Clementine commented wryly.

'Yes, a present from my father.'

Clementine raised an eyebrow. 'Wish my father was that generous. They have similar pieces in Nadia Goodman on the high street. Perhaps I should drag him in there one of these days.' Jennifer smiled awkwardly. Clementine smiled back knowingly. *Naughty Mr Atwood*, she thought to herself as she crossed the hall. *Or should I say,* stupid *Mr Atwood?*

For a moment her discovery lifted her spirits and she couldn't wait to tell Sylvia. Who would have thought that quiet Jennifer on reception was Mr Atwood's mistress? But as she walked through the sitting rooms to the conservatory, her thoughts returned to her departure and her spirits flagged once more. What was the point of leaving if she wasn't going to provoke a reaction? At the very least she deserved an apology from Rafa.

She ran her eyes over the tables. Her attention was drawn to a party of giggling girls in short, flimsy dresses and heavily applied make-up. She recognized Sugar from Devil's. Then she saw Rafa in their midst, like a peacock among peahens. Her resentment seethed as she watched him sip his cocktail and laugh at their comments, while Sugar wiggled her breasts in front of him with shameless exhibition. There was no doubt that he was enjoying the attention.

Suddenly, he raised his eyes, drawn by the magnetism of her fury. He stopped laughing and put down his glass. Clementine was appalled that he had caught her watching him, and turned and fled. With a racing heart she stormed through the hotel and out into the evening sunshine. She sensed he was right behind her.

'Clementine, stop,' he called. But she ignored him and climbed into her car. She fumbled for the key. 'Where are you going?'

'I'm moving in with Joe.' She tried to sound nonchalant.

'Not because of what I said last night?'

'Don't flatter yourself. Just forget it.'

He put his hand on the roof. 'I want to apologize. I was out of line.'

'Apology accepted.'

'You're still angry.'

'No, I'm not.'

'Then come and have a drink with me?'

'You seem a little busy.'

'I have all the time in the world for you.'

'Well, I haven't.'

'We can go to the house that God forgot. Come on, Clementine. Don't be cross with me any more. Life is too short.'

'You seem to know a lot about life.'

'I've picked up a thing or two.' He grinned at her, but her heart remained firmly shut.

'Look, another time perhaps. I've got to go.' He took his hand off the car and stepped back. She started the engine.

'Another time, then.'

She roared out of sight. Rafa watched her go, perplexed. He couldn't help but feel sad. When he had planned his journey, he hadn't imagined he'd meet a girl like Clementine.

Chapter 18

Marina, Jake and Grey sat in Marina's office. The atmosphere was heavy with an ominous sense of inevitability. Only Jake seemed impervious to it.

'So, Charles Roache is coming to check us out, is he?' said Grey, rubbing his chin. He stood by the window and gazed anxiously out to sea. He barely dared to look at his wife.

Marina sat at her desk chewing the end of a Biro. 'It's not a big deal. He makes us an offer, we refuse it.'

'It's not quite that simple, darling.'

'It never is,' said Jake.

'The truth is, we're losing money,' Grey continued. 'Our outgoings are vast. We have a heavy loan that I don't think we can sustain for much longer. The interest is beyond us.'

'We could lay off a few people,' Jake suggested.

'Like who?' Marina asked.

'I don't know,' Jake mumbled. 'Mr Potter, for a start.'

'Mr Potter?' Marina was indignant. 'That man has been in these gardens longer than you've walked the earth.'

'But he should have retired years ago.'

'He's not going anywhere. The day we say goodbye to him will be the day we bury him, probably beneath the roses, which is where his heart is. Get rid of Mr Potter? I've never heard anything so callous, after all the work he's done for us.'

'Bertha?' Jake ventured, knowing Marina didn't much like her.

'That won't save much. She's on a minimum wage and besides, she's a character.'

'Jake's on the right lines, darling. Unless we start making money . . .'

'What?' Marina felt her stomach turn to liquid. 'Unless we start making money, what?'

'Well, we'll have to rethink our options.'

'What are you saying, Grey?'

'That if Charles Roache makes us a good offer I think we should consider it.'

'Dad's right,' said Jake. 'It's just a hotel.'

'It's *more* than a hotel, it's our home,' Marina protested, ignoring Jake.

'I know, darling. But fundamentally it's a business. I love it like you do, but I won't let it pull us under. If Charles Roache wants to buy it and offers decent money for it, I think we should accept. We can set up more modestly somewhere else.'

Marina was horrified. 'We just need more time. If we could get our literary dinners off the ground and Rafa . . .'

'We're not going to suddenly start making a profit because of one handsome young man who teaches guests to paint. It's just not going to happen,' said Grey. 'I'm sorry.'

Marina stood up and began to pace the room. 'You're giving up too easily, Grey. If that man is going to come into our home, size us up like a prize cow and think he can buy us because he has pots of money to throw around, then I won't have him. I won't.'

Grey could see she was getting worked up. 'Calm down, darling.'

'Calm down! You're telling me to calm down? This is my home, Grey. This is where I belong. I've sweated blood into every piece of fabric and every piece of furniture. I've poured my love into every inch of it. It's not just a home, it's a person.' She turned on him, eyes welling with tears, and in a small, pleading voice, she said, 'It's not just a person, it's my *child*.' She clutched her belly as the unspeakable word escaped into the air. Grey and Jake stared in astonishment, as if seeing it materialize. For a long while no one said anything.

Marina blinked in surprise as it echoed in her ears. *My child . . . my child . . . my child.*

She wiped her cheeks and returned to her chair. 'I'm *not* going to give up,' she stated firmly, sitting down. She raised her eyes to her husband. He saw the determination in them and knew that the battle was far from over. 'I will explore every avenue, turn over every rock, and beg if I have to. I will not sell this place. You will have to bury me first.'

Jake coughed, embarrassed. 'So, are they coming or not?'

Grey looked to his wife. 'Let them come,' she replied. 'Let them offer all the money in the world. And watch me say "no", for "no" is the only answer I will give them.'

Grey and Jake left the room. 'I need a stiff drink after that,' said Grey to his son.

'Me too. Christ, she's emotional.'

'Yes, very hot-blooded sometimes.' They walked across to the stable block.

'Isn't she very exhausting?' said Jake, following him into the sitting room.

'Not all the time. Right now, she's going through a difficult patch. As you can see, she loves this place. It's the child she can't have.'

'That blew me away. I've never heard her mention her childlessness.'

Grey went to the drinks cabinet and poured them each a gin and tonic. 'She never talks about it. It's just something that's always there, simmering beneath the surface. She's a contradiction – on one hand very open and fiery, and on the other extremely secretive. I was as surprised as you when she artic-ulated it.'

'I feel sorry for her. You already have two children. She has none.'

Grey handed his son a glass and smiled at him affectionately. 'I appreciate that, Jake.'

'I can see why Clemmie's a disappointment to her.'

'Marina loves you both. You don't belong to her, but she's watched you grow up. It's a cause of great unhappiness that Clemmie and she don't get along.'

Jake took a sip and went to sit on the sofa. 'Clemmie's just confused.'

'Have you met this Joe?'

'No.'

'I wonder if he's any good.'

'I doubt it. She doesn't seem that inspired by him. Saying she's in love is bollocks.'

'When you get to my age you realize that you can't live people's lives for them. If it doesn't work out, she'll come back.'

'No, she won't. She's too proud for that. She'll earn her money and scoot back to India at the first opportunity.'

Marina remained at her desk. When she reached out to pick up her Biro she saw that her hand was trembling. She rubbed it as if nursing an injury. While she rubbed, she considered her options. There weren't many. But there *was* one. She bit her lip and turned her eyes to the window. Outside the sea was calm. The sky was clear. A few gulls hovered like gliders on the wind. If pushed, there was one card in her deck that she could still play. One person she could turn to for help. But did she dare go back and open the door she had so firmly shut years ago? Her eyes welled with tears and she put her head in her hands; she now realized that there was simply no other way.

*

The following morning Clementine awoke to the shrill ringing of the alarm clock. At first she wondered where she was. She opened her eyes to the unfamiliar surroundings: the beige curtains, the white walls, the unremarkable pictures hanging there. Then she inhaled the very masculine smell and remembered. Fighting a wave of homesickness, she propped herself up on her elbows. Joe lay groaning beside her. She watched him throw his arm over his face to shield it from sunshine breaking through the curtains and felt nothing but her sinking heart. She didn't love Joe and right now, as he moaned like a dying dog, she found him intensely irritating.

She climbed out of bed and staggered into the bathroom. Her legs felt heavier than ever. She washed her face and tied her hair up. She was only twenty-three but she looked old and tired. She thought of Rafa and the way she had rebuffed him. Her behaviour hadn't been very mature. He had apologized and she had made it very clear that in spite of her words, she hadn't forgiven him. Well, she'd put it right.

In a flurry of enthusiasm she washed and blow-dried her hair, leaving it loose to fall onto her shoulders. She applied her make-up with care, masking the shadows beneath her eyes with concealer and accentuating her lashes with mascara. *You never know*, she thought hopefully. *He might come looking for me in the office.* She chose an Emporio Armani navy suit that she had never worn, primarily because she felt too grown-up in it, and a pair of heels. Rafa would appreciate those. If he did come looking for her she was determined he'd find a woman in the place of the child he had rowed with. She didn't bother to kiss her lover goodbye; he had fallen back to sleep anyway.

She popped into the Black Bean Coffee Shop on the way to work. Standing in the queue she remembered the first time she had seen Rafa. She even remembered his smell of sandalwood. She cast her eyes around the café, hoping that by some miracle he had decided to have his morning coffee in town. But it

was full of the usual young mothers with toddlers and businessmen on their way to the office. She noticed a couple of
men raise their eyes above their newspapers and glance at her
appreciatively. She felt good in her suit.

Remembering that Mr Atwood had an important meeting
that morning, she arrived at Atwood and Fisher laden with
coffees, muffins and a hot chocolate for Sylvia. Mr Atwood
was sitting in the lounge area with a couple who had come in
search of a house to buy. He glanced at her, then did a double
take, losing his train of thought and stammering.

Clementine smiled. 'Good morning, Mr Atwood. I've
brought you coffee and muffins.' She placed them on the table
in front of them.

'Muffins! My favourite,' said the husband, picking one up
and taking a bite.

'Very efficient secretary,' said his wife, eyeing her suit enviously.

'I only employ the very best,' said Mr Atwood, puzzled.

'Thanks for the hot chockie,' said Sylvia, taking in the trans-
formation. 'I'm loving the suit. That look is really working for
you.'

'I've decided I no longer want to be me,' Clementine
declared, sitting down and switching on her computer.

'What's wrong with *you*?'

'Everything.'

'Not any more. It's good to see a woman in heels. It shows
you mean business.'

'That's exactly what I mean.'

'I gather you've moved in with Joe.'

'Yes.'

'It must be love.'

'Whatever it is, it's very convenient.'

'Having trouble at home, are you?'

'When aren't I?'

'Joe's a good lad. He'll look after you.'

'He was buried beneath the duvet this morning.'

'I didn't feel like getting up myself. The trouble with having an affair with a married man is that you never get a cuddle in the morning.'

'I didn't get so much as a "good morning".'

'But at least he was there. I think I should trade Freddie in for a single man. A man who can give me all of his time and all of his attention.'

'Quite,' Clementine agreed, not really listening. Her mind was being pulled back to the hotel. She wondered whether Rafa was on the lawn giving lessons.

'I might go up for a drink at your hotel this evening.'

Clementine frowned. 'Really? Why?'

'Everyone's talking about your Argentine.'

'He's not *my* Argentine.'

'Good. So the way is clear, then?'

'For you?'

'Of course. Latin men like curvaceous women, don't they?'

'I don't know. I know nothing about them.'

'Well, everyone's talking about him. Sugar was up there last night and now she's absolutely smitten.'

'I know. I saw her. Flaunting herself like an old tart.'

'That's not kind,' Sylvia chided. 'She's just playful.'

'Don't misunderstand me. *He* was loving it.'

'I'm sure he was. She says he's delicious. She's going to ask your stepmother whether they can have painting lessons at the weekend.' Sylvia giggled. 'Maybe *I* should learn how to paint.' She raised her eyebrows suggestively. 'I'm very happy to pose nude if he wants to paint *me*.'

Clementine tried not to feel jealous. It was always inevitable that Rafa would eventually sink into the perfumed posse of Dawcomb girls. With his good looks and charm he was like a honey pot to bees. She wished she hadn't provoked a row.

They had been getting along so well. Now she had blown it, they weren't even friends.

Mr Atwood finished his meeting and called Clementine into his office. He dictated a couple of letters, then gave her a tray of papers to file and a list of documents he needed for the afternoon.

'Good look,' he said with a nod.

'Oh, thank you,' she replied, glancing down at her suit in surprise.

'I like my secretary to look professional.'

'Well, I feel professional today. It's a novelty.' She laughed joylessly. 'Did your wife like the bracelet?'

'The bracelet? My wife? Oh, yes.' He coughed. 'She was very pleased. Yes. Well chosen, Clementine.'

Clementine grinned as she went to the filing cabinet. Now she knew who his mistress was she could have fun with him. If she hadn't been in such a grumpy mood she'd have confided in Sylvia. For the time being, she decided to keep the information to herself.

Having organized the files so efficiently, she found the documents he required with ease. She swiftly typed the letters and envelopes and took them through to his office. 'That was quick,' he said, taking the documents and looking them over to check they were the right ones. He murmured his approval. She placed the letters in front of him for his signature. He read them for errors, surprised to find none. He signed his name in his tight little writing at the bottom of each. 'Well done, Clementine. You're becoming quite a good secretary all of a sudden.'

'That's high praise from you, Mr Atwood.'

'Praise where praise is due.'

'Thank you.'

'I'd like you to come to the meeting this afternoon. It's time you learned a little more about the business.'

'Sure.'

'And in that suit, I think you're perfectly dressed to represent us.'

'OK. Where is it?'

'It's a massive property called Newcomb Bisset Manor, about half an hour away. If all goes well, Atwood and Fisher are going to put it on the market. The husband is a bit of a ladies' man. He'll like the look of you. If he has any doubt about being represented by us, he won't by the end of the meeting.' Clementine grimaced. 'All you need to do is smile,' he added firmly.

Back at the Polzanze, Rafa was giving a lesson to a group of twelve in the vegetable garden. Some were painting in watercolours, others with oils, a few drawing in charcoal. They all sat in front of the picturesque glass-and-iron greenhouse where Mr Potter was busy washing potatoes.

The Brigadier sat beside Jane. He'd made sure he was downwind so he could smell her perfume. He liked her company. She was sweet-natured and gentle, which reminded him of his wife. The more he talked to her, the more he realized she was mischievous too, which made him laugh. His wife, as much as he had loved her, hadn't been known for her sense of humour.

Grace, Pat and Veronica chatted in the sunshine. Fat bees buzzed about the lavender and the pink and yellow roses that climbed the south-facing wall of the greenhouse. Birds tweeted in the lime trees, intrepid squirrels played tag in the branches. The atmosphere was languid. Rafa wandered from easel to easel, giving advice here and there, sometimes taking the brush himself and showing how it was done.

When he had a moment to himself his mind drifted to Clementine. She was tugging his conscience like a kite on the wind. He had gone over and over their conversation and, as much as he regretted speaking his mind, he didn't regret trying to help her. He had definitely gone about it the wrong way, picked the wrong moment, but his intentions had been honourable. He had noticed Marina's tense shoulders that morning and the way she had smiled with her lips and not with her eyes. He wondered whether she was upset that Clementine had moved out. He resolved to go into town that afternoon and find her at work. Perhaps they could have tea together and make up.

After lunch he took a break from painting and drove into Dawcomb-Devlish. He knew that she worked for an estate agent on the high street. It wouldn't be hard to find. He parked the car on the seafront. The place was teeming with tourists and British holiday-makers on half term. Children sat on a low wall licking ice cream in cones, waiting for a man with a long ponytail to apply tattoos. Mothers in brightly coloured sweaters and shorts gossiped on the pavement, and a couple of dogs lay in the shade waiting for their owner to come out of Kitchen Delights. Rafa weaved through the slow-moving throng that ambled idly up the road, and scanned the shops for the estate agency. It wasn't long before he stumbled upon it.

Atwood and Fisher looked suitably prestigious, painted a discreet navy blue with shiny windows displaying fine, beach-front houses to rent or buy. He peered through to see a pretty redhead talking on the telephone at the front desk. There was no sign of Clementine. When he opened the door, the red-head glanced up. With a smile she swiftly wound up her conversation and put down her nail file. 'Hello, can I help you?' she asked.

Rafa approached her desk. Her green eyes devoured him hungrily. 'I'm looking for a girl called Clementine Turner. Does she work here?'

'Little Clemmie? She certainly does. You must be the artist-in-residence at the Polzanze.'

He grinned. 'Am I that obvious?'

'You are, lovely. It's the accent, distinctly *not* English.'

'Is she here?'

'I'm afraid not. She's gone for a meeting with Mr Atwood. I don't think she'll be back until late afternoon. They've only just left.'

He swore in Spanish. 'Can you give her a message for me?'

'Of course.' She picked up her pen. 'Fire away.'

'You don't need to write anything down. Just tell her I came by to see her.'

'I'm coming up to have a drink at the Polzanze tonight. I'll bring her with me.'

'OK. Then tell her I'll see her later.'

'Sure.' Eager to detain him she added breezily, 'So, how's it going up there?'

'Getting busy.'

'I bet it is. You're slowly getting to know the whole of Dawcomb.'

He laughed. 'It's a great town.'

'I like it. Clementine doesn't. She's just desperate to leave. But then she's a city girl. I prefer the quiet of the countryside. I'm a woman of simple pleasures.' Rafa took in her heavy make-up and manicure and smiled to himself. She didn't look like a woman who understood the word 'simple'.

'I'd better get back to the hotel. I have some very keen artists to teach.'

'I'm glad the weather's nice for you.'

'So am I.'

She watched him walk to the door, wishing she could entice him to stay and chat a little longer. 'My name's Sylvia, by the way.'

'See you later, then, Sylvia.'

She gave a little wave. 'Bye!'

*

Clementine sat through the meeting while Mr Atwood's client, Mr Rhys-Kerr, leered at her from the other side of the dining-room table. The discussion went on for well over an hour, the majority of it having nothing to do with business and everything to do with golf. It transpired that Mr Atwood and Mr Rhys-Kerr were both members of the same club.

Once the finer details of the sale were settled, Mr Rhys-Kerr insisted on showing them around the house. Mr Atwood had already seen it, but Mr Rhys-Kerr was keen for Clementine to appreciate the merits of a big country pile. Clementine rolled her eyes at his childish innuendos: bath 'wide enough for two'; shower 'that's seen a lot of loving'; bedroom 'if these walls could talk, I'd blush to the roots of my hair'. The two men clearly shared the same sense of humour as well as the same golf course, because Mr Atwood laughed at everything Mr Rhys-Kerr said.

'You were terrific, Clementine,' Mr Atwood gushed as he drove out of the electric gates. 'He really liked you.'

'Must be the suit,' Clementine replied drily.

'You're a pretty girl, no doubt about it. We'll make a fortune on that house.'

'It's very naff.'

'Naff?'

'Yes, no taste at all.'

'That's beside the point. The fact is, it's twelve thousand square feet with a sea view. Splendid.'

'It's still naff.'

'Are you telling me that if you had the money to burn, you wouldn't like to live there?'

'I'd hate to live there. The house is new, with no character or charm.'

'But it's big.'

'And soulless.'

'I can't work you out, Clementine.'

Clementine sighed and stared out of the window. 'You're not alone, Mr Atwood. Neither can I.'

When they returned to the office Sylvia was talking on the telephone to Freddie, doodling love hearts onto her notebook. She waited until Mr Atwood had left the room, then she told Clementine that her Argentine had come looking for her.

'What did he say?' Clementine asked, perking up.

'Just that he popped by to see you.'

'Oh.'

'He's gorgeous. It's the smile. Full of naughtiness. And his accent is as delicious as toffee banoffi pie.'

'I suspect he wanted to apologize.'

'About what?'

'Long story.' She sat down, disappointed that she had missed him. 'What do I do?'

'Go home to Joe. Rafa's a man who is bound to break a girl's heart.' Sylvia knew she should tell her that he expected to see her at the hotel that evening, but hard as she tried, she couldn't get the words out. They hung on her lips, refusing to budge. She knew jealousy didn't become her, but she convinced herself that Clementine wasn't interested in him. As she settled grumpily behind her desk, Sylvia decided that she'd probably decline his invitation anyway.

Chapter 19

That evening Sylvia changed into a red dress, reapplied her lipstick and motored up to the Polzanze, fighting her guilt that she hadn't invited Clementine to come with her.

She was greeted at the door by a porter who escorted her into reception.

'Good evening, can I help you?' said Jennifer, smiling politely from behind the desk.

'Yes, I've come to have a drink with your artist, Rafa . . .' She hesitated, not knowing his last name.

Jennifer recognized the buxom redhead, but couldn't place her. 'Sure, he's in the drawing room, straight through the hall.' She watched her slope off in the direction of the drawing room, her gait slow and sexy as if she were walking through a saloon in a cowboy movie. And then she remembered where she had seen her, through the window of Atwood and Fisher, and she breathed deeply, relieved that she had taken the incriminating bracelet off.

Sylvia found Rafa in the sitting room, talking to a group of old ladies and a ruddy-faced codger in a gold-buttoned blue blazer. He looked up as she walked over and acknowledged her with a smile. She noticed his eyes stray past her, expecting to see Clementine. She wasn't used to that.

'I'm on my own, I'm afraid. Clementine's busy,' she said carelessly, as he stood up to greet her. His face darkened with disappointment. She wasn't used to that either. Normally she eclipsed other women like a big, beautiful moon. 'You don't mind having a drink with me, do you?'

'It will be my pleasure. Let's go outside. Will you be warm enough?'

'I have a wrap,' she replied, flapping it in front of him. 'It's come all the way from India.'

'When were you there?'

'Oh, I haven't been. It was a gift.'

'It's pretty.'

She savoured the suede texture of his foreign accent and followed him through the conservatory. 'I could listen to your accent for ever,' she sighed. 'But I suppose all the girls have told you that?'

'So, there's no point trying to sound English?' he replied with a laugh.

'Oh, no, that would be foolish. You won't have any admirers at all if you sound like everyone else.'

'I'll lay it on thickly, then.'

The terrace was almost full. They sat at a small round table and looked at each other across the candlelight.

'So, what's this boyfriend of Clementine's like?'

'I introduced them,' Sylvia replied proudly. 'Do you mind if I smoke?'

'Not at all.'

'Can I offer you one?'

He shook his head. 'I'm surprised a beautiful woman like you smokes.'

She pulled the packet out of her bag and tapped it with a talon. 'I've tried to give up, so many times, but it'll take more than willpower.'

'Like what?'

'Love,' she stated simply, fixing him with feline eyes. 'If I fell for a non-smoker, hook, line and sinker, I'd give up for him.'

'I think you should give up for yourself.'

'Been there, done that, failed miserably.' She placed the cigarette between her scarlet lips and lit it with one of the tea lights set decoratively in purple tumblers in the centre of the table. He watched her puff a few times, then sit back as the nicotine loosened her up.

Jake decided to take their order himself. He liked the look of Sylvia, full-bodied and feminine, like a beautiful ginger cat. He had seen her up there once or twice before, but she hadn't noticed him other than to say a brief hello in response to his greeting. Now she tossed him a smile as Rafa ordered a Martini and a glass of Chardonnay. Then she settled her pretty eyes onto the Argentine again and blew a ribbon of smoke out of her mouth provocatively.

Jake withdrew inside as his gut twisted with jealousy. He resented Rafa more than ever. While Rafa resided at the hotel Jake didn't stand a chance. He gave their order to the waiter. Then stood a while, watching Sylvia from the conservatory, unwilling to tear himself away.

'You know, Clemmie's told me a lot about you.' Sylvia took a sip of wine.

'Has she?'

'Yes, she came rushing in after she'd seen you in the Black Bean Coffee Shop. She's a child, really. I'm like a mother to her.'

'It was such a coincidence, meeting like that.' He smiled at the recollection and Sylvia noticed his eyes sparkle. 'She's quirky, I like that. In Argentina we say, *un personaje*. So tell me, is her boyfriend good enough for her?'

'Absolutely,' she replied with emphasis. 'They're like two peas in a pod.'

'Her stepmother doesn't like the sound of him,' Rafa added.

'That's because they have a bad relationship. Clemmie says she's a drama queen because she likes to be the centre of attention. I fancy it's the stress of wanting children and not being able to have them that has driven her a little crazy.'

'How long have you known Marina?'

'I don't really *know* her. Only through Clemmie. The problem is she's from a different class to Grey and that bothers Clemmie. It's a very unattractive English trait, this class obsession. I'm sure you don't have anything like it in Argentina.'

'Believe me, prejudice exists all over the world.'

'Well, Clemmie thinks that Submarine – I mean, Marina – set her sights on Grey because she wanted to move up in the world, socially. I think they just fell in love. After all, they hardly hobnob with the aristos. But no child is ever going to love a step-parent, however hard the parent tries. I'm sure Marina has tried until she's blue in the face. Clemmie is very stubborn.'

While she spoke he listened attentively, his eyes steady and penetrating. 'This class thing, is it based on family or education?'

'The two go together. I suspect Marina's family are working class, or lower-middle class. She certainly wasn't privately educated. I should know because I wasn't either.'

'Have you met her parents?'

Sylvia shook her head. 'Clemmie's never met them. I think Marina keeps them well hidden, don't you?'

'You mean, she's ashamed of them?'

'Perhaps.' She laughed. 'I don't think they even attended their wedding. Clemmie once remarked that they married in the local registry office as soon as the divorce came through. For two people in love, that's not very romantic, is it?'

'Some people don't like to make a big noise.'

'Clemmie says Marina loves a big noise, if she's in the middle of it.' She lowered her voice, aware that she might be overheard. 'I imagine she didn't want her family there to let her down. She presents quite posh, doesn't she? I mean, her accent, it's rather pretentious, isn't it, like she's trying too hard?'

It was now twilight. The tea lights glowed in their purple glasses, the roosting birds were silent against the sleepy murmur of the sea. Rafa drained his glass, Sylvia lit another cigarette. He felt anxious about Clementine – every time he thought about her the knot tightened in his chest.

'Do you have Clementine's mobile number?' he asked.

'Yes.' Sylvia squirmed uncomfortably.

'Give it to me.'

With a groan she burrowed in her bag for her mobile and scrolled down for the number. She read it out and watched nervously as he punched it into his BlackBerry.

'Are you going to call her?'

'Why not? She can be busy up here.'

'I don't think Joe will like it. He's very possessive.'

'Then I will ask them both.'

'Why don't you text?'

'You think that would be more appropriate?'

'Absolutely, otherwise you might get her into trouble.'

C where are you? I was hoping you would come up with Sylvia for a drink. Are you really too busy? I want to tell you I'm sorry . . . Rafa

Clementine read the text. Her stomach flipped like a pancake. She read it again, blushing deeply. Her first thought was that Rafa wanted to see her. Her second was that Sylvia had deliberately failed to include her. She glanced at Joe, sitting in the armchair watching sport on Sky, and knew that she couldn't possibly get away right now. She wished Joe would disappear in a puff of smoke.

Can't now. Can you come to the house that God forgot tomorrow evening, after work? C

Rafa's BlackBerry bleeped with an incoming message. Sylvia reddened. 'Is that Clemmie? Is she coming?'

He read her text and narrowed his eyes. The house that God forgot, would he remember how to get there?

'Well? What does she say?'

'She's busy,' he replied.

Sylvia's shoulders relaxed. 'You see? I told you.'

'I'll see her tomorrow. What time do you finish work?'

'Five thirty.'

'OK.' He typed with his thumbs:

I'll come by your office and we can go together.

'Who are you texting?' Joe asked.

'Jake,' Clementine lied. 'I'm going to go up to the hotel after work tomorrow. There's something he wants to tell me.'

'Probably wants to persuade you to move back.'

'Maybe.' The only thing standing between her and going home was her pride. Joe turned his attention back to the television. She watched him as he sipped beer out of the can, feet up on a stool, eyes glued to the screen and thought how very coarse he was. Just as she was wondering what on earth had possessed her to move in with him, her telephone bleeped with a text. She read it eagerly. So, Rafa would pick her up tomorrow and they'd drive out to the old church, their secret place. At once her spirits soared.

She remembered walking down the little path to the beach, the way he had disentangled her from the brambles, the moment they had stripped off to their underwear and run into the sea. She remembered the way they had laughed, shared stories and returned to the Polzanze like schoolchildren trying not to be caught breaking the rules. She smiled wistfully and hoped that tomorrow would be just as special.

*

Sylvia noticed Rafa's glance at his watch. She could sense when a man wasn't interested in her and wasn't about to make a fool of herself. She looked at hers and gasped. 'Good Lord, is that the time? I should go. Freddie will be wondering where I am.'

'Freddie?'

'My lover. He'll be wanting dinner.'

'I should go, too.'

'Do you have a dinner date?'

'I'll join my students.' He grinned. 'That sounds odd as none of them is under seventy.'

She looked around. 'This place is really rocking.'

'It's a beautiful hotel.'

'Rumours indicate that it's struggling.'

'It doesn't look like it's struggling to me.'

'No, you're right. The air has changed, it feels happy. Makes me want to stay and soak it up.'

'You'll have to come again.'

'I'll drag Clemmie here next time.'

'You do that.'

She wondered why his face lit up. Clemmie was a peculiar creature, not a great beauty like *her*, and Rafa was clearly a man who could have any woman he wanted. 'It's been fun. Is it presumptuous to thank you for the drink?'

'Not at all, it's my pleasure.' He escorted her to the hall, glancing at his ladies as they walked through the drawing room, pleased to see that they were still heavily absorbed in conversation. The Brigadier's loud guffaws shot into the air like gunfire, filling the room with mirth.

'They're having a good time,' Sylvia commented.

'My dinner companions,' he laughed.

'Dinner won't be dull, then.'

'Neither will yours.'

'No, Freddie's a laugh a minute.' But as she left the hotel she was struck by a sudden stab of loneliness. There was no dinner with Freddie; he was at home with his family. There was no one at home for her.

Jake stood in the hall and watched her walk across the gravel to her car. He had said 'good night' but she had responded glumly, without even looking at him. Her evening with Rafa had clearly not gone well. He wished she had stopped to talk to *him*. He was sure he could have cheered her up.

The following morning Harvey drew up in front of the hotel in a gleaming Jaguar. With the roof down, he sat at the wheel, his arm resting casually on the window frame, a roguish grin carved into his happy face.

'Go and find Marina,' he called to Tom, who gave a low whistle before rushing off to get her.

Shane sauntered out to admire the car. 'It's a real beauty,' he gushed.

'Jaguar XK, with all the trimmings.'

'Nice. Whose is it?'

'My nephew's. He's lent it to me. I want to see Marina's face when she sees me in it.'

'Nice nephew!'

'He's done well for himself.'

'Will you take me for a spin later?'

'You bet. It'll take more than a few odd jobs to get me out of this today.'

Marina stepped onto the gravel and her mouth opened in a silent gasp as she saw Harvey at the wheel of a sleek racing-green Jaguar. 'I don't believe it!' she exclaimed, shaking her head in wonder. 'I never thought I'd see you in a sports car, Harvey. It's stunning!'

'Get in!'

'Are you going to take me for a drive?'

'I have a little time before I'm due to take Rafa and his

painters to the Powells' for lunch. Mrs Powell is putting on a picnic for them so they can paint the old dovecote.'

'What a good idea. So, where shall we go?'

'Wherever you want, m'lady.' Shane opened the passenger door and watched Marina climb in.

'How exciting.' She laughed like a young girl going out on a date. 'We'll be gone for some time,' she told Shane. 'Tell Jake to hold the fort.' With a purr the car crept smoothly into the drive. Shane and Tom watched it go.

'I'd like a car like that,' said Tom enviously.

'The only way you're going to get one of those is by stealing it, or robbing a bank,' said Shane.

'Or finding a rich bird to buy me one.'

'You won't find her here, lad. Rich birds go to the South of France not Dawcomb-Devlish.'

'What a beauty, Harvey. How long have you got it for?' Marina shouted over the roar of the wind.

'As long as I want,' he replied carelessly. 'My nephew won't be needing it. He's gone abroad for a few weeks.'

'It must have cost a bomb.'

'Sixty-three grand, new.'

'You've got to be joking!'

'Nope. Well, that's the retail price but this is second-hand. Still, it's got all the trimmings: leather seats, touch-screen sat nav, alloy wheels, and she moves like a big, beautiful cat.'

'She certainly does. You'd better keep it in the garage while that robber is on the loose.'

'I'm more worried about the boys running off with it.'

'Shane and Tom?'

'Yes, wouldn't trust them as far as I can throw them.' He winked. 'When it comes to those two, they're just a pair of schoolboys.'

They drove down the country lanes, the sun on their faces,

the wind tossing Marina's long hair playfully. After a while they ceased to talk. Occasionally she smiled at him and he grinned back at her fondly and in those moments she was able to forget about Clementine, the hotel, their mounting debt and the imminent arrival of Charles Roache. When she was with Harvey, she felt the weight of responsibility lighten, as if he was there to carry it all for her.

Clementine was furious with Sylvia for having deliberately excluded her from her evening with Rafa, but for once she decided not to create a scene. She was disappointed in her, having believed they were friends, but in her heart she was not surprised. Sylvia was a man's woman and their friendship counted for nothing when she set her sights on a new conquest.

She got to work early, having not wanted to spend more time than necessary lying beside Joe, who seemed to have nothing to get up for, and drank a latte at her desk. She wore her hair up and her navy suit, but had packed a Jack Wills sundress, cardigan and flip-flops in a bag for later. The very thought of spending the evening with Rafa had turned her stomach upside down. She had no appetite for breakfast and could barely sit still.

Sylvia arrived, looking guilty. Instead of flouncing confidently to her desk she shuffled in sheepishly.

'I feel dreadful,' she stated, coming straight to the point. 'I didn't sleep a wink last night.'

'Why?' Clementine asked breezily.

'Why? Because I've been a bitch, that's why. I didn't like who I was last night and I want to say I'm sorry.'

'It's OK, Sylvia. I understand why you did it.'

Sylvia was surprised. 'You do, and you're not upset with me?'

'Not at all.' Clementine's happiness made her unusually forgiving. 'I was with Joe anyway, so I wouldn't have been able to come.'

'Well, I should have told you. He's *your* friend, not mine.'

'He's everyone's friend, Sylvia.'

'No, I think he likes you more than anyone else. His face lit up when he spoke about you.'

'Really?'

'Really.'

'He's like that with everyone, don't be under any illusions.' But she allowed herself a *frisson* of excitement even though she was certain Sylvia was wrong.

Mr Atwood arrived in the early afternoon after a meeting in Exeter. The letters he had requested were waiting on his desk, a list of messages neatly typed up beside them. Clementine came in with a cup of coffee. He sat back in his chair and chewed on the end of his pencil, observing her through narrowed eyes.

'You're becoming a rather good secretary, Clementine. I'm impressed!'

'Thank you, Mr Atwood.'

'Let me ask you, why the sudden leaf turning?'

'No reason. I'm actually enjoying myself.'

'Good. That suit becomes you.'

Clementine noticed the lascivious glint in his eyes and recoiled. 'Thank you.'

'You're a pretty girl, Clementine.'

'Is there anything else, Mr Atwood? Because if there isn't, I'd like to get back to my desk.'

'Yes, yes. Of course. Don't let me detain you.' He gave a cheerful chuckle to show that he meant nothing by the compliments. 'I like a secretary who's keen to be at her desk.'

Back at the hotel, Bertha sat at the kitchen table with Heather, hugging a mug of coffee.

'I think the Brigadier is keen on Mrs Meister,' said Heather. 'I've been watching them closely. They always sit together and he's asked her to take a walk with him this evening. I'm ashamed to have eavesdropped, but it's gripping, I can't help it.'

'Love is in the air,' Bertha sang tunelessly.

'I've always felt sorry for him. You know, coming up for breakfast every morning on his own. No wife at home to go back to. Now he's all smiles. I think it's sweet.'

'Which one's Mrs Meister?'

'The little mousy one.'

'Oh dear, can she cope with the Brigadier? He's like a big walrus.'

'Her husband died, poor love, so she's on her own, too. I think it's a match made in heaven.'

'I've got my eye on Rafa.' Bertha grinned into her mug.

Heather was horrified. 'You're not going to do anything about it, are you?'

'I don't mean *I* fancy him. I like an older man, personally, and a little bigger. I'd squash him like a crêpe. I mean I'm *watching* him.'

'Why?'

'I think he's got a girlfriend back home.'

'Really?'

'Yes. When I was cleaning his room I came across a wad of love letters from a girl called Costanza. That's Constance, isn't it?'

'Must be.'

'So, I'm just keeping an eye on him in case he strays.'

'Why would you care if he strayed?'

'I wouldn't. I just want to make sure that I'm around to see it.'

'Really, Bertha. You're terrible, you are.'

'Just looking for a little entertainment. It's not often that exciting things happen down here in Devon.'

'I'd say Baffles is exciting.'

'If he comes here, which I doubt. Not a great deal to take

of any value, here.' She snorted disparagingly and slurped the last dregs of coffee from the bottom of the mug.

'Didn't you see Harvey's new car?'

'No.' Bertha looked put out. 'What new car?'

'A Jaguar, no less.'

'What's he doing with a Jaguar?'

'Lord knows, but if he's not careful he'll find it gone in the morning with nothing but a note saying "Thank you" in its place.'

By five thirty Clementine's insides were a tangle of nerves. She logged off her computer and took the tray of paperwork to the filing cabinets to file. As she put them away in the correct folders, all neatly labelled in alphabetical order, she noticed her hands were trembling. She heard Mr Atwood on the telephone, talking to his mistress, no doubt. She didn't imagine he called his wife 'cowgirl'. As she tuned into his saccharine sweet-talking she didn't hear the door open, nor the squeak of embarrassment from Sylvia, who was still at the front desk.

Rafa greeted Sylvia but his attention was drawn to the back of the room where a slim girl in a well-cut navy suit and stilettos was standing by the filing cabinets. It took him a moment to recognize her, at which point she turned.

'Clementine?' He looked surprised. She closed the drawer and walked over.

'Rafa.'

'*Dios mio*, you look fantastic.'

She flushed happily. 'Working attire. I have something less formal in my bag. Do you mind waiting while I change?'

He put his hands in his pockets. 'Of course not. Sylvia can keep me company.' But he didn't take his eyes off Clementine until she had disappeared into the ladies' room.

Sylvia smiled uncomfortably, hoping he wouldn't refer to the evening before. She wished Clementine would hurry up.

Rafa leaned on her desk and grinned down at her. 'Working hard today?'

Clementine wriggled into her dress and slipped her feet into flip-flops. She let her hair down and scrunched it between her fingers. She remembered with disbelief the afternoon day-dreaming that the handsome Argentine she had met in the Black Bean Coffee Shop would saunter into her office to find her. Now he had and the evening stretched out before her, full of promise.

Chapter 20

Clementine sat in the passenger seat of Rafa's hire car, barely able to believe that they were finally off together, just the two of them. She rolled down the window and let the sweet scents of summer billow in on the breeze. At first their chat was awkward, both talking at the same time, stumbling on their words, laughing to mask their nervousness. The atmosphere had changed. Clementine didn't know why it had changed, or when, but a *frisson* existed between them that hadn't been there before.

Rafa, casual in jeans and white shirt, glanced across at her every now and then and grinned. He wore dark glasses and his thick hair stuck up as the wind blew through it. She had always found him handsome, but now, knowing him a little better, she saw that his good looks ran so much deeper. He had a gift for seeing the best in everyone and a generosity of spirit that gave his eyes and smile an exceptional brilliance.

Above all, she liked who she was when she was with him, as if, in his eyes, she was a better version of herself: braver, wittier, prettier. She gazed out over the countryside and noticed how very lush it was. The bright green of the leaves and the dazzling blue of the sky filled her up until she was ready to burst with happiness.

They pulled up into the lay-by and Rafa walked round to open the boot. 'What have you got in there?' she asked, leaning on the gate and allowing her gaze to drift over the house that God forgot.

'Supplies,' he replied with a grin.

She turned to see him pull out a canvas bag. 'What's that?'

'A picnic.'

'Who made it for you?'

'Heather.' He peered inside. '*Qué bueno*, she's included a bottle of wine.'

Clementine's spirit swelled. 'Where are we going to have it?'

'Down on the beach, I think. Don't you?'

'Good idea.'

However, it hadn't been such a good idea to wear a dress. The path down to the beach was narrow and lined with brambles. She hadn't thought about practicalities when she had planned her wardrobe.

'I'll give you a piggy-back,' Rafa suggested.

'Oh, no, I'm far too heavy,' she protested.

'No you're not. The faces I pulled last time were in jest. You're tiny. I could swing you over my shoulder and barely notice you. Here, you carry the bag.' He crouched down. 'Climb on.'

Wishing she were a few stone lighter, she tentatively sat astride him. The blood boiled in her cheeks at the intimacy of their bodies, but she didn't have time to dwell on it. He stood up, hooked his arms beneath her legs, and set off down the path. 'You see, I barely know you're there.'

'Liar,' she laughed.

'Who said that?' He turned round, pretending to look behind him. She laughed again. He swung around the other way. 'And that? I thought I was alone.'

'Silly!'

'Who said that?'

'If you keep swinging round, you're going to make me seasick.'

'Ah, it's *you*.'

'Yes, it's me, so light you forgot I was on your back.' He strode on down the path, careful to keep her bare legs away from thorns. At last they reached the sand and he gently put her down.

'You see, I'm not even out of breath.'

They sat on the beach and watched the waves roll gently in. Gulls wheeled on the breeze, the more intrepid ones dropping onto the rocks nearby in the hope of scrounging scraps from their picnic. Rafa poured the wine and Clementine opened the sandwiches.

'Here's to our renewed friendship,' he said, raising his glass. 'I want to say how sorry I am that I interfered. Your relationship with Marina is none of my business. The truth is, I like you both and I want you to like each other.'

She raised her glass. 'I accept your apology, graciously this time.'

'So, we're friends again?'

'Yes. Definitely.' They drank a moment in silence. Then Clementine took a deep breath. 'You know you said that I should detach from the past so as not to ruin my present? What exactly did you mean?'

He looked at her anxiously. 'You don't really want to talk about this, do you?'

'Yes, I do.'

'You promise you won't run off in a fury?'

She laughed. 'I'm sorry I lost my temper. I promise I won't run off. Anyhow, you have the car keys.'

'OK, if you insist, I'll share my thoughts, for what they're worth.'

'I think they're worth a lot.' She took a bite of turkey sandwich. 'I might learn something.'

'First of all you have to understand my philosophy of life.'

'Which is?'

'I start from a belief in our ability to choose our destinies.

We come down here to experience life and learn to be compassionate, loving human beings. During our lifetime we have many choices which affect those around us as well as our own futures.

'Imagine a pebble dropped into a pond. You may think that the pebble simply sinks to the bottom, but you are wrong. The pebble causes ripples that run to the edge, where they nudge a leaf off the bank. A bumble bee is drowning in the water, but now he is able to climb onto the leaf and save himself. The bumble bee flies off and lands on the arm of a child, who watches in wonder and thus develops a love of nature. The child's parents are fighting, but the mother sees the bee and panics that her child will be stung. Both parents rush to help the child and forget their argument, united in their love for their child. The bee flies off and ... well, you can invent whatever story you like.

'The point is, nothing you do is in isolation. So you see, your choices are important. If you choose to hold onto grudges you will create a future that is unhappy, because every decision will be born out of your resentment. Marina fell in love with your father and married him. It doesn't matter any more whether she stole him from your mother, or rescued him from an unhappy marriage – and believe me, each person involved will have their own interpretation of the events and they will all be different. But you, Clementine, can choose how you react. You're an adult now with your own future to build. If you detach emotionally, give them your blessing, try to see the good in Marina instead of looking for the bad, you will forge a happier present for yourself.'

She thought about it a while, her gaze drawn out to sea. 'I've never given Marina a chance,' she said softly. 'I've always resented her for taking Daddy away from me.'

'Your father is still here. Perhaps *you* need to be the bigger person and reach out to *him*.'

'You make it sound so easy.'

'Look, we are not caricatures but complicated, flawed human beings. Love is bigger than all of us. Just understand that they had their reasons, probably not the reasons you think they had, and make a conscious decision to let them go. They're a great big liner you are pulling across the waves. Cut the rope. Release yourself. You can rise to great heights in spite of the terrible start you had in life,' he smiled with empathy. 'But more probably *because* of it.'

'You said I should ask Marina her side of the story.'

'Maybe one day, down here on the beach, when you're alone and uninterrupted, you might ask her to tell you what happened. But only when you're ready to listen without judging her. Only once you have detached enough not to bring it all back to you.'

'You're very wise, Rafa.'

'That's what everyone says, but I'm not. I'm still learning, still searching.'

'You seem to know a lot already.'

'The more you know the more you realize what there is to learn.' He poured another glass of wine. 'Need a refill?'

She nodded. 'You know, you're going to have to carry me back up the path.'

'A few more drinks and I might carry you all the way home!'

The tide crept in as they sat chatting on the sand. The orange sun sank low on the horizon, turning the clouds a deep purple against the pale blue of the sky. It was so romantic, against the hypnotic rhythm of the waves and the melancholy cry of gulls, that Clementine was sure he was going to lean over and kiss her. Inside, her heart began to thump with anticipation. The intense way he looked at her, the jaunty way he smiled, the playful way he teased, all indicated that he was attracted to her. The wine had made her senses more acute and

out and into the water. All the time Rafa spoke to him, encouraging him, coaxing him, praising him. Clementine swam the other side of the dog so that he felt protected on both sides. Slowly, they made their way round the corner. The wind had picked up and the sea was choppier now. It required more effort to swim, but Clementine gritted her teeth and kept her eye on the beach. The little dog swam with all his might, his nose in the air, nostrils dilating, eyes wide with anxiety. But on he swam, his courage greater than his fear.

At last they reached the beach. The dog trotted onto the sand and shook the water out of his fur, then wagged his tail so hard it looked as if his bottom would come off. Clementine and Rafa staggered out of the waves and collapsed onto their knees to pat him.

'Clever dog!' they exclaimed breathlessly and the dog seemed to understand, licking their faces with happiness.

'We've got to get him home. He'll be cold and dehydrated. God knows how long he's been tied up in that cave.'

'We've got water in our picnic bag,' Clementine suggested.

'Good. Come on, boy, let's get you home.'

The dog drank from the bottle and ate the remains of the sandwiches. He was indeed hungry and thirsty.

'You know, Marina hates dogs,' said Clementine.

'How can a person hate dogs?'

'I don't know. She just does.'

'We'll worry about that later. Let's get him dry first and then we'll talk to her. You can't have him at work, so she'll have to tolerate him being at the hotel.'

'She'll make you take him to a dog home.'

'This dog is staying with me. It's Fate, don't you see? We were meant to find him.' He grinned at her playfully. 'It's my choice to keep him.'

She smiled back, relishing having something that they alone shared. 'Then it's mine, too.'

They dressed over their wet bodies and shivered all the way up to the car. Rafa offered to carry Clementine, but she declined, explaining that the dog needed their attention. Coming down the hill with her on his back was one thing, but going up was an entirely different matter, and she didn't care how many thorns ripped her skin as long as she was spared the humiliation of having to be put down halfway because she was too heavy.

They put the animal on the back seat, where he lay like a sodden mop. After a while, the rumble of the engine lulled him to sleep.

In spite of the heating in the car, Clementine and Rafa were both still shivering when they reached the Polzanze. They were cold right through to their bones.

'Let me deal with Marina,' Rafa suggested as the car pulled up in front of the house.

'I'm not going to argue with that,' Clementine said, biting her lip nervously. 'I hope we can keep him.'

'We're going to keep him, don't worry.'

'I'll go and get some old towels and a blanket.'

'Do you have anything to change into?'

'I'll borrow Dad's dressing gown.' Tom strode out of the hotel. He stared at them in surprise as they climbed out of the car. 'Tom, will you stay with the dog while I go and get some blankets?' Clementine asked.

'Dog?'

'Yes. We found a dog tied up in a cave. He was going to drown. We had to swim out to rescue him. Now he's asleep on the back seat, poor thing.'

Tom shook his head. 'Uh-oh, you know what the boss thinks about dogs.'

'This is different. He's frightened and has no one to look after him.'

'Where is Marina?' Rafa asked.

'In the conservatory with the Brigadier and your ladies.'

'Right, I'm going to put on some dry clothes, then I'm going to see her.'

'Good luck,' said Clementine.

'You need more than luck,' Tom added.

Clementine emerged a little later, swamped in Grey's dressing gown and slippers, armed with an old towel and blankets. Rafa, in fresh jeans and sweater, was coming out of the hotel with Marina. It was clear from the look on her face that he hadn't told her. Clementine glanced into the back of the car. The dog was still asleep. He looked very sweet, his brown hair curled by sea water, his little body rising and falling as he breathed. How could anyone reject such a helpless creature?

'So, what's the surprise?' said Marina, approaching the car. Tom looked terrified and backed away quietly, but near enough to watch.

'We have rescued a dog,' said Rafa carelessly. 'He was tied up in a cave and left to drown. Clementine and I had to swim out to rescue him.'

Marina's jaw dropped in horror. 'A dog?'

'Yes, isn't he adorable? He's asleep now. He was so frightened.' Rafa was clearly trying to appeal to her compassionate nature.

She peered in, wringing her hands anxiously. 'You know I can't have dogs in the hotel,' she said, but Rafa sensed the weakness in her voice and pushed on.

'But he was going to die. We have a responsibility to look after him. He's very young, not much more than a puppy. We cannot give him away.'

Marina stared at him. The fear in her eyes took them all aback. Quite unexpectedly, Clementine felt a sharp ache in her chest and her heart flooded with pity. Marina looked so small, as if a gust of wind would blow her over.

'It's OK, Marina, I'll have him,' she volunteered. 'Mr Atwood will just have to put up with him in the office. He can sleep under my desk.'

'No, you can't have him at work,' said Rafa.

'I can ask my mother,' Tom suggested. 'She's got a cat, but you never know, they might get on.'

Marina seemed to be struggling with her conscience. 'I can't give him away,' she muttered. 'I can't. We have to take care of him.'

'I can look after him up in my room,' Rafa said gently. 'You've given me an enormous suite, Marina; there's room enough for both of us.'

She looked into the car and gazed on the sleeping mongrel. Then her eyes filled with tears. No one knew what to say. They had not expected her to react in this way.

'I'm sorry, Marina. I didn't realize you were frightened of dogs.'

'I'm not frightened of them,' she replied, straightening up and composing herself. 'He's very dear. What are you going to call him?'

'We hadn't thought,' Rafa replied, looking to Clementine for help.

'Biscuit,' she replied, grinning at her stepmother.

Marina gave a small smile and wiped her cheek. 'Biscuit.' She laughed. 'That's a good name.'

'I thought you'd like it.'

'Sure,' Rafa agreed, oblivious of the joke that passed between the two women. 'I'll carry him upstairs and put him to bed.'

Marina seized control. 'Tom, go and tell the kitchen to prepare something for him to eat and take up a bowl of water. Clementine, you go with Rafa and make up a little bed. I'm sure we have a basket somewhere – I'll go and have a look.' She marched off to the stable block.

They watched her go. 'What was that all about?' Rafa asked.

Clementine shrugged. 'I don't know. She's a mystery. At least we know now that she's not afraid of dogs.'

'If she's not afraid of them, what's the problem?'

'Perhaps it's the fur. She's very proud of her house.'

'No, it's more than that. She nearly lost it.'

'She does that occasionally. Usually Harvey or Dad is near to put her back together again.'

Rafa frowned. 'Why?'

'You ask too many questions, Rafa.'

But he stood staring at the stable block long after Marina had disappeared inside.

Rafa carried Biscuit upstairs and put him onto the blankets Clementine laid out for him on the spare bed. He was so sleepy he could barely keep his eyes open. Tom appeared a little while later with a bowl of water and some leftover chicken, and Marina had found an old wicker picnic basket as a temporary solution. Tomorrow they'd go and buy supplies at the pet shop. It looked like Biscuit was here to stay.

Clementine ignored the three missed calls on her mobile from Joe and agreed to stay for dinner while her clothes dried. They retreated to the stable block and sat around the kitchen table eating spaghetti with mussels, which Marina cooked better than any chef. Grey joined them, interested to hear about the dog, but more concerned about his wife and how she was reacting to her new guest. It astonished him that she had allowed the animal onto the premises at all. Rafa longed to ask why she didn't like dogs, but intuition told him that *that* particular avenue was dark and treacherous.

At eleven Rafa got up from the table. 'I'd better go and check on Biscuit, in case he wakes up and finds himself alone. He might be frightened.'

'After his adventure, I imagine he'll be nervous for quite a while yet,' said Grey.

'I should go, too,' said Clementine. 'Dad, can you give me a lift? I left my car in Dawcomb.'

'Of course,' said Grey, getting up.

Marina frowned. She sensed Clementine's reluctance and wished she had the courage to admit that she'd been wrong and come home.

'I'll walk you out,' said Rafa, then he turned to Marina. 'Thank you for dinner. You cook spaghetti better than an Italian.'

Marina smiled. 'Thank you. That's quite a compliment, coming from a half-Italian.'

Rafa accompanied Clementine onto the gravel. 'What a day,' he said, putting his hands in his pockets.

'Why is it that whenever I'm with you, I end up taking off my clothes and jumping into the sea?'

'If you can't work that out you're not as clever as I thought you were.'

She smiled. 'Then you go to extraordinary lengths to get a girl to undress.'

'Some girls require more guile.'

'Will you give Biscuit a kiss from me?'

'I'll give him more than one. Come up and see him tomorrow. After all, he belongs to both of us.'

'I will.'

'I'll call you in the morning to tell you how he is.'

'I hope he has a good night.'

'After the fright he had today, he'll sleep like a baby.' He laughed. 'And so will I.'

Clementine climbed into her father's car and they motored up the drive. She saw Rafa watching her in the mirror and waved out of the window. He waved back. She knitted her fingers and took a deep, satisfied breath.

Grey dropped her off outside Joe's, but instead of going inside, she waited for her father to leave, then slunk off to find her Mini. She didn't want to face Joe yet, she wanted to sit a while and feel close to Rafa, so she drove to the house that God forgot.

The moon was big and bright, drenching the landscape with enough light for her to see her way down the field. She didn't feel afraid on her own. It felt good to be out in the wind, blanketed by the night. It was too dark to enter the church, so she sat on the step at the entrance and leaned against the wall, listening to the rustling of leaves and the steady murmuring of the sea below. Moonlight caught the tips of waves as they rose and fell, splashing them with silver. Tonight, the beauty didn't make her feel melancholy, but happy. Her heart felt full and warm as if it were a cupcake, just out of the oven. She knew now that there was such a thing as Big Love and that it could creep up on a person very suddenly, almost before they recognized it. Well, she recognized it, all right, and, with a shudder of anticipation, she yearned to let it in.

Chapter 21

Tuscany 1971

Floriana lay on the beach, her gaze lost in eternity. She considered the stars, so bright and vibrant, and wondered how many of them had already burned themselves out long ago, leaving their light to shine on like memories. She imagined death like that. Her mother might just as well be dead, for she wasn't ever coming back. Floriana accepted that now. Once there had been an afterglow of memory as bright as those stars, but now it too had run its course. She could barely remember what her mother looked like. She certainly had no recollection of her little brother. But she did often wonder where they were and if her mother ever thought of her. Those meanderings of her mind used to cause her pain and, in a strange way, she had taken pleasure from the discomfort, like the tongue that seeks the hurting tooth. Now her heart had hardened and she felt nothing, not even resentment.

It had been almost five years since Dante had left and she thought of him every day. She was almost sixteen, a young woman, yet inside she was still the little girl peering in through the gates of La Magdalena; and she still loved him.

After he left she believed her world had imploded, and her will to live had collapsed. Without Dante in her life what was the point of going on? She had sought comfort in the church, for no one else cared but Jesus, and He had reached out and touched her heart, whispering quietly in her ear so that no one else could hear. He had told her to wait, that the day would surely come when Dante would return and ask her to marry him. So, she had dried her tears and straightened her shoulders and resolved to do exactly as He commanded, for Jesus and His mother, Mary, loved her – and in case They got diverted by someone else's troubles, she went to church every day to light a candle for Dante, and to remind Them that *her* prayers were a priority.

The following summer Costanza was invited up to La Magdalena to play with Giovanna, the youngest Bonfanti child. It transpired that Costanza's mother had approached Signora Bonfanti at Mass and suggested getting the girls together. Signora Bonfanti had been delighted, embracing Costanza's mother like a long-lost friend. Contessa Aldorisio had not mentioned Floriana. She was keen for her daughter to find girls of her own class to play with, now she was growing up. But Costanza had insisted. She was too frightened to go on her own, and well aware that it was Floriana who had captured their hearts, not her. The countess had relented on the condition that once she was comfortable with Giovanna she leave Floriana behind, and besides, now she and Signora Bonfanti were reacquainted, she would take her to La Magdalena personally so she was not in need of an escort.

It wasn't long before Costanza and Giovanna were firm friends. Like Costanza, Giovanna was timid and uncertain. She had none of her sister's confidence nor her brother's charm. Floriana hung around them but she soon grew bored of their games. She longed for Dante to walk through the trees, but he had gone and she didn't know when he'd be coming back. So, Floriana played with Good-Night. The dog was the little bit of Dante she could hold onto. She taught him to retrieve, to sit when he was commanded and to follow her as she weaved in and out of the trees. They played hide-and-seek and endless other games she devised for him, and sometimes she'd put on shows for Giovanna and Costanza, who would sit together in their fancy dresses and clap prettily as if they were at the theatre.

Damiana was delighted to see Floriana again and mothered her as she had done the summer before. She let her retrieve balls when she played tennis with her girlfriends and invited her up to her bedroom to help her choose which dresses to wear. But Floriana's heart longed for Dante and in spite of all the attention, Villa La Magdalena seemed empty without him.

If it hadn't been for Signora Bonfanti, Costanza's mother would have made sure Floriana stayed at home. But this fey, dreamy woman with the delicate beauty of a sylph, fell in love with *l'orfanella* in the same way that her two elder children had. She had heard her tragic story from Dante and resolved to embrace the child with all her maternal love, which she had in abundance, having longed for many more children than three.

On her initial visit, she took the little girl by the hand and led her into her mermaid garden, where Floriana had sat with Dante the first time she had entered the grounds of La Magdalena. There they had remained for the entire afternoon, watching the fountain, listening to the birds and sharing thoughts and ideas. Signora Bonfanti found in Floriana a child who shared her love of nature and her insatiable curiosity about the world. Floriana found in Signora Bonfanti a gentle mother who threaded flowers in her hair and read her poetry and stories. A mother who took trouble with her the way her own mother never had.

Little by little Floriana had become a permanent fixture at La Magdalena. As permanent as the stray dogs and cats that Dante had adopted. And like the stray dogs and cats she was patted and teased with affection by everyone, except Contessa Aldorisio, who resented her presence there, as if it threatened her secret ambitions for her daughter. She need not have worried, for Giovanna grew to consider Costanza a sister and they remained in contact during the winter months when Giovanna was back at school in Milan. Floriana visited La Magdalena every day, although the family had long since departed, and took Good-Night off into town to chase pigeons in Piazza Laconda. The dog became her constant companion and her greatest pleasure. Unlike Costanza, who was too grand to talk to staff, Floriana had made friends with the locals who worked at La Magdalena, and when she wasn't in school or at Mass, she often hung around the gardens, playing with the animals and talking to the gardeners.

Alone again, Costanza sought the company of her old friend, and Floriana was happy to be welcomed back. But now they had to meet in town, or on the beach, for Costanza's mother was doing everything in her power to separate them. Costanza was thirteen now and resented being told what to do and who to be friends with, and she felt a strong loyalty to Floriana. But Contessa Aldorisio was confident that one way or another the two girls would eventually grow apart. It was inevitable, considering their lives and the stark differences of their class. If it didn't happen naturally, she would give it a little helping hand.

Another summer blossomed, the second since Dante's departure, and Floriana felt his absence more acutely than ever. Long, languid days at La Magdalena ensued, full of beautiful people, large lunch parties and afternoons in the mermaid garden, reading poetry. Signora Bonfanti invited Floriana to help make a picture mosaic and they spent hours in the conservatory cutting out small squares of paper and sticking them onto canvas. Floriana loved being close to her, while Good-Night lay snoozing by her side. There were pictures of Dante all over the house and sometimes she would glean bits of news as Signora Bonfanti processed her thoughts out loud in rambling soliloquies. It seemed that Dante was doing exceedingly well in America but that his future lay here in Italy, where he was expected to rise to great heights in his father's company.

Floriana did not like Signor Beppe. He had none of his son's charm or benevolence. His face was handsome in a hard way, his frown low over dark, shrewish eyes, and his neck was thick like a bull's. His mouth was twisted in repose, cruel in mirth, and when he laughed, it seemed superficial, as if he did it for effect and not out of joy. His mind seemed constantly occupied by work and he was always being called to the telephone, or in his study talking to men in black suits, smoking cigars that reeked into the marble hall. Signora Bruno said that Beppe Bonfanti was part of the local Mafia and had actually had people killed, but even though his eyes were remarkably cold, Floriana dismissed the old woman's gossiping as rumour. She couldn't believe that Dante's father was a murderer. That he was fearsome was without doubt.

He was shadowed constantly by Zazzetta, a wiry, sinister little man with a bald head and aquiline nose who whispered in his ear and wrote things down in a black notebook. Signor Beppe listened to him more than anyone else, and he seemed to have the power to grab his attention with as little as a raised eyebrow. Signor Beppe relied on him for everything, calling him his *braccio destro* – his right-hand man. Floriana didn't like Zazzetta either.

Signora Bonfanti kept out of her husband's way and he never sought her out. He barely noticed Floriana, in the same way that he never noticed the stray animals who hung around the terrace at lunchtime, but he did notice Costanza. He seemed to enjoy his younger daughter's flowering friendship and asked Costanza endless questions about herself and her family. Costanza told Floriana that Beppe had invited her parents to dinner and that they were now close friends. Floriana didn't see the significance of this. She cared only for Dante, his mother and his dog.

Five long years had passed since Floriana first met Dante and now summer was here again. But this time it would be better than any other because he was coming home. She had heard from Costanza, who had heard from Giovanna, and there was to be a big party to celebrate his homecoming. Floriana lay on the sand and felt a shiver of excitement ripple across her skin. Dante was finally coming home. They would be reunited at last. It never occurred to her that he might have fallen in love with someone else, or that he wouldn't fall in love with her, because she had lit a candle every single day for almost five years and sent her wish up to Jesus. With such constant badgering it was inconceivable that He would have the heart to ignore her.

'So? Which do you think? The blue or the white?' Costanza asked the following afternoon, laying the dresses on her bed. They had taken care to sneak into the house while the countess was out and their mischief gave them a heightened sense of excitement.

Floriana sat back against the pillows and took a good long look at both. 'Well, the blue is pretty, the white is a little bridal, don't you think?'

'So, the blue?'

'Put it on.'

Costanza didn't need further encouragement. She hurriedly slipped it on and stood before the long mirror that leaned against the wall. She was curvier now, her breasts large, her hips wide above short, porcine legs and small trotter-like feet. She loved her food and ate copious quantities of bread and pasta for comfort while she lamented her clumsy body.

'Do I look fat in this?' she asked, biting her bottom lip and pulling her stomach in.

'Of course you don't,' Floriana lied. 'You look voluptuous. Italian women are meant to be voluptuous.'

'You're not.'

'I have hips and breasts.'

'Not like mine.'

'But you have the grand title and parents. Which would you prefer?'

'I should diet.'

'Then diet.'

'It won't make a difference in time for tomorrow night.'

'Then eat and be happy. The blue looks lovely, really it does.'

'What are you going to wear?'

'I have nothing special. I'll probably borrow a dress of Aunt Zita's. She's more or less the same size and she's very vain, so she'll have something pretty.'

'You can borrow some of my jewellery,' Costanza volunteered, suddenly feeling sorry for her.

'Really?' Floriana's eyes widened.

'Let's have a look.' She hurried to her dressing table and opened her jewellery box. 'These were my grandmother's,' she said, withdrawing a pair of diamond earrings.

Floriana gasped. 'They're exquisite.'

'Put them on.'

'I couldn't wear those.'

'Why not?'

'Your mother will have a fit.'

'She won't know until it's too late. Anyway, why would you care what my mother thinks? Here, put them on.'

Floriana clipped them onto her lobes. She pulled out the stool in front of the dressing table and sat down, then looked at her reflection with wonder. The white diamonds shone like icicles against her brown skin.

'See how they light up your face?'

'They're beautiful,' Floriana sighed, pulling her hair away from her neck. 'I love the way they catch the light and twinkle like stars.'

'Then borrow them.'

'Oh, I couldn't. They're too valuable.'

'Please, it would give me pleasure to see you in them.'

'I feel like someone else – an impostor.'

'But you look like a princess.'

Floriana stared at her reflection, her heart expanding with a sudden longing for something she could never be.

'My mother has a big jewellery box of gems, all inherited from my grandmother,' Costanza continued. 'I'm going to inherit them all one day.'

'You're very lucky.'

'I know. But that's all I'm going to inherit. Papà lost a fortune and still hasn't managed to make it back. Mamma hopes I'll marry money, then we'll be rich again.'

'I'm sure you will,' Floriana said vaguely, gazing dreamily at the diamonds.

Costanza flinched as they heard the front door slam downstairs. Floriana snapped out of her trance. 'Is that your mother?'

'It can't be.'

'You said she had gone out for the day.'

'She has.'

Floriana hastily pulled off the earrings and placed them on the dressing table. 'Well, if she catches me here, so what? What's the worst she can do? I'm certainly not going to steal out of the window like a thief.'

Costanza wrung her hands anxiously. 'You're my friend and that's that,' she said, trying to be brave.

They heard steps on the stairs, then the countess's familiar voice. 'Costanza!'

Costanza threw her friend a helpless look. 'I'm in my bedroom, Mamma.'

The door opened and the countess peered in. When she saw Floriana her initial reaction was one of horror, but she swiftly composed herself and forced a saccharine smile. 'Hello, Floriana,' she said tightly. 'What are you two up to?'

'I'm trying on dresses for the party.'

Her mother scrutinized her daughter. Distracted by her ambition she strode over to get a better look. 'I like the blue on you,' she said, grabbing the skirt and pulling it down. 'Though, it's a little tight.'

Costanza sighed. 'I'm holding my stomach in.'

'Not enough,' replied the countess briskly. 'Too much pasta, my dear.'

'I could wear the white.'

'And look like a meringue?'

Costanza's exuberance deflated like a balloon. 'What shall I wear, then?'

'You shall wear this one, but Graziella will let it out for you.' She noticed the diamond earrings on the dressing table and guessed that Floriana had been trying them on. She inhaled through dilated nostrils. 'And you can wear these,' she said. 'Floriana, the earrings, please.'

Floriana suffered a stab of disappointment. She lifted them carefully and dropped them into the outstretched hand.

'I was going to lend them to Floriana,' Costanza exclaimed without thinking.

'To Floriana? Whatever for?'

'For the party.'

The countess gave a little snort. 'My darling, Floriana isn't going to the party.'

Floriana's anger mounted. 'I *am* going to the party,' she interjected firmly.

'Oh, I'm so sorry, my mistake. I didn't know you'd received an invitation.'

Floriana flushed. 'An invitation?'

'Yes, you can only go to the party if you have an invitation.'

'You have one, don't you?' Costanza asked as her mother clipped the earrings onto her lobes.

'There, that's better. Nothing like diamonds to lift a frock.'

She smiled at her daughter. 'You look quite lovely, Costanza. You'll be the belle of the ball.'

Floriana felt dizzy with mortification. 'No, I don't have an invitation,' she replied quietly, and to her fury her eyes began to sting with tears.

'She can come with us, can't she?' said Costanza.

'I wish she could, darling, but if she hasn't been formally invited it would be rude.'

'But Signora Bonfanti adores her.'

The countess shrugged. 'I'm sorry, Floriana. What a disappointment. Still, it's only a party.'

Costanza bit her lip. She wanted to wrap her arms around her friend, but her mother stood between them.

Floriana drew back her shoulders and lifted her chin. 'You're right,' she said. 'It's only a party. And you, Costanza, are going to shine brighter than the brightest star.' She was damned if she was going to let the countess see her cry. 'I should go now.' There was an awkward silence as she stood up to leave.

'You don't have to,' said Costanza at last, bravely defying her mother.

The countess pulled a sympathetic smile, but it was void of any real feeling. 'She's very strong,' she said as Floriana closed the door behind her.

'Why haven't they invited her?'

'Because she's not of our world, darling.'

'Does it really matter so very much?'

The countess placed her hands on her daughter's shoulders and fixed her with eyes as cold as gun metal. 'Listen to me, Costanza. It matters more than you can imagine. You are from a good family, don't ever forget that. Money comes and goes but you'll always be an Aldorisio. Floriana is a nothing, a no one. She'll marry one of her kind and you'll forget you were ever friends. But you, my love, will marry one of *your* kind –

or at least a man worthy of you in terms of wealth. Life is tough. It will roll over you if you're not nimble enough to jump on top of it.'

Costanza nodded, but her eyes slid to the door.

Her mother pulled her by the chin. 'Look at me, Costanza, and tell me that you understand.'

'I understand,' she replied.

'Good. Now, diamond earrings, yes, they're very pretty, but I think we can do better. Come with me, I have far more beautiful diamonds in *my* jewellery box.' She tossed the earrings onto the dressing table.

Floriana ran down the hill, tears tumbling over her cheeks, a sob caught in her chest. It was only when she reached the beach that she let it out with a loud wail. She sat on the sand and hugged her knees to her chest, rocking back and forth. How could it be that she hadn't been sent an invitation? She thought Signora Bonfanti liked her, but she was just like the countess after all, dismissing her like a stray dog. She took a deep breath and gazed out over the sea. Somewhere, in the mist where the water met the sky, was Heaven. It was there that Jesus lived, in a palace of marble, too far away to hear her prayers.

Suddenly, a cold, wet nose pressed itself under her elbow. It was Good-Night. With a rush of affection she wrapped her arms around him and cried into his fur. He seemed to understand and leaned against her, sniffing her skin with his prickly muzzle. After a while she felt a little better. With Good-Night to give her strength she realized that it didn't really matter whether or not she went to the party. It was, after all, only one night. Dante would be down for the whole summer. She'd have ample opportunity to see him. And anyway, he'd probably be so busy talking to all his parents' friends that he wouldn't have time to talk to her.

'I'm still going to marry him,' she told Good-Night, drying her face on his ear. 'Then I'll officially be your mother.'

The countess ran herself a bath. Graziella had closed the shutters and drawn the curtains. She undressed and slipped into a silk dressing gown. It was old and a little stained on one sleeve, but she didn't have the money to buy another one. She couldn't afford that sort of extravagance. But, if she was cunning, Costanza would marry well and she'd be able to afford the very best of everything again.

She looked around her bedroom, at the peeling plaster, the watermark in one corner where the rain had come in through a broken tile, the general shabbiness of the place. If she started to renovate the villa, she'd never stop. It needed so much work. Her husband was making money, but not enough to restore them to their former glory. At least they still had the *appearance* of grandeur – and their illustrious name.

She walked over to her chest of drawers. It was an antique, bought in Paris in the early days of their marriage, placed in the master bedroom in their palazzo in Rome. She sighed as she remembered the palazzo in Via del Corso. What a prestigious house that had been and how very fitting to live there. It grieved her greatly to recall the week they had packed up and left. Dark, dark days indeed. She opened the top drawer and pulled out a stiff white envelope. The words had been written in the finest calligraphy: 'Signorina Floriana'.

She didn't feel bad. It was the right thing to do. When Signora Bonfanti had given it to her to pass on to Floriana, the countess had seized her opportunity. It was for the best. Why give the girl a taste of a world she was never going to be able to live in? Surely that was crueller? It would only raise her expectations. She replaced the invitation and closed the drawer. It was for the child's own good.

Chapter 22

The day of the party dawned. A perfect June morning to herald the return from America of Beppe's only son and heir, who had graduated from one of the finest universities in the world, studied for a master's degree and then learned the ropes of business with associates of his father's based in Chicago. The sky dazzled a sapphire blue and the sun poured her golden light over the magnificent yellow villa where an efficient army of staff bustled about importantly, putting the finishing touches to the preparations.

A midnight-blue canopy had been constructed at the end of the formal garden behind the villa, where two hundred guests would sit down to eat, listen to speeches and dance until sunrise. It was designed to light up after dark with a thousand twinkling stars. Inside, the tables were draped in deep blue cloths with antique silver cutlery and crystal glasses brought up from the cellars beneath the house. Extravagant displays of rare blue orchids were placed in the centre of each table in case anyone was in any doubt about the wealth and prestige of Beppe Bonfanti.

Outside, gardeners clipped the topiary and combed the borders for weeds that might have been overlooked. The stone steps descending from the villa were swept for the final time and lined with tea lights in midnight-blue tumblers. The effect was ravishing. Signora Bonfanti gave the garden one final touch of magic by placing the peacock beside the fountain, hoping that once guests arrived, he might open his tail and dazzle everyone with his beauty.

Floriana lay in bed, hiding her face beneath the sheet. As much as she had tried to convince herself that she didn't care whether or not she went to the party, she still wanted it all to be over and her disappointment to be gone. Her father slept on in the room next door, having drunk too much the previous night. She could smell the alcohol through the wall.

He was completely useless now, so crippled by his addiction that even the count had stopped employing him. If it wasn't for Aunt Zita and the money she reluctantly gave them from time to time, they would be forced to beg for help. Floriana managed to work here and there, helping in the kitchens of the restaurants on Piazza Laconda after school. Everyone knew her situation and was eager to help. Only her father, Elio, seemed not to want to help at all and took her money without a word of thanks, as if it were his due.

But Floriana knew she couldn't stay in bed all day. That was defeatist, and one thing she wasn't was defeatist. She washed and dressed, slipping into a simple cotton dress and tying her hair back with a band. Signora Bruno was outside in the courtyard, arguing with one of the other residents about the overwatering of his geraniums. When she saw Floriana's dejected expression she waved him away and shuffled over to meet her.

'What's that face for?'

'It's the party tonight,' Floriana said, slowly descending the staircase. She didn't need to say more, Signora Bruno had been there to comfort her after the countess had told her she wasn't invited.

The old woman put a sturdy hand in the small of her back and gave it a firm rub, everything ached nowadays. 'Curse the lot of them,' she scowled. 'You're too good for them.'

'*They* don't think so.'

'They don't know.'

'I wonder if Dante even remembers me.'

'Of course he does, *amore*. You're a young lady now, and so pretty he won't believe his eyes when he sees you.'

'I love him more each day,' she said and her gloom lifted at the thought of his smile and the tender way he looked at her. 'One day, I'm going to marry him and have a big party.' She grinned mischievously. 'I'll invite the countess, though.'

'Now, why would you do that?'

'To see her face and watch her squirm as I walk down that beautiful stone staircase in a flowing white dress.'

'You'd better get on with it, then, for I want to be there at the bottom to watch you.'

'Of course you'll be there, Signora Bruno. It wouldn't be a party without you.'

Signora Bruno chuckled. 'Don't leave it too long, I'm wearing thin.'

'Not *thin*, *signora*,' Floriana teased.

'Well, not thin, no – but I'm wearing out.'

'I won't tell Elio, though.'

'Wouldn't he give you away?'

She looked at Signora Bruno solemnly. 'I have to belong to him first for him to give me away.'

'Oh, Floriana.'

'I don't belong to anyone but Dante.'

'I hope he's deserving of you.'

'We deserve each other, Signora Bruno.'

'So, what are you going to do today?'

'I'm going to pretend it's any other day. I'm going to go to Mass and light my candle, just in case Jesus has decided to tune in. Then I'm going to spend the day with Aunt Zita at the laundry.'

'Really, that ludicrous woman. She's only ever done the

minimum for you. She should be ashamed of herself.' Signora Bruno had no patience for Zita.

'The busier I am, the faster the day will go.'

'You're not going to spy on that wall, then?'

'No.'

'Or go and see the little princess?'

'Costanza? No. I couldn't bear to watch her in those beautiful diamonds.'

The day passed slowly. Floriana knew that Dante must be home because Good-Night did not come to find her. She missed his eager face and gentle presence but she was pleased he was with his master and excited at the thought that soon she would be with him, too. She spent the day with Aunt Zita, who knew nothing of the party or her niece's love for Dante, and twittered on about the hopeless Elio and his lack of responsibility. Then Floriana wandered down to the beach to watch the sunset.

Costanza dressed alone in her bedroom. Graziella had let out her frock and it now fitted her perfectly. She still looked fat, but her breasts distracted from her convex waist and wide hips. Her mother had lent her a diamond necklace with matching bracelet and earrings worthy of royalty. She felt every inch a princess. However, alone in her room her thrill was dampened by the thought of Floriana. It would have been much more fun dressing together, sharing make-up and jewellery.

It seemed inconceivable that Signora Bonfanti would have forgotten to invite Floriana. But when Costanza thought about it long and hard, she remembered how Signor Beppe had ignored her, treating her with no more courtesy than the stray animals that wandered around the gardens. Perhaps she had been nothing more than a pet for Dante's mother, too – someone she could use for company and entertainment, but not for public display. Her mother was right: Floriana really wasn't accepted in their world. Once that thought would have afforded her pleasure, but now she felt only compassion and an unfamiliar sense of guilt.

The countess was thrilled by her daughter's appearance. The diamonds were impressive and the dress no longer pulled around the waist and hips. She'd have to supervise her diet in future. She was getting too grown-up now to get away with being fat.

The count returned from work. He showered and dressed, then the three of them departed for La Magdalena in a car driven by one of the boys from the office.

They approached the big, black gates of the villa behind a line of other grand cars: Alfa Romeos, Ferraris and Savoy-blue Lancias. Security guards stopped each driver, requesting to see both invitation and identification. One could never be too sure and Beppe Bonfanti was a man of caution when it came to his personal safety. The air was charged with anticipation and Costanza gazed out of the window excitedly. The countess commented on the magnificence of the drive lined with blazing flares, and the splendour of the yellow mansion at the end, and secretly envisaged her daughter residing there as mistress of it all.

They were dropped off at the front and taken through the marble hall and drawing room to the terrace where Beppe and his wife stood side by side greeting each guest. They took their places in the queue, their eyes drawn to the garden below, with its flamboyant fountain, and beyond, where the canopy stood ready for the banquet. Costanza recognized Michelangelo the peacock, wandering around aimlessly, dragging his tail on the ground, and felt her stomach churn with nerves because she didn't have Floriana to hide behind.

'Violetta,' gushed the countess at last.

Violetta Bonfanti took her hand and smiled serenely. 'It's so lovely to see you.'

'What a beautiful tent.'

'Yes, it's like a fairy tale. Costanza, my dear,' and she took the girl's hand and smiled in the same distracted manner.

Beppe shook the count's hand vigorously. 'No expense spared for my son,' he said, puffing out his chest, keen to show off his wealth to the aristocrat.

'I can see,' replied the count, finding it all highly ostentatious. 'It's magnificent.'

Beppe turned his eyes onto Costanza. 'You look radiant, my dear.'

'Thank you, Signor Bonfanti,' she replied timidly.

He chuckled. 'I think you know me well enough now to call me Beppe. I'm Beppe to my friends, no?'

The Aldorisios descended the sweeping staircase into the garden. The place was filling up with people, saturating the air with perfume and cigarette smoke. A quartet played classical music and guests greeted each other and talked, sipping pink Dom Perignon out of tall, crystal flutes.

Costanza was relieved when Giovanna found her and they fell on each other with excitement. Giovanna was a young woman now, being almost eighteen. Her curvaceous body glittered in a green Dior gown and her neck sparkled with emeralds.

'I have so much to tell you,' she said, pulling Costanza away by the hand. 'Come, let's go somewhere quiet where we can talk.'

The countess swelled with pride as she watched the two girls weave through the throng, hand in hand. This is what she had always wanted. She sighed happily and surveyed the glamour of her surroundings. This was where she belonged, among people of her own sort. Although the Bonfantis and some of their friends were rather vulgar, their wealth excused any lack of good taste. And there were enough aristocrats present for her to feel she was in the right company. She smiled contentedly and sipped her champagne. It was as if she had come home after a long exile.

'Shall we plunge in?' she asked her husband.

'I think that's a very good idea,' he agreed, giving her his arm. 'Ah, isn't that Conte Edmondo di Montezzemolo . . .?'

At last the guests were silenced. Beppe took his position at the top of the stone staircase. He smiled on the garden below like an emperor greeting his people. Then he held out his arms and in a very loud voice announced the arrival of his son. 'My friends, it gives me great pleasure to present to you my son, Dante Alberto Massimo Bonfanti, graduated with Honours from Harvard, America's finest university.'

There was a round of applause and Dante stepped out of the villa to embrace his father. Beppe patted him heartily, then kissed him on both cheeks. 'My son!' he bellowed, and the two men stood together, with their arms around each other, waving at their audience.

Floriana wandered down the beach, shoes in hand, feet in the water. She imagined Costanza at the party and gave in to a wave of resentment. How unfair that she was excluded just because she didn't have rich parents, or a grand title. Why couldn't a person be judged on what was on the inside? Why did it matter so much where she came from? Weren't they all God's children, equal in His eyes? Didn't she have just as much right to live and love as anyone? She watched the sun melt into the sea and turn it orange. The beauty was overwhelming and she stood in awe, watching the light fade to make way for the first star. Beneath so vast a sky she felt very small, and yet, weren't they all small when viewed from God's great height? Titles and wealth seemed so unimportant compared with the natural riches of God's creation. What mattered was the heart, for surely that was the only thing she'd take with her when she died.

As the day evaporated she felt her determination mount. It

was up to her to shape her own destiny, rather than allowing others to decide what shape it should be. With her resolve renewed, she put on her sandals and strode back up the beach.

Dante made his way through the crowd of guests, shaking hands with the men, standing firm as they patted him robustly on the back, and bending down to kiss the women. He enchanted them with his natural charm and wit. He had grown into a strikingly handsome young man. With his shoulders back, his head held high, his pale gaze clear and steady, he looked every inch a crown prince. Yet, there was no trace of arrogance in his expression. A sardonic amusement, perhaps, in the curl of his lips as if he thought the whole event slightly farcical, but he was too polite and aware of the trouble his mother had taken to let it show.

Five years in America had taught him a great deal about the world, but also about himself. He was smart, quick to learn and made friends easily. Girls fancied him – but he found to his cost that as simple as it was to get attached, getting *un*attached was a painful and complex operation. So, he had enjoyed countless flings where there was no danger of commitment. There had been enough women on campus who simply wanted to bed him, so he'd taken his pleasure, then moved on to the next.

He'd hung out with a group of boys who enjoyed sport like he did, learning American football and baseball, as well as excelling on the tennis and squash courts. He'd relished the novelty of living in another country. However, there was a part of him that had always been dissatisfied. An anxiety, like homesickness, that caught him when he was most vulnerable, like on waking in the morning, or sometimes when he was alone and pensive. As much as he tried, he couldn't identify it. He knew for certain it had nothing to do with his parents, and he didn't miss his home. But when his mind wandered to La

Magdalena he had suffered an aching sense of loss. Now he was there, he wondered whether that feeling would creep over him again, or whether his soul was finally satisfied.

Dinner was served beneath the canopy of stars. Dante sat beside two young women who flirted and twittered like a pair of pretty budgerigars. The countess noticed that Costanza was on a table at the other end of the room from Dante, with a group of youngsters her own age. She resolved to draw her to his attention after dinner. Her placement, however, pleased her very much, for she was on the next table to Beppe, with his cousin on one side and a very close family friend on the other. She sipped her wine and savoured the moment, feeling a warm sense of belonging.

After dinner Beppe gave a long and pompous speech, another sign of his lack of respectability, the countess thought smugly. Not that it mattered. The guests laughed at his jokes and clapped loudly when he had finished. Wealth glossed over his flaws as surely as her mother-in-law's diamonds glossed over the Aldorisios'. Glasses were raised, toasts were given, Dante stood up and gave a witty, self-deprecating speech, which made everyone love him more. The girls secretly hoped to win him, the mothers planned their strategies like colonels.

Costanza thought of Floriana and her impossible dream. If she could see him now she would realize how ridiculous she was to harbour hopes of capturing his heart. A man like Dante would never notice a local girl like her.

The countess watched the other mothers of young daughters with a growing sense of competitiveness. There were some extremely lovely girls in her midst, slimmer and more beautiful than Costanza. She would have to assert more control over her diet if there was to be any hope of fulfilling her dream. As soon as the opportunity arose, the countess took Costanza by the hand and almost dragged her to the other end of the garden, where Dante was talking to a small group of attractive young people. He recognized Costanza immediately and broke away from his friends to greet her.

'You've grown up,' he laughed, kissing her cheek. 'Where's your crazy little friend?'

The countess bristled. 'Hello, Dante, what a divine party.'

'I'm glad you could come, Contessa.' He took her hand and kissed it formally.

'Costanza has been seeing a great deal of your sister Giovanna,' she continued. 'They're intimate friends, aren't you, darling? They write to each other all winter when Giovanna's at school in Milan.'

'Is Floriana here?' He raised his eyes and swept them over the guests, who now mingled in the candlelit garden.

Costanza hesitated, knowing her mother would not want her to speak of Floriana. 'No, she isn't,' she said carefully.

Dante was surprised by the force of his disappointment.

'I don't know what she's up to these days,' the countess continued with a smile. 'Dear little local girl. You know how things are, all very well playing with those sort of people when one's little, but now Costanza is a young lady it's only right that she mixes with her own sort.' She gave a little sniff.

'I see,' said Dante. 'Well, it's good of you to come. I hope you enjoy the rest of the party.' And he went back to join his friends. However, his thoughts were drawn away from their conversation to the point in the wall where Floriana used to climb up and spy.

Struck by the silliest idea, he strode into the house to get Good-Night. The dog was lying asleep in the kitchen. He whistled for him, and Good-Night, always eager to be part of an adventure, trotted happily into the park at his side. The music had started and guests were beginning to move onto the dance floor. Some wandered around the gardens, others sat at tables and chairs now placed on the terrace, to drink coffee and talk where it was quieter. The sky was bright with stars, the moon bathing the earth in a soft, silver light. Dante was tired of talking to endless people, bored of having to play the role of hero when he felt he had done nothing that hadn't been done by so many others, a million times before. But his father liked to make a fuss. He enjoyed the fanfare and relished any excuse to beat his chest and show everyone how rich and important he was. He expected a great deal from his son, but most of all he wanted to be a proud father, because to Beppe, face was everything – hadn't he earned it? Every lira?

As he approached the wall Dante's stomach began to twist with anxiety. The ghost of the little girl danced before his eyes, silhouetted against the night. He felt his throat tighten and wondered why he felt such a crippling sense of loss.

Distracted by something at the wall, Good-Night bounded off. Dante saw a shadow move, like a cat catching the light before jumping lithely down. But it wasn't a cat. As he got nearer, he saw that it was a beautiful young woman.

'Floriana? Is that you?'

'Dante,' she said in a low voice. Good-Night rushed at her excitedly. She laughed and ran her hands over his ears.

Dante watched in astonishment as she bent down to caress the dog as if she wasn't at all surprised to see him. For a moment he was too stunned to speak. 'He's happy to see you,' he said at last.

'He's always happy to see me. He's my dearest friend.'

'So, you did look after him while I was away?'

'Of course, we're almost inseparable.' She grinned up at him and he was struck by how lovely she looked in the moonlight. 'I knew you were back today because he didn't come to see me.'

'So he runs off to find you, does he?'

'He's very clever.'

'Because he's a stray. They're more streetwise than those who are raised at home.'

He watched her closely as she stood up and smoothed down her dress. Her body had lost the straight lines of girlhood and expanded into gentle curves. He was surprised to see that she had breasts and a little waist. Five years had transformed the grubby child into an arresting young woman and he felt his heart inflate with wonder.

'Have you tired of your party already?' she asked, and the twinkle in her eyes was so familiar to him.

'I sensed we were being spied on. I came to check our defences.'

'You remembered the weak spot in the wall, then?'

'And the insurgent who knows how to climb in.'

'So what do you do when you catch one of these insurgents?'

He rubbed his chin and considered his answer. 'I take her prisoner.'

Floriana's heart thumped against her ribcage. 'I think she's more cunning than you give her credit for.'

'I suppose you may be right. If she's a stray like Good-Night, then she'll most certainly out-wit a home boy like me.'

She laughed. 'What if the insurgent agrees to call a temporary truce?'

'You mean, put down her weapon and enter into peaceful talks?'

'Yes, that sort of thing. Only temporary, of course.'

'I think that can be arranged. Perhaps we had better walk on neutral ground.'

He jumped onto the wall and reached out his hand. She took it and let him pull her onto the top. Touching him felt like the most natural thing in the world, as if they had been familiar with each other's skin for ever, and she felt her spirits expand with happiness that they were finally reunited, as God had so clearly intended.

Once on the other side, they began to stroll up the track,

side by side, Good-Night at their heels. There was a strange intimacy between them, as if they knew each other so well they didn't need to talk.

'Did you miss me?' he asked, sensing, as she did, that he was being carried along by a strong current.

'Yes,' she replied. There was no point hiding the truth. 'Did you miss *me*?'

He paused and took her hand. 'I didn't think I did,' he said, surprised by a sudden rush of tenderness. 'But now I realize that I did. You have no idea how much.'

Chapter 23

Floriana knew now that those five years of waiting had not been in vain. Nothing could keep them apart, because the superior forces of Fate would always draw them back together again, as inevitably as the pull of gravity. It no longer mattered that she hadn't been invited to the party, because Dante had sought her out in the one place he knew where to find her.

They ambled slowly up the track, hand in hand, closing the gap that those five years had opened. Then they sat on the rocks overlooking the ocean and the moon lit a path across the water all the way to Heaven. Floriana thought the night had never been more beautiful. The stars were clearer than ever before, twinkling like shiny new memories, and the breeze was warm and sweet with the scent of pine.

'I didn't expect to find a woman at the wall,' Dante confessed, sweeping his eyes over her features.

'What did you think, after five years?'

'That you'd be the same little girl lost, with knotted hair and big, frightened eyes.'

'I was never frightened,' she laughed, nudging him playfully.

'Yes, you were. You just knew how to hide it.'

She shrugged. 'I can't allow myself the luxury of fear, Dante.'

He put his arm around her, drawing her against him. 'I'll never forget the first time I saw you at the gates. You were like a little prisoner, all grubby and dishevelled, gazing through the bars at freedom. I'd taken the gardens for granted until I saw them through your eyes. Everything touched you and you gazed in wonder at the simplest, most overlooked things, like the birds in the trees, or the water whooshing out of the fountain. And now, you're a young woman, a *beautiful* young woman, but inside you're still the same little girl lost, and I want to take care of you.'

He took her face in his hand. He had spent the last five years adrift, not knowing the reason for his disquiet, like a sailor so busy navigating the sea that he cannot hear the small voice calling him home. Looking into her eyes, he knew that voice had been Floriana's all along and that now he was with her, he was home where he belonged.

Slowly, he bent his head and brushed her lips with his. She closed her eyes and shut out the world, her senses aware only of the warm sensation of his mouth parting her lips and kissing her deeply. Every nerve tingled with the novelty of his touch and the naked intimacy of his kiss, and she gave herself to him joyfully. Dante wrapped his arms around her and held her fiercely, determined to cherish and love her as no one else had ever done.

The countess was disappointed that Dante had dismissed them so swiftly. She had hoped that he and Costanza would have more to talk about. But he had mentioned Floriana and from that moment on, an air of distraction had blown him out of their reach. Her one consolation was the sight of her daughter and Giovanna sitting by the fountain, heads close together as they giggled and shared secrets. *That* was a friendship time would only make stronger. If her daughter didn't manage to win the heart of Dante, she would win the heart of another like him, for with Giovanna she would be sure to meet the very best society had to offer.

The count looked at his watch and saw that it was past two o'clock, time to gather his family together and go home. The countess was ready to leave. She had talked to everyone she felt might be useful to her and made some important new friends.

Costanza was not ready to go. She had just been invited to dance by a shy young man with thick brown hair and glasses, and had drunk enough champagne to give herself the confidence to accept. Reluctantly, she followed her parents to the front of the villa where their car waited on the gravel, the young chauffeur fast asleep in his seat. They weren't the only ones leaving. Most of the adults were sweeping off in their big, shiny motors, leaving the young to dance until sunrise.

Costanza stared out of the window, feeling strangely melancholic. The night had been magical and now it was over. She had never had such an enchanted evening in her life and she was sorry that it had come to an end. Dazzling in diamonds, she had felt beautiful for the first time. Without Floriana at her side to eclipse her, she had found she had a light of her own and the confidence to shine. Giovanna had introduced her to all her friends and she had felt part of the group and no less rich or glamorous; she had looked and felt every inch one of them.

Her mother was right. Floriana didn't belong there, and Costanza knew that if she was to secure the future her mother wished for her, she would have to let Floriana go.

The countess noticed Costanza had gone very quiet. 'Did you enjoy the party, darling?'

'I loved it, Mamma. I wish it hadn't finished.'

'All good things come to an end,' said her father.

'And because of it good things will start. You'll see,' added her mother, determinedly.

'Do you think so?'

'Of course, my dear. I have taken all the important telephone numbers. I'll make sure that you are invited to all the
grand houses in Tuscany.'

'Out with the old, in with the new,' said the count, thinking of the new contacts he had made and the business
opportunities they might give him.

'I think this summer is going to be very special, darling. A
turning point for you now that you're a young lady.'

'I felt I belonged tonight.'

'And, darling, you *did* belong. I watched you and Giovanna
and thought how very like sisters you are.'

'She's my best friend.'

'Indeed she is, and I can't think of a nicer friend for you.'
Floriana's name rested unspoken on both their lips.

Dawn was seeping into the sky when Dante and Good-Night
walked Floriana back to her home on Via Roma. The stars
were beginning to fade, the moon now as pale as a spectre.
The town was slowly waking, the odd Cinquecento rattling
over the cobbles, dogs gathering outside the *panetteria* that
smelled of freshly baked bread.

'So, this is where you live,' he said, stopping in front of the
portone – the big wooden door that once opened to cars, but
now remained firmly bolted. Floriana hesitated by the
smaller door cut into it. She did not want him to come in
and see the simplicity of her apartment, nor her inebriated
father.

'This is it,' she replied. 'Signora Bruno doesn't like visitors.'

'You need to get some rest.' He ran his thumb over her
cheek. 'I'm glad I found you, Floriana.' He kissed her again,
not wanting to let her go, drunk on love.

'I must go,' she said, aware that her father could come weav-
ing down the street at any moment.

'Come to La Magdalena today.'

'Perhaps.'

'Good-Night will want to see you. And so will I.'

'Then I'll come with Costanza.'

She slipped in and closed the door behind her, leaning against it and shutting her eyes to hold onto the magic.

'So, you went to the party after all,' came a low voice from the stairs. It was Signora Bruno in her dressing gown, her wide feet squeezed into slippers. 'You look like you've just been kissed by a prince.'

'What are you doing up at this hour?'

'I'm always up. I find it hard to sleep in the heat.'

Floriana ambled over, her hips swinging playfully. 'I *have* been kissed by a prince,' she laughed.

Signora Bruno forgot all about her insomnia. 'The devil strike me down,' she exclaimed. 'Little Floriana, of all people!'

'I didn't go to the party. I spied from the wall and he found me.'

'He must have been looking for you.'

'I think he was.'

Signora Bruno chuckled. 'Well, that'll teach them.'

'Our love is too strong to keep us apart.'

'So, tell me. What does he look like?'

Floriana sat down on the step below. 'He's tall and fair-skinned with pale green eyes, the colour of a tropical sea.'

'Well, you must be in love if you see his eyes like that.'

'But I love his mouth the best, the way it curls at the corners, and when he smiles it's so wide, showing all his teeth.'

'So, you've just enjoyed your first kiss.' Floriana blushed and touched her lips with her fingertips. 'I remember my first kiss. It was the nicest kiss I've ever been given. If I could put it in a box and take it out now and then I'm sure I'd sleep better. It's never like that again, you know. Innocence once lost is lost for ever. Enjoy it while it lasts.'

'You're an old cynic.'

'Perhaps, but a wise cynic. After you make love he'll never bother to kiss you like that again, for hours and hours. It turns into something else and kissing is no longer the goal, but the means to an end – and in my experience men usually prefer to skip that bit altogether and jump right to the end as fast as possible. Mind you play hard to get.'

'He's already got me.'

'No, he hasn't. Don't go giving in too easily. A man like that might suppose a girl like you is something she's not.'

Floriana was appalled. 'I'll be a virgin on my wedding day, if that's what you mean.'

'Well, of course you will. Still, this is the time you need a mother to tell you the story of the stork.'

'But I have you, Signora Bruno.'

'I knew there must be some purpose to my life. If I wasn't intended to marry a prince myself, I was charged with making sure you do.'

'When I marry him you're going to come and live with me at La Magdalena.'

'Oh, good. I'll die happy.' She pushed herself up with a groan. 'Right, the day is beginning. I can't sit around in my dressing gown all morning. There are things to be done – and that *cretino* has overwatered his geraniums again.' She clicked her tongue.

Floriana lay on her bed fully clothed, but she was too excited to sleep. She replayed the night over and over, dwelling on the kiss and closing her eyes to relive it. Dante was back and he loved her; nothing in the world mattered any more. She could hear her father snoring in the room next door. What a useless, selfish man he was. She longed to have a father who loved her, with whom she could share her innermost thoughts and wishes. A father she could be proud of. But nothing would convince her to introduce Elio to Dante.

*

Dante appeared for breakfast on the terrace where a round table had been set up in the shade. His mother was sipping coffee in a wide sunhat, her pale skin shiny with moisturizer, eyes hidden behind big sunglasses. Giovanna sat sleepily, nibbling toast while Damiana drank coffee and ate a bowl of fruit. Beppe presided over the table like a king, surveying the remains of the party from the lofty height of the terrace.

Already the team was back to dismantle the tent and take away the tables and chairs – and the guest who had fallen asleep in the corner. By evening the gardens would be restored to their former perfection and the view of the park once again unbroken.

'Ah, my son,' exclaimed Beppe. 'Come and sit beside me and tell me what you thought of your party.'

A butler pulled out his chair. Dante sat down and asked for a black coffee. 'I had a blast, Papà.'

His father beamed proudly. 'Good boy. No one throws a party like I do. Any girls worth mentioning?'

Dante hesitated. The one girl he wanted to mention was unmentionable. 'Many.'

Beppe patted his son's back. 'That's my boy. Many.' The butler poured Dante a cup of coffee just as breakfast was interrupted by a telephone call. Beppe disappeared off to take it in his study.

'So, girls, how was it for you?' Dante asked.

'It was magical,' said Damiana, brightening up now her father had left the table.

'It was the best night I've ever had in my life,' enthused Giovanna.

'I saw Costanza was here,' said Dante carefully. 'She's grown up, hasn't she?'

'But little Floriana didn't come,' his mother interjected mournfully. 'I can't say I wasn't disappointed.'

Dante was surprised. 'You invited her?'

'Why shouldn't I? Really, Dante, you're as bad as your father. She's adorable and I'm extremely fond of her.'

'Do you know where she lives?'

'So, she lives in a modest house in Herba – why should that make a difference? In fact, I don't know where she lives so I gave her invitation to Costanza's mother.'

It didn't take Dante long to work out what had happened. 'I doubt that woman ever gave it to her.'

Violetta took off her glasses. 'What are you suggesting?'

'That she's a terrible snob.'

'You really think she would be capable of such unkindness?'

'Absolutely.'

Violetta's face relaxed into a smile. 'I do hope there is some mistake, but not misconduct. I thought it odd that Floriana didn't come.'

'She would have loved to come,' Damiana reassured her. 'She adores it here and she adores you, Mamma. You're the mother she has never had.'

'I'm sure Costanza's mother wouldn't have done it on purpose,' said Giovanna. 'Perhaps she just forgot or mislaid it.'

'Perhaps,' said Violetta, draining her coffee cup. 'Anyway, I shan't ask her. I'm sure it's an innocent mistake. But I will tell Floriana that she wasn't excluded. If she didn't get the invitation she will be hurt that she wasn't invited. Will she be coming today with Costanza?'

'I don't know,' Giovanna replied. 'I asked Costanza and she said nothing about Floriana'

'I'm sure she will,' said Damiana. 'They usually come together, don't they?'

Dante sat quietly, letting the women discuss the likelihood of Floriana turning up to swim, knowing for sure that she would. He wondered what his parents would think of him courting her. His mother adored her, but would she consider her good enough for her only son?

He watched her across the table. Violetta was from a middle-class family in Venice. Dreamy and idealistic, she was a woman who loved nature and animals like he did, and considered all creatures equal in God's eyes. How extraordinary that she had chosen to marry Beppe, a man who had left his working-class home in Turin and built a fortune in Milan, making packaging for food and liquids.

They were opposites: one strong, the other fragile; one ambitious, the other unmoved by ambition; one loud and pompous, the other quiet and unassuming. For Beppe, reputation and social standing were all important; for Violetta it was only the heart that mattered. It was all very well having ideals, accepting people for their natures, not for their credentials, but when tested, would she be able to live by them? For the time being Floriana would have to be a secret Dante kept to himself.

After breakfast Dante went into the house with the intention of going up to his room, when he bumped into Zazzetta in the hall. The little man smiled – a crooked smile, which revealed a sharp eyetooth that was slightly longer than the others, like a wolf's.

'Good morning, Dante,' he said, giving a barely perceptible bow.

'Zazzetta,' Dante replied. He had never liked his father's fixer. There was something shifty about him.

'Your father wants to see you.'

'Now?'

'If you have nothing better to do.' Dante bristled. Zazzetta knew he had nothing better to do. He cursed under his breath and strode into the study, the black-clad adviser following silently behind.

'Ah, Dante, come in,' said his father, putting down his pen and looking up from the document he was signing. 'Done,

Zazzetta.' He dabbed his signature with a blotter and handed him the paper. Zazzetta placed it carefully in the black leather folder he was carrying and slid away, closing the door behind him.

'Let's talk about your future.' Beppe was not a man to waste time with small talk. 'You have finished your studies and your apprenticeship and made me proud, Dante. I was never given the opportunities you have been given.'

'I know and I'm grateful, Father.'

'You've excelled yourself.' He appraised his son with satisfaction. 'You are everything I have ever wanted in a son. You're handsome, intelligent, athletic and shrewd. You've inherited the best of me and the best of your mother. It's lucky that you haven't inherited her flaws, eh?'

'Her flaws?'

'Don't look so alarmed. No one is perfect. If you had inherited your mother's gentle nature you would be no good to me.'

'Her gentle nature is an advantage in a woman.'

'Indeed. But in a man it is a weakness and there is no room for weakness in the world of business. I didn't make my millions being kind and gentle, but shrewd and formidable. As Machiavelli so brilliantly put it: Fear is the way a man commands respect. So, Dante, you will join me in Milan on the first of September.'

Dante was not surprised by his father's instructions. In fact, he had always known he would be expected to join the family firm. However, he still felt apprehensive, as if a heavy barred door had just closed on his freedom.

'It will be reassuring to know that my son and heir will take over when I retire. I didn't build my fortune to have it passed on to an outsider. So, what do you say?' His father did not anticipate a refusal.

'I'm ready, Father,' Dante replied dutifully.

'*Bravo!* Now, how about a game of tennis, eh? You might be

younger and fitter than me, but I have the cunning of an old fox.'

They played a set on the rich red sand of the tennis court, assisted by Piero and Mario, the chauffeur's sons, who made very fine ball boys. Halfway through the set, when Dante was winning and about to serve game point, he saw Giovanna walking in the garden with Costanza. His heart inflated at the prospect of seeing Floriana and he served an ace, passing his father on his backhand. Beppe was not a good loser and swore furiously, whacking his racket through the air. The distraction, however, caused Dante's game to decline as he had one eye on the garden, searching for Floriana.

'You see, there's still life in this old dog,' Beppe taunted, as Dante hit another ball into the net. Keen to finish and find Floriana, Dante focused, pulled it together, and finally beat his father 6–4. Beppe was gracious in defeat because there was no shame in that score. He shook hands with his son, patting him firmly on the back. 'I hope you are as impressive in the board-room as you are on the tennis court.'

'I'll do my best,' Dante assured him.

'I'm sure you will.'

Then Beppe noticed Zazzetta slinking through the olive trees towards them. 'What now, Zazzetta?'

Dante left them together, talking in low voices, their heads together like a pair of thieves. He found the girls by the pool, but there was no sign of Floriana. 'I came on my own,' Costanza explained when he asked after her. Dante noticed a new confidence in her deportment, the way she stood with her back straight and her gaze steady.

'Did she not want to come?'

'I don't know. I haven't seen her,' Costanza replied carelessly.

Dante frowned. 'Well, Good-Night wants to see her,' he said, striding off towards the steps built into the rock. If she didn't come on her own, he would go and get her.

Chapter 24

Dante climbed into his silver Alfa Romeo Spider, a present from his father on his return from America. Good-Night jumped onto the back seat and sat, tongue out, ready for another adventure. With the roof down and the wind raking through his damp hair, Dante roared between the cypresses towards the gate. He was astute enough to notice a change in the air around Costanza. It was no coincidence that Floriana hadn't come to the party and wasn't invited with Costanza today. She was being deliberately excluded. Well, he'd show them. He gripped the wheel determinedly and drove down the coast towards Herba. In a few minutes he was driving up the cobbled stones between the ancient buildings, waving at the locals, who stared at the beautiful car in wonder.

He parked right outside Floriana's building on Via Roma and rang the bell. When no one appeared he rang it again. Finally, the doleful voice of an old lady was heard on the other side. 'All right, all right, I'm coming. Be patient.' The door opened and the round face of the woman Dante took to be Signora Bruno squeezed into the crack. When she saw Dante she recognized him at once. His eyes were, indeed, the colour of a tropical sea. She opened the door wide and smiled sweetly.

'I've come for Floriana. Is she here?' His gaze strayed into the courtyard.

'No, she left about half an hour ago.'

'Do you know where she went?'

'I assumed she went to see you.'

Dante's face darkened with frustration. 'I don't suppose she walks up the road.'

'Of course not. She takes the short cut through the poppies.'

'Thank you, *signora*, you've been very helpful.'

'Signora *Bruno*,' she said, introducing herself. 'I'm like a mother to Floriana. Have been ever since Loretta disappeared with the child's little brother.'

Dante was astonished. 'Floriana has a little brother?'

'*Had* a little brother.'

'She never said.'

'Well, she wouldn't. It's too painful, and children have a way of blocking out the nasty things. God only knows what's become of them now.'

'That's unspeakably cruel to choose one child over the other. What sort of woman could do that?'

'A very selfish one. I don't suppose her tomato man wanted an older child. Little Luca was very sweet and Floriana worshipped him.'

'What was the name of the tomato seller?'

Signora Bruno noticed the purposeful glint in his eyes and put a podgy hand on his arm. 'Don't go there, Dante. I know you want to put it all right, but you can't. They are long gone. If Loretta wanted to come back and find her, she could, at any time. She knows where she is. But she doesn't want to, does she? It is better that Floriana forgets about the past and concentrates on her future. She's a bright, determined young woman. It's only a shame that her mother can't see her now, because she'd be very proud of the person Floriana has become, in spite of all the obstacles.'

'She's lucky to have you, *signora*.'

'I know.' She waved away the compliment. 'I'll reap my rewards in Heaven, no doubt about that.'

Dante drove back up the road, his mind full of Loretta's malice and the tomato man who lured her away. He'd give anything to find them. The truth was that he *could* find them. All he had to do was ask Zazzetta and it would be done. He didn't doubt the capability of that shady man. But perhaps Signora Bruno was right. What good would it do? Why rake it up and cause Floriana to feel rejected all over again?

As he drove up the road to the gates of La Magdalena Good-Night began to bark. At first Dante thought he was excited to be home again, but then he saw Floriana's familiar figure walking slowly up the hillside towards the gates. She was wearing a floral sundress, her feet in sandals, her hair loose about her shoulders, carrying a handful of poppies and a small canvas bag. He tooted the horn and she looked up, shielding her eyes against the sun. He waved and tooted again, stopping the car.

Good-Night leaped out and galloped down the slope to meet her, nearly knocking her over as he crashed against her legs.

In a moment Dante was gathering her into his arms and kissing her. 'Where have you been?' he asked, burying his face in her neck.

'I went to find Costanza first.'

'She's already here.'

'I suspected she was.'

He looked into her face. 'Did she not invite you to join her?'

'I don't care. Look at your fancy car!'

'Come for a drive?'

'I'd love to. I bet it goes really fast.'

'If it goes too fast Good-Night might fall out.'

'Darling Good-Night.' She patted him fondly. 'He became my best friend while you were away. Look, he's going grey around the muzzle.'

'He's getting old.'

'But he's still agile and swift.' As if to prove she was right, he trotted up the slope to the car.

Inside it smelled of new leather, warmed by the sun. Good-Night jumped onto the back seat again, wagging his tail expectantly. Floriana slipped into her seat and ran her fingers over the wooden dashboard.

'It's a stunning car, Dante.'

'Father bought it for me.'

'How generous of him.'

Dante grinned cynically. 'Generous, yes. But he sees me as an extension of himself, so it's rather like giving *himself* a new car.' He started the engine. It growled like a lion, then the car sped off up the road, leaving the gates of La Magdalena far behind. Good-Night cowered on the back seat as the car lurched forwards. Floriana laughed above the rumble and threw back her head as the wind seized her hair and tossed it about. After showing off its speed, Dante slowed down so they could talk.

'You were invited to the party last night,' he said solemnly.

'No, I wasn't,' she replied. 'But I don't mind, really.'

'No, you misunderstand me. You *were* invited. Mamma sent you an invitation, but she gave it to the countess.'

Floriana grew serious. 'You mean, there was an invitation for me all along?'

'Yes. I suspect the countess forgot to give it to you.'

'I bet she did,' Floriana replied in a tone that suggested she didn't believe it at all. She turned to look at the passing countryside. 'That woman has never liked me.'

'She's jealous, that's all.'

'She looks down on me. But I'm used to it and I don't care. What harm can she do me?'

'She can't do you any harm at all.' He took her hand across

the gear box. 'You're with me now, Floriana, and no one will ever hurt you again.'

Costanza was surprised when Floriana came down to the pool with Dante. She was suddenly beset with guilt, wishing she hadn't been so fickle and unkind in excluding her.

'Look who I picked up on the road,' said Dante, smiling triumphantly. He wandered into the changing room to put on his swimming shorts.

Costanza hurried over to her, desperate to excuse herself. 'I'm sorry, Floriana,' she said in a low voice. 'I expected you to be here already.'

Floriana tossed off her apology with a shrug. 'How was the party?'

Costanza frowned. 'It was wonderful. I so wish you could have been there.'

'I was invited, you know, but your mother forgot to give me the invitation. Easy mistake.'

'My mother?' Costanza stared at her in disbelief. 'Are you sure?'

'Perfectly. Signora Bonfanti said she gave it to your mother to give me.'

'I don't understand. Then why didn't she give it to you?'

'She obviously didn't want me to come.' Costanza looked horrified and Floriana took her hand to reassure her. 'It's OK, I understand. I'm not from your world, Costanza. I don't blame you, but I won't pretend I like your mother.'

'Do you want me to say something to her?'

'No.'

Costanza was relieved – the thought of confronting her mother terrified her.

'Leave it alone. It doesn't matter any more. What's done is done.' Floriana smiled and Costanza was pleased to see her fighting spirit restored.

'Come swimming. Giovanna and I are seeing how many lengths we can do underwater.'

'How many can you do?'

'One and a half.'

'And Giovanna?'

'Two.'

'So, I will do three.' And Floriana marched off to the changing room to slip into her bathing suit.

Dante dived into the pool and swam a couple of lengths of front crawl. When Floriana emerged in a pale blue swimsuit, Dante stopped swimming and trod water to watch her. She had developed curves in the five years that he had been away. Her waist was narrow, her hips wider, thighs fuller and her breasts were plump and round. She was no longer the child he had said goodbye to, but a girl hovering on the brink of womanhood. He felt the familiar stirring of excitement in his loins and swam over to meet her.

Floriana jumped into the water. When she came up for air Dante was right beside her, grinning broadly. He wanted to gather her into his arms and kiss her wildly, but he restrained himself for they weren't alone. Instead, he whispered his desire into her ear then pulled her underwater again to steal a kiss where no one could see.

Damiana came down to sunbathe with a couple of friends and soon the pool was full of young people, splashing in the water, drinking juices on sun loungers and chatting in the sunshine. Costanza played with Giovanna. They tried to include Floriana, but after proving to everyone that she could hold her breath underwater longer than anyone else, she swam off to be with Dante. This didn't surprise Costanza. Dante had always been fond of Floriana and she knew Floriana was in love with him. It didn't occur to her that Floriana's feelings were reciprocated.

When they went up for lunch, Violetta was overjoyed to see

l'orfanella, as she was now known in the family. She swept her into her arms and kissed her happily.

'I'm so sorry there was a muddle over your invitation, Floriana,' she said, looking genuinely unhappy about it. 'I gave it to the countess because I didn't know where you live. My fault entirely, I should have asked you – or given it to you directly. I'm mortified that you might have thought we didn't want you.'

'I would have loved to come, but I'm happy I wasn't forgotten,' Floriana replied truthfully.

Dante put his arm around her shoulder. 'She's here now,' he said, and only his mother detected the unfamiliar tone in his voice.

She watched them sit down together and could almost see the vibrations quivering between them like heat evaporating off a hot road in midsummer.

Beppe presided over the lunch table. He made a great fuss of Costanza. Floriana was down the other end, but he wouldn't have paid her any attention had she been seated on his right-hand side. Costanza was the daughter of a count and the niece of a prince, and that was all there was to it. Dante and Floriana might as well have been on a table of their own. With their heads together, chatting and laughing like old friends, they had no interest in anyone else. Violetta watched her son with interest, and a little sadness, because there was no possibility of this young love maturing into anything greater. She considered her husband's wealth and position, and pondered on the divisive force of money. Once, Floriana would have been acceptable. Now, Beppe would have his sights on a girl like Costanza.

That afternoon Dante gave Floriana a tennis lesson. Giovanna lent her a pair of tennis shoes and a racket, then returned to the pool to lie in the sun with Costanza, Damiana and her friends. Alone on the court, Dante stood behind her, his arms around hers, showing her how to hold the racket. He placed her hands on the grip, but his lips digressed to her neck and he kissed her there where her skin was soft and warm. She laughed and shrugged him off playfully. 'You're meant to be giving me a lesson.'

'I am. A lesson in love.'

'*Stupido!*'

'I can't help it, you're too delicious.'

'So, I hold it like this. When can I hit a ball?'

'I like your spirit,' he said, reluctantly letting her go. 'For every ball you miss, I get a kiss.'

'You're expecting me to be very uncoordinated.'

'I'm counting on it.'

'But if I'm a natural?'

'I'll claim them by force!'

'Dante!'

He shrugged. 'Because I can.'

He walked around to the other side of the net. She put the racket out, determined to show him that it wasn't going to be that easy. He tossed a ball. She watched it bounce, drew her racket back and hit it.

'Looks like I'm a natural,' she said, grinning at him triumphantly.

'Beginner's luck.'

'Try again.'

He tossed another ball. She drew her racket back and hit it. He pulled a face. 'This won't do.'

'You're just a very good teacher.' He threw another ball, this time on her backhand. She missed.

'You haven't taught me that stroke!'

'Rules are rules and you have to forfeit a kiss!' Jubilantly, he jumped over the net and lifted her off her feet, pressing his lips to hers.

'If you do this every time I miss a ball I'm never going to learn how to play,' she protested, coming up for air.

'That was never my intention.'

'It wasn't?'

'No, I just wanted to get you on your own.'

'Aren't there simpler ways of doing that?'

'I couldn't think of one.'

'I can.' He put her down and she took him by the hand. 'Let's take a walk.'

Down on the beach she knew so well, she led him to a little inlet sheltered from the wind. They sat together, watching the speed boats slicing through the water in the distance.

'Now I truly have you all to myself,' he said, drawing her into his arms. Floriana made no protest this time. She wrapped her arms around him and let him kiss her.

That evening, as Floriana and Costanza walked through the poppy field, Floriana's happiness spilled over into her walk, causing her to bounce with each step. Her face glowed and her arms swung freely at her sides. Every now and then she bent down to pick the wild flowers that grew among the long grasses.

Costanza was still distressed about the lost invitation. Could her mother *really* have been so devious? What harm could Floriana have done by turning up to a party? She didn't understand, and yet she felt desperately guilty, as if she had in some way conspired against her friend. She regretted her decision to let Floriana go and decided to make it up to her somehow, as soon as she was in a position to do so.

'I'm in love,' Floriana sighed, unable to keep her feelings secret.

'I know you are,' Costanza replied.

'And he loves me back.'

'Well, he's very fond of you. I know that.'

'No, he loves me. He's told me.'

Costanza stopped walking. 'What? He's told you he loves you?'

'Yes. Last night I came to spy on the wall and he found me there. We walked and talked for hours and then ...' She blushed, almost too afraid to articulate it. 'He kissed me.'

Costanza was astonished. 'He kissed you?'

'Yes. It was divine!' Floriana began to twirl round and round with her arms out. 'God heard my prayers and answered them. I love Dante. I love him I love him I love him and I don't care who knows it.'

Infected by her friend's exuberance, Costanza began to laugh. 'I don't believe it. But he's so much older than you.'

'What does that matter? Love has no boundaries!'

'You're right. It doesn't. If he loves you back, then you will marry him. You'll have a jewellery box much bigger than Mother's.' That thought gave Costanza a strange sense of satisfaction.

'I don't want a jewellery box. I just want *him*. I have nothing but love and I'm the happiest girl in the world!'

Costanza took Floriana's hand and they ran down the field together. 'Then you shall have him!' Costanza shouted, and they both laughed until they were out of breath and had to stop.

Costanza accompanied Floriana to church. Floriana wanted to light another candle, in gratitude, Costanza in remorse. She'd never betray her friend again, so help her God. Padre Ascanio was in the nave, preparing for Mass, shadowed by Father Severo, the sacristan. When he saw the girls, Padre Ascanio wandered over to greet them, his robes polishing the stone floor as he swept across it. He had always kept a close eye on Floriana, as was his duty as shepherd of his flock. He had listened to her in the confessional every week, pouring out her hopes and dreams, her little heart so full of faith, her spirit unshakeable. Now she lit her candle with her eyes closed, a beatific expression on her face, he knew something good had happened.

'Hello, my children,' he said softly.

'Hello, Padre Ascanio,' said Costanza. She flushed guiltily and lowered her gaze, expecting the priest to know her innermost thoughts.

Floriana finished her prayer and opened her eyes. 'Good evening, Father.'

'God is delighted by your happiness,' he said with a smile.

'I *am* happy, Father,' Floriana replied. 'I'm grateful, too. He has answered my prayer.'

Father Ascanio frowned. Had her mother returned after all these years? Or had the young Dante Bonfanti reciprocated her love? Father Ascanio knew all the secrets in Herba – and Father Severo knew all Father Ascanio's.

'Dante loves me, Father.' She beamed so brightly that Father Ascanio couldn't help but take pleasure from her joy. God had looked favourably on His little daughter at last. However, his pleasure was tinged with foreboding. Theirs was an unlikely union and one that would undoubtedly be frowned upon by Dante's family.

'You must ask for God's guidance, my child.'

'He is already guiding me, Father. It is because of Him that I have arrived at this point.'

He watched the two girls skip out into the sunshine and shook his head. 'Father Severo, I fear that is not going to end well.'

'Indeed,' said Father Severo, dabbing his bald head with a handkerchief. Even he could detect the alcohol in his sweat. He hoped he could rely on Father Ascanio's poor sense of smell.

'It troubles me that Floriana's heart might be broken again,' Father Ascanio continued. Father Severo nodded. 'I shall be there, though, to pick up the pieces and put them back together again. Her father has taken up with the Devil and is not to be relied on. She relies on us.'

'She has her faith,' Father Severo added.

'It is very strong. But is it strong enough to endure another heartbreak? I don't know. I shall pray for her.'

'And so shall I,' Father Severo agreed. 'Most ardently.'

That evening Costanza ate in the dining room with her parents. Her mother rattled on about the party, discussing the extravagance of it all and the new friends they had made. Costanza didn't mention Floriana but she was constantly in the back of her mind. If her mother knew that Dante had kissed her and confessed his love, she'd be horrified. It was almost worth baiting her, just to watch her squirm, but her fear overrode temptation and she kept quiet. She didn't need to fight Floriana's battles for her; the girl was more than capable of fighting for herself.

Dante swung by Floriana's house in his Alfa Romeo Spider and tooted the horn. Signora Bruno bustled out to admire the car, running her hands over the shiny bonnet as if it were made of real silver. Children pushed past each other to get a better look, daring one another to touch it.

Dante noticed the smallest child, who was standing on his tiptoes at the back of the throng, and waded through to get him. 'Do you want to sit inside?' he asked and the little boy nodded excitedly.

When Floriana stepped out, she found Dante in the front seat with the child on his knee, showing him what all the buttons were for.

'You be careful with Floriana,' said Signora Bruno, wagging a stout finger at Dante.

'Trust me, she'll be cherished like a jewel,' he replied, lifting the little boy off his knee and placing him on the ground.

'I'll wait up,' she added, as Dante started the engine.

The children stepped back in wonder. Floriana waved and

Dante tooted again. As they drove slowly up the street the children followed, like a pack of playful dogs.

'Where are we going?' Floriana asked.

'Anywhere you want.'

'Let's just drive.' She took his hand and he lifted it to his lips.

They drove as the sun set on the olive groves and vineyards of Tuscany. The light grew mellow and the sky paled until it was dusk and the first twinkling of a star could be seen high in the sky. They found a little trattoria and dined on pasta beneath a trellis of tomato plants. The candle glowed as the natural light diminished and the crickets sang their nocturnal chorus. It was late when they left their table and drove back towards home.

Dante parked the car on the cliff top, overlooking the sea. The moon shone a path of silver light across the water. He turned off the engine and they sat in silence, gazing out at the beauty before them. For a long while neither spoke, and their stillness was as comfortable as the stars and the moon above them.

'It's always going to be like this,' he said at last, drawing her close. 'We're going to sit here when we're old, discussing our children. We're going to grow old together.'

'And we'll tell them how we met.'

'Yes, we'll tell them about my *piccolina*, pushing her nose through the gates to gaze longingly at the house and her gardens.'

'I'll be a good mother,' she said wistfully. 'I'll give our children everything I never had.'

He kissed her forehead. '*I'll* give you everything you never had.'

She gazed up at him and her eyes glistened. 'You already have.'

Chapter 25

Two months went by. Floriana still had to work to support herself and her increasingly inebriated father. Some days she helped her aunt in the laundry, other days she waited on tables in the *caffè* in Piazza Laconda. She wasn't too proud to wash dishes or sweep, anything that would earn her cash to buy food and clothing, and the locals knew they could call on her at the last minute if they needed something doing. Dante was unaware of her plight, having never been acquainted with someone who had nothing, and Floriana didn't tell him; she would have been deeply embarrassed to receive his charity.

Costanza spent most days with Giovanna, either at La Magdalena or at other beautiful houses nearby. The summer stretched into one long lunch party and soon Giovanna's name was barely mentioned without Costanza's attached to it, like a pair of decorative birds who were always together. Costanza had never had such fun, and her happiness allowed her to feel genuinely happy for Floriana. They didn't see so much of each other now, for Floriana was excluded from all the grand social events, but when they did, Costanza watched her flowering romance with pleasure and a sense of intrigue.

Dante couldn't hide his love. He wanted to spend every minute with Floriana. They'd go for drives, or picnic on the beach, or simply lie on the grass in his mother's mermaid garden and read out loud, with Good-Night snoozing contentedly beside them. Those were magical evenings, when the crickets chirruped, the birds settled down to roost and the light grew soft and golden, and Floriana basked in them, fully aware of God's blessing.

Violetta watched her son's summer romance with growing unease. They were clearly besotted with each other, which was touching to see, but she worried that Floriana's heart would break when it all came to an end. In September Dante would return to real life in Milan, leaving Floriana behind and bereft.

She didn't discuss it with Beppe. As far as he was concerned their romance was nothing more than one of the many flings Dante would enjoy in his life, before he settled down with an appropriate spouse. It didn't surprise him, nor did it interest him.

Not everyone was as heartless as Beppe. Father Ascanio anticipated the catastrophe hovering in the wings, awaiting its cue to swoop and destroy, and decided to speak to Floriana when she came in to light her daily candle.

Floriana had great respect for Father Ascanio, whom she had known for as long as she could remember. She also held him in awe, being the most senior man in Herba and the closest to God. When he said he wished to speak to her, she immediately felt guilty and tried to work out what she had done wrong as she followed him into a little side chapel, where they could talk in private.

'You look fearful, Floriana,' he said, sitting down on one of the wooden chairs arranged in front of the altar.

'I feel I must have transgressed for you to need to speak to me like this.'

His kind old face crinkled indulgently. 'You're not a child any longer, Floriana. The days when you used to leap off cliffs and skip your classes are far behind you. You're a God-fearing

young woman on the threshold of your sixteenth birthday and
I'm proud of you.'

'So, I've done nothing wrong?'

'Nothing at all.'

'Then why do you need to see me, Father?'

He hesitated and silently asked God for guidance; young
love was something he knew nothing about. Flaring his nostrils, he inhaled deeply then plunged into the cold pool of
reason. 'My dear child, in the absence of a mother to guide
you as you teeter on the brink of womanhood, I feel it's up
to me, as Father of this parish, to give you some fatherly
advice.'

Floriana's heart contracted with dread, for she knew at once
that it must be about Dante. Father Ascanio registered her
apprehension and took her hand in his large, doughy one. 'I
know that you and Dante Bonfanti enjoy a deep friendship.'

'Yes, Father.'

'But I feel I would not be doing my duty, as God bids me,
if I did not speak to you about the impossibility of it.'

'Impossibility?'

Father Ascanio frantically searched within himself for
strength as Floriana's eyes welled with tears, which spilled over
onto ashen cheeks.

'He will return to Milan in September to work for his
father, and your life will return to the way it was. You are so
very young, my dear, and he is now twenty-three, a man ...'
His voice trailed off as Floriana's heart broke right in front of
him. 'I'm sorry to have to tell you this, but I want to spare you
the hurt by opening your eyes to the truth.'

'But, Father, Dante loves me.'

'I'm sure he does. But do you really think he'll get his
father's blessing to marry you?' Floriana lowered her eyes,
defeated. 'You are from very different worlds, my child. This
is an experience for you to treasure, but you will move on and

settle down with someone from your own class. Dante Bonfanti is not for you.' The sight of her crumpling with sorrow like an autumn leaf was too much for Father Ascanio. 'I shall leave you here to compose yourself,' he said gently, patting her hand.

'But I love him, Father.'

'Sometimes love isn't enough, Floriana.'

'But Jesus—'

He lowered his voice. 'You are right, Jesus taught us to love our neighbours as ourselves, but unfortunately Beppe Bonfanti hasn't yet learned that lesson.'

Floriana remained alone in the little chapel. She buried her face in her hands and tried to feel God's presence, but she felt nothing other than her wet cheeks and leaden heart. Was it really impossible for them to be together? Could something as trivial as wealth keep them apart? For a moment she felt defeated. Beppe Bonfanti rose up before her like a giant, his dark and powerful figure standing firmly between her and the man she loved. Father Ascanio's kindly face floated in front of her eyes, shaking his grey head help-lessly. It seemed everyone was against her. But then the gentle countenance of Violetta shone through the dark and smiled at her with motherly love. Surely, *she* would give them her blessing? Perhaps she could even persuade her husband to give his?

Clinging onto this small flicker of hope, Floriana dried her eyes on her skirt. It wasn't fair that she bear this misery alone. She would tell Dante what Father Ascanio had said and he would reassure her and kiss away her fears. Everything would be all right; she just knew it. Father Ascanio was doing what he thought was right, but he was ignorant of the circum-stances. He was unaware of the strength of the love they felt for each other. Her spirits lifted once more as she reasoned with herself; her heart had survived against all odds, she wasn't about to let Beppe Bonfanti crush it now. If Father Ascanio had taught her anything, it was that all human beings were equal in God's eyes – she was as precious as everyone else.

It was dusk when she reached La Magdalena. Good-Night rushed up the drive to greet her as the big iron gates opened to let her in. Trembling, she bent down to stroke him, burying her face a while in his fur, composing herself as her fears now reared up to overthrow her again. She wandered up the avenue of cypress trees, where she had walked with Dante for the first time as a little girl. But she was too anxious to savour the smells of the garden, as they lingered seductively in the evening air.

Dante, who had been waiting for her, ran out of the house to meet her. When he saw her stricken face, he gathered her into his arms.

'What's happened?' he asked.

Defeated by the strength of his concern, Floriana collapsed into sobs. She was too distraught to speak.

'Come, let's go somewhere we can talk in private.' He led her through the trees and sat down beneath a tall umbrella pine. 'Is it your father?'

Floriana shook her head. 'I wish it was!'

'Then what is it?'

'Father Ascanio warned me that we have no future together.'

Dante was appalled. 'He warned you *what?*'

'That we come from such different worlds, and I am so young, that it will end in September . . .'

'What does he know?' Dante was furious, which made Floriana feel a lot better.

'He said your father would never give us his blessing.'

Dante held her upper arms and looked deep into her eyes. 'Listen to me, Floriana. No one is going to tear us apart. Do you understand? I love you. I'll never love anyone else, ever. You leave my father to me. Don't listen to Father Ascanio. He's never been in love, so what does he know?' Floriana smiled and wiped her eyes with the back of her hand. 'There, that's better. If he wasn't a priest, I'd go and have it out with him in the square for meddling in what does not concern him.'

'He was only doing what he believed was right.'

'The world has changed. I can't believe he thinks two people can't be together because of their class. He's an old fossil. Trust me, Floriana. You and I have a beautiful future together. So what if you're young? You'll grow up. It's nearly your birthday.'

'The fourteenth of August.'

'How shall we celebrate?'

'I don't care.'

'*I* do.' He got to his feet and pulled her up by the hand. 'Come on. We're getting out of here. I don't want to see you sad again.'

'I'm better now.'

'Good. Don't ever suffer alone, Floriana. Always come to me, because I'll be here for you. Do you understand?' She nodded. 'Now, where's Good-Night? He'll be very cross if we leave him behind.'

Floriana believed Dante when he said that they would always be together. If he loved her, then nothing could stand in their way, because Dante was the master of his own destiny. She pushed her fears to the back of her mind where they lay in shadow for the time being, ignored.

The sands of summer slowly seeped away with each hour, and Floriana and Dante spent as much time together as they could. When she met Costanza at La Magdalena, they'd sit and chat, and Floriana would share the details of her romance, which delighted Costanza, not least because she knew how much it would annoy her mother, were she to find out.

Costanza had won a few admirers of her own. There was tall, dark, brooding Eduardo from Rome; fair, blue-eyed Alessandro from Milan; and handsome Eugenio from Venice.

But no one was quite good enough for the countess. She had her eye on the biggest prize of all. Because of this, Costanza couldn't help but divulge the truth to her mother, although she knew that in so doing, she would put her friend's romance at risk.

They were in the back of the car, returning home from a lunch party where Eugenio had taken Costanza into a corner and talked to her for most of the afternoon. Costanza rather liked Eugenio. He was quiet and intellectual, with a sweet smile. His family were well known and established, living in a beautiful palazzo in the centre of Venice. But this did not seem enough for the countess.

'Mother, I'm very young,' Costanza said. 'I have years ahead to meet the man I'm going to marry. Can't I just have some fun like Floriana?'

The countess flinched at the mention of Floriana. 'How is *she* having any fun?'

'Because she is in love with Dante.'

'Really, that's absurd.' The countess laughed scornfully.

'Actually, you're wrong. He's in love with her, too.'

'You can't be serious?'

'I am very serious. They've been seeing each other all summer.'

'But she's a child.'

'He'll wait and marry her when she's older.'

The countess gnawed at her thumbnail. 'I'd have thought a young man like Dante would go for something a little more sophisticated than a local stray.'

'She's pretty and funny. I'm not at all surprised that he loves her; everyone loves her but you.'

The countess was stunned by the aggression in her daughter's voice. She had never dared speak out like this before. But the countess was a shrewd woman. She knew that fighting with Costanza would only push her away.

'Darling, I know she's pretty and funny, and you're wrong about me disliking her. I'm only protecting you as any mother would do in the same circumstances. Look what fun you've had with Giovanna this summer. Do you think you would have enjoyed all those parties if you were still attached to Floriana? I don't think so. You and Giovanna share a deep bond because you have so much in common. You have nothing in common with Floriana any more, except memories, which you must treasure because they're special. But you must also be savvy enough to look forward to your future. I like Eugenio very much. He's a delightfully charming young man and a nice escort for you. If you want to be friends with him you have my blessing. I only want your happiness.' She took Costanza's hand. 'And I only want you to have what you deserve and nothing less.'

Costanza was suitably wooed. 'I know Mamma, and I'm grateful.'

'I'm old now; I don't have to think about myself. I wake up every morning and think, what can I do for Costanza today?'

'You're very unselfish.'

'That's what motherhood is all about: putting one's children above oneself. So, this romance between Floriana and Dante – is it really that serious?'

'Well, they are joined at the hip. They spend every available moment together.'

'And what do Beppe and Violetta think about it?'

'Giovanna says that her mother loves Floriana very much, as a daughter even, but that her father barely notices her.'

'Beppe would never allow his son to marry a girl like Floriana.'

'Perhaps they'll elope.'

'Don't be ridiculous, Dante isn't going to throw his inheritance away.'

'Giovanna says her brother is besotted.'

'Besotted he may be, but if his father is against the union, which I have no doubt he will be, then their plans are thwarted before they've even begun.'

'Poor Floriana,' Costanza sighed.

'It's a beautiful love story, but it has an unhappy ending, as the best love stories do. She'll get over it. She's a strong girl. I suspect she'll end up marrying someone in Herba and forgetting all about Dante. Really, it was a hopeless dream from the very beginning.'

'Can't she go and live in Milan?'

'And do what? Stay with whom? Of course she can't. I imagine that Dante will come to his senses once he is back in his world. Can you imagine Floriana in Milan? It's unthinkable. No, this is a lovely summer romance but it will end. It pains me to say it, really it does.' She put a hand on her heart and pulled a sad face. 'I can't bear to think of little Floriana suffering after all she has already been through, but it is inevitable. You would be a good friend to her if you were able to warn her.'

'I couldn't do that!'

'Then leave it to Fate.' *Or me,* the countess thought maliciously.

When Dante told his mother that Floriana's birthday was fast approaching, Violetta decided to throw her a surprise dinner party with the family. Beppe was conveniently in Milan, giving her free rein to spoil Floriana. The table was set up on the terrace with a silver balloon attached to the back of each chair. A cake was made in the image of Good-Night and tall flutes were arranged for champagne. Violetta was sure that Floriana had never been given a birthday party and wanted to make it special – overcompensating, perhaps, for the disappointment that would surely strike come September. She bought her a gold bracelet, which rattled with little charms, and took great care in wrapping it with pretty pink paper and ribbon. The chef cooked a buffet-style dinner that was laid out like a banquet.

Dante kept Floriana away, taking her down to the beach until it was time to return to the villa. She knew he had a surprise for her, and she was sure he was going to take her out to dinner at a fine restaurant. She had put on her best dress especially. But when they returned to La Magdalena she realized that he had planned something else and hadn't a clue what it could be.

They walked through the house hand in hand. As they entered the drawing room she saw the table and balloons through the French doors and put her hand to her mouth in astonishment. Outside, the family awaited her: Giovanna and Costanza, Damiana and her two best girl friends, Rosaria and Allegra, and Violetta, gift in hand and smile lighting up her delicate face.

Floriana's fears were now swept away for good. Violetta could not have given her blessing more clearly had she voiced it out loud. With tears in her eyes and pink-cheeked with pleasure, Floriana approached the table. She noticed everything: the little flowers scattered over the tablecloth, the gifts piled onto her plate, beautifully wrapped with pretty paper and ribbons tied in bows, and the bounty of food. All for her.

Violetta embraced her affectionately and held out her gift. 'Darling child,' she said, 'you deserve this more than anyone I know. I wish you happiness and health and many fruitful years ahead.' She briefly touched Floriana's cheek with the back of her hand, gazing onto her face as a mother to a daughter.

Floriana sat down and opened the gift. She pulled out the bracelet and stared at it in disbelief. Violetta attached it to her wrist. 'I chose the charms individually. Look, here's Good-Night, and F for your name, a bird, a cricket, a flower, a little house that opens to reveal two hearts, a church and a cross.'

Floriana laughed through her tears and shook her head, and everyone laughed too, realizing her emotions prevented her from speaking.

She opened her other gifts: a dress from Damiana, a necklace from Giovanna, a poetry book from Rosaria and a bottle of Yves Saint-Laurent perfume from Allegra. The countess had taken Costanza shopping and bought Floriana a pretty leather handbag with a matching purse, leaving Costanza in no doubt that her mother was really very fond of her.

Drunk on happiness, Floriana sipped champagne and ate from the delicious spread of food. Dante sat beside her, squeezing her hand under the table every now and then to remind her that he loved her. As the light faded and the candlelight grew stronger, the chef stepped out of the house with the cake. The table cheered at the sight of Good-Night recreated in sponge and icing, and Floriana clapped her hands in delight. She blew out the sixteen candles and reluctantly plunged the knife into the dog's paw, closing her eyes to make a wish.

Violetta knew what she was wishing for and her pleasure was at once marred with apprehension. She wished this night could go on for ever, then no one would get hurt.

But time ticked on without consideration for Violetta's feelings, and at the end of the evening Dante drove Floriana home.

They stopped in a secluded place, overlooking the sea and Dante pulled a little box out of his breast pocket. 'And this is my gift to you,' he said, handing it to her.

'What is it?' she asked, turning it over.

'Open it and see.' Floriana did as she was told and carefully opened the wrapping. Inside was a little red box. With trembling fingers she lifted the lid to reveal an eternity ring glittering with white diamonds. Without a word he lifted it from the velvet cushion and took her hand in his. 'We're too young to marry, Floriana, but with this ring I promise you that

I will love you for eternity.' He solemnly slipped it onto the third finger of her right hand.

Floriana gasped and watched it sparkle like little stars in the moonlight. 'It's the most beautiful thing I've ever seen.'

'Well, it's the second most beautiful thing *I've* ever seen.'

She wrapped her arms around him and kissed him. 'Thank you, Dante. I've had the most wonderful day. The best day I've ever had in my life. I won't ever forget it.'

'This is only the beginning, *piccolina*. I'm going to have such pleasure in spoiling you.'

When Floriana returned home there was no one to share her day with. Her father slept noisily in the room next door and Signora Bruno's apartment was dark. So, she sat by the window and gazed up at the stars. She wondered whether the same moon was shining down upon her mother and whether she ever looked up at it and thought of her.

'Mamma,' she said softly, 'I'd like to tell you about Dante ...'

Chapter 26

As September drew closer, like a river flowing inescapably towards a sharp waterfall, Dante began to feel the cold chill of the approaching descent. The summer had been a blissful plateau of long, lazy days in the sunshine, romantic drives through the Tuscan countryside, idle walks up and down the beach, and wishes tossed into the poppy fields like magical seeds to flower into happy endings. But now those poppies had withered back into the ground and the last days of August finally drained away. Beppe summoned Dante to Milan.

Dante didn't know how to say goodbye to Floriana. He loved her with all his heart and soul, but he hadn't considered the practicalities of sustaining a long-distance relationship. He wished he could take her with him to Milan but that was as impossible as his father giving his consent to marry her. Until she was twenty-one they were bound by law to his command – and even then, he couldn't imagine disobeying his father. In his daydreams, he swept her into his arms and ran off with her, to marry in some foreign country far away where no one could stop them. But they were only fantasies. The reality remained: Dante had to go to Milan to work with his father, and he loved his home and family too much to elope.

The day before his departure he found Floriana at home, alone. Her father was out, or slumped against a wall somewhere. Signora Bruno let him in and showed him up to her small apartment. At first Floriana was mortified that he had witnessed her poverty, but her mortification quickly dissolved when she realized he had come to say goodbye.

Fearful that her father might suddenly appear, she took him into her bedroom where they could speak in private. The room was small and simple, with a large cross on the white wall behind the bed and cool floor tiles beneath their feet. A chest of drawers stood opposite the iron bed and the window was wide open, but neither was aware of the sounds of the town that blew in on the breeze.

They remained a moment staring at each other, suddenly daunted by the scale of all that stood between them. The languid summer days seemed far away now, gone with their carefree laughter and courageous dreams, and they searched each other's eyes for confirmation that their love could be nurtured, like hands cupped around a fragile flame as the wind blows closer.

He pulled her into his arms and clung to her. 'I'll write and drive down as often as I can,' he explained, closing his eyes and savouring the vanilla scent of her skin with a sharp sense of longing for what was soon to be lost.

'I'll wait for you, Dante,' she replied. 'Whatever happens, I'll wait.'

Those words 'whatever happens' struck his heart with the full force of their implication and he let his grief consume him. He no longer thought rationally. He imagined her alone in Herba, without anyone to protect her from the lurid intentions of malevolent men. The thought of her vulnerable to predators filled him with a raging jealousy and an unbearable sense of helplessness.

Dizzy with homesickness, he let his passion carry him away. He kissed her deeply and she held him tighter than she had ever held him. A wild, uncontrollable desire overcame him, so that his instincts took over where his reason should have prevailed. He carried her onto the bed and lay down beside her. Floriana was willing to give herself to Dante, to do whatever he wanted. Without a mother to guide her, she barely knew what was happening, aware only of the deliciously warm feeling that saturated her loins as he ran his hands over her dark and secret places. And then he was inside her, moaning as he moved rhythmically to his own escalating pleasure. Beads of sweat gathered on his brow as he thrust deeper, claiming her for himself. Floriana bit her lip and withstood the initial discomfort, sure that *this* union would tie them together for all eternity.

When it was over, they lay entwined. Dante trembled with remorse, suddenly aware of what he had done. Floriana smiled in her ignorance, flushed with happiness, for now they really belonged to each other in all but name.

'This must remain a secret,' he said seriously. 'I didn't mean to do it.'

'I'm glad you did, Dante. I gave myself to you willingly.'

'But you're only sixteen. I could go to prison!'

'I won't tell a soul. It'll be our secret, I promise.'

Encouraged by her words, he kissed her forehead. 'Now you're really mine.'

'I always have been. From the moment you let me into your gardens, I was yours.'

'Did I hurt you?'

'A little.'

'I'm sorry.' He kissed her again, pulling her closer.

'Don't be sorry. Isn't that the way it *should* be?'

Dante didn't know, having never deflowered a woman before. As reality shone an unforgiving light onto his recklessness, he was left with the suffocating sense of having made a very deep commitment. He wrapped his arms around her more tightly and kissed her temple, whispering, 'I love you,' over and over again.

Then he was gone.

*

Floriana waited for rain, but it did not come. She wanted the skies to cloud over and the rain to wash the summer away, so it couldn't linger to torment her. But it lingered in long, hazy days and golden evenings, and she felt Dante's absence as sharply as a knife to her chest.

When she went to La Magdalena the family had left for Milan. The house was quiet, only the staff were there tidying up, closing shutters and laying dustsheets over the furniture. Good-Night welcomed her in the same affectionate way he always had, but Violetta, Giovanna, Damiana and Dante were all gone. She wandered around the gardens like a pining dog, besieged by the ghostly echoes of summer carried mournfully on the autumn wind.

School started again, but Floriana got a full-time job in a restaurant. The countess hired a private tutor for Costanza as the count's summer of networking paid off, rewarding him with various offers of work. They began to discuss the very real possibility of returning to Rome. The two girls saw each other very rarely. Once they had shared everything, but now the gap between them widened and their brief meetings, outside church after Mass, or sometimes in the town when Costanza came in to shop, were awkward. Costanza had made many friends over the summer; Floriana's one friend was gone, leaving her isolated and alone.

Dante wrote daily and Floriana replied, expressing her enduring love in small, deliberate handwriting. She treasured his letters and kept them in a drawer in her dressing table, tied with the pink ribbon Violetta had used to wrap her bracelet. Her diamond ring was her most vital link to him and she cherished it, taking comfort from its value, which surely reflected his intentions to marry her eventually.

When she began to feel sick she thought it was the result of not eating properly. But even the smell of food made her want to vomit. After a few days of constant nausea she worried that she might be very ill and went to see Signora Bruno. The old woman asked her a few probing questions about how often she had thrown up and for how long she had felt like this, and Floriana answered earnestly, afraid she was perhaps dying.

But Signora Bruno took her into her apartment and sat her down in the sitting room, closing the door behind her. She looked as stony as a grave and asked whether Dante had made love to her. At first Floriana was evasive, remembering the promise she had made. But when Signora Bruno suggested that she might be pregnant, Floriana admitted that he had.

'Is that how it happens?' she enquired innocently.

Signora Bruno shook her head, appalled. 'Didn't anyone ever tell you?'

'Who was going to tell me?'

'Your aunt?'

'Zita? No, we never discussed it.'

'Curse that woman for her incompetence. What about Costanza?'

'She doesn't know.'

'It's not possible. Do you realize how serious this is? You're going to have a child. How will we hide it?'

'Why would I want to hide it?'

'Because *you* are a child, my dear, and it's against the law. Dante could go to gaol. He's a grown man, he should have known better. What came over him?' Signora Bruno wrung her hands. 'What will Beppe Bonfanti do when he finds out? God help you.'

Floriana's initial joy at not being terminally ill slid away as she now realized the gravity of her situation. 'What am I going to do?'

'You go and speak to Father Ascanio at once. He is the only one who can help you.'

'Won't I get Dante into trouble?'

'Father Ascanio's a priest, he's bound to secrecy. There's not a secret of mine he doesn't know. In fact, I suspect he knows all the secrets in Herba. He won't tell and I won't tell, so help me God.' She crossed herself. 'But I can't help you. I'm not equipped. He is the only one who will know what to do.'

'I must tell Dante.'

Signora Bruno rounded on her like a spitting yak. 'You'll do nothing of the sort. I knew that family were bad news right from the start. I should have warned you instead of letting your heart run away with you. Don't breathe a word of it to Dante, do you understand? Not before you tell Father Ascanio. You need to take advice from him and him alone.'

Floriana should have felt fear, but she ran her hands over her belly and felt nothing but awe and happiness. She was going to have Dante's baby. His father would not be able to deny them his consent now that she was carrying his grandchild – a son, perhaps, and heir to his great fortune. She smiled, musing on Fate and how very clever it was to give her the one thing that would irrevocably tie her to Dante for ever.

This was all *meant* to happen. God had answered her prayers and given her something that only He could bestow: a new life that belonged exclusively to her and Dante.

Ignoring Signora Bruno's advice, Floriana wrote at once to Dante. A few days later the butler from La Magdalena appeared at her door with a message: Dante had telephoned to say he was coming down to see her. Overjoyed at the prospect of being with him again she set about cleaning her apartment, humming a merry tune as she went about her work. She looked around at the modest room and simple furnishings and thought of the future that would take her away from her father and this pitiful place. She envisaged sitting in the mermaid garden with Dante beside her, reading poetry, while their son floated his toy boats in the fountain. Good-Night would be lying at her feet, snoozing in the sunshine.

Perhaps she'd be expecting another child. They'd have many. In a house the size of La Magdalena she could have as many as she wanted.

However, she was to be disappointed. The Dante who appeared in her doorway was not the radiant, overjoyed young man she had expected. Instead of sweeping her into his arms with excitement, he looked grey and terrified. Her heart plummeted like a stone.

'Are you all right?' she asked, tentatively wrapping her arms around his waist.

'We need to talk, Floriana. I came as soon as I heard. Are you sure you're pregnant?'

'I think I am, but I'm not entirely sure.'

'Who have you told?'

'Signora Bruno. I *had* to tell someone.'

'I understand.' He turned to face her. She had never seen him look so defeated. 'And *she* thinks you're pregnant?'

'Yes.' She frowned up at him. 'I thought you'd be happy.'

'Happy? My darling Floriana, you have no idea what this means.'

'We can get married.'

'This is no time for fantasy. My father will never allow that.'

'But I'm carrying his grandchild.'

'He doesn't care about his grandchild. He barely cares about his children. He's as sentimental as one of those silly statues in the garden. All he cares about is money and reputation.'

'So, you're not going to tell him?' Floriana's chin began to tremble. She took a deep breath and puffed out her chest, willing herself to overcome her disappointment.

'I don't know what I'm going to do.' He took her hands in his, overpowered by the sight of the woman he loved and the knowledge of the seed he had sown inside her. 'But I'm not going to desert you. We'll think of something.' He drew her into his arms and held her tightly against his chest. 'It's my responsibility. I got you into this and I'll get you out of it. Somehow we'll be together, I promise.'

'I'm happy, Dante. I feel no fear at all. I realize now that all I have ever wanted is a child. Someone to love and care for. A little part of you that will always be with me, no matter what.'

He put his hand on her flat belly. 'Hard to imagine there's a child in there.'

'I know. Signora Bruno says I won't show for at least six months.'

'Then that gives us time, at least. Don't breathe a word to a soul, do you understand?' She nodded. 'I'll find you somewhere else to live, far away from here.'

'But I want to be with *you*.'

'That's just not possible, Floriana. Can you imagine the scandal? No one must ever know.'

'But our child will be born out of wedlock.'

'There is no other way.'

Floriana blanched. 'We can't have a child out of wedlock. It's a sin.'

'We have already committed the greatest sin, Floriana.'

His words slapped her in the face and stung, but she lifted her chin and fought for her unborn baby. 'We can marry in secret.'

He pulled away and strode over to the window as if searching for a means of escape. 'It's all so simple for you because you've got nothing to lose.'

She sat on the bed and folded her arms. 'All that matters is that I love you and our child.'

'But life is more complicated than that.'

'Only if you let it be.'

'I am my father's heir.'

'Can't you just walk away?'

'And what will we live on?'

'I've lived on nothing all my life and I've been happy.'

'I have a responsibility to my parents. I am set to inherit my father's company. I can't throw it all away and ride off into the sunset. My father will disown me. My mother's heart will break and I'll have nothing. Don't you see? I'll lose everything.'

'You'll only lose what doesn't matter.'

Dante felt like a drowning man. He didn't doubt his love for Floriana, but he did doubt his ability to stand up to his father. All his life he had done what was expected of him and earned Beppe's love, which was entirely conditional. He held his father in the highest respect, but if he searched deep inside his soul where all truth lies hidden, he'd find the residue of fear that remained at the very bottom, left over from his boyhood, with the same old need to please. He cursed his weakness but there was nothing he could do. Confiding in his father about Floriana was inconceivable. His mother would probably be more sympathetic, but even she, with her sentimental heart, could not condone marriage to Floriana, even if she were the right age.

Dante gave Floriana money to use the public telephone to call him, and promised that he would go away and think about how best to deal with the situation. However, he had no idea how he was going to resolve it. If only he could just turn his back on it all and return to his old life – but that possibility no longer existed. His love bound him to Floriana, and the knowledge that his child was growing inside her made walking away impossible. He was responsible for them both. Never before had he felt the weight of duty so heavily upon his shoulders.

He cursed himself for not having the courage to elope and start again in a new place. But marriage was impossible whichever way he looked at it. He could set her up in a flat somewhere near Milan so she could give birth in secret, but then what? The future was grim for both of them. He stopped the car on the side of the road just outside Herba and put his head on the steering wheel, closing his eyes in desperation, wishing to lose himself. What had he been thinking? He should never have fallen in love with Floriana. It was doomed from the beginning. His mind whirred with images that grew large and distorted: the scandal, his father's wrath, his mother's disappointment, Floriana's hopes dashed yet again. It was all too horrible to bear.

Then a tiny pinprick of hope glimmered through the darkness. He sat up and stared at it. The more he stared the bigger it got, until he was sure that light would show him the way. He turned the car round and drove back into Herba.

Father Ascanio was surprised to see Dante. The family had long gone back to Milan and didn't usually return until the following summer. When he saw the young man's stricken face, he was sure there had been a death in the family, and that Dante had come to inform him personally.

'My son, what has happened?'

'I need to speak with you urgently,' Dante replied.

'Of course. Please.' The priest led the way to the little chapel where, not so long ago, he had advised Floriana that nothing could come of her love. They sat down. Dante inhaled deeply. He noticed a faint smell of alcohol waft in from behind him and turned to make sure that they were alone. 'How can I help you?' Father Ascanio asked, his tone soft and reassuring.

'I'm in terrible trouble, Father. I have sinned.' Dante put his head in his hands.

'Don't be afraid. God forgives those who repent.'

'Oh, I do. I regret my transgression wholeheartedly.'

'Would you not prefer to use the confessional?'

He sat up and gazed at the priest in despair. 'No. I need more practical help.'

'I see.'

'Father Ascanio, you have known me since I was a child.'

'I have.'

'And you have always guided me to the best of your ability, with the greatest wisdom and tact. Is that not so?'

'I have always done my best.'

'Well, I need your wisdom now, but I fear your judgement.'

'My son, I'm not here to judge you. That is not for me to do, but for God, in His wisdom. Tell me what troubles you have and I will do my best to advise you.'

Dante swallowed hard. He could no longer look into the priest's eyes and dropped his gaze onto the flagstone at his feet. 'Floriana is pregnant.'

Father Ascanio caught his breath. His hand shot to his chest where a sharp pain caused him to wince. He stifled a groan. His first thought was for Floriana, so innocent and trusting and brave, and his heart flooded with compassion. His second thought was for Dante and his foolishness, and he tried very hard not to condemn him to the harshest criticism.

Dante felt the priest's horror without having to look at his face. He buried his head in his hands, overcome with shame.

Father Ascanio stood up and walked over to the altar. He put his hands on the white linen cloth and closed his eyes in prayer. What was the right thing to do for Floriana? He tried to remain detached, like a surgeon poised to cut through the flesh of a patient, but his heart swelled and contracted as he explored every alternative.

Finally, he returned to his chair. Dante raised his eyes. 'What shall I do?' he whispered, feeling worse for having shared his problem.

'There is only one thing you *can* do,' the priest replied with a sigh.

'Anything. I'll do anything for Floriana.'

'There is a convent not far from here where she can go for the duration of her confinement. I have known the Mother Superior for many years and it is not uncommon for her to take in girls like Floriana.'

There followed a heavy pause and Dante knew what he was going to ask, for the question hovered in the air between them like a bright red balloon.

'Do you intend to marry her?'

'I don't know.' He shrugged helplessly and dropped his head. 'I've dreamed of marrying her. I thought I'd wait until she was old enough and then . . .' his voice trailed off. 'Love blinded me to the reality of my situation. My father would never accept her as his daughter-in-law. I'd have to give up *everything*.' He choked on his words for he was well aware that sacrifice was the way of the Lord. 'Father, I am weak!'

Father Ascanio drew on all his strength. He wanted to shake the boy and berate him for having ruined the girl's life. 'But you will support her financially?' he asked with forced calmness.

'Of course. I will look after her and our child. She will live like a princess.' His words sounded hollow and he wished he hadn't said them. 'I will wait until I am rich enough in my own right and then I will marry her.'

'So, you must tell Floriana what you have decided and she must make ready to leave as soon as I have arranged it with the Mother Superior.'

'I will.'

'She must not tell a soul.'

'She has told only Signora Bruno.'

'Teresa is a good, discreet woman. You can count on her to keep it to herself.'

'I'm humbled, Father, and deeply in your debt.'

'There are no debts to repay, Dante, only amends. Go and look after Floriana, and love her very dearly. You are responsible for her predicament and for her future. It is human to transgress, but you can raise yourself up by doing your duty before God – repent, pray for forgiveness and put it right.'

'I will, Father.'

'Now go.'

Dante left the little chapel and strode over the flagstones towards the door. He did not notice the sacristan who kneeled in prayer in the chapel next door. The alcohol seeped through his pores and evaporated into the air to mingle with the smell of burning wax.

As Dante's footsteps grew faint, he raised his head and narrowed his eyes. So, Floriana was pregnant. *That* was a surprise. Out of all the secrets he had overheard during the many years he had worked in the church, this was by far the most shocking. But he was a man of discretion. He prided himself in keeping secrets. He fished behind the confessional, in the cracks between walls and doors, and picked up little pieces of information, then saw how deeply he could store them away. So far, he had never let a fish slip out. The trouble was, this fish was the biggest and most slippery fish he'd ever caught.

Chapter 27

Floriana knocked on Signora Bruno's door. The smell of frying onions seeped out and under her nose, causing her stomach to churn with nausea. She wondered how long the sickness would last. Putting a hand on her belly she silently told her child that she would suffer whatever nature threw at her in order for him to be born healthy and strong.

The door opened and Signora Bruno's anxious face peered out. 'Ah, Floriana. What news?' she asked, pulling the girl in by her skirt. 'Have you spoken to Father Ascanio? What did he say?'

'I have spoken to him,' Floriana lied. Well, she had, *indirectly*.

'Well?'

'I'm going to a convent.'

'That's the best thing for you. Thank God.'

'It's called Santa Maria degli Angeli. Padre Ascanio will arrange it for me.'

'I told you he would know what to do.'

'I am happy. I will give thanks to God every day for the gift of my child.'

Signora Bruno sucked in her cheeks. 'When do you leave?'

'As soon as he has organized it.'

'Who will take you?'

'Dante.'

'Dante knows?'

'Of course. It's his child, too. Once the baby is born he will buy us a place to live and one day, when he's independent of his father, we will marry. God will forgive us for having a child out of wedlock – and anyway, it is His gift, so He can't be cross.' She smiled excitedly. 'I'm so happy, Signora Bruno.'

The old woman frowned. How was it possible to feel happiness in her situation, her future being so uncertain? She didn't believe for a minute that Dante would ever marry her; that kind of happy ending did not happen for girls like Floriana. She chewed on the inside of her cheek thoughtfully. 'Well, that's as much as we can hope for.'

'I'm going to be a mother.' Floriana sighed dreamily and flopped into a soft chair. 'It's a boy, I just know it. A beautiful little boy. I talk to him all the time.'

'I doubt he has ears to hear you.'

'He hears me with his soul.' Floriana's smile was peaceful, as if she wanted for nothing. Signora Bruno couldn't help but admire her optimism, and fear the moment life would disappoint her and snuff it out for ever.

'Are you hungry?'

'No, I'm living off air and thriving.'

'You look skinny.'

'I feel sick in my stomach but well in my heart.'

'You'll harm the baby if you don't get something down you. Come on, I've made soup.'

Reluctantly, Floriana followed her into the kitchen. The smell of onions was overpowering. 'I don't think I can eat anything. Perhaps a cracker. Do you have a cracker?'

'And some cheese.'

'Just a cracker.'

'I'll butter it.'

Floriana grinned at her fondly. 'You're acting like a mother.'

Signora Bruno scowled to hide her emotion. 'You need a mother.'

'How lucky then that I have you.'

'I don't suppose you're going to tell Elio?'

'Of course not. One day he'll wake up and find me gone.'

'You really feel nothing?'

'Nothing.' Floriana turned away and picked up a piece of onion peel. 'He's no father to me.'

'Perhaps being a grandfather will set him on the straight and narrow.'

'No, it won't. Nothing will. He's well and truly lost. No wonder my mother left him. Sometimes I think she must have hated me very much to leave me at his mercy.'

Signora Bruno was horrified. 'You don't believe that?'

Floriana shrugged. 'It doesn't matter. They're all losers because they'll never know the precious little child that I am going to bring into the world. I need nothing, Signora Bruno, nothing and no one, because I'll have my son. I'll never be alone again.'

Signora Bruno found her bravado heartbreaking.

Dante remained in Milan, confident that his child would be born in secrecy. He no longer felt that clawing fear in his stomach because the burden had been lifted and arrangements had been made. His father wouldn't find out. Floriana would be safe and cared for. They could continue their relationship in a new town where no one knew them. As for the future, he didn't have to think about it yet. For the time being things were fine. However, in the quiet moments before he fell asleep at night and when he awoke in the morning, he shuddered at the thought of how close he had come to ruin.

Floriana's pregnancy was a delicate issue and Father Ascanio didn't want to speak to the Mother Superior on the telephone. He arranged to go and see her instead.

As he drove through the Tuscan countryside he mulled over

the unfortunate situation. Floriana would give birth within the safe walls of Santa Maria degli Angeli, then Dante would whisk her away to some far-off town, to start a new life where she knew no one. Of all the people in his parish, Floriana was the least well equipped psychologically to cope with that sort of change. He feared for her, all alone with a small child and no daily support. Perhaps Dante would arrange for help, but still, she'd be emotionally close to no one.

He wrestled with anger when he thought of Dante's foolishness. One moment of pleasure and he had potentially destroyed a young girl's life. Of course, Floriana wouldn't see it that way. She loved him and trusted that he would look after her and possibly even marry her one day. But Father Ascanio was old and wise, and had instantly recognized the weakness in the boy's demeanour, having seen it so many times before in others. The way he hadn't been able to look him in the eye, the way his shoulders had slumped in defeat – and Father Ascanio *knew* the boy. He had watched him grow up beneath the forceful authority of his father. To break that kind of influence took a will of fire and a courage of steel, neither of which Dante possessed, for all his charm and geniality.

He arrived at the imposing gates of the convent and hesitated before getting out and ringing the bell. Once Floriana walked through these gates he might never see her again. His heart contracted and he was stunned by the sudden rush of emotion. Only now that he was on the point of losing her did he realize how deeply he cared.

Floriana telephoned Dante often from the public telephone in Luigi's. They couldn't speak for long, but Dante's voice was enough to reassure her. In her free time she'd wander up to La Magdalena and find Good-Night. Together they'd walk through the fields and she'd tell him of the future she was going to have with Dante. They'd sit on the beach as the water gently lapped the rocks, and she'd sing to her unborn child, and the dog that had grown to love her above all others.

Father Severo took another swig from the bottle he had hidden beneath a floorboard in his bedroom. Many times he had told himself that this swig would be his last. He knew that if he was caught, Father Ascanio would throw him out, being a man of the highest principles. But he was unable to stop, and Father Ascanio's poor sense of smell enabled him to continue undetected.

Tonight Father Ascanio was out. He had disappeared in his car that afternoon and hadn't come back. Father Severo wondered whether the outing had anything to do with Floriana. He felt the slippery fish of his secret and relished the pleasure it gave him, knowing something that he shouldn't and not having weakened and told anyone. His discretion gave him a buzz.

He took another swig. It was a beautiful evening. The light was mellow, the air warm and autumnal. The sounds of children playing echoed off the ancient stone walls and made him think of his own isolated childhood and the boys who refused to play with him because they sensed that he was different. He decided to go for a walk and get some air. He considered Father Ascanio as he weaved slowly up the narrow street towards the Piazza. How he admired him. But he could never rise to such heights, being the inadequate man that he was. He knew his failings and was content living in the shadow of a great man of God, giving his life to the service of others, hoping to redeem himself through his work. He repressed the sexual feelings he had for other men and prayed daily to be cured. But the pain persisted and only the alcohol helped stifle it.

At the end of the street he saw a man crouched on a doorstep, head in hands. He recognized him instantly.

'Elio,' he said as he approached. 'Are you all right?' The man looked up at him and the suffering on his face yanked the sacristan out of his internal world with a jolt.

'Father, help me.'

The sacristan sat beside him. The stench of alcohol seeping from Elio's pores was pungent. 'How can I help you?'

'I have lost my wife and son and now I am losing my daughter, too.'

'What do you mean, your daughter?'

'She doesn't care for me. I have let her down. I should be working to support her, but here I am, a slave to alcohol. I have hit the bottom, Father, and I don't know how to lift myself up. I want to take care of her but she won't speak to me any more. I know that one day she will leave me, like her mother did, and I'll die alone like a common tramp.'

'Elio, you have taken the first step to recovery. By acknowledging that you have a problem, you have already moved towards resolving it.'

'I won't drink ever again.'

'That takes a very strong will,' he said, thinking of his own weakness and once again vowing to overcome it.

'So, what am I to do?'

'You need something to live for, a goal that will keep you from the bottle and inspire you to get back to work and live a clean life.' He felt the slippery fish in his throat and a sudden bolt of excitement as it slowly worked its way up.

'I have nothing but Floriana and she despises me.'

'You have to prove to her first that you can do it. It's no use telling her over and over that you will give up drinking because you have failed to do so countless times in the past. You have to show her that you seriously intend to change.'

'She doesn't love me any more. Once love is dead it cannot be revived.'

'Nonsense. Father Ascanio says that love is always there, at the very heart of all of us, even those who don't know it. We just have to let go of all negativity.'

'I don't deserve her love. Look at me.'

'Of course you do. It's human to make mistakes. Jesus taught forgiveness. Floriana is a good Christian. She loves you in her heart, even if she is not aware of it. You're her father and the only family she has.'

'And what have I done for her?'

'Don't ask yourself what you have *done*, but what you can *do*.' The slippery fish was now on his tongue and wriggling about so furiously it took all his strength to hold it there. The pleasure was overwhelming and he began to sweat little beads onto his nose and forehead. Never before had he had to wrestle with such a big one.

Elio lifted his chin. 'I'm no fool, you know. I am aware that she has a boyfriend. She thinks I don't know but I have eyes and ears like everyone else. She won't tell me, of course. She doesn't tell me anything these days. Once, when she was a little girl, she used to share her thoughts, but I didn't listen. I didn't take any notice.' He crumpled again into a heap of self-pity. 'What sort of father am I? She'll marry one day and who knows whether she'll want me there at her wedding. I should walk her down the aisle to give her away, but what man is going to ask for her hand from me, when I have no right to give it? I have failed her.' His shoulders began to shudder.

'Let's get you home.' The sacristan got to his feet. The slippery fish slid enticingly onto the tip of his tongue.

Elio gazed up at him forlornly. 'I have nothing,' he said, and with that final declaration of despair the fish glided out.

'You're going to be a grandfather, Elio,' announced the sacristan. To his surprise he discovered that the pleasure of divulging the secret far outweighed the pleasure of keeping it. Elio stared up at him in astonishment. 'Yes, Floriana is pregnant,' he repeated gleefully.

'Pregnant? Floriana?'

'It is Dante Bonfanti's child.'

Elio sobered up as he digested the news. 'Are you sure?'

'Trust me, I know. You see, you do have something to live for.'

'But she's so young.'

'She is young, but I suspect the boy will marry her.'

'He'll take her away.'

'Surely not.'

'Of course he will.' Elio struggled to his feet.

The sacristan gripped his arm to steady him. 'Now, you mustn't say a word to anyone, do you understand?' Elio barely heard him. 'I shouldn't have told you, but when you looked up at me with such misery I felt you needed something to live for. Now you have it. You are going to be a grandfather. Floriana will need you. Now is your chance to make amends.' The sacristan felt a sudden sense of satisfaction at doing something good.

'Dante Bonfanti?' Elio muttered, scratching his head. 'Beppe Bonfanti's only son?'

'Yes, that's the one. Now remember, I told you not to say a word!'

'Not a word,' Elio repeated vaguely.

'Good. Let's get you home. I want you to give me all your bottles and we'll pour them down the lavatory. From now on you are going to be a different man. No more drinking and feeling sorry for yourself. God has given you another chance. You have it within your power to change your life and be the father you've always wanted to be.'

Elio stumbled over the cobbles, leaning heavily on the sacristan. Did he really say Floriana was pregnant by Dante Bonfanti? Was it possible? He grunted and nearly tripped. The sacristan caught him before he fell. In his inebriated state much was unclear. However, there was one thing that shone out from the mist as clear as quartz: Beppe Bonfanti would never allow his only son to marry his daughter.

The following day Dante spoke to Floriana via the public telephone in Luigi's. 'Everything has been arranged,' he explained. 'I will drive down on Friday the nineteenth of November and pick you up Saturday morning. I think it's best that we meet at the wall. We can spend the day together, then I'll drive you to the convent.'

'Will you be able to visit me there?'

'Of course I will. It's not a prison, you know.' He paused a moment. She could hear him breathing down the line. 'You're not frightened, are you, *piccolina*?'

'No. I'm excited. At the moment he's not showing at all. If I didn't feel nauseous all the time, I'd wonder whether I really was pregnant.'

In spite of her excitement, Dante dearly wished it was a false alarm. 'Once you've seen a doctor we'll know for certain.'

'Oh, I know for sure. I can feel him inside me although he's just the size of a seed.'

'And you think he's a boy?'

'For certain. I'm going to give you a son, Dante.' When he didn't reply, she grew anxious. 'Are *you* frightened?'

He didn't want to admit his fear. 'I feel guilty for having got you into this mess in the first place.'

'Don't feel guilty, my love. No child comes into the world by accident. God wouldn't be so careless. Every child is precious however he is conceived. Our son is more precious than most, because he was conceived with love.'

Dante couldn't help but smile at her idealism. He wondered whether she'd be so carefree once the child was born and crying through the night. 'I love you, Floriana.'

'And I love you, too, Dante.'

'Do you remember that day on the bench, when I took your hand and asked you your name?'

'Of course. I'll never forget it.'

'I sensed then that you were going to be a part of my life. I didn't know how, but I just knew we'd somehow be connected.'

'I sensed it, too.'

'You were lost and I wanted to look after you.'

'I'm not lost any more.'

'As long as I live, my *piccolina*, you'll never be lost.'

Elio watched his daughter like a lion watches an unsuspecting gazelle. He watched her come in humming to herself and he watched her leave with a skip in her step. Then he sat down and wrote a letter; the letter that was going to transform his fortunes for ever.

The sacristan had poured all Elio's bottles down the toilet. There wasn't a drop of alcohol left in the apartment, but Elio didn't care, his thoughts were on a higher goal, and for that he needed to be focused and alert. For the first time in years he had woken with a sense of purpose. A tingling sensation rippled over his body as he considered his daughter's predicament and what use could be made of it.

Beppe Bonfanti was one of the richest men in the country. There was simply no way that he would allow his son and heir to marry a local girl from an obscure little town in Tuscany. She might have deluded herself otherwise, and Dante might have convinced himself that they could run away together and live happily ever after, but the reality was blatant to anyone who had lived as long as he had. It wasn't going to happen. So, if his daughter wasn't going to become the wife of a millionaire he had to take what he could from the situation.

He chuckled as he wrote his letter to Beppe. He'd never been within sight of such easy cash in all his life. He had been a terrible father, but now he had the chance to make it up to his daughter. He couldn't demand that Dante make an honest woman of her, but he could demand money to support her and their bastard child – with a little extra for good measure.

Floriana decided that she wasn't going to tell anyone but Signora Bruno that she was leaving. She would simply go. Signora Bruno could inform her father that she had moved away to start a new life somewhere else and he could tell Aunt Zita. However, she was deeply indebted to Father Ascanio and it was right that she should go and thank him for his kindness.

The day before she was due to leave, she skipped over the cobbles with a light heart. Her future didn't frighten her at all. In fact, she looked forward to moving to a new town and starting over. There, no one would pity her for the mother who had left her and the father who got drunk every night and cheated at cards. No one would know anything about her. She'd reinvent herself as a mother with a small child and a handsome young husband who worked in Milan – no one would have to know that they weren't married. No one would have to know anything at all. She'd create a whole new identity.

That cold November morning Father Ascanio was giving Mass. Floriana sidled into the back of the church and waited until it was over. The usual party ensued in the square and it was another half-hour before the last stragglers dispersed. Father Ascanio smiled warmly at the sight of her. She stood a little apart, a coat wrapped tightly around her shoulders, arms folded against the autumn chill. Her hair blew about her face, which was pale and thin, and more beautiful than he had ever seen it. She no longer looked like a child.

'Floriana,' he said, taking her hands.

'I've come to thank you.' She lowered her eyes and found to her surprise that they were welling with tears. Father Ascanio and his church had been home to her. Now she was leaving, she didn't know when she would see them again.

'Don't cry, my child. God will always be with you wherever you are in the world.'

'You have been so generous and understanding and wise. I realize only now how much I have depended on you.' Her voice thinned and she couldn't go on.

'Come, let's go inside. It's getting cold.'

'May I confess, Father?'

'If it would make you feel better.'

'It would. One last time.'

She sat in the dark confessional and opened her heart in a way she had never done before. She spoke about her mother and the desperate sense of abandonment she had suffered as a consequence of her leaving. She spoke about her brother, the sorrow of his sudden disappearance and the jealousy she had felt that he had been chosen over her. And she spoke of her father and her deep shame.

Father Ascanio listened compassionately as she cut through the defensive outer shell she had forged for herself and delved into the soft, tender flesh of her sorrow. When she had finished they both sat in silence as the words settled around them like flakes of snow. She felt better for having opened her heart and released her grievances; less bitter towards her father, less resentful towards her mother, and in the light of her new life with Dante, her heart grew warm.

'Now you can see why my child is so important to me, Father. I do believe God has given him to me to make up for all that I have lost. And I will love him with all my heart and soul.'

Father Ascanio silently prayed for the angels to carry her into a bright and happy future.

Chapter 28

Beppe and Dante arrived at the office at nine a.m., as they did every morning. Beppe's driver picked them up from the family home on Via dei Giardini and drove them the twenty-minute journey to the factory, situated in a high-security, purpose-built business park on the outskirts of Milan. Beppe was proud of his son. He was a quick and enthusiastic learner and had wasted no time in rolling up his sleeves and getting to know every aspect of the business, from the factory floor to the boardroom. He cut a dash in his navy-blue suit and crisp white shirt, and looked every inch a figure of authority. One day he would step into his father's shoes and Beppe was more than satisfied that he was the right man for the job.

The sky was grey, it looked like it might rain, but inside the lights were bright and the building buzzed with activity. Beppe's employees were well aware of his high expectations and made sure they arrived at their posts before him. Too many workers had been dismissed without explanation for anyone to be complacent about his job. Beppe marched through the open-plan office of cubicles where heads were down over typewriters, telephones were ringing, cigarettes smoking and employees furiously looking busy. He smiled to himself, taking pleasure from their fear, which generated such high levels of productivity.

Dante strode into his office, leaving his father to his crisp and doting secretary, Signora Mancini. She greeted him with black coffee and a crimson smile and followed him into his office with the post. There, Beppe Bonfanti sat in splendour in a room designed to look as sumptuous as his own drawing room at home. There was a walnut drinks' cabinet with crystal decanters, a finely upholstered coffee table laden with glossy tomes, a suite of sofas and armchairs in the finest silk, and paintings on the walls from artists all over the world. His antique desk was vast, to reflect his importance, and behind him large windows gave out onto an ornamental pond complete with swans and geese.

'Your nine o'clock meeting is ready in the boardroom,' Signora Mancini said, placing the letters on his desk. 'Signor Pascale has just called to say he is running a little late.'

'Pascale is always late,' Beppe growled, taking off his loden coat and hat. Signora Mancini hung them on the stand by the door, as she did every morning, then awaited his instructions like a well-trained Labrador. Beppe dropped his gaze onto the pile of letters and frowned. Sitting on the top was a hand-written envelope stating 'Private and Confidential' in bold black ink. 'We'll start the meeting without him,' Beppe continued, picking it up and opening it. 'He's probably over-slept. He should invest in a better alarm clock.'

Signora Mancini watched her boss pull out a small white sheet of paper. His eyes narrowed as he scanned the page. After a moment, he inhaled deeply and flared his nostrils. Signora Mancini felt her blood chill as the air in the office grew cold.

'Bring me Zazzetta,' he said in a low voice, without taking his eyes off the letter. Signora Mancini left, heart pounding. When Beppe Bonfanti was angry, he didn't lose his temper as others did, but turned cool and steady, as if aiming a gun.

A moment later Zazzetta was standing before him. Signora Mancini closed the door and went back to her desk. She wondered what the letter could possibly contain to inspire such a powerful reaction in her boss. However, it wasn't her job to dwell on it, nor to wonder how Zazzetta would deal with it. It was better not to know.

Beppe handed him the letter. Zazzetta read it. He showed no emotion at all, but the sallow holes where his cheeks should have been were stained a pale, reluctant pink.

'So, the old drunk has sobered up enough to try to black-mail us,' said Beppe, lighting a cigar. He chuckled cynically. 'He must think he's holding the winning lottery ticket.'

'Are we sure Dante is the father?'

'It could be any man in Herba. Trouble is, we can't risk it, can we?'

'We don't want a scandal,' Zazzetta agreed.

'I am perplexed that my son should be so very stupid.'

'He is young and in love.'

'His brain is in his cock. If he wasn't my son, I'd slice it off.'

'If he wasn't your son, you wouldn't care.'

'But he is my son, so, what do we do, my friend?' Beppe shrugged and exhaled a cloud of smoke.

'We deal with it, *Capo*.'

'Yes, we deal with it in the simplest way. We pay the old scoundrel to shut up and we get rid of the problem.' He fixed Zazzetta with the cold eyes of a man who has ordered the efficient removal of enemies many times before. 'We make her disappear.'

'Do we have to take such drastic measures? She is a young girl . . .'

'Make it look like an accident.'

'But, *Capo*—'

'It is the only way or we'll have the father sucking our blood for the rest of his life. This is not the last time he'll come asking for money. I don't want this hanging over us, nor over Dante, the fool. The problem has to go away, full stop. There is only one way to be sure that it won't come back to haunt us again and again.' He turned to look out of the window. 'I wonder whether the old soak will consider it was worth it when he realizes his golden goose is gone for ever.'

'Won't he try to find her?'

'A man who is capable of selling his daughter in this way has no heart. You know as well as I do that Elio is a drunk, hopeless idiot. He'll take the money and run – and hopefully we'll never hear from him again.'

'Consider it done, *Capo*.'

'Good.' He turned back to Zazzetta. 'And not a word to my son. Perhaps we can pay someone to say that she ran off with a tomato seller.'

As Floriana left the church she spotted Costanza crossing the square weighed down with shopping bags. The girls stared at each other warily. It had been awkward between them for so long now. Instead of hurrying on, Floriana waved. Her heart was so full of happiness as she hovered on the brink of her new life that there was no room for bitterness. 'Do you want a hand?' she asked, smiling. Costanza looked at her anxiously. 'You don't have to worry, your mother's nowhere in sight.'

'It's not like that, really it isn't,' Costanza protested, but Floriana shook her head dismissively and briskly relieved her of one of the bags.

'What have you got in here?'

'I'm sorry, it's really heavy.'

Floriana peered inside. 'Fruit?'

'Mamma has put me on a diet.' Costanza shrugged. 'I'm not sure it's working, though.' She gave a pathetic smile.

Overcome with nostalgia for the way things used to be, Floriana suggested they go down to the beach. 'We can sit and chat like old times.'

'I don't know. I should be getting home.'

'Please.'

'Well, maybe quickly. If you don't mind carrying that bag.'

'I'm stronger than I look.'

'OK then. I'll come, but not for long or I'll get into trouble.'

They set off along the road that led out of town. 'So, your mother is really determined to marry you off, isn't she?'

'She's scheming and plotting.'

'In the end you'll marry who you want to marry and that'll be that.'

'No, I'll marry who *she* wants me to marry. I know that's my fate. I don't have the strength or the courage to go against her will.'

'You have time to grow strong.'

'I'm her only child. She has pinned all her hopes on me.'

'Are you still going to move back to Rome?'

'Papà's going to become an industrialist,' Costanza declared proudly.

'An industrialist?'

'Yes, we might move to Milan.'

'Milan?' Floriana thought of Dante and her stomach lurched.

'I only pick up bits and pieces. No one tells me anything. They still think I'm too young to understand. Or too stupid. Anyway, I think he's going to do something for Beppe Bonfanti. Consultancy work, I imagine. He's very well connected in the one area that Beppe isn't.'

'It all boils down to class,' said Floriana quietly.

'Yes, I'm afraid it does.'

They sat on the sand, two girls who had once shared so much, and gazed out across the ocean. 'I'm leaving, too,' said Floriana.

Costanza was astonished. 'Where are you going?'

'I don't know. I need to start afresh somewhere new.'

'What about Dante?'

Floriana longed to confide in her, but Dante had begged her

not to tell anyone. 'What about him? It was just a summer romance,' she replied carelessly.

Costanza looked genuinely sorry. 'Are you very sad?'

'No, I'm fine. I'm looking to my future now. No point dwelling on the past.'

'But you were so in love. I thought you were going to marry him and live happily ever after. I was hoping you would because that would have infuriated my mother more than anything else.'

'Perhaps your mother was right all along. I should find someone from my own world.'

'No, she's not right. Love has no boundaries of class or age or anything else.' Costanza took her hand. 'Wherever you go, will you promise to keep in touch?'

'How will I know where to find you if you move to Milan?'

'I'll leave my address at Luigi's. You can get it from him. So, when are you thinking of leaving?'

'Tomorrow.'

'So soon?'

'Yes, it's all arranged.'

'So, you weren't even going to say "goodbye"?'

'I was planning on slipping away quietly.'

'But where are you going?'

Floriana had to think quickly. 'I have a cousin in Treviso, so I shall go there.'

'I didn't think you had anyone besides Elio and Zita.'

'Neither did I until recently. Zita mentioned her and I seized the opportunity. She's married with children my age. She's agreed to take me in until I find a place of my own.'

'But what are you going to do?'

Floriana felt a stab of guilt as she embellished her lie. 'That's the difference between us, Costanza. I'm happy to do anything. Anything at all: cleaning houses, waitressing, gardening.

I'm ready to put my hand to anything. Girls like you are too grand to stoop that low.' She laughed. 'Don't worry about me, I'm very resilient.'

'I've always admired that about you, Floriana.'

'Don't tell anyone I'm going, though, please.' Costanza frowned. 'I mean it. Not a soul. I can trust you, can't I?'

'You know you can. But why mustn't anyone know?'

'Because I don't want my father coming after me.'

'I see.'

'I just want to leave without any fuss.'

'But Zita must know.'

'Yes, Zita knows, but she won't know that *you* know. So please don't mention it to her.' Floriana was almost breathless with spinning such a complex web of lies. 'Just keep it to yourself.'

'I shall.' Then in a small voice, Costanza added, 'I'll miss you, you know.'

'I'll miss you, too.'

'We had fun, didn't we?'

'We certainly did.'

'Until Mamma set us apart. I'll never forgive her for that.'

'Don't hold onto bitterness, just make sure that you don't become as snobby as she is.' Floriana pulled a comic face and they both laughed.

'No one makes me laugh any more,' Costanza complained. 'I'll miss your wit.'

'Then you must be the witty one.'

'I'll try.'

'If you're fun to be with you'll always be popular and then you can marry whoever you choose.'

'If only!' Costanza looked at her watch. 'I'd better go. It's been nice sitting here talking, just like old times. Are you coming?'

'I'll accompany you to the fork in the road. Then you'll

have to go the rest of the way on your own. I don't want to bump into your mother.'

'Neither do I!'

At the fork Floriana handed over the bag of fruit. 'Don't eat them all at once,' she said, suddenly feeling tearful.

'I wouldn't be allowed to do anything so rash.' Costanza looked at her friend sadly. 'Look after yourself, Floriana.'

'You too.'

Suddenly, Costanza put down the bags and flung her arms around Floriana's shoulders. She squeezed her hard and long. 'I hope your new life makes you happy. I hope it gives you everything you've ever wanted. I hope the angels keep you safe.' When she pulled away Floriana saw that she, too, was crying.

Floriana watched her walk up the road, her tread slow and heavy. Unable to bear it, she turned and hurried off towards home. She had to pack her things and make ready for the morning. Determined to keep her mind off the past she was leaving, she remained focused on the future ahead.

When she arrived back at her apartment, she was met by her father. He didn't appear drunk or hung-over but he wore the most unfamiliar expression on his face. Before she could speak, she noticed a stranger in the room with them, a strong, burly man with thick black hair and oily skin.

'What's going on?' Floriana asked, sensing danger but not knowing what form it took.

'My daughter,' said Elio, reaching out for her. She flinched and narrowed her eyes. 'I know you are expecting a baby.' The world spun out of control and she put her hand on the wall to steady herself. 'Don't be alarmed. I'm happy, Floriana. I'm going to be a grandfather. This man is here to take you somewhere safe so you can have your baby without scandal. When you are ready, you can come back and we'll be a family again.' She stared at the stranger and her mouth went dry. Where was

Dante? How had her father found out? She noticed he was holding a thick brown envelope. 'Oh, this?' he said, tapping it against his hand. 'This is a little gift from Beppe.'

'You blackmailed him?' she hissed, incredulous that her own father could betray her.

'You might not be happy now, but you'll thank me later.'

'Where's Dante?' she asked. 'Where is he?'

'He is waiting for you up at the house,' said the stranger.

'But I was to meet him tomorrow.'

'The plan has changed,' the stranger continued. 'You are to come now.'

'Can I pack my things?'

The man nodded. 'Of course.' She marched past them into her bedroom and closed the door behind her.

Her first instincts were to climb out of the window and run away. But what if the man *was* speaking the truth? What if her father *had* informed Beppe and he had given him money to support her? What if Dante *was* waiting for her at La Magdalena? After all, there was no way of letting her know with no telephone in the house. Perhaps Beppe was now taking control of the situation, which would surely be a good thing? In which case they wouldn't have to skulk about any more but could declare their love openly.

With these thoughts she began to put her few belongings into a bag. It didn't take long. She was anxious to get out of the house and as far away from her father as possible. There was something callous about his eyes, something she didn't recognize or like.

When she emerged, her father tried to embrace her, but she recoiled in disgust and hurried down the stairs after the swarthy man, who smelled of cheap cologne. She looked around for Signora Bruno, but she was nowhere to be seen. She climbed into the little black car that was parked in Via Roma, as her spirits fluctuated between excitement and fear.

It didn't look like the sort of car Beppe Bonfanti would own and she hesitated, her instincts crying out that something wasn't right. But she was incapable now of doing anything about it. As Floriana's pulse thumped in her temples, the stranger started the engine and the car rattled up the street.

Floriana didn't say a word. She was too frightened. She kept her eyes on the road ahead. At least they were going in the right direction. She noticed the man's hands. They were large and strong and gripped the steering wheel very tightly. Then her gaze strayed past them to the door and she saw that it was locked. They were *all* locked. Her breath caught in her chest and her head grew dizzy with terror. The gates of La Magdalena reared up in front of them and she felt a tremendous wave of longing wash over her, forcing her back in her seat. She began to knot her fingers and her palms grew damp with sweat. Slowly they approached, so slowly it was as if she was outside her body, looking down. As if she was watching a movie of someone else's life.

At that moment, Good-Night ran out into the road, breaking the spell. She sat up and gazed at him in desperation. He seemed to know that she was in the car and strained his neck to see her. The car didn't slow down, but sped past the dog and the gates of La Magdalena. She swivelled around in her seat and banged on the window. 'Good-Night! Good-Night!' The dog recognized her at once and bounded speedily after her.

'Sit down!' commanded the man. 'Or you'll make me crash.'

'Where are you taking me?' she demanded. When he didn't reply she began to sob. 'You're not taking me to Dante, are you?' She stared out of the rear window as the dog slowed down to a trot and grew smaller and smaller, until he was a little dot on the tarmac. 'What are you going to do with me?' Still he didn't answer. He had his orders. He clutched the steering wheel until his knuckles turned white.

*

The following day it poured with rain. Dante waited for Floriana under an umbrella by the wall, as they had arranged. He paced up and down, up and down, every now and then looking at his watch, wondering why she didn't come. Good-Night stood in the middle of the road, ears back, tail between his legs, as restless as his master. He whined, trotting in circles as Dante grew ever more anxious, but he had no way of letting his master know what he had seen.

Heavy-hearted, Dante drove into Herba. He encountered Signora Bruno at the door, but she was as mystified as he was. She had assumed the girl had gone to see *him*.

He found Elio drinking at the bar in Luigi's. The old man was sobbing into his glass. 'I've lost my daughter,' he wailed.

'Where has she gone?' Dante demanded.

'Just like her mother,' said Elio.

'What are you talking about?'

'Run off with her lover.'

'What lover?'

'A man she met at the market.'

'You're confused,' snapped Dante.

'No, she's a whore!' The old man cackled. 'And you thought the child was yours. Ha! That's the funniest part of the story. I'd laugh if I wasn't so bloody miserable. Just like her mother. Now I am well and truly alone.'

Dante left the bar, reeling. He knew in his heart that what Elio said could not possibly be true. The man was drunk and hallucinating. He *had* to find her, but where in the world would he start looking?

When he arrived back at La Magdalena Good-Night was waiting for him at the gates in the pouring rain. At first Dante barely recognized him: he was sodden and bedraggled, and the fur about his face was grey, making him look old and sad. Dante climbed out of the car and ran over, lifting the animal into his arms. But as he staggered back to the car he was overcome with loss, and sank to his knees. He buried his face in the dog's soggy neck and cried.

'Where is she? Where has she gone?'

Good-Night wriggled out of his embrace and limped into the middle of the road. Then he lay down with a whine and placed his head between his paws.

Chapter 29

Devon 2009

Rafa awoke to Biscuit jumping onto his bed with an enthusiastic leap. For a second he defended himself, forgetting about the rescue the evening before. Then, just as suddenly, it all came rushing back, and he laughed, pulling the dog into his arms affectionately.

'Oh, it's you, Biscuit!' he said in Spanish. 'You want to go out, I suppose?' Biscuit seemed to understand, for he sprang off the bed and waited by the door, wagging his tail.

Rafa dressed and made his way downstairs with his new companion. The hotel was gently stirring to life. He could hear the creaking of the water pipes beneath the floorboards and the gentle clatter from the dining room where a few early risers were already having breakfast. Shane was in the hall with Tom, while Jennifer was at reception, checking her mobile telephone for messages. When Biscuit clattered down the stairs they all stopped what they were doing and greeted him enthusiastically.

'He's none the worse for his fright,' said Shane, giving him a firm pat.

'He's had a good sleep,' Rafa informed him.

'Isn't he adorable?' Jennifer gushed, crouching down to tickle his ears. 'I'm glad he's allowed to stay.'

'By the skin of his teeth,' said Tom with a smirk.

Rafa took Biscuit round to the front of the hotel and

watched him run down the lawn. It was a beautiful June morning. The sky was veiled in a light mist, the sun already burning through to reveal patches of blue. He put his hands in his pockets and thought of Clementine. The mental picture of her made him feel light inside. He imagined her smile and the way it transformed her face. Then his thoughts clouded a moment as he remembered why he had come. He knew it wouldn't be in his interests to get too close, especially at this stage. But he was beginning to feel a warm sense of belonging and he was beginning to *care*. The thought of seeing her later filled him with anticipation, and he wasn't sure he'd be able to wait until the end of the day. He strode into the vegetable garden while Biscuit sniffed the ground excitedly, taking in all the new, unfamiliar smells.

Rafa pulled out his BlackBerry. He felt the urge to call her, just to hear her voice. He scrolled down to her number and pressed it. It rang a few times before going through to her voicemail. He grinned as he listened to her recorded message: 'Hi, it's Clemmie. Not a good moment. Sorry. You know the drill.' There followed a long bleep.

'*Buenos días*, Clementine,' Rafa said. 'I'm in the garden with Biscuit. It is a beautiful day. I don't feel right taking our dog for a walk without you. He's just found a very interesting hole in the grass. Luckily it is not big enough for him to climb into. We need to buy him food, no? Let me know when you are free. Have a good day in the office. *Ciao*.'

As he hung up, he saw Biscuit accosting Harvey as he came out of his shed at the bottom of the vegetable garden. The old man was surprised to see a dog on the property and looked around anxiously to see where he had come from. Rafa hurried down to explain. 'Ah, Rafa. Does this little fellow belong to you?'

'He's called Biscuit. Clementine and I rescued him from the rocks last night.'

'Has Marina seen him?' Harvey looked concerned.

'She says we can keep him.'

'She does?'

'Yes. She wasn't too happy about it, but his owner tried to murder him.' Rafa shrugged. 'I guess she felt sorry for him.'

'I'd keep him away from her as much as possible, all the same,' Harvey advised. 'I think she's afraid of dogs.'

'A bad experience in the past perhaps.'

'Perhaps.' He bent down to stroke him. 'Affectionate dog, isn't he? I don't think it'll be long before he wins her over.' Then he spoke to Biscuit. 'You're not going to frighten anyone, are you?'

'I don't think he'll see off Baffles, do you?'

Harvey chuckled. 'You're right about that. He's no Rottweiler. Still, a dog is better than none. He may surprise us and bring the thief in by the collar.' Rafa watched him straighten his tweed cap then walk slowly up the garden. Biscuit ran off in the opposite direction and Rafa was left no alternative than to follow him.

As he walked down the path to the beach his BlackBerry bleeped with a message. He knew it was from Clementine before he pulled it out of his pocket, and his heart swelled with joy.

Good morning indeed! You're out early. We'll have to train Biscuit to sleep in. Pick me up after work and we'll go together. Don't forget to bring the client. He might be choosy. C

He returned to the hotel with a spring in his step. Jennifer informed him that a group of six girls were arriving on the train from London for a hen weekend and might be keen to do some painting. She added that a couple of bird-watchers from Holland were due that evening and might be interested, too. Rafa shrugged nonchalantly. If there were enough paint brushes he was happy to tutor them all.

He breakfasted with the Brigadier, Pat, Jane and Veronica,

while Grace had hers in her bedroom. Biscuit lay obediently at his feet, oblivious that he was the subject of their conversation.

'How could anyone be so cruel?' said Veronica when she heard how Biscuit had been left in the cave to drown.

'There are some very nasty people in the world,' Pat added. 'Sue McCain says you can't trust a person who doesn't like dogs, and I think she's right. Anyone who ill-treats a dog has a heart of stone.'

'Hear hear!' exclaimed the Brigadier, winking at Jane, who hid her blush behind her cup of coffee.

The Brigadier and Jane had much in common. Rafa noticed the enthusiasm with which she told him about her childhood in an army garrison in Germany, and how the Brigadier listened with great interest, nodding his agreement and reminiscing about his own army days. It was as if they were at a table of their own. He wasn't surprised when they declared they'd pass on their painting lesson and walk to Salcombe instead. The look that passed between them was at once tender and mischievous. Pat was on the point of suggesting she go too when Veronica interrupted briskly, proposing another outing in Grey's boat. Nothing could tempt Pat as surely as the sea, and the Brigadier breathed a heavy sigh of relief and smiled gratefully at Veronica.

The morning passed slowly. Rafa took his students down to the beach and they positioned themselves on the rocks to paint the sea. The six girls on their hen weekend giggled and flirted with him so brazenly that they barely touched their paints, while Grace scowled from the other end of the beach and complained about their lack of refinement to Veronica and Pat.

After lunch, Rafa retreated to his bedroom for some time on his own. He looked out of the window, at the magnificent view of the ocean, which never ceased to capture his attention, when he was suddenly distracted by the unexpected sight of Marina wandering across the lawn towards Biscuit, who lay asleep in the shade of the cedar tree. He remained staring as she trod slowly, hands in pockets, shoulders a little hunched, then stood a while gazing down at him, alone with her thoughts. He wondered what she was thinking – and if it wasn't fear that made her recoil last night, what was it?

After a long while, she sat beside him and rested her hand on his head. Rafa could feel the weight of her sorrow as if it fell on his shoulders, too. The dog slept on, but Marina gently stroked his fur, never taking her eyes off him. Rafa could barely take his eyes off *her*. He wanted to go down and sit with her. He wanted to ask her why the dog made her feel so sad. But he knew it would be intrusive. He didn't know her well enough – and he didn't want to break the moment. Eventually, he dragged himself away and went into the bathroom to freshen up for his afternoon lesson.

Clementine had wanted to tell Joe about Biscuit but she couldn't trust herself not to give away the growing feelings she had for Rafa. The two were intertwined: Biscuit was the excuse that would throw them together, and she couldn't think of the dog without recalling Rafa's heroism. So, she had made up a story about helping her father with his boat and falling into the sea, which is why she was in his dressing gown with her wet clothes in a plastic bag.

Joe had bought it, because he had *wanted* to buy it. If he suspected she was lying, he hadn't let it show. He had put his big arms around her and if he had felt her body stiffen, he had ignored it.

She had spent a long time in the bath, recalling every moment of the rescue – the way Rafa had swum so bravely, the way he had encouraged her so confidently, the way he had cared so deeply for the endangered animal. He had touched her heart and she had flung wide the door and let him in. Only, he didn't know that he was in.

So, why didn't she just end it with Joe? She had asked herself that question many times, and always got the same answer: but then she'd have no one.

In the morning love had awoken her early. She had left Joe asleep, spread-eagled in the bed, but she was too wound up to feel any regret. Her belly was full of tingling nerves like the mad crawling of a whole nest of ants. She wasn't hungry, but she stopped at the Black Bean Coffee Shop anyway, to feel close to Rafa even though he wasn't there. When she had received his voicemail, her stomach had lurched with excitement. The thought of their afternoon outing to the pet shop had propelled her through her day.

She had sat at her desk dreamily, half listening to Sylvia whingeing on about Freddie and whether or not he'd ever leave his wife, half replaying the rescue over and over again. She glowed with the infectious light of love and every man who came into the office sensed it and was drawn to it, leaving with a little sprinkle on his shoulders and a spring in his step. Mr Atwood lingered as much as possible, hovering around her desk like a mosquito. Clementine barely noticed him.

Joe telephoned but Clementine managed to avoid his calls. Sylvia glanced at her suspiciously, wondering why she was too busy to speak to him. But when Rafa appeared at 5.30 p.m. with Biscuit, she realized why: Clementine was in love – but not with Joe. She felt the air vibrate between her and Rafa like a whole orchestra of violins, and couldn't help but feel a stab of jealousy. Why didn't Big Love ever happen to her?

Clementine cuddled the dog affectionately, recounting to Sylvia how they had saved him from drowning. Rafa rejoined that if he ever found the person who had tied him up in that cave, he'd personally beat him to a pulp. Clementine looked on proudly as Sylvia's admiration glowed on her face. He was not only handsome, but heroic, too. Biscuit had recovered from the shock of his near-death experience, as only a dog can. He wagged his tail and panted, pushing his nose under Clementine's hand whenever she got distracted and paused her stroking. He was clearly happy with his new owners.

Sylvia watched them all leave. She had read about another robbery in the *Gazette*. A small one, this time, at the private home of Edward and Anya Powell, who happened to be great friends of Grey and Marina. The only thing taken was an enormous diamond engagement ring Anya always put in an ashtray on the kitchen window sill when she was washing up. The only proof that it was stolen at all and not mislaid was the note saying 'Thank you' in the unmistakable hand of Baffles, the gentleman thief. The journalist reporting said there was a chance that it was a spoof, a copycat burglary, for why would Baffles bother to break in for one small piece of jewellery, unless he was getting a buzz out of once again slipping through the net?

Clementine and Rafa went straight to the pet shop. They filled a trolley with dog food, biscuits and toys. Rafa pulled treats off the shelves and took them out onto the pavement for Biscuit to sniff. Clementine watched, amused, while Rafa was certain the dog had the ability to choose from the packet what he liked best. She realized she hadn't ever had such fun. Sure, people made her laugh, but never with such abandon. Most of all she felt *she* was fun to be with. Rafa brought out the best in her and she liked who she was when she was with him.

They stuffed Rafa's boot with their goods, then drove to Salcombe to give Biscuit a run. It didn't seem right to take him to the beach where they had first heard him cry for help, so they took him to a pebble beach nearby and let him off the lead to explore freely. They wandered up and down, chatting contentedly, then found a pub nearby and sat outside in the fading sunlight to enjoy a light dinner. Clementine didn't feel the need to drink copious amounts of alcohol. She no longer felt the desire to lose herself.

When her telephone rang, she looked at the name on the screen and pulled a face.

Rafa raised his eyebrows. 'Joe?' he asked. Clementine nodded. She wished he'd mind but he simply smiled at her. 'Aren't you going to answer it?'

Reluctantly she put it to her ear. 'Hi, Joe.'

'Where are you?'

'I'm at a pub with a friend.'

'The Argentine and his dog,' Joe stated flatly. Clementine was taken by surprise. She hadn't expected him to know. 'I came by your office but you had already left. Look, Clemmie, we need to talk.'

'You're right, we do.' She watched Rafa stroke Biscuit, but she knew he was listening.

'When are you coming back?'

'Soon.'

'We'll talk then.'

'OK.' She hung up. 'Sylvia told him I went off with you. He's not over the moon about it.'

Rafa sat up and looked at her, his brown eyes full of understanding. She remembered the first time he had gazed into her eyes like that, in the church when she had told him she believed Marina had stolen her father, and he had been as irresistible then as he was now. 'You should move back in with your parents.'

'I know.'

'You don't love him.'

'That obvious, eh?'

'I'm afraid you don't have to be a rocket scientist to see that you used him just to get at your stepmother – and perhaps to get at me, too.'

She blushed but brushed aside his analysis. 'I've only just moved in.'

'That's irrelevant. You cannot stay in a relationship if your heart isn't in it.'

'I'm very proud.'

'Pride only hurts the proud. Let it go. Everyone makes mistakes, there's nothing wrong with that. It's Life. But if you hold onto unhappy situations just because you're too proud to relinquish them, then you're the fool.' He took her hand in his. 'Don't be the fool, Clementine. You're way too clever for that.'

She felt her blush deepen. Nothing else existed but his hand and the feel of his skin touching hers. She tried to act as if it meant nothing, but she was sure her heart was jumping through her T-shirt like a cricket trying to find its way out. He was looking at her so intensely she could barely hold her ground, but she was determined not to look away. 'You're a very special girl,' he said softly. 'The trouble is you don't see yourself that way. You have to start looking at yourself through my eyes.'

'What do you see?'

'I see a very beautiful smile. I see blushing cheeks and pretty blue eyes, but I see beyond all that to the person you are inside, and I like that person very much.'

Clementine shuffled on the bench. 'I don't know what to say.'

He shrugged. 'Then don't say anything at all. I'm simply stating things the way they are.'

'Do you say these things to everyone?'

'Only if I mean it.'

'But do you see blushing cheeks and pretty eyes in everyone? Or . . . or . . .' she hesitated. 'Or is it just me?' She laughed to hide her embarrassment.

'It's just you, Clementine,' he said seriously, and his gaze felt like a caress as it swept across her face.

They drove back into town with Biscuit at Clementine's feet. The air was highly charged now that they had both gone some way towards declaring themselves. And yet they hadn't, quite. Clementine wished Rafa would just stop the car and kiss her, then it would clear the air like a thunderstorm after days of heavy humidity. But he pulled up outside Joe's house and got out to open her door. She stepped onto the pavement.

'Would you like me to wait for you?' he offered.

She wanted to run upstairs, grab her bags and drive off into the sunset with him. 'No, I'll be fine, thank you,' she said instead. 'I don't know how long this is going to take.'

'Do you want me to warn Marina?'

'No, don't say anything. I'll say it myself when I see her.'

'She'll be very pleased, you know. I think she's missed you.'

Clementine sighed heavily. 'To tell you the truth I've missed them all, too. I knew from the beginning that I was making a mistake. I feel bad for Joe.'

'Text me if you need support.'

'After your heroics in the sea, I have no doubt that you would come to my rescue if I needed you.'

'You know I would.' He watched her unlock the front door.

'Here goes,' she mouthed, before disappearing inside and closing it behind her.

Rafa drove back up to the Polzanze. He took his time, taking pleasure from the lush countryside and cotton clouds that caught the wind and raced across the darkening sky like sailing boats. He was beginning to love it here, but most surprisingly of all, he was beginning to love Clementine.

He bit the inside of his cheek as he recalled how close he had come to kissing her. In any other time or place he would have swept her into his arms and kissed her days ago. He would have kissed her in the house that God forgot, he would have kissed her in the sea, he would have kissed her when she was furious with him and asking him to leave, and he would have kissed her many times since – countless opportunities, desire growing steadily stronger – but one thing was standing in his way.

He kept his eyes on the road ahead and drove on.

Chapter 30

Marina and Grey were sitting at the kitchen table finishing supper when Clementine's car drew up outside the hotel. She got out and stood a while in the dark, mustering up the courage to face them. Moving in with Joe had been an act of defiance, but she admitted now that it had also been a cry for help. It hadn't extracted the reaction she had hoped for. Or if it had, her father and stepmother hadn't let their feelings show.

She thought of Rafa and the advice he had given her. It was time she talked to Marina. The English were great avoiders. They were happier plodding on pretending issues didn't exist. Her family was worse than most. They had never discussed the past or opened up about the way they felt. But Rafa had given her the courage to do it. She would listen to her stepmother's side of the story, accept it, then let it go.

She pulled her bag out of the boot, and with a deep breath strode over to the stable block. Marina heard the door open and assumed it was Jake. When Clementine stood in the doorway she was caught off guard.

Grey noticed her suitcase in the hall behind her. 'Clementine!' he exclaimed happily. 'How nice to see *you*.'

'Is everything all right?' Marina asked, reaching for her glass of wine.

'I've come home,' Clementine stated.

Marina knew her reaction was crucial if she didn't want the

girl running off again. 'Do you want to talk about it?' she asked carefully.

'I broke off with Joe.'

'Come and sit down, darling. I think you need a drink, don't you?' said Grey, getting up to find her a glass.

'I should never have left in the first place.'

Marina noticed the heavy cloud that usually accompanied her everywhere was no longer in evidence. She had put down her sword and come in peace. 'I'm so pleased you're back,' she said truthfully. 'I'm sorry you and Joe didn't work out. That must be a great disappointment. But I'm happy you're home.'

'It's not a disappointment at all. I never cared about Joe. I never really cared about myself. But I do now.' A smile like that of a smug cat crept onto her face. 'I see the world through different eyes. I'm never going to settle for second best again.'

Marina didn't have to ask who was behind the change of perspective. Grey, however, was oblivious and frowned quizzically. 'That's good,' he said and poured her a glass of Pinot Grigio.

'Marina, I'd like to talk to you alone. Do you mind, Daddy?'

'I'll give her some fortification, then,' he said, replenishing Marina's wine. The two women stood up.

'Let's go outside,' Clementine suggested.

Marina refused to give in to temptation and catch her husband's eye. She could feel his baffled stare. She assumed Clementine wanted to talk about Rafa and felt her heart swell with pleasure that the child was at last looking to her for guidance. She'd tell Grey later when they were alone.

'I'll just get my coat,' she said, striding into the hall.

'Me too. It's a chilly evening, but it's so beautiful. I want to sit under the stars.'

Grey did notice the change in Clementine's tone of voice, however; the way she said 'beautiful' was different, as if she said it with her heart and really meant it.

THE HOUSE BY THE SEA 383

The night was deep and dark but as soft as velvet. A brisk
wind swept off the sea but it was a warm wind that smelled of
salt and damp grass, and the roar of waves crashing against the
rocks below was a distant, friendly rumble. The moon shone
brightly, every now and then hidden from view by swift clouds
that rolled across the sky. Clementine and Marina walked
down the lawn to sit on the bench. They were quite exposed
there, overlooking the ocean and far-off peninsula where the
lighthouse shone its warning light through the inky blackness.
They wrapped their coats around them and sat down.

'I never understood why you loved it here so much,' said
Clementine with a contented sigh. 'I was a town girl, happier
on pavement than on grass. Yet now, it's as if a veil has been
lifted from my eyes and I see the extraordinary beauty of this
place.'

'You do?'

'Yes, and it makes me feel good inside.'

'Nature is a wonderful healer. If ever I'm unhappy I come
out here and absorb it. I always return feeling better.'

Clementine took a gulp of wine. 'Marina, I want to apologize for being such a cow.'

Marina took a gulp, too, astonished by her stepdaughter's
admission. She didn't think she had ever heard her say sorry in
all the years she had known her. However, she wasn't entirely
convinced and decided not to say anything until she was sure
that there wasn't an ulterior motive to her apology.

'I know what you're thinking,' Clementine continued.
'And I deserve it. If I was in your position I wouldn't believe
me either. But I really feel sorry. I do. Ever since I was little
I've believed that you broke up my family and stole my father
from under Mummy's nose. And I felt that you stole him
from me, too. But there are always two sides to every story
and I want to hear yours, if you'll tell me. I'd like to understand from your point of view and put an end to my childish

interpretation. I'm adult enough to know that nothing is ever black and white.'

Marina felt her throat constrict and blinked back tears. She took her stepdaughter's hand. 'I don't know what to say. I never thought we'd ever have the chance to sit alone like this and be honest and open with each other. You have no idea how long I have wished to talk to you, woman to woman, and beg your forgiveness.'

Clementine was surprised how tender her heart felt. For a moment she wondered whether it was the wine that had turned her all soft, but then she felt the warmth in Marina's hand and realized it was love that had thawed the ice there and opened it up like a tulip. 'You don't need my forgiveness,' she said softly.

'I do. When I fell in love with your father he was married with two small children. I could have walked away and left him in his unhappiness, but I didn't. I don't suppose your mother ever spoke of the acrimony. According to your father, you were a family intact, but so broken.

'Grey and I found each other because I, too, was lost. I recognized the loneliness in him because I felt it so profoundly myself. There was a big difference in age and he was very well educated, while I was not. But we shared something and together we found we had the power to heal one another. I never set out to steal him and I certainly never wanted to destroy a happy family. But, Clemmie, you *weren't* a happy family and in the end our love eclipsed everything else. I carry that on my conscience.

'What we did wasn't right, but we felt it was best for everyone, including you and Jake. I don't know whether children are better off with unhappy parents, or with happy step-parents. I don't have the answer. But you can be sure your father has always loved you and Jake above all others, including me. You might not have felt it, as a little girl you were always so angry you pushed him away whenever he reached out to you. I expected you to push me away, but I tried all the same. You must know that his love for you is unconditional.'

She drained her glass and swallowed hard, though her throat was so tight it hurt as the wine went down. She stared out over the sea and Clementine felt a chill ripple across her skin from the inside.

'As you know, Clemmie, I cannot have children. It is my deepest sorrow and something that claws at my heart every day and every night. Sometimes, I can barely function because the desire to love is so strong. Most of the time I throw myself into the hotel and give that all the care and nurture I would give a child. It is a poor compensation, but it is all I have. You and Jake will never be mine. I have inherited you and I thank Fate for that blessing. We haven't had it easy, you and I. But I understand. I can never be a mother to you, and I wouldn't expect to be. But I do very much want to be your friend.'

Clementine began to cry. She realized then that she had so misunderstood her stepmother. The facts of her parents' marriage break-up were irrelevant, as were the facts of Marina and Grey's affair – *they* had never been the issue. When the artichoke of her life was peeled away, petal by petal, the core was love and the fact that Clementine had felt she had not been given enough.

'I've been so selfish,' she sniffed. 'I've only ever thought about myself and how little attention I'm getting. That's all it is. I feel such a fool.' She thought of Rafa and how he had seen past the prickly petals to the core all along. 'And, Marina . . .?'

'Yes?' Her stepmother put her arm around her and drew her close. 'What is it?' Clementine was crying so much now she was unable to speak. 'It's OK, you mustn't feel bad. It's only natural to feel like you do. Every child wants their parents to love them above all others, and marriage break-ups—'

'It's not that.' Clementine wiped her face with her sleeve and sat up.

'Oh, I see. There's something else.'

'Yes. I'm in love. I'm desperately in love and I don't know what to do about it.' Her breath caught in her chest.

'Rafa?'

She nodded. 'I don't know how he feels about me. One moment I think he's going to kiss me, then he pulls away. I don't know whether he leads everyone on like that, or whether I'm special. It's been such a short time but I'm crazy about him.'

'I can't say I haven't noticed that you're keen on him. But I haven't seen you together enough to tell you how I think he feels.'

'Today he told me that I'm special. He took my hands and told me I'm beautiful. Then, when I asked him if he said that to all the girls or if it's just me, he said that it was just me. I could have sworn he was about to lean over and kiss me. He looked at me so intensely. But we got up and drove back into Dawcomb, where he dropped me off outside Joe's flat. He knew I was going to break up with him.'

'And he didn't suspect that he's the reason?'

'I don't think so. He said he could tell that I wasn't in love with Joe.'

'I think we all worked that out.'

'So, what shall I do?'

Marina didn't hesitate. 'Absolutely nothing.'

Clementine was surprised; she was expecting a long lecture on how to play hard to get.

'You're lovely, Clemmie, just the way you are. He'd be a very stupid man to let you go.'

Clementine wanted to cry again, with gratitude. 'Thank you.' She put her arms around her stepmother's small shoulders and hugged her tightly. 'I'm so happy we're friends.'

'Me, too,' Marina agreed, closing her eyes.

When the two women returned to the stable block, Grey was still up, watching a documentary about sea creatures on Sky. He was surprised to see them both red-faced and shiny-nosed. Without a word of explanation, Clementine marched up to him and put her arms around his neck. She gave him a long, hard squeeze and planted a kiss on his cheek. 'I'm going to have a bath, my feet are freezing.' He watched, amazed, as she walked lightly out of the room.

'What's she taken?' he asked Marina.

'Come upstairs and I'll tell you. I need to warm up, too.'

'What the devil have you been up to?'

'Long story, but I feel wonderful.' She sighed heavily, unburdening years of pain, and grinned at him broadly. 'You're never going to believe it.'

'The hotel's heaving,' said Bertha the following morning, settling onto the kitchen chair like a nesting hen. 'Shame it's in such trouble.'

'What do you mean, trouble?' Heather asked, hugging her mug of coffee.

'I've heard they've run out of money,' Bertha said in a low voice. 'Though you didn't get that from me.'

'Who did you get it from then?'

Bertha pulled her ear lobe. 'Ear to the ground. Apparently, some bigwig is coming down from London to make them an offer.'

Heather's jaw unhinged. 'Are you sure?'

'Well, I heard Jake talking to his father in the stable block, and it sounded to me like they don't have much choice in the matter.'

'They'll have to bury Marina first. She won't give in without a fight. What'll happen to us?'

'I don't know. They might get rid of some people, but not us. We're independable.'

'You mean indispensable?'

'That's what I said, indispensable.'

'*You* might be, Bertha, but I'm not so sure about me. Anyone could do my job.'

'It's not anyone they'd want, now, is it? They'd want experienced staff who know their way around.'

'Hope you're right. Keep your ear to the ground and let me know if you hear anything else.'

Clementine was no artist, but the only way to spend time with Rafa was to join his class. He was pleasantly surprised when she appeared on the cliff top to paint the lighthouse with Pat, Grace and Veronica. 'I've got nothing else to do this weekend,' she said, sitting on a blanket with Biscuit.

Rafa gave her a sketchpad and some watercolours.

He bent down and whispered in her ear, 'You've made it more fun for me.'

'I'm really bad, though,' she replied, smiling at his compliment.

'Don't stunt your ability with your negative attitude.'

'Well, I haven't painted since school.'

'You're here to have fun and to enjoy this peaceful place. I bet you haven't sat and observed every wave and every cloud, every blade of grass and flower?' She looked at him quizzically. 'Most of the time we race through life with our eyes closed, absorbed in endless thought. We miss the simple magic of a buttercup hidden in the grass. Now you can really take the time to look around you with your eyes wide open and enjoy the beauty of nature. You can fully exist in the present.' He grinned and stood up.

She dipped her brush into the water. 'Very well, I'll exist in the present. But I'm not sure my picture will be any better for it.'

He put his hand on her shoulder. 'But *you* will be.'

The six hen-weekend girls had gone to spend the day at a spa, and the bird-watchers from Holland had gone in search of the solitary sandpiper. 'I'm glad we're not having to spend our last couple of days with those vulgar girls,' said Grace, tying a Hermès scarf under her chin to preserve her hair from the wind.

'They're young, Grace,' said Veronica. 'They're just having fun.'

'Still, they have no style. In our day there was no such thing as a ladette.'

'I came pretty close,' said Pat. 'I was a tomboy.'

'That's different. You didn't go throwing yourself at young men.'

'Had I had your looks and Veronica's grace, I think I might have,' Pat retorted.

At first Clementine was unable to lose herself in her sur-roundings. As much as she tried she was too aware of Rafa walking up and down, giving advice. It was only when he sat down beside her and began to lose himself in his own paint-ing that she was able to relax. The silence was comfortable. She didn't feel the need to fill it with chatter. Rafa seemed to fall into an all-absorbing world and soon she joined him there, noticing every seagull and every rock until she ceased to notice herself.

It was sunset when they returned to the hotel. Rafa was impressed with Clementine's painting.

'You're just being kind,' she protested.

'You have an interesting way of using colour.'

She laughed. 'Interesting, certainly, but not very good.'

'Let me be the judge of that.' His gaze lingered on her for what felt like a long time.

'Why are you looking at me like that?' she asked, suddenly embarrassed.

'The light is golden tonight.'

'Yes, it is.'

'I'd like to paint you.'

'Oh, really, Rafa, I'm not sure that even you could turn me into Botticelli's *Venus*.'

'I wouldn't have to. You're lovely just the way you are.' She frowned at him. Marina had said the same thing. Could it be possible that he was beginning to believe it? 'I mean it. I want to paint you before the sun goes down.' He threw the rug onto the lawn and insisted she sit down. Biscuit lay beside her and rolled onto his back, hoping she was going to take the hint and stroke his tummy. Pat, Veronica and Grace walked on up the lawn, leaving them alone.

Rafa opened his box of oils and found a fresh sheet of paper. 'What do you want me to do?' she asked.

'Talk to me,' he replied, looking at her intently.

She sighed. 'I think he's really going to draw us,' she said to Biscuit.

'I'm going to draw *you*,' he corrected. Then he grinned as he swept the oil pastel across the page. 'You know, you're a very beautiful girl, Clementine. But you're typically British in that you cannot accept a compliment. In my country girls thank a man when he flatters her.'

'All right, thank you.'

'My pleasure. Now talk to me.'

The sun seemed to hover above the tree line just for Rafa. The light was soft and mellow, the air infused with the scents of cut grass and honeysuckle, and in the tallest branches the birds settled down to roost.

'I did as you advised and talked to Marina,' said Clementine. 'You know, you're the only person who has ever given me proper advice.'

'I don't believe that.'

'You're the only person who has ever suggested I talk to her. My friends loved hearing my stories, and I'm ashamed to admit that I enjoyed telling them, and exaggerated wildly to get attention. My mother was always petty and small-minded, preferring that I ganged up with *her* rather than persuading me to build bridges. She's never been magnanimous and I suppose it must have given her pleasure that I never bonded with the woman Dad had fallen in love with. The truth is that no one ever told me to make friends with her. It had never occurred to me. And I never thought to listen to what *she* had to say.'

'But you did.'

'Yes, and you were right. There are always two sides to every story. She isn't a wicked stepmother after all, so I shan't call her Submarine ever again.' She dropped her gaze and rubbed Biscuit's stomach. 'I think I understand a little more about love.'

'You do?'

'Yes. Love is like a bright light that burns away all negativity. You know, like sunshine on mist. I felt my heart open when I listened to Marina, and all the heavy, unhappy fog simply evaporated. It was extraordinary. So, it got me thinking, happy people are full of love, unhappy people have very little, perhaps none at all. That's all there is to the world – those who love and those who don't. It's really very simple. If everyone loved there'd be no wars. Everyone would live in peace.'

'I think you should run for Prime Minister.'

She laughed. 'But how do you teach people about love?'

'There have been many teachers, like Jesus, Mohammed, Buddha, Gandhi, to name but a few. Now we can add Clementine Turner to the list.'

She watched him sketch, his hand moving confidently across the paper, and thought how attractive it was to be so talented. 'Rafa, have you ever been in love?'

'I've been in love many times,' he said, grinning at her. 'There's a very big difference between being "in love" and "loving". "In love" is infatuation. Loving begins when the infatuation passes and you really *know* the person. Otherwise, how can you love them if you don't *know* them?'

'So, have you ever *loved*?'

'Once.'

'What was she like?'

He thought for a moment. 'She was very sweet.'

'Blonde, brunette?'

'Brunette.'

'What happened?'

'I wasn't ready to commit.'

'Did she want to marry you?'

He shrugged. 'She was Argentine, that's all she thought about.'

'Did that put you off?'

'Not really, but I was restless. The timing was wrong.'

'So what happened?'

'She finished with me, found someone else and married him.'

'Were you very sad?'

'Of course, but what could I do?'

'Do you ever think about her?'

'Sometimes.'

'Do you regret that you didn't marry her?'

'Never.'

'Do you keep in touch?'

'No.' He narrowed his eyes and his lips curled at one corner. 'Any more questions or is the inquisition over?'

'You're very shady.'

'Shady?'

'Yes, you don't give away much about *yourself*. Sure, you talk about your parents and Argentina, but you don't talk about *you*.'

He sighed dramatically. 'All right. I'm a spy working under-cover for the Argentine government. But that is all I can tell you, otherwise I have to kill you.'

She stared at him pensively. He looked steadily back at her. For a moment neither spoke. Everything stilled. The sun finally dipped behind the trees, leaving them in shadow. They both felt the energy build between them. But Clementine was used to the warm feeling of desire and the anticipation of the kiss that never came. It took all the willpower she could summon to tear her eyes away. 'Are you nearly done now?' she asked, breaking the spell. 'I'm getting rather stiff.'

'The light has changed.'

'Shall we go in?'

He sighed regretfully. 'If you want to.'

She got to her feet. Biscuit rolled over and stretched. She could feel Rafa's disappointment as the energy drained away and the wind picked up.

'Can I see it?'

Rafa handed her the sketchbook. She looked at his picture and gasped in surprise. The girl in the golden light was beautiful. He gathered his paints and crayons and stood up. 'Do I really look like that?' she asked, staring at it.

'You do to me, Clementine.'

She frowned at him, wondering why, if he saw her like that, he didn't take her in his arms and kiss her. 'I don't know what to say.'

'Yes you do,' he replied.

'Thank you.' She handed back the book. 'Are you coming in?'

'In a minute. I want to make a telephone call.'

'Good night, then. I'll see you tomorrow.' Clementine marched up the lawn with Biscuit. She could feel Rafa's eyes on her back, but she didn't turn around. It had taken as much will as she could muster to walk away; she wouldn't have enough to do it a second time.

Rafa watched her disappear around the hotel, a frown rumpling his brow. He felt dissatisfied. He didn't know how much longer he could continue like this. Clementine was beginning to consume him. Whenever he tried to think of something else she popped back into his head. He thought he could control his feelings, but it was becoming increasingly clear that he could not.

He pulled out his BlackBerry and called his mother. At times like this he missed her dreadfully. He missed the sound of her voice and all that it represented. 'Mamá.'

'Rafa, *mi amor*. Is everything OK?'

'Mamá, I'm in love.'

There was a moment's silence. Then she spoke with surprising calmness. 'Is she very special?'

'She's unique.'

Maria Carmela might not have understood his motives for being there, but when it came to love, she understood very clearly indeed. 'So, why do you sound so sad?'

'I'm confused. I came here for one thing and one thing only. I didn't come here to fall in love.'

'Follow your heart, Rafa.'

'I want to. But I can't if I'm unable to be honest with her.'

'Then you have to come clean, Rafa. You have to tell her why you're there. You have to tell all of them the truth.'

'It could go horribly wrong.' Another moment of silence ensued. Maria Carmela did not know what to advise. *This* was beyond her. 'They know nothing. *Nothing*. And I'm still not sure. I need more time.' He sighed heavily. 'Am I being selfish? They're a happy family and I like them all so much. Then there's you. You're the most important person in my life – if you doubt me, then I cannot do it.'

'I've been thinking, if this is really so important to you, then you must do it and I will support you. Your father wouldn't be happy, but I'll deal with him when I see him in the next life. Leave him to me. Right now, you have to find peace. That is all that matters. It is your right and I am beside you all the way.'

He was almost too choked to speak. 'Thank you.'

'It is love that gives me the courage to let you go.'

'You're not afraid any more?'

'No. I am resigned and I am content. I don't know why I ever doubted you.'

He rubbed the bridge of his nose. 'You don't know how much that means to me.'

'Oh, yes I do. Now, do you want to hear what that silly parrot did today?'

He laughed and wiped the damp from his eye. 'Yes, tell me.'

When Clementine arrived at work on Monday morning, Sylvia was at the filing cabinet, her face hidden by a cascading wall of wavy hair. On close inspection Clementine could see that she was crying.

Mr Atwood wasn't in yet, neither was Mr Fisher. Clementine ignored the telephone, put the coffees on her desk and approached her.

'Are you OK?' she asked.

Sylvia sniffed and nodded. 'I hear you've broken up with Joe.'

'Yes, I'm afraid I have. It wasn't going anywhere. It was unfair of me to lead him on.'

'And you're in love with Rafa, aren't you?'

Clementine frowned. 'Is that why you're crying?'

Sylvia looked up from the drawer and pulled a sorry smile. She nodded. 'I don't love Freddie,' she confided. 'I never have. To be honest, I've never loved anyone, really. But the other day ...'

'Come and sit down.' Clementine put her arm around her. Sylvia allowed herself to be led to her chair. Clementine gave her the carton of coffee, which she began to sip half-heartedly.

'I saw you and Rafa together and, well, I could feel it.'

'Feel what?'

'Feel this incredible thing you have together. I've never had that. I've never believed in it.' She gazed at Clementine help-lessly. 'I want it.'

Clementine felt relief. It wouldn't be fun chasing the same man. 'So, you're not in love with Rafa?'

'Oh, I could be, he's very sexy, but no, I'm not in love. I just want to be.'

'Then stop being so cynical and wait for someone to rock your boat hard!'

Sylva's scarlet lips curled into a small smile. 'I doubt Freddie is ever going to leave his wife.'

'I don't know, but you shouldn't break up a marriage if you can help it.'

'I'm a bad person.'

'Misguided, that's all.'

She sighed. 'What must I look like! Have I got mascara half-way down my face?'

'You'd better hit the loo before Mr Fisher gets in. Hasn't he got a nine-thirty meeting?'

'Oh Lord, I forgot. Do me a favour, lovely – go and get some buns? And if you bump into another handsome foreigner, for goodness sake bring him back for me!'

Clementine hurried out into the street. It was a warm, sunny day, pigeons dropped onto the pavements to scrounge for scraps, and gulls circled high above like gliders. She sighed happily, filling her lungs with fresh sea air. Today she felt lighter inside, as if she had been relieved of a heavy burden. She walked with her shoulders back and her chin held high, and noticed the interested glances of the men she passed in the street. It had little to do with her clothes or high heels, and everything to do with her attitude. She liked herself, and that confi-dence radiated around her like sunshine. As she stepped into the Black Bean Coffee Shop she resolved to follow Marina's advice and just be herself. Rafa thought she was beautiful – that was a good start – and hadn't he said it was impossible to love someone without knowing them properly? They had the whole summer to get to know each other – and she looked forward to lying on her stepmother's bed and confiding her progress.

'They're on to him,' Jake told his father as Grey prepared to take some guests out in his boat.

'Your mole in the police force?'

Jake nodded importantly. 'Apparently, they have a lead.'

'Do they now? Well, that's good.'

'He's getting a little complacent.'

'Complacency will be his downfall in the end.'

'He should quit while he's ahead.'

'They never do. It's like a drug. They can't stop.'

'It shouldn't be long before they catch him, but keep it to yourself. They don't want him going to ground.'

At that moment Marina appeared at the boot-room door. 'I've got good news for you, darling.' Grey raised his eyebrows. 'William Shawcross has just telephoned.'

Grey's eyes lit up. 'And?'

'He'll be very happy to come and give a talk at our first literary dinner.'

'Well, that's just fantastic news.'

'I've got his number so you can call him back.'

Grey patted his son firmly on the back. 'Great idea, son.'

'Thanks, Dad.' They watched Marina walk off down the corridor.

'Though I'm not sure it's going to be enough to save us,' Grey added in a low voice.

'What are you thinking?'

'I'm trying hard *not* to think at the moment, but it's not

looking good. The bank is hot on my tail. It's only a matter of time before we have to make a tough decision.'

'You could retire.'

'I'm not rich enough to retire.'

'Buy a lottery ticket.'

'We need more than luck,' said Grey darkly. 'We need a miracle.'

Chapter 31

'I can't believe it's come to an end,' said Pat mournfully. 'It's gone too fast!'

'I wish we were staying another week, don't you, Grace?' added Veronica, leaning over to take one last sniff of the lilies. 'Oh, I do love the smell of this place.'

'You'll have to come again next year,' said Marina.

'I've had a lovely time,' Jane said, trying to sound jolly when inside she felt full of concrete. 'Thank you so much, Marina.'

Marina sensed her heavy heart and wondered whether it had anything to do with the Brigadier. They had been joined at the hip for the past few days but she had noticed his absence at breakfast.

'You can come any time you like,' she replied in a low voice so the others wouldn't hear. 'You can stay as my guest.'

Jane's cheeks reddened at Marina's implication and she hastily brushed it off. 'Oh, I wouldn't want to be a burden. I'm sure we'll all come again next summer.'

'If we're still around,' Grace interjected drily.

Marina accompanied them out onto the gravel where the people carrier waited to take them home.

'It's an oasis here. One forgets oneself,' said Pat, sweeping her eyes over the house one final time.

'I know. Heaven, isn't it?' agreed Veronica. 'Now I'm beginning to remember myself again.'

'What hell,' quipped Grace.

'Not so bad. I feel like a different person,' Veronica retorted. 'I shall miss my lovely room, though.'

'And I shall miss the maestro,' said Grace as Rafa appeared up the track, followed by an exuberant Biscuit.

'I'm sorry you're all leaving,' he said to the departing ladies. He tried not to look at Marina, who was staring pensively at the dog.

'Biscuit looks a lot better than he did the night you rescued him,' said Pat, whistling heartily and slapping her thighs. Biscuit trotted over eagerly.

'So, you're going to keep him,' said Veronica.

'Of course,' Rafa replied. 'He has nowhere to go.'

Pat bent down and gave his curly back a vigorous rub. 'What a good dog you are. Yes, you are, a very good dog.'

Grace rolled her eyes. 'Why is it the English all think their dogs understand what they're saying?'

'Oh, but he does,' Pat insisted.

Grace tutted. 'It's all in the tone of the voice. Look, Pat.' She approached the dog and in the same excitable voice as Pat, she gushed, 'You're a very *bad* dog, yes, you are, a very *bad* dog.' Biscuit wagged his tail so hard he nearly took off like a helicopter. 'See, said with the same intonation the silly animal doesn't know the difference.'

'You're an old cynic,' said Pat. 'Or should I say in my most jolly voice: You're a silly old bag, Grace.'

They said their goodbyes and climbed into the vehicle. The driver started the engine. Marina, Rafa and Biscuit stood back to wave them off. Just as they were drawing out of the drive, the Brigadier's old Mercedes swept round the corner, tooting the horn, demanding that they stop. 'He's late for breakfast,' observed Marina, glancing at her watch.

'I don't think he's come for breakfast,' said Rafa.

The Brigadier leaped out of the car like a young officer,

reached into the back seat, and extracted an enormous bouquet of white roses. The door of the people carrier slowly
opened and a blushing Jane stepped lightly down.

'I want to ask you to stay,' said the Brigadier, presenting her
with the flowers.

Jane pressed them to her nose, not knowing how to reply.
She felt foolish in her awkwardness. 'They smell wonderful,'
she said. 'How very sweet of you to think of me.'

'I went to a lot of trouble to find smelly ones,' he said. 'I
chose them because they smell like you.' A warm glow spread
across her face and she smiled self-consciously.

The Brigadier rocked back and forth on his heels as he
worked up the courage to deliver the short speech he had been
rehearsing all night. He cleared his throat. 'It's been a long time
since I've asked a girl out.'

'It's been a long time since I've been asked.' Jane's blush
deepened.

'I'd like to marry you, Jane.'

'Marry me?'

'Well, of course. We haven't got all the time in the world,
why beat about the bush? I like you very much. Very much
indeed and I think you like me, too.'

'Yes, I do.'

'So how about it?'

Jane looked around her, embarrassed to be the centre of
attention. Marina put her hand to her mouth, stunned by the
Brigadier's sudden proposal. They had known each other only
a week. Rafa was smiling broadly. Veronica, Pat and Grace
were practically hanging out of the car in their eagerness to
hear her response. Jane bit her bottom lip to stop it wobbling.
'Well, yes,' she replied timidly. 'Why not? Yes, please.'

'Sue McCain would be very proud of you,' said the
Brigadier, winking at Pat. 'Her motto must be something like
"seize the day".'

Pat chuckled and shook her head. 'Very funny, Brigadier. I'm not sure what her motto is, to tell you the truth. I'll remember to ask her.' She climbed down to join them.

'Well, young man,' Grace barked to the driver, 'don't dilly-dally, take Jane's suitcase off the bus! She's staying right here.'

'Oh, lucky lucky girl! She gets to stay in Devon!' gushed Veronica, dabbing her eye with a hanky. 'Oh dear, now we have to say goodbye all over again.'

Finally, the people carrier disappeared up the drive. The Brigadier carried Jane's case into the hall as she looked on anxiously. 'What do we do now?' she asked. 'I'm going to have to go home at some stage to sort myself out and tell my family.'

The Brigadier took her hand. 'Don't worry, my dear, you have all the time in the world for that. Right now, we'll go and have a jolly good breakfast.'

'That would be nice.' Jane had hardly eaten anything earlier.

'It's on the house,' said Marina. 'So is the champagne.'

'Champagne?' Jane repeated in surprise.

'Of course. A champagne breakfast is the only way to celebrate an engagement.'

'A champagne breakfast, at our great age,' Jane laughed.

'Which is why we're getting on with it,' said the Brigadier heartily. 'I suggest we tie the knot as soon as possible. Where would you like to go on honeymoon?' he asked.

'I'd like to stay right here,' she replied.

'Really? Right here, at the Polzanze?'

'Yes, Brigadier. I'm very happy here.'

'Then we'll come back after the wedding. But this afternoon I'm taking you home.' He raised his fluffy eyebrows. 'And I think it's time to call me Geoffrey, don't you?'

'Geoffrey,' she said softly. 'It suits you.'

'Geoffrey and Jane. That's got a nice ring to it.'

'Do you mind if I move you into a prettier room for your honeymoon, Mrs Meister?' said Marina, thinking of the room Grace had just vacated.

'I'm very content where I am,' Jane protested.

'Well, I'm not,' Marina replied. 'I'd be happier if you and the Brigadier spent the first days of your marriage in our best suite.'

'All right, if you insist.'

'Then that's settled. Now, let's open the champagne.'

Mr Atwood pulled the tights over his head. They were thick enough to mask his face, but thin enough for him to see through. He wore black trousers, a black polo neck and black shoes, soft soled so as not to make any noise when he crept into the house. He tiptoed round the building to where a ladder had been placed in the garden against the back wall. It was dark enough for him to blend in with the night, but the neighbour's window threw a shaft of light onto the lawn, which he was careful to avoid. He felt like a cat, treading softly over the dew.

Slowly he mounted the ladder. One rung at a time. It wouldn't do to fall and hurt himself – his wife thought he was out at a business dinner. Being driven to hospital in a burglar's outfit might give the game away. He grinned with satisfaction, pleased that he was able to keep so many different strands of his life together. It was entertaining to assume diverse personalities. He was a father, a husband, a businessman, a lover – and now a robber. He reached the window, which had been left ajar, and slid his fingers through the crack. Quietly, he lifted the bar and pulled it open wide enough for him to climb through.

As he rather clumsily scrambled in, not quite the cat burglar he was trying so hard to emulate, he heard a sharp intake of

breath and an excited squeak. His heart pounded with anticipation, for there, lying naked and spread-eagled on the bed,
was Jennifer. Her arms and legs were tied to the four posts, her
pale skin, sporran of golden pubic hair and round breasts
loomed out of the darkness, and she shivered expectantly.

'What do I see here?' he said in his coldest voice.

'Don't hurt me,' she wailed.

'Hurt you? I'm going to *pleasure* you to death.'

'Oooooooh, no!'

'Yes, I'm going to have fun, my little play-thing.'

'Please, leave me be!'

'And you're all tied up and ready for me.'

She pulled her arms and tried to wriggle her legs, but to no
avail. She was well and truly bound. He stood beside her and
ran a gloved finger down her neck, over the mound of her
breast, around her nipple, which grew hard with desire, down
her stomach, through the sporran and between her legs, where
it lingered.

So great was their focus on their game that they didn't hear
the rustle in the garden below or the loud whispers of the
police, who now surrounded the house. The neighbour
watched enthralled from her bathroom window. Hastily an
officer climbed the ladder. When he reached the window he
peered in to see the burglar about to descend onto his victim
with a very large erection.

With the swift, nimble movements of the cat that Mr Atwood
could never be, the officer leaped into the room and wrestled
him to the floor. Before Mr Atwood knew what was happening he was cuffed and helpless on the ground, the tights ripped
off his head with such force they bruised his nose. The lights
were turned on and the room filled with the familiar faces of
the Dawcomb-Devlish police force, gawping at them in astonishment. They looked from Mr Atwood to Jennifer, bound and
displayed like a pig at the butcher's, but only one or two had the

decency to avert their eyes. At last one of the officers threw a towel over her exposed body and set about untying the ropes.

'This is a terrible mistake,' gasped Mr Atwood.

'. . . Anything you do say may be given in evidence.'

'I'm not robbing the house, I'm role-playing with my mistress. For God's sake, this is ludicrous.'

'Come on!' said PC Dillon, lifting him to his feet.

Mr Atwood looked down to see his once proud erection shrivelled like a little pink worm. 'Well, if you insist I come with you can you please do up my trousers!'

The following morning word had got out and Dawcomb-Devlish could talk of nothing else.

Mr Atwood did not come into the office, which was just as well, for a group of photographers had gathered outside with the nation's press. The crowd of onlookers grew until PC Dillon had to put up barricades to keep the traffic moving.

'They thought they'd caught Baffles,' said Sylvia, her eyes brimming with mirth. 'Can you imagine, Mr Atwood of all people!'

'It's beyond the powers of my imagination,' agreed Clementine, watching the heaving throng outside the window.

'Fancy him dressing up and pretending to break into your receptionist's house.'

'I knew he was having an affair with her. The silly fool took me with him to buy her a bracelet. Didn't it occur to him that I'd recognize it on her wrist and put two and two together?'

'Perhaps he doesn't think you're very good at maths!'

'Maybe he *is* Baffles and this is a double bluff,' Clementine suggested.

'He's not that clever.'

'I wonder whether we'll see Jennifer today?'

'Or ever!'

'I'd leave the country if that happened to me.'

Sylvia giggled. 'I think it's quite an inspired idea. I could get rather turned on with the right man.'

'Not Mr Atwood, then?'

They both laughed. '*Not* Mr Atwood! Say we close up shop for the day and go and have a nice lunch?'

'Now *that's* inspired,' Clementine agreed, picking up her handbag. 'The goldfish bowl is not a life for me!'

'So, how's it all going with Rafa?' Sylvia asked, sipping a glass of Pinot Noir on the terrace of the brasserie.

'Oh, nothing to report.'

'But it's only been a week!'

'I know. I shouldn't expect things to move so swiftly. I just feel I've known him for ever.' She shrugged, not wanting Sylvia to know how much she cared.

'You need to go away so that he misses you.'

'I'm not going anywhere until September.'

'That's too late. You need to go away now.'

'And where do you think I should disappear to?'

'Anywhere, down the road – so long as he thinks you've gone away.'

'I don't have enough money – or time off.'

'Shame. Absence makes the heart grow fonder.'

'Or it makes the heart forget altogether.'

'Not likely, lovely. Trust me, I know. I'm a master at playing hard to get.' Clementine laughed, assuming she was being ironic, but Sylvia was looking at her very seriously.

She coughed. 'I'm sure you're right,' she said hastily. 'If anyone can play it cool, you can.'

Rafa watched Marina disappear up the drive in her car before wandering furtively into the stable block. Grey was out in his boat, the painters were busy in the vegetable garden, and Harvey was on the roof mending one of the chimney pots with glue, baler twine and Agritape. Mr Potter was having his tea and digestives in the greenhouse with Biscuit, and Bertha was making up Rafa's room, taking as long as possible to fold and hang his clothes from the night before.

He climbed the stairs and walked across the landing to Marina and Grey's bedroom. The smell of her perfume wafted into the corridor and it clung to his nostrils as if she were right there with him. He glanced around anxiously before entering. But he needn't have worried, he was quite alone. Inside, the bed was unmade, awaiting the arrival of Bertha, and the window wide open, boasting a magnificent view of the sea. With his heart pounding loudly, he began carefully to lift things up. She didn't keep many trinkets and as far as he could tell there was nothing out of the ordinary.

He began to open her drawers and run his hands along the bottom and across the back to check for hidden items. But there was nothing squeezed behind the clothes and he felt ashamed for having invaded her privacy. When he reached her cupboard his heart lurched at the sight of a pretty floral box file that lay partially hidden beneath her shoes. He delved within, removed the shoes and pulled it out. With trembling hands he opened it. Inside, it was stuffed full of letters. The paper was yellowed, indicating that they were old. He caught his breath. He lifted the one at the top. But his heart deflated for it was a love letter from Grey, dated 1988. He burrowed deeper, but they were all either letters from Grey or childish pictures from Jake and Clementine.

He found her marriage certificate and a couple of photographs of their wedding day. He dug his hand into the very bottom and pulled out the final letter, hoping for something revelatory. What he found was a poem torn out of a book, entitled 'My Marine Marina', dated 1968, by John Edgerton. He read it and his eyes watered; it could have been written about her.

Oh mournful soul that craves the sea,
Restless will forever be,
What relics of your dreams lie there,
Beneath the waves of your despair . . .

It was a poem about love, but also about loss. He wondered if she had known the poet and whether he had written it for her.

Suddenly, he heard the front door open and slam shut. Hastily, he thrust the box back into the cupboard and replaced the shoes on top. He hurried out of the bedroom. As he stepped onto the landing the floorboards creaked loudly into the silence. Jake heard him and peered up from the hall below. 'Rafa! What are you doing here?' he demanded, staring at him suspiciously.

'I'm looking for Biscuit,' Rafa replied, trying to sound casual. He thrust his hands into his trouser pockets. 'He sometimes likes to come in here and lie on your father's bed.'

'Does he?' Jake wasn't convinced.

'He's not here.'

'Why do you want him?'

'I want my students to paint him.'

'Really?' Jake watched him come down the stairs. 'Tell me, didn't Harvey take you to Edward and Anya Powell's house not so long ago?'

Rafa nodded. 'Yes, we went to paint the dovecote.'

'Hmm.'

'Why?'

'No reason,' Jake replied, rubbing his chin thoughtfully.

He watched the artist leave the house and walk across to the hotel. He had a sudden, uncomfortable feeling that Rafa was not all that he seemed.

Chapter 32

That evening Jake took Clementine aside. 'I need to talk to you,' he said seriously.

She followed him into the library. 'What's the matter?'

'It's Rafa.'

'What about him?'

'I caught him snooping around the stable block this morning.'

'What do you classify as "snooping"?'

'Well, he wasn't in the kitchen making a cup of tea.' Clementine shot him a withering look. 'He was upstairs on the landing.'

'Did you ask him what he was doing?'

'He said he was looking for Biscuit.'

'Perhaps he was.'

'Rubbish! He wasn't looking for Biscuit. He was looking around.'

'Are you sure?'

'Positive. He looked really shifty.'

'What are you suggesting?'

'You know Harvey took him to the Powells' house before it was robbed.'

Clementine gasped. 'You're not suggesting he's Baffles?'

'Don't you think it's a bit of a coincidence that the very house he visits is later robbed?'

Clementine was too shocked to answer.

'He did a recce to see if it would be a good place to take his painters. He must have gone into the kitchen and seen the ring on the window sill.'

'I can't believe you're even suggesting such a thing! It's not in his nature to be dishonest,' Clementine said, horrified.

'Do you really believe he's an artist happy to spend the summer teaching old ladies how to paint for his board and lodging? Think about it. What was he doing down here in the first place? Robbing big houses and hotels. Then he sees Marina's ad in the local paper and thinks: Aha, I'll go under-cover for the summer and no one will suspect me.'

Clementine narrowed her eyes incredulously, but Jake continued, pleased with the way his hypothesis was snowballing. 'Look, he's right in the middle of Devon, surrounded by big, expensive houses, most of which he has access to because Marina insists on showing him off to all her friends. This is the perfect decoy. No one is going to point the finger at him, are they?'

'I'm not sure about this, Jake.' But Clementine was ashamed to sense a little seed of doubt taking root.

'I've always thought him dodgy. Right from the start, he was too good to be true.'

'Well, you have no proof.'

'I'll get it.'

'He's a very good painter.'

'Coincidence.'

'If he was a robber, wouldn't he wear an expensive watch, drive a snazzy car?'

'Only if he was a very stupid robber, which he clearly isn't.' He grinned at her. 'And *you've* fallen for him, haven't you?'

Clementine was infuriated. 'You know, if he was the low-life you think he is, he would have seduced me weeks ago.'

'No he wouldn't. That would distract him from his purpose.'

'I don't believe you, Jake. You've never liked him because you're jealous. He's more handsome than you, cleverer than you – which, I might add, isn't hard – and he's a great deal more charming. It's no surprise that you can't bear him.'

'I've got a good nose for disingenuous people.'

'So, are you going to tell Marina?'

'Not yet.'

'Good, because she won't believe you.'

'I'll get proof.'

'The Roaches are coming this weekend. Don't give her something else to worry about.'

'Ah, the Roaches.' He pulled a face. 'They've got their sights on this place, for sure.'

'If they make an offer Dad can't refuse, Marina will throw herself off the cliff.'

'Don't be so dramatic. She'll be fine. They'll buy somewhere else.'

'You just don't get it, do you?' she rounded on him crossly. 'This is more than a home to Marina. This is her child.' Jake had the decency to look a little ashamed. 'Don't think she'll be fine, because she won't. She'll be destroyed and broken, and nothing will ever be able to put her back together again.'

Jake watched in astonishment as she stalked out into the hall.

Clementine sat in her bedroom mulling over what Jake had told her. Her instincts reassured her that he was wrong. Rafa wasn't a burglar. He was gentle and kind and compassionate. If he was a burglar he'd be ruthless and duplicitous, which she was sure he was not. However, she couldn't ignore the niggling feeling that he was hiding something. Jake had brought that doubt into the open and she now admitted that it had always been there, lying at the bottom of her happiness like clay. Was he too good to be true? And if he wasn't the burglar, what was he?

More worrying than Jake's suspicions about Rafa was the threat to the Polzanze and what such a loss would do to Marina. She found, to her surprise, that the thought of Marina being forced to give up what she treasured most gave her a sharp pain in the middle of her chest. She put her hand there. If only she could help, but there was nothing she could do. If her father really was in financial trouble and the Roaches made a generous offer, he'd sell. Poor Marina would be devastated. She'd never get over it.

A sudden inspiration assuaged the pain: she'd stay with her and not go abroad. That's what she'd do. She'd help Marina set up somewhere else. They'd build a new place together, a place more beautiful even than the Polzanze.

With that thought she felt happier. She turned her attention back to Jake and his ludicrous theory. As if Rafa could be Baffles; the very idea was absurd.

On Friday 12 June Charles Roache and his glacial wife, Celeste, arrived for the weekend. Marina had begged Grey to say they were fully booked, but he had refused her. As hard as it was for him to admit it, he needed them.

It poured with rain, which Marina hoped might put them off, for the place looked very grey in bad weather. Heavy black clouds hung low over the sea and a cold wind whipped up the cliffs and over the roof, groaning as if in protest at the new guests.

Marina loathed Celeste on sight. She was almost six foot tall, and so skinny she nearly disappeared when viewed from the side. She had the remains of an icy beauty, with pale blue eyes, heavily made-up with kohl and mascara, and white hair blow-dried into a stiff shoulder-length bob. Her cheekbones were high and as sharp as the big diamond studs that glittered on her ear lobes and long, wrinkled fingers. Her lips were thin and pursed into the disapproving pout of a very unhappy woman. In spite of her luxurious cream cashmere sweater, black crocodile Birkin and matching Ralph Lauren shoes, she looked utterly disenchanted with her life.

'What a quaint little place,' she said in a nasal voice as she stepped into the hall, leaving Tom and Shane to stagger behind with her Louis Vuitton luggage. 'And you must be Marina.' She looked down her nose and pulled a tight smile, as far as her recent facelift would allow.

Marina extended her hand and smiled politely, though her eyes remained hostile. 'You're very welcome,' she said.

The Roaches were the enemy, inveigling their way into her home to snatch it for themselves. Grey greeted her warmly, for nastiness was not in his nature. Marina glanced out of the open door to see Charles Roache pacing the gravel with his BlackBerry pressed to his ear, while his driver walked behind with a large golfing umbrella. He was short and portly, with the big belly of a man who spends a great deal of time in restaurants. His head was bald, his face fleshy and broad like a toad. When he came in at last, he shook the rain off his trench coat and complained in a strong cockney accent about the lack of signal.

'You'd have thought we were out in the sticks. You know, I was in the back of beyond in India last week and the reception was one hundred per cent. What does that tell you about Britain, eh?'

'You're welcome to use the phone in your room,' said Grey.

'It looks like that's what I'll have to do.' He shook Grey's hand and smiled. 'Nice place you've got here.'

'Thank you,' Grey replied. 'It's Marina's place, really.'

'Pleased to meet you,' he said to Marina, shaking her firmly by the hand. 'I've heard a lot about it so I had to come and check it out for myself.'

'May I introduce you to the manager, my son, Jake.' Grey was aware of his wife's mounting resentment and keen to keep her as far away from the Roaches as possible.

'A family business, I like it,' said Charles. 'Have you met my wife, Celeste?'

By contrast, his wife spoke in a croaky, upper-class whine. 'Of course we've met,' she retorted. 'You've been nattering on the telephone for ten minutes – what was I supposed to do, watch the flowers wilt?'

'Let me show you to your room,' said Grey.

Marina watched them leave the hall and bristled like a territorial tigress. Celeste's heavy floral perfume lingered in the air and Marina insisted that the door remain open until the smell had gone. She looked at the magnificent display of white lilies and roses, none of them anywhere near wilting, and thought Celeste Roache the rudest woman she had ever met.

The telephone rang and Jennifer, back at her post after her embarrassing episode with Mr Atwood, answered it in her most professional voice.

'It's for you, Mrs Turner. It's Clementine.'

Marina took it at the desk. 'Clemmie.'

'Are they there yet?'

'Yes, they've just arrived.'

'What are they like?'

'Ghastly.'

'If she was an animal, what would she be?'

Marina laughed. 'An albino hyena in diamonds.'

'Lovely. And him?'

'A toad in suede and cashmere.'

She lowered her voice. 'Do you need any moral support? I can leave at any time. After Mr Atwood's robbery charade I can do whatever I want.'

Marina glanced at Jennifer, busy with the diary, and suppressed a smile. 'I'll be fine, don't worry. It's nothing I can't handle. Grey has insisted we entertain them royally so I'm going to kill them with kindness.'

'Can't you just leave them to get on with it?'

'Trust me, these are the sort of people who demand to be entertained.'

'OK, but call me if you need support. I'm dying to leave the office, it's a miserable day and nothing's happening.'

'Come home early and join us for tea. If the situation wasn't so tragic we could have a good laugh about this.'

'We're all in this together, Marina. One for all and all for one. Don't forget that.'

'I won't, darling. And thank you for calling. Your concern means a lot to me.'

She wandered into the sitting room where the fire was lit to keep out the damp. It was cosy and warm, and the air smelled pleasantly of wood smoke. She perched on the club fender and thought about Clementine and how much she had changed. She had almost forgotten the dark shadow that had once accompanied her stepdaughter everywhere. The girl was transformed. Marina looked through to the conservatory, where Rafa was teaching a group of young women from London, and knew that she had *him* to thank. Somehow, his presence there at the hotel had changed everything.

It wasn't long before the tranquillity of the sitting room was disturbed by the whining tones of Celeste. 'It's jolly cold for June,' she complained, making her way towards one of the sofas. When she saw Biscuit lying comfortably on the armchair she screwed up her nose in horror. 'Goodness me, a dog. Do you allow animals into the hotel?' She directed her question at Marina.

'Of course. But Biscuit lives here. He's part of the place.'

'So, he's yours?'

'Well, he belongs to all of us and none of us.'

'Lucky I didn't wear my smart trousers.' She brushed a hand over the sofa before sitting down.

'You needn't worry, he's only taken a liking to the armchair.'

Celeste swept her eyes over the room. 'The Somerlands had very good taste in decoration, didn't they?' she said. Marina didn't bother to tell her that the taste was all hers. 'What's the name of that beautiful flower?' She pointed to the display of purple orchids on the coffee table at the other end of the room.

'Orchid,' said Marina.

'No, my dear, I mean the grown-up name.'

'I wouldn't know,' Marina replied, biting her tongue. 'I have yet to grow up.'

At that moment Grey appeared with Charles, who was ruddy-faced with excitement. 'Grey's going to give me a tour of the garden,' he declared.

Marina panicked. The idea of being stuck here with Celeste was more than she could bear. 'Would you like to go, too?' she asked hopefully.

But Celeste settled back into the sofa and folded her arms. 'I'm not going out in the rain,' she replied, appalled. 'You go and be boys, but we girls are going to stay by the fire, aren't we, Marina?' Heather entered with tea. 'Good timing. I could murder a cup of tea. Is it Earl Grey?'

'Yes, ma'am,' said Heather, placing it on the coffee table.

'Oh, biscuits. I won't be touching those.'

'They're homemade shortbread,' said Marina.

'I'm sure they are. Typical of these provincial little places. Delightful, I'm sure, but I'll pass. I didn't get to be as slim as I am by gorging on shortbread.'

Heather poured her a cup of tea. 'Would you like milk, ma'am?'

'Is it soya?'

'No, cow's milk.'

'Full fat or skimmed?'

'Full fat.'

Celeste blanched. 'I'll have it with a slice of lemon, then.'

Marina rolled her eyes at Heather. It was going to be a tiresome weekend.

*

When Rafa sauntered into the sitting room, Celeste sat up keenly. Marina introduced them and watched as Celeste began to flirt like a young girl. Clearly used to being admired, she seemed not to care that it was inappropriate to behave that way with a man young enough to be her son. She giggled shyly and blinked up at him from beneath her thick black lashes. Rafa flattered her and asked her about herself, looking into her eyes in that intense way of his, making her feel she was the only person in the room he wanted to talk to. Marina wondered whether he was doing it on purpose as a favour to *her*, or whether he did it unconsciously.

'Do you paint, Celeste?' he asked.

'I was once a very good painter,' she replied. 'I have a good eye for detail.'

'Then come and paint.'

Marina was quick to encourage her. 'Oh, you must, Celeste. You can show those girls in there how it's done.'

'Oh, I haven't painted for years.'

'You never forget how to paint,' said Rafa.

'It's like riding a bicycle,' rejoined Marina.

'I'd have to change out of my clothes.'

'I have an overall for you,' said Rafa. 'Come, it will give me pleasure.'

Celeste got up. 'What a wonderful idea, having an artist-in-residence, Marina.'

'Thank you,' she replied, waiting for the insult. But it didn't come.

Celeste followed Rafa into the conservatory and Marina made her escape – but not before Rafa had looked over his shoulder and tossed her a wink.

At midday Charles returned with Grey, full of enthusiasm. They had walked all the way along the cliff top to Dawcomb-Devlish and enjoyed a cup of coffee in the Wayfarer.

'Charming place,' Charles gushed, inhaling with delight.

'Nothing like the sea and the smell of ozone to clear the airways and soothe the mind. This place has a special energy. I like it. I like it a lot.'

Grey was keen not to be overbearing and left him to lunch with his wife in the dining room.

The sommelier had at last found someone who knew about fine wine. They discussed the list in great detail and Charles chose a red Cabernet Sauvignon blend, Chateau Palmer '90, one of the most expensive wines available on the menu. The sommelier almost danced around the tables in his eagerness to go and fetch the bottle from the cellar.

Celeste had enjoyed a couple of hours in the conservatory with Rafa and was now an expert on watercolours. She told her husband that the young artist had encouraged her to paint because he had recognized a kindred spirit in her, someone with natural flair and talent like him.

'The trouble is,' she explained as the sommelier poured a little wine into her husband's glass and waited for him to taste it, 'there just isn't time enough in the day to do all the things I'm good at.' Charles swirled it around, then put the glass to his lips. The sommelier waited, barely daring to breathe. This particular Cabernet Sauvignon blend was a favourite of his and he was sure a sophisticated businessman like Mr Roache would appreciate it.

'Full bodied, complex and fruity,' he declared and tapped his glass.

The sommelier filled Mrs Roache's glass first before filling her husband's. He was dismayed to see the woman take a sip without so much as a smile of pleasure. She was too busy talking about herself to notice the exceptional taste of the wine.

After lunch Celeste was keen to continue painting. Charles retreated to his room to make some calls. Grey and Marina returned to the stable block. It had stopped raining and the sun had come out, shining onto the wet leaves causing the raindrops to glitter like glass. Neither wanted to talk about the Roaches. The implications were too painful. So they skirted around the subject, although it hung between them like a bright neon sign.

At tea time Clementine roared up the drive in her Mini Cooper, eager to see what the Roaches were like. She found Rafa in the conservatory, putting away the paints and brushes.

'So?' she hissed, surprising him from behind.

He turned round. 'Oh, it's you,' he laughed. 'I don't suppose you're referring to the Roaches.'

'Go on, what are they like?'

'*Pesados*,' he replied. 'Heavy.'

'Where are they now?'

'I don't know. Marina and your father have gone back to the stable block. The atmosphere is very tense.'

'I know. I can feel it.' She cast her eyes around the drawing room, at the other guests who sat in small clusters drinking cups of tea and nibbling on little egg sandwiches, and wondered whether they felt it, too.

'I can't believe my father will actually agree to sell.'

'He doesn't want to, Clementine.'

She looked at him seriously. 'It's that bad, isn't it?'

'I think so. I wish there was some way I could help.'

'Me too.' She placed a hand on his arm. 'But there isn't. All we can do is support – and hope the Roaches loathe the place.'

He grinned at her sadly. 'Unfortunately, that is impossible. The Polzanze has a certain magic you don't find very often.'

'A magic Marina will take with her if she has to leave. They'll end up buying a shell.' She walked over to the glass and looked out onto the sun-drenched gardens. 'Fancy taking Biscuit for a walk?'

'You've read my mind, Clementine. There's nothing I'd like to do more.'

*

Clementine spent the weekend by Marina's side, protecting her from the hyena's barbed comments and making fun of her behind her back to make her stepmother laugh.

But it was of no consequence that Celeste had enjoyed her painting lessons or that Charles had relished going out in Grey's boat and catching fish, because if they liked the bones of the hotel and bought it, they'd gut it anyway, as they had done to all their others, and change it in every way.

On Sunday, Grey and Charles spent a great deal of time in the library discussing books. Then the door was shut and they remained there until lunchtime and no one knew what they were talking about. Marina had had enough and refused to join them. She sat in her kitchen with Clementine, Rafa and Biscuit, drinking cups of strong tea and eating the shortbread Celeste had declined to taste. 'I know he's making Grey an offer he can't refuse,' she said, wringing her hands.

'He always has the power to refuse,' said Rafa hopefully.

'Not if we're broke.' She sighed. 'There, I've said it. You might as well know, Rafa. We've borrowed up to our eyeballs and we're simply not making money.'

'But the place is full now,' Clementine protested. 'We must be making money.'

'Unless you have a fairy godmother who can wave her wand and give us a great big cash injection, we are incapable of paying back the money we owe.'

'There has to be a way,' said Rafa.

Marina shook her head. 'If there is, I haven't managed to figure out what it is.' She began to gnaw the skin around her thumbnail, for that wasn't entirely true. There *was* a way; it had occurred to her many times in her most desperate moments. At first it had just been the frantic meandering of a desolate mind. Then, as the possibility of losing the Polzanze had become a reality, those meanderings had grown more direct and strategic.

Yet, beneath her desire to rescue the hotel was a need more visceral. At first she had been too afraid even to contemplate it, but little by little the idea had grown into a possibility and her heart had filled with hope. Was her plan to save the hotel merely an excuse to enable her to go back and right that terrible wrong? She pictured the little box at the top of her cupboard and shivered at the prospect of stepping back into her past.

Clementine confused her shudder for helplessness and took her hand. Marina smiled at her feebly.

At last the Roaches left in their chauffeur-driven Bentley and Grey appeared at the kitchen door. Even Biscuit lifted his head to hear what he had to say.

'Well?' Marina asked. But she could tell by the doleful expression on his face. 'Oh God, he's made an offer, hasn't he?'

Rafa caught Clementine's eye. They were both thinking the same thing. They turned to Marina and watched powerlessly as she seemed to wither before their eyes.

'Is it a very big offer?' she asked in a trembling voice.

'It's the biggest offer we're ever likely to get,' Grey replied. He was too ashamed to admit that part of him felt relieved that there was at last a way out of their financial nightmare.

'What are you going to do?'

Clementine squeezed Marina's hand. 'You can't sell, Dad. There has to be another way.'

Grey sighed and scratched his head. 'I can't think of one.'

Marina closed her eyes. In that brief moment she saw her life flash before her. She watched the building of the home she cherished as if it were a reel of film passing across her mind. Harvey and she were laughing as they painted the hall; Mr Potter was mowing the lawns on the new tractor they had bought; Grey was coming down on weekends and admiring the progress; they were sitting in the greenhouse as the rains battered the glass, chewing on Mr Potter's digestive biscuits,

discussing what plants to buy and where to place them. They
had planned together: she, Harvey, Mr Potter and Grey. They
had been a team, a family. She had realized her dream with the
very force of her will and watered it with love. It had grown
bigger and more beautiful than she could have ever imagined.
No one was going to take it from her. Not now. Not when
she needed it the most.

'There is one person who can help,' she said, lifting her chin.
'One person, if you'll let me ask.'

Chapter 33

The kitchen fell silent. Rafa, Clementine and Grey stared at Marina in amazement.

'Who?' Grey asked. He thought they had explored every avenue.

Marina looked embarrassed. 'An old friend.'

Grey frowned. 'What do you mean, an old friend?'

'It's complicated. He's someone I knew a long time ago.'

'Well, where is he?'

She hesitated, knitting her fingers. 'Italy.' The word was released into the air for them to gaze on in astonishment. No one was more astonished than Marina.

'Italy?'

'Yes.'

'Who on earth do you know in Italy, let alone someone capable of bailing you out?' Grey gazed at her across the table. 'Darling, this is a big surprise. Why didn't you tell me about him before?'

The corners of her mouth twitched with emotion and she took a deep breath to steady her nerves. 'You have to trust me, darling, and not ask any more questions. Please. It's a long story. I wouldn't have even considered him if I wasn't desperate. But I *am* desperate.' In the silence that ensued she felt something pull in the deepest depth of her heart. She realized she had been desperate for a very, very long time and only now, as she teetered at the frontier where past and present collide, did she recognize the real motive behind her plan — and it wasn't the Polzanze. The little shoebox hidden away at the top of her cupboard surfaced again and her eyes welled with tears.

Grey was appalled by her plan. 'I won't have you crossing Europe to beg for money from a man I have never met.'

'This is different, darling — and I won't be begging.'

Grey pulled out a chair and sat down. He didn't like the idea of his wife keeping secrets from him, especially when it came to money. He looked at her steadily. Then he saw something in her eyes that changed his mind — the same longing he had seen when he had comforted her after her nightmares, the same craving that drove her to pace the beach and stare for hours across the water. He knew then that the root of her unrest lay in Italy, and for that reason, she had to go.

'All right,' he conceded gently, taking her hand. 'But I can't go with you.' She understood that he wasn't comfortable asking a stranger for help. 'This is your business, Marina.'

'I'll go on my own. I'll be fine.'

He smiled at her fondly. She didn't realize how fragile she looked. 'Darling, I don't think it's wise to travel alone. Why don't you take Clemmie with you, or Jake?'

'No, really, I'll be fine,' she insisted.

'I'll go with you.' Rafa suggested. Marina and Grey looked at him. They had almost forgotten he was there. 'I speak the language, for a start.' He shrugged. 'And I'm a good chauffeur.'

'That's very generous of you to offer, Rafa,' said Grey. He turned to his wife. 'I think that's a sensible idea. I'd be much happier if I knew you had someone with you.'

'Then that's settled,' said Marina. She smiled weakly, as deflated as a tyre that has run many thousands of miles and can run no more. 'It's our last chance.'

Grey nodded. 'If it's unsuccessful we will agree to sell to Charles Roache. We can set up again somewhere else.' But

Marina wasn't listening. She was already in Italy, walking back down the avenues of her past.

Later, when Clementine and Rafa walked Biscuit along the cliff top, they discussed the extraordinary episode in the kitchen. 'What was all that about?' Clementine asked.

'I have no idea. It's bizarre.'

'Who's she going to see in Italy? An old lover, perhaps?'

'Anything's possible.'

'You must text me. I'll be longing to know.'

'He must be a very *special* old lover if she's hoping he'll write her such a vast cheque.'

'Who has that sort of money to toss away?' She was aware that he was looking at her strangely. 'Why can't she just call him up? If he's such a good friend, why doesn't she just telephone him and ask for a loan?'

'Clementine, there's something I need to tell you,' he said suddenly. She turned to find his face had grown pale, right down to his lips.

'Are you all right?'

'No.'

Clementine didn't want his confession. If he was Baffles she'd rather not know. He could go on robbing in secret and their friendship could continue undisturbed. She liked the way things were. If he confessed, he'd ruin everything.

'I was in the stable block—' he began.

'I know. Jake found you.'

'I said I was looking for Biscuit.'

'But you weren't?'

'No.'

'I'm sure Jake just misjudged you. Don't worry about him. He's a little jealous of you, as you've probably worked out.'

'Jake didn't misjudge me. I was looking for something else.'

'I don't want to know,' she blurted, putting her hands over

her ears. 'Don't tell me. If you have a secret, keep it to your-self, please.'

He looked at her in astonishment. 'But I want to tell you. I want to come clean.'

'Why? What good will that do? You'll confess something terrible and then we won't be friends any more.'

'No, it's not like that.' He took her hands and pulled them away from her ears.

'Yes, it is. You didn't come here to teach old ladies to paint, did you?'

'No ... but—'

'You targeted us for a reason?'

'Yes.'

Clementine felt a surge of emotion rise up her chest and tore her hands away. 'So, don't tell me the reason. I can't bear it. I trusted you.' In her confusion she began to run up the beach.

'Clementine, wait! It's not what you think. My intentions are good.'

She stopped and turned, the wind whipping her hair from behind and tossing it across her cheeks. 'You just don't get it, do you?' *You don't get that I love you*, she called silently. Then out loud she added, 'I hope you find what you're looking for.'

He watched her go. He could have run after her and told her everything – he was now pretty sure that he was in the right place – but Grey knew nothing of Marina's past, and Rafa hadn't anticipated that. How would they feel if he suddenly turned their reality upside down and told them who he really was? He sat on the sand and put his head in his hands. Part of him wanted to pack his bags and return to Argentina, putting the whole messy business behind him. But part of him knew he had to go to Italy with Marina. If he had any hope of winning Clementine, he had to know the *whole* truth.

*

Clementine sobbed into her pillow. She knew she should have waited to hear what he had to say. Her performance had been as bad as in the worst soap opera, where the characters always walk out on one another before waiting to hear their explanations. But she couldn't bear to watch him topple off his pedestal. She couldn't risk the chance that she had fallen in love with a mirage, a cleverly constructed image. She didn't want to be like Sylvia, with her cynical view of love. So now what? How could they ever go back to the way they were? She might as well have listened because now everything had changed between them and she didn't even have the satisfaction of knowing what or who he really was.

Marina and Rafa left for the airport early the following morning before dawn, while the Polzanze slept on. They took a train to Heathrow via London, and flew to Rome.

There were so many questions Rafa longed to ask, but he knew better than to intrude in what Marina believed to be her own secret adventure. She wasn't aware that it was Rafa's, too.

Marina was nervous. She bit her nails, fidgeted and failed to read the magazine that remained open on the same page for the entire duration of the flight. She was unusually quiet, replying to his comments in monosyllables. The croissant on her tray remained untouched. At Rome airport she asked him to organize the hiring of a car, which he did in fluent Italian while she paced up and down like a greyhound preparing for a race. Finally, with a map and two cups of takeaway coffee, they drove through the Tuscan countryside towards an obscure little town called Herba.

Rafa concentrated on the road while Marina stared outside at the inky green cypress trees, towering umbrella pines, and Italian farmhouses with their red tiled roofs and sandy-coloured walls. A warm breeze blew through the open windows, carrying with it the scents of wild thyme, rosemary and pine. She rested her elbow on the window frame and clenched her finger between her teeth. She felt as if she were driving towards an enormous door with only one chance to open it. If she failed, it would close for ever on the very thing she had waited most of her life to find. Now she was in Italy the Polzanze seemed very far away and somehow less important. Her focus had changed, the mask was slipping – perhaps the Polzanze had been nothing but a screen all along, hiding the only thing that mattered – the only thing that had *ever* mattered. She wiped away a tear and tried to focus on her plan.

It was early evening when the car drew up at the gates of La Magdalena. The light had grown soft, the shadows long. The yellow palace at the end of the drive peered out of the avenue curiously. A security guard leaned into the window.

'Marina Turner,' she said. The man nodded and returned into his hut to open the gates electronically. 'Drive on,' she instructed.

Rafa did as she asked and motored up the track. He dared not look at Marina; he knew without looking that she was crying. He drew up in front of the house.

'Why don't you drive into Herba and take a look around?' she suggested. 'Give me a couple of hours.' He watched her get out and take a while to gather her courage. She swept her eyes over the façade, straightened her dress and smoothed her hair. Then she walked up the steps to the front door where she was met by a butler in uniform.

Rafa drove down the coast into Herba, the little town he knew so well from his father's memories. He had described it in detail during those long rides across the pampa and Rafa could see now that it hadn't changed very much since his father was a boy, running barefoot with his brother across the cobbles. So, this is where it all began, he thought, feeling a strange sense of nostalgia wash over him.

*

The butler greeted Marina formally then led her over the che-
querboard floor, stopping outside an imposing pair of wooden
doors. He knocked briskly. A voice called from within,
'*Avanti.*' Marina caught her breath and blinked the mist from
her eyes. The butler opened the door. She lifted her chin,
pulled back her shoulders and stepped inside.

The man behind the desk put down his pen and raised his
eyes. He blanched in astonishment at the sight of the woman
who now stood before him. 'My God,' he gasped, standing up.
For a moment he believed his eyes were deceiving him.

'Dante,' she said softly. She couldn't take another step, for
her legs were numb. She remained frozen and trembling. The
man walked slowly around his desk and towards her, without
taking his gaze off her – afraid that she would disappear as suddenly as she had come. When he stood a few inches away, his
eyes misted, too. He took her hand and seemed not to care
that a tear had escaped and trickled over the lines on his skin.

'Floriana.'

Chapter 34

They remained a long while staring at the past. Dante had grown old, as had she. His hair was grey and receded, the crow's feet entrenched deep and long into his temples. He had weary bags under his eyes and the shadows there betrayed a life defined by hard work and disappointment. He ran his gaze over her features in wonder, the questions falling over each other to be asked, but his voice was lost in the turmoil of his emotions. He didn't let go of her hands but remained as she did, frozen and trembling.

At last he pulled her into his arms and embraced her so fiercely for a moment she was unable to breathe. It was as if the last four decades had simply dissolved, leaving them as they once were, only changed on the outside.

He pressed his wet cheek to hers and closed his eyes. 'You have come back,' he whispered. 'My *piccolina. L'Orfanella.* You have come back.' When he released her, they both laughed through their tears, a little embarrassed that two mature people could behave in such a manner. 'Come and sit outside where I can see you in the light. You haven't changed at all, Floriana, except your hair, it's lighter!'

'I dye it,' she replied, sheepishly. 'Don't you like it?'

'It's different, and you speak Italian like an English-woman.'

'I *am* an Englishwoman.'

He took her hand and led her through the house to the terrace. 'Do you remember your birthday party?'

'Of course.'

He looked down at her hand. 'You're not wearing my ring – nor Mamma's bracelet.'

Her eyes welled again and she began to explain, 'I gave them—'

He smiled and dismissed it with a wave. 'It doesn't matter. Nothing matters. Come, sit down. We have so much to talk about. Would you like tea, coffee? I don't know what you drink these days.' He suddenly looked deflated. 'Once I knew everything about you.'

'I'll have coffee and bread. I'm suddenly rather hungry.'

He called to the butler. 'Coffee, bread and cheese for both of us.'

Dante and Marina sat side by side, looking out over the gardens. Memories rose up from the grass like butterflies and scattered on the breeze. 'I can't believe you're here,' he said, staring at her incredulously. 'I think my eyes deceive me. And yet, here you are, more beautiful now than when I knew you.'

'I never thought I'd see you again. I read and reread your letters, and hoped you'd come and find me. For years I waited.' She shook her head, not wanting to revisit that bleak and lonely time. 'What happened to Good-Night?'

'He pined for you, Floriana. He just lay in the road and stared ahead.'

She pressed her hand against her heart, horrified. 'He pined for me?'

'Yes. We carried him inside eventually, but he wouldn't eat. Floriana, I didn't know what had happened to you. I looked everywhere but no one knew anything about it, except Elio.'

'What did he tell you?'

'That you had run off with another man, just like your mother.'

'Did you believe him?'

'Of course not. Tell me now, where did you go?'

The butler brought coffee in a silver pot and a tray of home-baked bread, cheese and quince. Marina waited for him to pour the coffee and leave them alone before she replied to Dante's question. She had never spoken about this before – even remembering had been too painful. But now, as she brought those memories to light, she realized that time had diminished their power.

'The evening before I was due to meet you at the wall, a stranger came to the apartment. My father told me he knew that I was pregnant with your child. He held in his hand a brown envelope. He said it was a gift from Beppe Bonfanti.'

'He blackmailed my father?'

'I'm afraid he must have.'

'So my father knew?' Dante lost his gaze in the gardens. 'My father knew all along?'

'I don't know how *my* father found out because the only two people who knew the truth were Father Ascanio and Signora Bruno, neither of whom would have betrayed me.'

'So, then what happened?'

She faltered a moment, for Dante's face seemed to have fallen with the weight of his sorrow. 'The man told me he had come to take me here, to you, and I believed him. What alternative did I have? He claimed your father was going to take care of me – of us.'

'Where did he take you?'

'We drove up here and there was Good-Night in the road, his tail wagging at the sight of me. But then the car passed the gates and Good-Night ran after the car.' Her chin began to wobble. Dante took her hand and stroked the skin with his thumb, silently imploring her to go on. 'Good-Night couldn't keep up. He ran and ran but soon he was a little dot until he had disappeared altogether. That was the last I ever saw of him.'

'And why he remained in the middle of the road, expecting you to come back.'

'I missed him so much, Dante. I almost missed him more than you.'

She sipped her coffee and Dante cut them both a slice of bread. They ate in silence as Marina remembered Good-Night and Dante remembered his demise. 'He took me to the convent, Dante.'

'Santa Maria degli Angeli?'

'Yes, the very same.'

'But I pounded on the door. For the love of God, I pounded on that door day and night.'

'You knew I was there?'

'I *hoped* you were there. It was the only place I had to look. Father Ascanio promised he had arranged for the convent to take you in, so when Elio said you had run away, I prayed that you had gone there. You had nowhere else to go. But they turned me away, claiming they had never heard of you. Of course, I didn't believe you had run away. I thought perhaps something had frightened you or that you had lost faith in me.'

He looked so dejected, her heart buckled. 'No, Dante . . .'

'But I never suspected my father knew. He never let on. To his dying day he never let on . . .' His voice trailed off.

'Yes, I read that he had died.'

'You did?'

'Six months ago. I keep all press cuttings about your family – and now with the Internet it's a lot easier.'

'Oh, Floriana,' he groaned.

'I'm sorry for your loss.'

'I'm not sorry at all. I never liked him.' He cut a wedge of cheese. 'Let's not talk about him. Go on. The puzzle is taking shape.'

At this point Marina found it hard to speak. It was as if a weight had descended onto her chest. 'I gave birth to a son.'

'We have a son?'

'We *had* a son, Dante.' Her neck began to grow hot and itchy. 'A beautiful little boy I nursed for five months, there at the convent, until he was finally taken from me.'

'Who took him?'

'Father Ascanio.'

'So Father Ascanio knew where you were all along?'

'He arranged everything,' Marina told him.

'I don't understand. He said he didn't know where you had gone. He said he was praying for your safe return.' He shook his head. 'He lied to me.'

'He was only trying to protect you, Dante. He said he feared for our lives . . .'

'He feared for your lives?'

'Yes, he said he couldn't protect us if we stayed in Italy.'

'Protect you from whom?'

'From Beppe.'

He looked at her askance and rubbed his chin. 'It doesn't add up, Floriana.'

'You mean, there was no danger?'

'I'm not saying that at all.' He seemed to dismiss the one piece of the puzzle that wasn't fitting. 'Go on.'

'Father Ascanio said that the only way to protect us was to give the child up. He sent me into hiding in England and I don't know where he sent our son . . .' Her voice cracked. 'I was hoping you might know.'

Dante gazed back at her helplessly. 'I didn't even know we had a son.' Then his face hardened and he lost his focus among the statues in the garden. 'However, I think I know someone who does.'

'Father Ascanio? I wrote but he never wrote back.'

'Father Ascanio died years ago.'

'Then who?'

'You never spoke to anyone else before you went to England?'

'Only the Mother Superior.'

'No one else?' She shook her head. 'Of course you didn't. It's beginning to make sense. After all these years, it's beginning to add up. Leave it with me.'

'Who?' she persisted.

He took her hand. 'Leave it with me, Floriana. You have to trust me.'

Her shoulders dropped. 'I do.'

Suddenly, she remembered Rafa. 'Oh goodness, Rafa might be back at any minute.'

'Rafa?'

'He's an Argentine artist who's come for the summer to teach painting to our guests. My husband wasn't happy for me to come on my own. I told him to drive into Herba for a couple of hours.'

'I'll ask Lavanti to look after him when he comes back. Don't worry.' Dante called the butler and instructed him to show Rafa into the drawing room. Then, as Lavanti left the terrace, Dante's gaze fell fondly on Marina again. 'When you spoke to my secretary and told her that you had information about Floriana, I realized that although I thought I gave up looking for you long ago, in my heart I had never stopped,' he said. 'But I had to cut you out of my consciousness eventually.'

'Did you marry?'

'Forgive me.'

She frowned at him. 'What is there to forgive?'

'I married Costanza.'

Rafa parked the car and wandered around the town. The air was thick and damp, the evening light turning the old Etruscan walls orange. Pigeons flocked on the cobbles, bony mongrels scavenged in packs, women gossiped on their doorsteps while children played. He reached the Piazza Laconda, where locals sat at tables under umbrellas, drinking Prosecco. He felt the allure of the church and walked inside. Incense still lingered from Mass and a gaggle of old widows remained in their chairs, chatting quietly. He put his hands in his pockets and stepped slowly over the flagstones, remembering Clementine and their first visit to the house that God forgot. He felt the pain of longing in his heart.

A young couple stood in front of the table of candles, holding hands. He envied their happiness. The man smiled at him and handed him a taper. Rafa took it and thanked him. The couple walked away, leaving him alone in front of the table of dancing flames. He thought of his deceased father, who must have lit candles here as he was now going to do. Then, as he lowered the burning taper onto the wick, he thought of his purpose and asked God to give him the courage to go through with it.

Marina felt as if a cold hand had squeezed all the air out of her lungs. For a while she couldn't speak. She stared at him in disbelief.

Dante was quick to explain. 'Oh, Floriana, it's not like it sounds. I never set out to marry your friend. It just happened by default because, I suppose, in a way I was always trying to find my way back to you. I couldn't leave the past alone. Constanza was my only link to you.' He raised his eyes and gazed at her sadly. 'Every time I looked at her, I thought of you, Floriana – until it dawned on me that she was a dead end, leading nowhere.'

'Costanza,' she whispered. 'I can't believe it.'

'We made each other utterly miserable.'

'Where is she now?'

'We divorced after fifteen years of marriage.'

'I'm so sorry.' She reached out and touched his hand. He squeezed it and smiled sadly.

'Fifteen wasted years, Floriana. Years I should have spent with you.'

'I have learned that nothing is a waste, Dante. Do you have children?'

'Three daughters, who bring me trouble and joy in equal measure.' The fondness he felt for his daughters restored the colour to his cheeks. 'But mostly joy,' he added.

'Costanza, a mother,' Marina said wistfully. 'I'm happy for her. Whatever became of the countess?'

'The countess.' He grimaced. 'I loathed her, until my loathing grew so great that I could no longer bear to be in the same room. Her husband worked for my father for a while, but he was useless and finally, when my father retired, I cut him loose. I bailed them out a few times until I lost patience. They live with Costanza in Rome and she takes care of them. But the countess is old and unhappy, and her disappointment has made her ugly in every way.'

'She was always going to be unhappy. Materialistic people are never satisfied.'

'Costanza talked of you constantly. She missed you. I could never let on the extent that I missed you, too. I had to hide my sorrow in my work. I thought if I worked every hour God gave me, there would be no room to think of you.'

'Oh, Dante.'

'Perhaps Costanza sensed it and talked about you in the hope of making me happy, but it only made it worse, like rubbing my wound with sandpaper.'

'The only thing wrong with Costanza was her mother. When I arrived in England, I had no one. I pined for her, too.'

'I could never have been happy with Costanza, Floriana. I married her to please my father and to maintain some sort of link with you. I'll never love anyone else but you.' He smiled at her forlornly. 'The only one who knew the secrets of my heart was Mother, although we never discussed it.'

'Violetta. How is she?'

'In a world of her own. She doesn't come here any more. She lives in Milan and rarely goes out. Tell me, do you have children?'

'No.'

He frowned. 'No?'

'God punished me for giving away the one entrusted to my care.'

'That's not true.'

She lowered her eyes, ashamed. 'I turned my back on God.'

'But, Floriana, you had no choice.'

'I should have fought harder for him.'

'You were a child yourself.'

'I begged to be allowed to keep him. I loved him with all my heart.' Her shoulders began to shake. 'So I put the bracelet your mother gave me, and the ring, along with a letter from me, in a box and . . .'

He wrapped his arms around her. 'It's OK. We'll find him.'

She gripped his shirt and gasped for air. 'I've never told anyone.'

'Not even your husband?'

'No one. I couldn't speak of it. I ran away from myself, Dante – from my guilt.'

He held her tightly and she shut her eyes. She remembered the little baby she had nursed against her breasts. The new soul she had watched as he lay sleeping, humbled by the miracle of his birth. She tried to picture his face but she couldn't. As much as she tried, his face was veiled in mist, which grew denser the more she tried to lift it.

As the shadows lengthened and the light grew dim, they talked. She told him about her life in England and how Grey had appeared like a guardian angel to lift her out of her dark pit with love and understanding.

'I've never told him about my past. He doesn't even know

I am Italian. I lived with a foster mother who taught me English and helped me build a new life. I set about learning the language with such dedication that by the time I met Grey I spoke English so well that he never suspected I was in hiding. I tried to look forward and become a different person. I thought if I left Floriana behind in Italy, I'd leave her pain there too. I tried to forget our son. I tried to forget you, too, Dante.' She closed her eyes. 'But the heart can never forget and wounds never really heal completely.'

'So, what made you come back? Why, after all these years, did you choose now to come home?'

'Because I need help. You always said I could turn to you, no matter what.'

'You still can, Floriana.' She took a deep breath. But then something stopped her before she could ask. 'What is it you need?'

She wiped her eyes and smiled to herself. 'Nothing,' she replied firmly. 'I don't need anything at all.'

He frowned at her quizzically. 'Are you sure? You know I'd do anything for you.'

She had thought the Polzanze was her life, but suddenly, in that joyous moment of self-discovery, she realized that bricks and mortar could never be more than bricks and mortar. Material things were meaningless without their associations; hence the Polzanze was nothing without her longing.

She took his hand and held his eyes in her gaze. 'Find our son, Dante, wherever he is.'

As they walked back inside, Dante put his hand in the small of her back. 'Floriana, this has been one of the happiest days of my life.'

'I should never have left it so long.'

'What are you going to do now?'

'I'm going to return to England and tell my husband everything.'

'Is he the sort of man who will understand?'

'I know he will. He's a good man, which is why I owe him an explanation for all my irrational behaviour over the years. He's been incredibly patient.'

'Do you love him, Floriana?'

She looked at Dante, aware that her answer would wound him. But she couldn't lie to spare his feelings. 'Yes, I do. I love my husband very much.'

'I'm happy that you found love with a good man, *piccolina*.' He smiled to hide his disappointment. 'Why don't you stay the night?'

'Rafa doesn't even know I speak Italian.'

'Does it matter?'

She shrugged. 'Not any more, I suppose.'

'Then we will have a nice dinner with fine wine and good food, and you and I will not talk about the past. You will rest and recover. You've just climbed an emotional mountain. It wouldn't be right for you to stay in some impersonal hotel on the road back to Rome, and anyway, it's late.' He grinned at her and she couldn't help but smile back. 'Please, stay.'

'All right. We'll stay. But you have to call me Marina.'

He looked appalled. 'That is too much to ask. I will call you nothing at all.'

Rafa returned in a sombre mood. He had taken a table in the square and sat for an hour over a glass of wine, wondering whether his revelation, when he finally told Marina, would be gratefully received. The butler met him at the steps and showed him into the drawing room. He waited a while, wandering around the room, looking at all the family photographs. Tanned and glossy people smiled out of silver frames, and Rafa got the impression of a rarefied world where it was always

summer and always happy. He gazed at the impressive paintings on the walls, then lingered a long time in front of the large
family portrait hanging above the fireplace. It was dated 1979:
mother, father and their three little girls in pretty white dresses
and pink satin shoes. He moved closer and scrutinized the
man. So absorbed was he in the picture, he didn't hear the
door open as Marina and Dante stepped into the room.

'Rafa.' Marina's voice extracted him from his thoughts with
a jolt. 'Come and meet Dante, my old friend.' Rafa wasn't surprised to hear Marina speaking fluent Italian; it just confirmed
what he had suspected all along.

But Marina misinterpreted his pallor and felt the need to
explain. 'I grew up here,' she said. 'Dante is part of my past.'

Rafa took Dante's outstretched hand. 'It's a pleasure to meet
you.'

'We have agreed that you will both stay the night here at La
Magdalena, then return to Rome in the morning,' said Dante.

Rafa was unable to tear his eyes off him. He was older than
the man who smiled out from the family photographs, but he
was still handsome, with a powerful charisma that filled the
room.

'I gather you are an artist. Come, let me show you some of
the works of art my family has collected over the generations,
and then I'll take you around the gardens before it gets dark.
I find this time of day particularly beautiful.'

Rafa followed Dante into the hall. He caught Marina's eye
and frowned, but she averted her gaze, leaving him to ponder
the nature of their relationship.

He was enchanted by La Magdalena, and felt his fears sub-
side when they wandered out into the serenity of the gardens.
Marina hung back, allowing her memories to float about her
in the smells and sounds of the place she had loved above all
others. Some she held onto while others she let go, but with
every recollection she felt a little lighter. They strolled into the

mermaid garden where she and Dante had first become friends, and into the olive grove where she had tamed Michelangelo the peacock. They walked around the fountain and admired the statues, but they didn't approach the wall where it was still crumbling. The memories that lingered there were too raw for both of them.

They dined on the terrace in the candlelight and Marina told Dante about Clementine and Jake. Rafa went quiet, remembering his clash on the beach with Clementine. He wanted to text her – she'd love to hear that her stepmother spoke fluent Italian – but he couldn't act as if nothing had happened. He had to come clean and tell her the truth, now that he knew for sure.

He watched Dante and Marina, the way they interacted with the ease of intimate friends, the way she moved her hands when she spoke Italian, the way she didn't really have much of an accent at all. Although they included him in conversation, they didn't pay him much attention, so engrossed were they in each other. Dante's tender gaze was unmistakable, and she seemed to swell beneath it, shedding the years with each peal of laughter.

Rafa grew subdued, withdrawing into the background while they basked in the strange magic they generated. How peculiar, he thought to himself, that sometimes when one question is answered, another is raised; and the answer to *that* question was the very thing he feared the most.

Chapter 35

Clementine did not go into work. She telephoned Sylvia and in her croakiest voice explained that she was feeling rotten with a mystery bug and didn't want to contaminate the office. 'I think Mr Atwood is in enough trouble at home already,' she said.

Sylvia knew she was faking, but she didn't mind. She imagined Clementine wanted to spend the day with Rafa, and she didn't blame her. She switched on her computer and wondered whether there was a Rafa out there for her.

But Rafa had left that morning for Italy and the hotel echoed with his absence. Clementine wandered through the rooms like a lost dog, aching with longing and loneliness. She took Biscuit for a walk along the cliffs and took her phone out of her pocket more than once to see whether Rafa had sent her a text. She thought of calling him to say she was sorry she had run off without waiting to hear his explanation, but each time she stopped herself mid-dial, afraid of what he had to tell her.

She found her father in the library, replacing the books the Brigadier had returned.

'He hasn't been reading so much since he asked Jane Meister to marry him,' said Grey, climbing the ladder to put Andrew Roberts's *Masters and Commanders* back in the military section. 'He's a happy man.'

'Lucky him.'

He glanced down at his daughter's disgruntled face. 'What are you so gloomy about?'

She folded her arms and looked out of the window at the sea. It was a beautiful day, blue skies and the ocean as flat as a mirror. 'Dad, do you fancy taking me out in your boat?'

Grey stopped what he was doing and came down the ladder. 'I'd love to.'

She smiled feebly. 'I'd really like to spend some time with you.'

Grey gently patted her shoulder. This small gesture of tenderness struck Clementine with a sudden wave of neediness, and she threw herself against him. He froze in surprise, not knowing how to respond. It had been many years since he had embraced her, he had forgotten what it felt like. But she didn't pull away. Tentatively he wrapped his arms around her and held her close. He didn't ask what the matter was, for he sensed that once she was out in the middle of the sea, she would tell him.

The following morning Marina awoke to the long-forgotten sounds of Italy. The birds chirruped high in the umbrella pines and the scents of the garden wafted in on a warm, sea breeze. She could smell pine and soil, rosemary and cut grass, and the sound of gardeners watering the borders with hoses was a distinctly foreign one. She opened her eyes and let her gaze wander leisurely around the bedroom. It was extravagantly decorated with tall ceilings and elaborate mouldings, delicate antique furniture and silk curtains in a pale, duck-egg blue.

Once, she had believed she would live here with Dante and have many golden-haired children to love, but that was long ago – another life. Now, as she lay in the big, luxurious bed with a view over the gardens she had once believed to be paradise, she didn't feel the old sense of longing or loss, but something different: a contentment of sorts. It was as if she could at last put the past behind her, because now she was back, she realized it no longer had the power to hurt her.

She got up and pulled open the curtains. Gazing into the sunshine she let the breeze brush her skin with soft caresses. She viewed the grounds with detachment and realized how much she had changed. She wasn't Floriana any more. She was Marina, with an English husband and an English life. Although there had been a moment last night when she had believed Marina to be the mask, she now realized that she *was* Marina, and Floriana no more than a memory she gave life to in her thoughts. The past was gone and she could never get it back.

But she didn't want it back. She inhaled deep into the bottom of her lungs and closed her eyes. She didn't want *the past* back, only the son she had left there, and she yearned for him with all her heart. The early days of her exile, when the grey English skies and cold, penetrating rain had sent her into a frenzy of home-sickness, were long gone. The hours pacing the beach in frustration while she waited for news of her son from Father Ascanio were gone, and the old priest was now dead.

The trauma of beginning again in a strange country, learning a new language and remaining in isolation because her heart was too broken to make friends, had also gone – and, like a tree in winter, she had remained frozen until spring had revealed little green shoots and finally blossom, and she had grown strong. She now knew that she could survive anything, even the loss of her beloved Polzanze, because she had lost her son and yet she still had the capacity to take pleasure in life, and love.

She gazed into the azure sky, where a bird of prey circled silently on the wind, and felt an expansion in her chest, a sense of something greater than herself; a sense of God. Closing her eyes again and feeling that warm presence on her face, she let Him back into her heart. And she sent up a prayer for the only thing that really mattered now: her child.

When she stepped out onto the terrace she found Dante and Rafa already enjoying a hearty breakfast. They were chatting away like old friends. Rafa noticed at once the change in Marina. She had a lightness of being, which made her look younger, almost girlish.

After breakfast they returned to the car. The butler had put their bags in the boot and now stood holding the passenger door open. Dante suggested they drive into Herba, but Marina refused. She had seen enough.

She took his hand and quietly, so Rafa couldn't hear, she whispered to him softly, 'I'm not that girl any more, Dante.'

His eyes grew foggy and he squeezed her fingers. 'But I'm the same boy who loves you.'

Rafa watched them embrace. They held each other tightly and for a long time. He turned away and cast his gaze into the coppice of pine trees where a couple of squirrels were chasing each other up a skinny trunk, disappearing into the thatch of green needles. He felt a stab of jealousy and shoved his hands into his trouser pockets.

Dante did not want to let her go. She still looked the same, in spite of her honey-coloured hair. When she had stepped out that morning he had caught his breath at the sight of her, and had gripped the table as he was suddenly whisked back forty years. He regretted not having the courage to elope when he had had the chance all those years ago, and he regretted not trying harder to find her. He watched her climb into the car and waved as it motored slowly down the drive. He could still smell her scent on his skin and feel her soft body in his arms, and his longing surprised him, for time had in no way diminished it. Fate had intervened and taken her from him once; now it took her from him again. But this time she wasn't lost –

and they had a son. He rubbed his chin. How he had ached for a son.

With a purposeful stride he climbed back up the steps into the house. 'Lavanti, I'm going back to Milan,' he shouted to his butler, then disappeared into his office.

Marina glanced back one final time as the car swept through the gates of La Magdalena. She watched them close behind her, shutting on the past, relegating it to the attic of her mind to be boxed up and put away with the rest of Floriana's life.

'You seem happier today,' Rafa commented, a little bitterly.

'I am,' she sighed. Rafa chewed on her words pensively. 'But I didn't get what I came for. I never asked.' She looked out of the window, at a mother with two small children wandering slowly down the road. 'If I lose the Polzanze, so be it. It is only a house. I can take all the important things with me.' *Because all the important things have been within me all along.*

'I don't suppose Grey knows that you speak fluent Italian.'

'No, he doesn't. I have a great deal of explaining to do.'

'I suppose it would be presumptuous to ask you to explain to me?'

'It would, Rafa.' She looked down at her ring. 'It is only fair that I come clean with my husband first. Then, I will come clean with all of you. I don't want to hide who I am any more.'

He frowned at her, feeling an odd sense of rejection. After that, neither spoke. They both stared out of the window, alone with their thoughts.

They arrived back at the Polzanze that evening. Grey, Clementine, Jake, Harvey and Mr Potter were all waiting in the conservatory to hear whether she had saved the hotel. Marina suddenly felt the heavy weight of responsibility, as if she had just donned a cloak of lead. So many depended on her and the Polzanze, and she had failed them. She looked at their eager faces and was suddenly deflated.

'I need to talk to Grey,' she said.

'Did you get it?' Clementine asked, unable to contain her impatience.

'No, I didn't,' she replied.

The air sank around them like damp snow. She wanted to reassure them that it didn't matter. But it *did* matter. It mattered terribly, to them.

Clementine pulled a sympathetic smile. 'We'll be OK,' she said, fighting tears. She hadn't realized until now how much the Polzanze meant to her. She looked at Rafa but he was unable to meet her eye. He looked so sad, as if the night in Italy had piled on a decade. She wanted to shake him. Didn't he know by now how much she loved him?

Marina looked at her husband. 'Grey, will you walk with me? There's something I need to tell you.'

Grey had known right from the beginning of their courtship that she was keeping something secret from him. The recurring nightmares when she cried out in her sleep then sobbed in his arms, hinted at something dark and terrible that she was unable to share. He hadn't ever asked her what it was for he had trusted that in time, when she was ready, she would tell him. He hadn't expected it to take so many years. Now she took his hand and they walked down to the beach where she had spent so many hours gazing out to sea, mourning her inability to conceive. They strolled up the sand and Marina took her time.

'Will you promise me one thing, Grey?'

'Of course.'

'Will you try not to judge me?'

'I won't judge you, my darling.'

'Yes, you will. It's only natural. Please don't think less of me because I hid this from you. It was the only way I could cope.'

'All right.'

'And you know that I love you.' She stopped and took both

his hands in hers. 'I love you for your patience, your compassion and for the fact that you have always loved me, in spite of knowing there was a depth in me that I never let you reach.'

'Marina, darling, whatever it is, I'll still love you.'

She took a deep breath and without being aware of it, she gripped his hands tightly. 'My name is Floriana Farussi. I'm Italian. I was born in a little seaside town called Herba in Tuscany. My mother ran off with a tomato seller from the market, taking my little brother with her, leaving me with my inebriated father, Elio. I was as good as an orphan but I always dreamed of something more.'

She was so intent on telling her story that she hadn't noticed her husband had gone as grey as a carp.

She talked at length and she told him everything. They sat on the sand and she described the summer she fell in love with Dante, the time she nearly killed herself jumping off the high cliff into the sea, and the moment he had made love to her. She told him about Good-Night and Costanza, and the wickedness of her mother, the countess.

As she told him about her pregnancy, her hopes for her future with Dante and the loss of her child in the convent, Grey began to understand her more profoundly. He realized now why she had paced the sand, mourning the loss of her child whom she had nurtured for such a short time, and why her later inability to conceive had nearly destroyed her. He understood why she had suffered night terrors and why she had, at times, seemed so haunted by loss.

'So, when I finally saw Dante I realized that I couldn't ask him for money. I just couldn't.'

He pulled her into his arms and kissed her temple. 'Of course you couldn't.'

'It would have reduced everything else to dust. He would have thought it a cynical ploy to exploit him. But what we had was precious, and the son we made together is out there

somewhere and so much more important than the Polzanze.'
She turned round and smiled at him. 'You see, it all became
very clear to me in Italy. *You* are important to me, Grey. You,
Jake, Clementine, Harvey, Mr Potter – *you* are my family and
I carry you in my heart wherever I go. So, it doesn't really
matter whether we continue on here, or start again somewhere
else. As long as we're together we'll be OK.'

'But your son, darling.'

'I might never find him.' She turned away and her eyes glittered in the reflection of the sea. 'I hope he's happy. I hope he
knows nothing about me.'

'I know it's late but I think you should tell Jake and
Clementine,' he said as they walked back up to the house.

'You're right. I hope they are as understanding as you are.'

'I'm glad you told me. You make more sense to me now. I
think you'll find you make more sense to them, too.'

Clementine and Jake reacted very differently to her confession.
Clementine was fascinated by the romance and tragedy of it.
She felt every bit as desperate as Marina as she described her
love affair and the loss of her son, while Jake found the emotions hard to comprehend. As a man who had never been in
love, who had never suffered, he failed to grasp the enormity
of it all. The fact that she had withheld it gripped him far more
than the story itself. It seemed little more than a great adventure. However, he admired her for not asking Dante for
money, and vowed that wherever Grey and Marina chose to
begin again, he would go with them and support them one
hundred per cent.

Rafa paced his room while Biscuit lay uneasily on his bed,
watching him stride back and forth as if the floor were made
of hot coals. Suddenly, he was unsure. When he had set out
from Argentina he had been so certain of the validity of his

quest. He had set about his search with the enthusiasm and curiosity of a young detective on his first case. But he hadn't considered the emotional consequences of the truth, once discovered. He hadn't imagined he would fall in love with Clementine, he hadn't considered that he might love Marina, too. He hadn't anticipated the terrible fear the answers would expose.

He wanted to call his mother. He wished he could speak to his father. He wished he had never set out in the first place. The cowardly part of him wished things could go back to the way they were, before his head had grown muddled and confused, before his heart had taken it upon itself to get involved.

He began to toss his clothes into his suitcase.

The following morning he awoke late. He looked at his watch. It was ten o'clock. He hadn't slept that long since his university days. He showered and dressed and began to finish what he had started the night before. He'd make up some excuse and leave as quickly as possible; that way he could put this whole business behind him. When he thought of Clementine he felt a sharp pain in his chest – the thought of never seeing her again was unbearable.

He was interrupted by a soft knocking on the door. He glanced at his case lying open on the bed and then back at the door. He was left no alternative but to open it. There, standing on the landing, was Clementine.

'Do you mind if I come in?'

He shrugged. 'You might as well, now you're here.'

She was surprised to see that he was packing. Her heart lurched with panic. 'You're leaving?'

'Yes.'

'When?'

'Today.'

She gazed at him, horrified. 'Where are you going?'

'Home.'

'But I thought you were going to stay the whole summer?'

'My plans have changed. It's complicated.'

'Not as complicated as the story Marina told us last night. Or should I say Floriana Farussi from Italy.'

He sat down on the window seat and rubbed his temple.

'Did you know?' she asked.

'What did she tell you?'

'Everything.' She sat beside him and hugged her knee against her chest. 'I had a lot of time to think while you were away. I'm sorry I ran off up the beach and didn't give you time to explain. It was cowardly of me. I'm ready now if you still want to tell me.' She looked at him intensely. 'Why are you running away, Rafa?'

Marina was gathering herbs from the trough outside the stable block when the shiny black Alfa Romeo pulled up in front of the hotel. The engine stopped and footsteps could be heard on the gravel, but her attention was on the job at hand. There followed a brief conversation in low voices and then the footsteps grew louder. She looked up to see Grey striding towards her with Dante. Her heart leaped in surprise and she dropped her secateurs.

'Dante?'

'Floriana. I couldn't wait and I didn't want to tell you over the telephone,' he said in English. 'Besides, I wanted to be here with you when I told you.'

'Told me what?' But she knew and her eyes filled with tears.

'Our son.'

Her fingers shot to her lips. 'You know where he is?'

'Yes.'

'Where?'

'He's here.'

She felt her head spin. 'Here?'

'Yes.'

'But I don't understand.'

'His name is Rafa Santoro.'

Marina was speechless. Her emotions rose in a great tidal wave and she let out a loud wail. Both men rushed forwards to catch her as her knees buckled. But Dante saw her reach out to Grey and caught himself. He stood back as her husband helped her inside and settled her on the sofa in the sitting room.

'I'm fine,' she said as he released her. 'Please go and get him. Bring him to me.'

Grey strode out, his own head whirling with the astonishing sequence of revelations.

She patted the sofa. 'Dante, how did you find out?' He sat beside her. She took his hand and smiled, although her eyes were streaming.

'When you told me that Father Ascanio had sent you to England because he feared for your life, it suddenly occurred to me that this was *not* my father's doing. You see, my father would never have involved a priest and his ways of dealing with problems such as ours were way more brutal. If my father had promised to look after you, there would have been nothing to fear. You wouldn't have been sent away and our son would never have been adopted. So, it got me thinking, if not my father, then who? Father Ascanio would never have had the means to set you up in England and arrange for your passport and change of identity. The only man I know capable of all that is Zazzetta.'

'Zazzetta?'

'I took the helicopter straight back to Milan and confronted him. All these years he kept the secret, surreptitiously sending money when needed to an old flame of his who had agreed to look after you here.'

'Katherine Bridges was an old flame of Zazzetta?'

'She worked as a governess in Milan when Zazzetta first

started working for my father. You owe your life to him, Floriana. When my father received the letter from Elio, black-mailing him, he told Zazzetta to make the problem go away. He told him to make it look like an accident.' Marina blanched. 'But Zazzetta is a religious man and it was more than he could do to kill a young girl and her unborn child. So, he arranged everything in utmost secrecy with Father Ascanio, whom he knew he could trust, and sent his own brother to fetch you. You see, Floriana, they couldn't tell you the truth, they couldn't trust anyone, because their lives depended on it, too. Were my father to find out that his most trusted aide had betrayed him, he would have done away with the lot of you. He would have tracked you down and he would have buried Zazzetta without so much as a backward glance.' He lowered his eyes. 'I cannot begin to tell you the wickedness of that man. I'd like to say that money and power corrupted him, but I think he was just born wicked.'

'Don't tell me, Dante. He's dead now. He can't hurt anyone ever again. And you have found my son. *Our* son.'

'All the time you were looking for *him*, he was looking for *you.*'

'And he found me. I just didn't know it.'

Dante grinned. 'There is a small slice of justice, however.'

'What's that?'

'My father entrusted his whole life to Zazzetta. He did everything for him. Therefore it was easy to take money from my father to pay Lorenzo Santoro in Argentina and Katherine Bridges in England. So, you see, my father financed your new life and our son's without ever knowing.'

'And here we are, after all these years, reunited. That is jus-tice, God's way.'

Chapter 36

'You're Marina's son, aren't you?' said Clementine. Rafa nodded. 'Why didn't you tell her?'

'Because I wasn't sure it was her. The only information I had was a letter signed "Floriana", a bracelet and a ring, and the box of personal items belonging to Father Ascanio, my father's brother, sent out after he died.'

'Father Ascanio was your uncle?'

'Yes. I'm Italian Argentine, don't forget.' He walked over to the suitcase and pulled out a file. 'Here are the letters. There are countless ones from Costanza in Rome, written to my uncle in Herba, begging to know Floriana's whereabouts, and letters to Floriana, which she asks him to forward. Of course, he never did, for here they are, bundled up with a half-written letter to Floriana that he wrote but never sent.

'It gave me my first lead. You see, he mentions Beach Compton, a little seaside town here on the coast, so that is where I started my search. I knew she was about seventeen when she left Italy so I presumed she would have gone to school. There is only one school in the town and the old headmistress still lives there. However, Floriana didn't go to school, but the headmistress knew her foster mother, Katherine Bridges, well, for she had taught English there and they had become friends. She remembered Floriana, although of course she wasn't called Floriana. That's why I couldn't be sure. And when I met her, she was so English, she wasn't at all what I was expecting.'

'Did you find Katherine Bridges?'

'She married and moved to Canada fifteen years ago.'

'I never even knew she existed. Do you think she kept her hidden away on purpose?'

'Possibly.'

'So how did you find Marina here?'

'The headmistress, Christine Black, keeps scrapbooks on everything. She showed me a magazine article on the Polzanze, written not long after it was opened.'

'So, why are you leaving?'

He rubbed his temples. 'Clementine, does Marina really want the past dug up? Does she want Grey to know her secret? Does Dante even know she had his child? She returned to Italy to save the Polzanze, not to unearth painful memories. Perhaps I'm a painful memory she would rather not remember.'

There was a knock on the door. Clementine huffed irritably, she didn't welcome the intrusion. She was surprised when her father peered around the door.

'Rafa, will you come over to the stable block? There's someone I think you ought to meet.'

Rafa glanced at Clementine, who raised her eyebrows, as baffled as he. Grey saw the open suitcase on the bed, but said nothing. They followed him down the stairs, past reception, where Rose was watching the mysterious comings and goings with curiosity, and across to the stable block, where Jake had now joined them.

Rafa noticed the Alfa Romeo on the gravel and the driver in uniform who was proudly polishing the bonnet. He did not expect to see Dante. When he entered, the sitting room fell quiet. The air grew suddenly still. Dante and Marina stood up. Rafa could see that Marina had been crying. He realized then that she knew who he was, and the relief was unexpected.

She looked at him with such tenderness that he was caught off guard. 'My son,' she said.

Rafa was too overwhelmed to reply. He had suspected she was his mother, then in Italy all doubt had been erased, and yet, hearing it said out loud made it real.

He looked at Dante. '*Mio figlio*,' he said, and reached out his hand.

'You came looking for me?' Marina whispered as she moved hesitantly towards him. All he could do was nod dumbly as the two people who had brought him into the world wrapped their arms around him.

'So, you're not Baffles, the gentleman thief,' said Jake, finding the intensity of emotion intolerable.

Rafa laughed. 'Of course not.'

'Then what were you doing in Marina's room?'

'Trying to find proof that she was my mother.'

'And did you?' Marina asked.

'No. Just a poem. "My Marine Marina".'

'Ah, wrong box. That was how I got my name. I chose it out of Katherine Bridges' book of poems that was on my bed-side table when I arrived in Beach Compton. Of course, I didn't understand it, speaking no English, but Marina is also an Italian name from *mare*, meaning sea. The sea was the only thing I could find that England had in common with Italy, so I chose it as my name and tore it out to keep. Let me get the *right* box and show you how I clung to your memory all these years.'

She left the room and hurried upstairs. Her heart was so light she could feel it bouncing in her chest like a big helium balloon.

Rafa sat beside his father, still holding the file he had been showing Clementine. Now he showed Dante. 'There was no mention of you anywhere in my uncle's file,' he told him. 'But I'm glad I've found you, too.'

Dante withdrew a little velvet pouch and peered inside. There, glittering through the dark, was the diamond ring he had given Floriana, and the charm bracelet from his mother. He turned the ring over in his fingers, remembering the night he had given it to her, beneath the stars overlooking the sea. He had once thought they'd grow old together.

'Now that I know who you are, I can see you have Marina's eyes,' said Jake.

'Good God, I think you're right,' Grey agreed. 'I can't think why we didn't notice before. The resemblance is startling.'

'And my colouring, not that you can see because I'm now so grey,' Dante added.

'*I* never thought you were Baffles.' Clementine smiled at him affectionately. He grinned at her and allowed his eyes to linger before Marina returned with an old shoebox, and he had to tear them away.

She kneeled in front of the sofa and opened the lid. The contents no longer afflicted her with guilt. Like grenades, they had been defused. 'These are small treasured things from our brief time together. A photo of you the Mother Superior took.' She lifted it out and stared at it, amazed that the little baby in the photograph now sat before her as a man. 'There, you see how sweet you were. And your blanket.' She pressed it to her nose then pulled out an envelope. 'A lock of your hair. Look how blond you were. You had such fine, silky hair. Silly things,' she said dismissively, feeling foolish as she rummaged about with trembling fingers. 'But they were all I had.' She lifted out a wad of letters tied with the pink ribbon with which Violetta had wrapped her birthday present. 'And these, how I treasured these.' She caught Dante's eye and smiled wistfully.

'What did you call me?' Rafa asked.

'You were christened Dante.'

He looked down at his buckle. 'Well, that has always been

my middle name. Rafael Dante Santoro. R.D.S. When you introduced me to Dante in Italy everything fell into place. It was then that I knew where I came from. But I wasn't sure I could go through with telling you. I wasn't sure you'd want to know. I wasn't sure *I* wanted to know – I hadn't anticipated feeling a sense of rejection. But now I know the truth, I understand why I was given up. I understand that you were given no choice.'

There were so many questions Marina wanted to ask, she didn't know where to begin. So she took his hand and asked him the one question that had worried her more than any other. 'Have you had a happy life?'

He smiled down at her. 'Very,' he replied.

'I am also here for another purpose,' said Dante.

'What more could there possibly be?' Jake asked, weary of yet more revelations.

'I would like to invest in your hotel.' Marina looked at Rafa and pulled a face. 'Yes, Rafa told me before you came down to breakfast. Don't be cross. I asked him why you had come and he told me. I respect you for not having asked, but now let me make you an offer.'

'I'm embarrassed,' she said, replacing the lid on the box.

'There is nothing wrong with loving a place and doing all you can to hold onto it. I love La Magdalena and would fight with all my resources to keep it, were I in danger of losing it. Let me do this for you, because I can.' He smiled at her fondly. 'And because I want to.'

She nodded in resignation, secretly pleased, for all their sakes. 'Then I will hand you over to my husband,' she said, pushing herself up from the floor. 'Grey understands the finances better than I do. Why don't you talk business with him while I go and arrange lunch? I suggest we all eat together. One big family.' She looked around. 'Where's Harvey? Has anyone seen Harvey this morning?'

'He went to visit his mother yesterday evening,' said Jake. 'Maybe he's not back yet.'

'Then I must call him straight away.' And she strode off into the kitchen.

Grey invited Dante over to the hotel to discuss business in the library. Jake returned to his duties, pleased to leave the stifling atmosphere of the little sitting room. Clementine and Rafa were left alone.

'So, are you still going to leave today?' she asked, thrusting her hands into her trouser pockets.

'How can I?'

'Well, you've found what you were looking for.'

'I've found *more* than I was looking for.' He gazed at her in that intense way of his. She averted her eyes, not wanting to hope and be disappointed. 'Clementine, I found *you*.'

'But you didn't want me.'

'I always wanted you. I wanted you so much it ached.' He took her in his arms. 'I couldn't expect you to love me when I was hiding my identity from you. I couldn't risk hurting you.'

'But you did all the same.'

He traced his fingers down her face. 'I'm sorry, *mi amor*. I never wanted to hurt the woman I love.'

'So what do we do now?' She lifted her chin defiantly.

'I suggest we enjoy the rest of the summer here. I want to spend time with Marina and share her memories. Then I will take you on a long trip around South America.'

'That's presumptuous.'

'We will start in Argentina, then go across to Chile on horseback, up to Brazil and Mexico and Peru.' He bent his head and softly kissed her neck.

'That's going to take a while. What will Mr Atwood say?'

'You're not going to work there any more.' He placed his lips on her jaw line.

'I'm not?'

'No, because you are made for better things than that.' He moved his mouth up to her cheekbone and lightly brushed her skin.

'What things might they be?' she asked weakly.

'I don't know, but we'll discover them together. That will be the fun of it.' Before she could say another word he pulled her against him and pressed his lips to hers. As he kissed her, all the disappointment and longing that had built up over the last weeks evaporated like summer mist.

Marina telephoned Sun Valley Nursing Home and asked for Mrs Dovecote. There was a lengthy scuffle, the mumbling of voices, then the receptionist returned on the line to tell her there was no one of that name in the home.

'But there must be some mistake. Perhaps she's registered under another name. Her son, Harvey Dovecote, goes to visit her regularly. Recently he's been going several times a week.'

'I'm sorry, there's no one by that name and everyone who visits has to sign in. There hasn't been anyone by that name. I'd remember a name like Harvey Dovecote.'

Marina put down the telephone, perplexed. She thought of his nephew's beautiful Jaguar and her heart began to pound. He had only started mentioning his nephew recently. Wouldn't he have mentioned him before? And if he wasn't going to visit his mother, where was he going? If his mother wasn't at Sun Valley, what else was he lying about? Did he have a mother at all? He was past seventy himself.

Suddenly, she had the most terrible vision. Hot with anxiety she hurried over to her office and rummaged around in her drawer for the key to Harvey's shed. She wasn't sure whether she had one, having not been in it for years. However, it lay there among all the other keys, tagged and labelled. She clutched it tightly, hoping her fears were unfounded. Perhaps Harvey had a plausible explanation. However, the vision refused to go away. Without a word to anyone she stole down the garden to Harvey's little shed, nestled at the back of the vegetable garden in the shadow of a giant horse chestnut. With a trembling hand she slotted the key into the lock and turned it.

The door whined grudgingly as the contents of Harvey's secret life were brought into the light. She gasped in astonishment. There, in neat piles among the baler twine and Agritape were jewellery, paintings and silver, pilfered from the grand houses he had robbed. On the shelf nailed to the wall was a neat pile of books by E. W. Hornung about Raffles, the Amateur Cracksman.

Hurriedly, she closed the door and locked it, her heart thumping frantically in her chest. *No one must know about this*, she thought to herself, feeling sick. *At least, not until I've spoken to Harvey*. She slipped the key into her pocket and made her way back up to the house.

Maria Carmela heard the telephone ring and knew instinctively that it was her son Rafa. She hurried into the kitchen and picked it up. '*Hola*.'

'Mamá.'

'What news? I haven't heard from you for a week.'

'I have found my biological parents.'

Maria Carmela sat down. 'You have found them? Both of them?'

'Yes. Marina, the woman who owns the hotel, is Floriana. She fell in love with a man called Dante. They're here, both of them.'

'Are you all right?'

'I'm happy, Mamá. I know where I come from now, but I also know who I belong to.'

'You do?' Her voice sounded strained.

'I belong to you, Mamá. I always have.'

Maria Carmela's heart felt as full as it could possibly be. 'I have been so worried. You see, when Father Ascanio asked us to adopt you, I had to confide in my employer, Señora Luisa. When she took you under her wing, I feared she would take you from me for she was the only person who knew you did not belong to us and she was enchanted by you. When you set out on this quest to find your biological mother, again I feared I'd lose you. I have always been aware that you were entrusted to us, but not one *of* us. I've always feared I would lose you one day.'

'But that makes no sense. You were the mother who kissed me goodnight, who read me bedtime stories, who bandaged my knee when I fell off Papa's mare. You were the mother I ran to when I was unhappy, to whom I poured out my heart when it was broken. You are the woman who has been a mother to me in all the ways that are important. I had no other mother but you.' He sensed her emotion down the line and understood that she was too moved to speak.

'Listen, you know the girl I told you about? Clementine?'

She sniffed and composed herself. 'Of course, Rafa.'

'I want to bring her to meet you.'

'You're coming home?'

'Yes, I'm coming home.' There was a pause. Rafa could feel his mother's happiness and his heart swelled with joy. 'She's incredibly special. I know you'll love her, too.'

'If you love her, then so will I. How wonderful to think that you went in search of one woman and you have found two. Tell me, *hijo*, was your biological mother very happy to see you?'

'Yes, she was.'

'Did you tell her how well I looked after you?'

'I told her that I have had the happiest life possible.'

'We weren't rich.'

'Neither was she. But like you, she is rich in everything that matters.'

'I think your father would be very proud of you.' Rafa didn't reply. 'I mean it, *mi amor*, he would consider you very brave. You took a risk, one he would have advised against, but it has paid off.'

'I miss him.'

'And I miss him, too. He wouldn't have approved of me giving you his brother's box of personal items, but he would be happy to know the outcome. That you are safe, that you know where you come from, but that, above all, you still know where you belong.'

Rafa put down the telephone and pulled the little pouch out of his pocket. He tipped the ring and the bracelet into his hand. He had always wondered about the woman to whom these had once belonged. He lifted his eyes to the window and saw Marina and Clementine beneath the cedar tree with Biscuit. He had arrived with a sense of dislocation, as if the truth about his birth had cut him off by the roots. Now he realized that those roots had never really been severed, for Maria Carmela and Lorenzo would always be his parents.

What changed now was his future. In his search for his mother he had found Clementine, and she had altered everything. Suddenly, he felt the desire to commit, to settle down and raise a family of his own. Floriana and Dante had not enjoyed a happy ending together, but he and Clementine could. He clenched his fingers around the jewellery. With Marina's blessing, he'd give the jewellery that had once meant so much to Floriana, to Clementine.

That night, in order to distract herself from Harvey's hoard of stolen treasure, Marina sat on the bench at the bottom of the garden with Costanza's letters and the half-written letter Father Ascanio had never sent. The sea murmured gently below her and the moon lit a silver river across the water to Jesus' marble kingdom where He had finally answered her prayer. She pulled her shawl around her shoulders and opened Father Ascanio's first. She switched on the torch and read his tidy, looped writing.

My dear Floriana,

I trust this finds you well in your body and healing in your heart. You are a very brave girl and I am immensely proud of you. You have conducted yourself throughout your ordeal with great dignity and strength.

I would have given anything for you to have remained in Herba where I could keep a fatherly eye on you, but as I explained at the convent, your life and the life of your son are in grave danger. This was the only way. Beppe Bonfanti is a very powerful man, capable of silencing his enemies in the most brutal manner. Therefore, I'm afraid I cannot forward any of your letters to Costanza – as her father now works for Beppe, it is too dangerous. No one must ever know where you are.

It grieves me greatly to inform you that Father Severo, who I have trusted for over fifteen years, overheard my conversation with Dante and let slip our secret to your father. He has confessed and is full of remorse. I felt it only right that he should leave Herba.

Trust me, my dear child, when I tell you that your little boy has been given to the most loving couple and will be brought up in the Catholic faith by an Italian family. You have given him the best possible start in life by your sacrifice. God knows what it has cost you and I pray that He comforts you as you settle into your new home.

I gather Beach Compton is on the sea. I hope you are able to make a fresh start there. Miss Bridges is a kind and godly woman, who I'm sure is taking good care of you. You have great inner strength and a strong, solid faith. Keep God in your sight and in your heart and you will put this all behind you.

As for me

He had stopped there. Only now did she understand the lengths that Father Ascanio had gone to in order to save her. He had sent her son to his own brother in Argentina, the only person he trusted to look after him properly. He couldn't have found a better home had he scoured the earth for one. He had put his own life at risk. Now she knew why: for love.

She closed the letter and replaced it in the envelope, saddened that Father Ascanio was no longer alive so that she could thank him. Then she took the bundle of letters Costanza had written and read them one by one, surprised by the extent to which her heart ached for her old friend.

The following morning Harvey appeared at the Polzanze. While Dante breakfasted in the dining room with Grey, Clementine and Rafa, Marina summoned him into her office.

'I need to talk to you, Harvey,' she said solemnly.

'Is everything all right?'

'I think you should sit down.' She perched on the armchair and watched him sink into the sofa, her old friend and confidant, the man who had been almost a father to her. She couldn't believe he was capable of lying. She wanted him to explain it all away. She was ready to believe any excuse he tossed her.

'I tried to call you yesterday at the nursing home.'

He looked surprised. 'You did?'

'They said they had never heard of a Mrs Dovecote.'

'You must have got the wrong home.'

'No, Harvey. I *know*.' She gazed at him sadly.

He averted his eyes. 'What do you know?' But she could tell from his grave features that he realized he had been found out.

'I know about your shed.' She lowered her voice. 'You're

Baffles, or Raffles, or whatever you call yourself. Harvey, how could you lie to me?'

He turned to her, his face full of remorse. 'I did it for you, Marina, for the Polzanze. When I saw you were in real danger of losing it, I decided I had to do something to help. I know how much this place means to you. I feared if you lost it, you'd lose your mind.'

'Oh, Harvey.'

He shrugged. 'So, I got a little carried away.'

'A little?'

'The Jag was second-hand. I got it for peanuts.'

'Do you even have a nephew?'

He shook his head.

'Or a mother?'

'No, she died years ago.'

'But, Harvey, you could go to prison for this.'

'I thought I'd only do it once. But it was too easy. So I did it again . . . and again. I admit it was fun. Macavity the Mystery Cat. I defied them all.' He grinned roguishly. 'It gave me a buzz to think of buying you out of your problems. Old Harvey, creeping into people's properties like James Bond.'

'Or Raffles.'

'I've always loved those novels. It began as a game.'

'But the game has gone too far.'

He looked at her wretchedly. 'What are you going to do, Marina?'

'I should call the police.'

'But you wouldn't turn in an old codger, would you? I'll die in there.'

Marina stiffened her jaw and lifted her chin. The thought of being without Harvey caused something to twist painfully inside her chest. She stood up and walked over to the window. She had lost too much in her life to suffer losing him. 'I won't turn you in, Harvey. But on one condition.'

'What's that? I'll do anything.'

'You have to give it all back.' His mouth opened in a silent gasp. 'If it was so easy, you can do it again. It has to go back, all of it.'

'But what about the Polzanze?'

'Ah, yes, you don't know, do you?' She sat down again. 'A lot has happened while you've been away. Goodness, where do I start?'

Chapter 37

Sylvia sat at her desk and gazed forlornly at the empty chair beside her. Clementine had come into the office on 31 August to pack up her things and say goodbye, which had been the arrangement from the beginning, as Polly was due back from maternity leave on 1 September. Only now, none of them wanted her to go. She had turned out to be the most efficient secretary – and a good friend to Sylvia. Mr Atwood had offered her an obscene amount of money to stay on, but she had declined. After all, what sort of woman would put money above a six-month trip around South America with the man of her dreams?

Sylvia was surprised that Mrs Atwood hadn't issued her husband with divorce papers. She wondered what sort of deal they had struck. Perhaps he had promised to don his robber suit for *her*. Maybe his wife was more game than he had thought. How many other guises did he assume? Those thoughts made Sylvia smile through those days when she missed Clementine.

Autumn had crept upon them without the slightest warning, because frankly, it had felt like autumn for the whole of July and August with the dampest skies and persistent drizzle. Polly had returned, unable to say a single sentence without squeezing her little girl into it somewhere. It was Doodlums this and Doodlums that, and Sylvia couldn't understand why she couldn't use her daughter's proper name, Esme, which was really very nice.

Clementine had looked radiantly happy. Sylvia hadn't felt jealous, because jealous implies resentment and Sylvia couldn't ever feel resentful towards Clementine, but she felt something close to envy. Not only did love make Clementine look prettier, it also gave her an air of insouciance, as if nothing in the world mattered as long as she was with the man she loved. The shadow had lifted and taken her defensiveness with it. No more unhappiness, no more bitterness, no more wallowing in self-pity.

Sylvia now booked in for lunch at the Polzanze on weekends. Before, no one had ever needed to book, but the hotel was very busy and the only way to get a table was to reserve one in advance, or call Jake on his mobile telephone, which he only gave out to very special clients, of which Sylvia was one. The artist-in-residence had gone, but the place now buzzed with Devon's most fashionable, and the rooms were always full. Marina had put an advert in the *Dawcomb-Devlish Gazette* for another artist, and William Shawcross had entertained everyone at the first literary dinner, which had been a sell-out. Not only was he an articulate and engaging speaker, but he was devilishly handsome, too. Sylvia had managed to corner him for the longest while, and he had politely indulged her as she told him her favourite subject at school had always been history.

She chewed the end of her Biro and considered how life had so suddenly changed for Clementine. After South America they were going to get married and settle down in Italy. They had thought long and hard about where to lay down their roots, as Rafa was anxious to remain close to Maria Carmmela, but his father, Dante, was very keen for them to live with him at La Magdalena. In the end they had decided to divide their time between Argentina and La Magdalena, flying Rafa's

mother over to Italy every summer. Sylvia thought how fabulous it must be to discover one's real father is one of the
richest men in Italy. She glanced at Polly, who was busily
scrolling down the Mothercare website, and scowled.
Clementine was so lucky. Now Sylvia didn't even have Freddie
to snuggle up to. She had never felt lonelier.

Just then the door opened and in walked Jake from the
Polzanze. It was funny to see him out of context, in a pair of
jeans and casual shirt. She was struck by how dashing he
looked with his fair hair flopping over his forehead and his blue
eyes as clear as a lagoon.

'Well, hello, Jake,' she said brightly. 'What are you doing
here?'

He looked around a little nervously. 'I came to see you,
actually.'

Sylvia straightened. 'Really?'

'I was wondering whether you'd let me take you out for
tea?'

She was surprised. 'Now?'

'If you're not too busy.'

She turned to Polly. 'Be a lovely and man the phones for
me. I'm going to take a break. It's not healthy to sit inside all
day.'

Jake grinned at her boyishly. 'Is Devil's good for you?'

'My favourite place.'

'I hear they do very good scones with clotted cream and
jam.'

'They most certainly do. Haven't you ever been there?'

'I'm ashamed to admit that I haven't.'

'Oh, Jake, you have a treat in store.' She shrugged on her
coat and grabbed her handbag.

They left the office and set off down the pavement. 'I've
been wanting to ask you out for a long time,' Jake confessed.

Sylvia bristled with pleasure. 'Really?'

'Yes, ever since you first came up to the Polzanze. I thought you were the most sensual woman I'd ever laid eyes on.'

'Goodness, Jake, I'm flattered. No one's ever called me sensual before.'

Her smile encouraged him to go a little further. 'It's the truth. I was just working up the courage to ask you out.'

'But what took you so long?'

'You're a beautiful woman, Sylvia. I wasn't sure you'd say "yes".'

She laughed incredulously. 'In that case, Jake, let's consider Devil's to be our first date.'

Devil's was warm and smelled of freshly baked cake. They sat at a table by the window and ordered scones and tea. Jake was delighted to see her tuck into the cream and jam with healthy abandon. 'I like a woman who's not afraid to enjoy her food,' he said.

'Oh, I couldn't deny myself this,' she enthused, licking a creamy finger.

'You look very good on it, I must say,' he added, admiring her full bosom as it strained against the stretchy fabric of her dress. 'So, why's a beautiful girl like you not married?'

She looked down at her ringless finger and sighed. 'I'm divorced, actually, yet to find the right man. I'm an old-fashioned girl at heart. You see, I believe in Big Love – the kind of love that sweeps you away, like in those romantic novels. There's no point compromising. I'd rather be alone than with a man I don't love.' She grinned as she thought of Clementine and what she'd say if she could hear her now. 'I want the fairy tale,' she added firmly. 'And nothing less.'

Grey motored the little fishing boat into the secluded bay. Seagulls dropped out of the sky to swim beside it, hoping to share the spoils of the picnic Marina had prepared. The water was calm, the sky cloudy but for patches of bright blue that gave them the occasional, fleeting glimpse of heaven. The wind was autumnal and Marina pulled her coat around her shoulders and shivered, hugging Biscuit closer to her body to keep warm.

Grey steered the boat onto the sand and switched off the engine. He leaped out and pulled it further up the beach, making sure that it wouldn't slip back into the sea. Marina handed him the rugs and the picnic basket, and laughed as Biscuit jumped over the stern and began to sniff the rocks excitedly. Grey gave Marina his hand and helped her down. 'So, this is it,' he said proudly. 'The place I've dreamed of bringing you.'

'It's lovely,' she enthused, taking a blanket and shaking it out onto the sand.

'It doesn't look like anyone ever comes down here.'

'Then it will be our secret place.'

'I like the sound of that.' He sat down beside the basket. 'What's in here?'

'All your favourite things,' she replied, joining him on the blanket.

'Ah, bread, pâté, smoked salmon, cheese and chocolate mousse.' He laughed. 'Darling, you think of everything.'

'Most importantly, the wine.' Snug in a cooler was a chilled bottle of Sauvignon Blanc.

Grey pulled out the glasses and poured the wine. He raised his glass. 'To absent friends,' he said meaningfully.

'To absent friends.' She took a sip. 'I miss them, but in a happy way.'

'They sound like they're having a wonderful time travelling around South America.'

'That's the great thing about email. In my day we had only letters and they took ages to arrive.'

'You never told me you still have all the love letters I wrote you.'

'I keep everything. I can't help it. It's in my nature to hold onto all the evidence of my life.' She grinned at him wistfully. 'Probably because I'm always a little scared of losing it.'

'Clementine has a beautiful diamond engagement ring, thanks to your magpie instincts.'

'It was strange seeing those pieces of jewellery again. They had meant so much to me at the time. Now they are just pieces of jewellery.'

'But Clemmie will imbue them with her own associations and they will be special to her in the same way that they were once so special to you.'

She took his hand. 'Grey darling, you've been wonderfully understanding through all of this.'

'Don't forget how many years I waited for you to open up.'

'Patience, then, is your most admirable quality.'

'I'd have waited for ever if I'd had to. But you know, it would have been so much easier if you had told me at the start. I'd never have judged you.'

'I know. But it was so raw it was unspeakable. Now I can talk openly about my son.' She smiled contentedly and took a deep, satisfied breath. 'My son — the words are very sweet on my tongue.'

'Who'd have thought, Rafa and Clementine? Your son and my daughter.'

'I'm going to have to suffer your ex at the wedding in May.'

'She's going to have to suffer the wedding being held at the Polzanze, I think that's worse.'

'And I'm going to meet Maria Carmela.' She trembled with excitement. 'She's going to bring photos of Rafa when he was growing up. How lucky that he fell into such a nice nest. I owe Father Ascanio so much, and Zazzetta, who I'd always believed to be the bad guy.' She took another sip of wine. 'You know, my life has been so rich because I have lived twice. If it wasn't for that one terrible twist of fate, I wouldn't have met

you, Clemmie and Jake – or Biscuit,' she added as the dog lay
down on the rug and began to sniff the basket.

'Who's to say what sort of people we'd be if we had never
met?'

'That's a very deep question.'

'Isn't it good then that we have the whole afternoon to discuss it?'

When they returned to the Polzanze it was already getting
dark. The days were shorter now, the sunlight weaker, the grass
strewn with crispy brown leaves and prickly conkers. Only the
pigeons cooed on the rooftops as if it were still summer.

Marina gazed upon the house she loved so dearly and
thought of Dante, who had made it all possible; Dante, who
was once again part of her life. She could now remember it
all with pleasure, and as she did so, memories buried deep
beneath the rubble surfaced again like flowers, finding their
way through the debris into the light where she feasted her
eyes on them nostalgically.

There was only one beautiful rose that came up through the
wreckage, thick with thorns. It gave her pain to look on it, so
she ignored it, even though it grew bigger and more alluring
with each day that passed. Until one wintry afternoon in
December she strode into the hall to find Jennifer on the telephone.

'Ah, here she is,' she said, making a face at Marina. 'It's for
you.' She held out the receiver.

'Who is it?'

Jennifer shrugged. 'I don't know. She says she's an old friend
of yours. Her name is Costanza.'

Epilogue

Rafa and Clementine wandered around the gardens of La
Magdalena. It had only been two months since they had
moved in and yet they already felt as if they had lived there
all their lives. Maria Carmela had come for the summer, settling herself in the little mermaid garden to read on the
bench where Violetta had liked to sit, and Dante's daughters
visited often with their husbands and children, filling the
pool once again with laughter. They had left Biscuit at the
Polzanze with Marina, but La Magdalena was full of stray
dogs and cats Dante had rescued, and Rafa and Clementine
loved them all.

The sun hung low in the west, turning the sky a translucent
pink and throwing inky green shadows across the grass.
Crickets and roosting birds squabbled noisily as they positioned
themselves for the night. The scents of pine and eucalyptus
hung thickly in the humid air and Clementine breathed it in
contentedly, savouring the smells of the foreign land she had
adopted. It wasn't long before they came across the part in the
boundary wall where the stones had fallen away, leaving it low
enough to scale.

'I wonder why Dante doesn't want this repaired,' said Rafa,
striding forwards. He picked up a loose stone, tossed it into the
air and caught it.

'It's obviously special to him. Did you notice the look on his face when he told us we could do whatever we liked to the house and gardens, but that this wall has to remain exactly as it is?'

'I would guess it has something to do with Floriana,' said Rafa. 'But somehow I don't feel we can ask.'

Clementine reached the wall and looked through the gap. Beyond, the hills of Tuscany undulated softly in the orange light and she could see the red rooftops of Herba in the distance and the tower of the church rising above them. Suddenly, she felt the urge to climb to the top and sit there a while. It was peaceful with the breeze in her hair and the sun warming her skin.

'Come and join me,' she said as she settled on the stones. 'It's lovely up here.'

Rafa scaled the wall and sat beside her. 'You're right, it's a beautiful spot.' He put his arm around her and gently pulled her close. They watched the sun sinking slowly in the sky and the subtle changes in colour as the day gave way to dusk. It was then, in the face of such splendour, that he knew. His parents had sat on this wall in the same way and witnessed the splendour of sunset as they did. The ghosts of the past were still here.

'Do you remember Veronica Leppley?' he asked after a while.

'Of course.'

'She once told me that I wouldn't feel complete until I had found my soul mate. Back then, I was searching for my mother. But now I have you, I realize she was right. Finding Marina gave me a sense of identity, I discovered who I really am and where I come from, but finding you gave me a sense of wholeness. I feel you complete the circle. Where I finish, you begin, and where you finish, I begin. Do you understand?'

Clementine lifted her chin and kissed his neck. 'I totally understand.'

'I love you, Clementine. I think we're going to be very happy here.'

She sighed contentedly, remembering her yearning to run away but unable now to recall exactly what it felt like. 'I love you, too, Rafa,' she replied, nuzzling closer. 'There's nowhere else in the world I'd rather be.'

THE DAWCOMB-DEVLISH GAZETTE

'BAFFLES' GENTLEMAN THIEF CASE DRAMA

– NEW MYSTIFYING DEVELOPMENTS – POLICE BAFFLED (AGAIN!)

The spate of burglaries in the Dawcomb-Devlish area, targeting family treasures in stately homes and country house hotels has been dubbed the 'Baffles' case after the eponymous hero of the movie, *Raffles*, who is a Gentleman Thief. But the case, which has generated both fear and amusement across Devon, has confounded the police. Now it has taken a dramatic turn.

If anyone thought the Baffles case could not get any more mysterious, they were wrong. In a sensational twist, it seems the thief was indeed something of a gentleman: he has started to return his ill-gotten gains.

The first item returned was the silver from Mr & Mrs Greville-Jones of Cherry Manor, Salcombe. Last Thursday, they discovered their silver service, worth £20,000, laid up on their dining-room table with a note that read: *Sorry the silver polishing took so long. Baffles.* 'It was as if it was laid up for one of my usual dinner parties,' said Mrs Greville-Jones.

Mrs Powell of Watertown Park, Thurlestone, found her diamond ring on the window sill: *This will put the sparkle back on your finger. My advice, never take it off again! Baffles*, read the note.

The police however are unamused: 'The perpetrator in this incident may find this amusing,' said Detective Inspector Reginald

Bud. 'But we regard this as a serious incident of breaking and entering.'

One victim who wishes to remain anonymous commented: 'I leave my front door unlocked now to make it easier for him, and my ten-year-old son leaves cakes and a glass of milk on the kitchen table in case he's feeling hungry. A bit like Santa Claus.'

COMING SOON

If you enjoyed *The House by the Sea* you will love

The Summer House –

the new novel from Santa Montefiore,
coming soon.

Read on for a sneak peek . . .

Chapter 1

Hampshire 2012

The beginning of March had been glorious. The earth had shaken off the early-morning frosts and little buds had emerged through the hardened bark to reveal lime-green shoots and pale-pink blossom. Daffodils had pushed their way up through the thawing ground to open into bright-yellow trumpets, and the sun had shone with renewed radiance. Birdsong filled the air and the branches were once again aquiver with the busy bustle of nest-building. It had been a triumphant start to spring.

Fairfield Park had never looked more beautiful. Built on swathes of fertile farmland, the Jacobean mansion was surrounded by sweeping lawns, ancient bluebell woods and fields of thriving crops and buttercups. There was a large ornamental lake where frogs made their homes among the bulrushes and goldfish swam about the lily pads. Towering beech trees protected the house from hostile winds in winter and gave shelter to hundreds of narcissi in spring. A nest of barn owls had set up residence in the hollow of an apple tree and fed off the mice and rats that dwelt on the farm and in the log barn, and high on the hill, surveying it all with the patience of a wise old man, a neglected stone folly was hidden away like a forgotten treasure.

Abandoned to the corrosion of time and weather, the pretty little folly remained benignly observant, confident that one day a great need would surely draw people to it as light to lost souls. Yet, today, no one below could even see those honey-coloured walls and fine, sturdy pillars, for the estate was submerged beneath a heavy mist that had settled upon it in a shroud of mourning. Today, even the birds were subdued. It was as if spring had suddenly lost her will.

The cause of this melancholy was the shiny black hearse that waited on the gravel in front of the house. Inside, the corpse of Lord Frampton, the house's patriarch, lay cold and vacant in a simple oak coffin. The fog swirled around the car like the greedy tentacles of death, impatient to pull his redundant body into the earth, and on the steps that led down from the entrance his two Great Danes lay as solemn and still as a pair of stone statues, their heads resting dolefully on their paws, their sad eyes fixed on the coffin; they knew intuitively that their master would not be coming home.

Inside the house, Lady Frampton stood before the hall mirror and placed a large black hat on her head. She sighed at her reflection, and her heart, already heavy with bereavement, grew heavier still at the sight of the eyes that stared back with the weary acquiescence of an old woman. Her face was blotchy where tears had fallen without respite ever since she had learned of her husband's sudden death in the Swiss Alps ten days before. The shock had blanched her skin and stolen her appetite so that her cheeks looked gaunt, even if her voluptuous body did not. She had been used to his absences while he had indulged his passion for climbing the great mountains of the world, but now the house reverberated with a different kind of silence: a loud, uncomfortable silence that echoed through the large rooms with a foreboding sense of permanence.

She straightened her coat as her eldest son, now the new Lord Frampton, stepped into the hall from the drawing room. 'What are they doing in there, David?' she asked, trying to contain her grief, at least until she got to the church. 'We're going to be late.'

David gazed down at her sadly. 'We can't be late, Mum,' he said, his dark eyes full of the same pain. 'Dad's ... you know ...' He looked to the window.

'No, you're right, of course.' She thought of George in the hearse outside and felt her throat constrict. She turned back to the mirror and began to fiddle with her hat again. 'Still, everyone will be waiting and it's frightfully cold.'

A moment later her middle son, Joshua, emerged from the drawing room with his chilly wife, Roberta. 'You OK, Mum?' he asked, finding the emotion of such an occasion embarrassing.

'Just keen to get on with it,' David interjected impatiently. Joshua thrust his hands into his pockets and hunched his shoulders. The house felt cold. He went to stand by the hall fire where large logs entwined with ivy crackled in the grate.

'What are they doing in there?' his mother asked again, glancing towards the drawing room. She could hear the low voice of her youngest son, Tom, and her mother-in-law's formidable consonants as she held forth, as usual unchallenged.

'Grandma's demanding that Tom show her how to use the mobile telephone he gave her,' Joshua replied.

'Now? Can't it wait till later?' Her chin trembled with anguish.

'They're finishing their drinks, Antoinette,' said Roberta with a disapproving sniff. 'Though I'm not sure Tom *should* be drinking with his history, should he?'

Antoinette bristled and walked over to the window. 'I think today of all days Tom is entitled to consume anything he wants,' she retorted tightly. Roberta pursed her lips and rolled her eyes at her husband, a gesture she wrongly assumed her mother-in-law couldn't see. Antoinette watched her arrange her pretentious feather fascinator in front of the mirror and wondered why her son had chosen to marry a woman whose cheekbones were sharp enough to slice through slate.

At last Tom sauntered into the hall with his grandmother, who was tucking the telephone into her handbag and clipping it shut. He smiled tenderly at his mother and Antoinette immediately felt a little better. Her youngest had always had the power to lift her high or pull her low, depending on his mood or state of health. A small glass of wine had left him none the worse and she ignored the niggling of her better judgement that knew he shouldn't consume any alcohol at all. Her thoughts sprang back to her husband and she recalled the time he had managed to telephone her from the Annapurna base camp just to find out how Tom was after a particularly bad week following a break-up. She felt her eyes welling with tears again and pulled her handkerchief out of her pocket. George had been a very *good* man.

'You haven't turned the heating off, have you?' exclaimed the Dowager Lady Frampton accusingly. '*I* never let it get so frightfully cold!' In her long black dress, wide black hat and mink stole Margaret Frampton looked as if she were off to crash a Halloween party rather than attend her only son's funeral. Around her neck, wrist and dripping from her ears like elaborate icicles was the exquisite Frampton sapphire suite, acquired in India in 1868 by the first Lord Frampton for his wife, Theodora, and passed down the generations to George, who had loaned it to his mother because his wife refused to wear such an extravagant display of wealth. The Dowager Lady Frampton had no such reservations and wore the jewels whenever a suitable occasion arose. Antoinette wasn't sure Margaret's son's funeral was quite such an occasion.

'The heating *is* on, Margaret, and the fires are all lit. I think the house is in mourning, too,' she replied.

'What a ridiculous idea,' Margaret muttered.

'I think Mum's right,' interjected Tom, casting his gaze out of the window. 'Look at the fog. I think the whole estate is in mourning.'

'I've lost more people than I can count,' said Margaret, striding past Antoinette. 'But there's nothing worse than losing a son. An *only* son. I don't think I'll ever get over it. At the very least, one would expect the house to be warm!'

Harris, the old butler who had worked for the family for more than thirty years, opened the front door and the Dowager Lady Frampton stepped out into the mist, pulling her stole tighter across her chest. 'Goodness me, are we going to be able to get to church?' She stood at the top of the stone stair and surveyed the scene. 'It's as thick as porridge.'

'Of course we will, Grandma,' Tom reassured her, taking her arm to guide her down. The Great Danes remained frozen beneath the weight of their sadness. Margaret settled her gaze on the coffin and thought how terribly lonely it looked through the glass of the hearse. For a moment the taut muscles in her jaw weakened and her chin trembled. She lifted her shoulders and stiffened, tearing her eyes away. Pain wasn't something one shared with other people.

The chauffeur stood to attention as Tom helped his grand-mother into one of the Bentleys. Roberta followed dutifully after, but Antoinette hung back. 'You go, Josh,' she said. 'Tom and David will come with me.'

Joshua climbed into the front seat. One might have thought that his father's death would unite the two women, but it seemed they were still as hostile as ever. He listened to his wife and grandmother chatting in the back and wondered why his mother couldn't get along with Margaret as well as Roberta did.

'That woman is so trying,' Antoinette complained, dabbing her eyes carefully as the cars followed the hearse down the drive and through the iron gates adorned with the family crest of lion and rose. 'Do I look awfully blotchy?' she asked Tom.

'You look fine, Mum. It wouldn't be appropriate to look polished today.'

'I suppose not. Still, everyone's going to be there.'

'And everyone is going to be coming back,' grumbled David from the front seat. He didn't relish the idea of having to socialize.

'I think we'll all need a stiff drink.' She patted Tom's hand, wishing she hadn't referred to alcohol. 'Even you. Today of all days.'

Tom laughed. 'Mum, you've got to stop worrying about me. A few drinks aren't going to kill me.'

'I know. I'm sorry, I shouldn't have mentioned it. I wonder who's come,' she said, changing the subject.

'Perish the thought of having to chat to Dad's dreadful aunts and all the boring relatives we've spent years avoiding,' David interjected. 'I'm not in the mood for a party.'

'It's not a party, darling,' his mother corrected. 'People just want to show their respect.'

David stared miserably out of the window. He could barely see the hedgerows as they drove down the lane towards the town of Fairfield. 'Can't everyone just bugger off and go home afterwards?'

'Absolutely not. It's polite to ask your father's friends and relatives home after the funeral. It'll cheer us all up.'

'Great,' David muttered glumly. 'I can't think of a better way of getting over Dad's death than having a knees-up with a bunch of old codgers.'

His mother began to cry again. 'Don't make this any harder for me, David.'

David peered around the seat and softened. 'I'm sorry, Mum. I didn't mean to upset you. I just don't feel like playing the glad game, that's all.'

'None of us do, darling.'

'Right now, I just want to be alone to wallow in my sorrow.'

'I could kill for a cigarette,' said Tom. 'Do you think I have time for a quick one round the back?'

The car drew up outside St Peter's medieval church. The chauffeur opened the passenger door and Antoinette waited for Tom to come round to help her out. Her legs felt weak and unsure. She could see her mother-in-law walking up the stony path towards the entrance of the church where two of George's cousins greeted her solemnly. *She* would never cry in public, Antoinette thought bitterly. Antoinette doubted whether she had ever cried in private. Margaret considered it very middle-class to show one's feelings and turned up her aristocratic nose at the generation of young people for whom it was normal to whine, shed tears and moan about their lot. She condemned them for their sense of entitlement and took great pleasure in telling her grandchildren that in her day people had had more dignity. Antoinette knew Margaret despised her for continuously sobbing, but she was unable to stop, even to satisfy her mother-in-law. But she dried her eyes before stepping out of the car, and took a deep breath; the Dowager Lady Frampton had no patience with public displays of emotion.

Antoinette walked up the path between her two sons and thought how proud George would be of his boys. Tom, who was so handsome and wild, with his father's thick blond hair and clear denim eyes, and David, who didn't look like his father at all, but was tall and magnetic and more than capable of bearing his title and running the estate. Up ahead, Joshua disappeared into the church with Roberta. Their middle son was clever and ambitious, making a name for himself in the City, as well as a great deal of money. George had respected his drive, even if he hadn't understood his unadventurous choice of career. George had been a man who loved natural, untamable landscapes; the concrete terrain of the Square Mile had turned his spirit to salt.

She swept her eyes over the flint walls of the church and remembered the many happy occasions they had enjoyed here. The boys' christenings, Joshua's marriage, his daughter Amber's christening only a year before – she hadn't expected to come for *this*. Not for at least another thirty years, anyway. George had been only fifty-eight.

She greeted George's cousins and, as she was the last to arrive, followed them into the church. Inside, the air was thick with body-heat and perfume. Candles flickered on the wide window ledges and lavish arrangements of spring flowers infused the church with the scent of lilies, freesias and narcissi. Reverend Morley greeted her with a sympathetic smile. He sandwiched her hand between his soft, doughy ones, and muttered words of consolation, although Antoinette didn't hear for the nerves buzzing in her ears like badly played violins. She blinked away tears and cast her mind back to his visit to the house just after she had heard the terrible news. If only she could rewind to before ...

It seemed that every moment of the last ten days had been

leading up to this point. There had been so much to do. David and Tom had flown out to Switzerland to bring back their father's body. Joshua and Roberta had taken care of the funeral arrangements. Antoinette had organized the flowers herself, not trusting her daughter-in-law to know the difference between a lilac and a lily, being a Londoner, and her sister, Rosamunde, had helped choose the hymns. Now the day was upon them Antoinette felt as if she were stepping into a different life; a life without George. She gripped Tom's arm and walked unsteadily up the aisle. She heard the congregation hush as she moved past and dared not catch anyone's eye for fear that their compassion would set her off again.

While Tom greeted their father's aunts, David settled his mother into the front pew. He glanced around the congregation. He recognized most of the faces – relations and friends dressed in black and looking uniformly sad. Then amidst all the grey, pallid faces, one bright, dewy one stood out like a ripe peach on a winter tree. She was staring straight at him, her astonishing grey eyes full of empathy. Transfixed, he gazed back. He took in the unruly cascade of blonde curls that tumbled over her shoulders, and the soft, creamy texture of her skin, and his heart stalled. It was as if a light had been switched on in the darkness of his soul. It didn't seem appropriate to smile, but David wanted to, very much. So he pulled a resigned smile and she did the same, silently imparting sympathy for his loss.

As David left the church again with his brothers and cousins to bear the coffin, he glanced back at the mystery blonde and wondered how she fitted into his father's life. Why had they never met before? He couldn't help the buoyant feeling that lifted him out of the quagmire of grief into a radiant and happy place. Was this what people called 'love at first sight'?

Of all the days it should happen, his father's funeral was the most inappropriate.

Phaedra Chancellor knew who David Frampton was, for she had done her research. The eldest of three sons, he was twenty-nine, unmarried and lived in a house on the Fairfield estate where he managed the farm. He had studied at Cirencester Agricultural College, for while his father had found the life of a country squire unexciting, David was as comfortable in the land as a potato.

Phaedra had only seen photographs of George's sons. Tom was without doubt the most handsome. He had inherited his father's blue eyes and the mischievous curl of his lips. But David was better-looking in the flesh than she had imagined. He was less polished than Tom, with scruffy brown hair, dark eyes and a large aquiline nose that did not photograph well. In fact, his features were irregular and quirky and yet, somehow, together they were attractive – and he had inherited his father's charisma, that intangible magnetism that drew the eye. Joshua, on the other hand, was more conventional-looking, with a face that was generically handsome and consequently easy to forget.

She looked down at the service sheet and her vision blurred at the sight of George's face imprinted on the cover. He had been more beautiful than all his sons put together. She blinked away painful memories and stared at the man she had grown to love. She could see Tom and Joshua reflected in his features, but she couldn't see David; he looked like his mother.

She sniffed and wiped her nose with a Kleenex. Julius Beecher, George's lawyer, who sat beside her, patted her knee. 'You OK?' he whispered. She nodded. 'Nervous?'

'Yes.'

'Don't worry, you'll be fine.'

'I'm not sure this is the right day to drop the bombshell, Julius,' she hissed, as music began to fill the church.

'I'm afraid there's no avoiding it. They're going to find out sooner or later and besides, you wanted to be here.'

'I know. You're right. I wanted to be here very much. But I wish I didn't have to meet his family.'

The choir walked slowly down the aisle singing Mozart's Lacrimosa. Their angelic voices echoed off the stone walls and reverberated into the vaulted ceiling as they rose in a rousing crescendo. The candle flames wavered at the sudden motion that stirred the air and an unexpected beam of sunlight shone in through the stained-glass windows and fell upon the coffin as it followed slowly behind.

Antoinette could barely contain her emotions; it was as if her heart would burst with grief. She glanced down the pew to where George's aunts Molly and Hester, one as thin as the other was fat, stood with the same icy poise as the Dowager Lady Frampton. Even Mozart was unable to penetrate their steely armour of self-control. Antoinette was grateful for her sister, Rosamunde, who howled with middle-class vigour in the pew behind.

Antoinette felt a sob catch in her chest. It was impossible to imagine that her vital, active husband was contained within those narrow oaken walls. That soon he'd be buried in the cold earth, all alone without anyone to comfort him, and that she'd never again feel the warmth of his skin and the tenderness of his touch. At that unbearable thought, the tears broke free. She glanced into the pew to see the flint-hard profile of her mother-in-law. But she no longer cared what the old woman thought of her. She had toed the line for George, but now he was gone, she'd cry her heart out if she wanted to.

When the service was over, the congregation stood while

the family filed out. Antoinette walked with Tom, leaning heavily on his arm, while David escorted his grandmother. He passed the pew where the mysterious blonde was dabbing her eyes, but he didn't allow his gaze to linger. He desperately hoped she'd be coming back for tea.

Outside, the fog had lifted and patches of blue sky shone with renewed optimism. The grass glistened in fleeting pools of sunlight and birds chirped once again in the treetops.

'Who's the blonde?' asked Tom, sidling up to David.

'What blonde?' David replied nonchalantly.

Tom chuckled. 'The really hot blonde you couldn't have failed to noticed about six pews behind. Very foxy. The day is suddenly looking up.'

'Come on, darling. Let's not linger outside the church,' said Antoinette, longing for the privacy of the car. The two brothers glanced behind them but the congregation was slow to come out.

Margaret sniffed her impatience. 'Take me to the car, David,' she commanded. 'I will greet people back at the house.' She strode forward and David was left no alternative but to escort her down the path. As she carefully lowered her large bottom onto the rear seat David's eyes strayed back to the church where the congregation was now spilling out onto the grass. He searched in vain for the white curls in the sea of black. 'Come, come, don't dawdle. Good, here are Joshua and Roberta. Tell them to hurry up. I need a drink.'

'Beautiful service,' said Roberta, climbing in beside Margaret.

'Lovely,' Margaret agreed. 'Though Reverend Morley does go on, doesn't he?'

'They all love the sound of their own voices,' said Joshua.

'That's why they're vicars,' Roberta added.

'I thought what he said about Dad being every man's friend was spot on,' Joshua continued, getting into the front seat. 'He loved people.'

Roberta nodded. 'Oh, he was terrifically genial.'

'We certainly gave him a good send-off, didn't we, Grandma?'

'Yes, he would have enjoyed that,' said Margaret quietly, turning her face to the window.

David returned to Fairfield Park with his mother and Tom. The house was restored to its former splendour now that the sun had burnt away the fog. Bertie and Wooster, the Great Danes, were waiting for them on the steps. It seemed that the sun had lifted their spirits, too, for they leaped down to the car, wagging their tails.

Harris opened the door and Mary, who cleaned for Lady Frampton, stood in the hall with her daughter, Jane, bearing trays of wine. The fire had warmed the place at last and sunlight tumbled in through the large latticed windows. The house felt very different from the one they had left a couple of hours before, as if it had accepted its master's passing and was ready to embrace the new order.

David and Tom stood by the drawing-room fire. David had helped himself to a whisky while Tom sipped a glass of Burgundy and smoked a sneaky cigarette – his mother and grandmother abhorred smoking inside, probably one of the only opinions they had in common. Little by little the room filled with guests and the air grew hot and stuffy. At first the atmosphere was heavy but after a glass or two of wine the conversations moved on from George and his untimely death, and they began to laugh again.

Both brothers looked out for the mysterious blonde. David had the advantage of being tall, so he could see over the herd, but, more dutiful than his brother, he found himself trapped in conversation first with Great Aunt Hester and then with Reverend Morley. Tom had thrown his cigarette butt into the fire and leaned against the mantelpiece, rudely looking over Great Aunt Molly's shoulder as she tried to ask him about the nightclub he ran in London.

At last the mystery guest drifted into view, like a swan among moorhens. Tom left Molly in mid conversation; David did his best to concentrate on Reverend Morley's long-winded story, while anxiously trying to extricate himself.

Phaedra suddenly felt very nervous. She took a big gulp of wine and stepped into the crowd. Julius cupped her elbow, determined not to lose her, and gently pushed her deeper into the throng. She swept her eyes about the room. What she could see of it was very beautiful. The ceilings were high, with grand mouldings and an impressive crystal chandelier that dominated the room and glittered like thousands of teardrops. Paintings hung on silk-lined walls in gilded frames, and expensive-looking objects clustered on tables. Tasselled shades glowed softly above Chinese porcelain lamps, and a magnificent display of purple orchids sat on the grand piano among family photographs in silver frames. It looked as if generations of Framptons had collected beautiful things from all over the world and laid them down regardless of colour or theme. The floor was a patchwork of rugs, cushions were heaped on sofas, pictures hung in tight collages, a library of books reached as high as the ceiling, and glass-topped cabinets containing collections of enamel pots and ivory combs gave the room a Victorian feel. Nothing matched and yet everything blended in harmony. George's life had been here, with his family, and she hadn't been a part of it. Just as she was about to cry again, Tom's grinning face appeared before her like the Cheshire Cat.

'Hello, I'm Tom,' he said, extending his hand. His eyes twinkled at her flirtatiously. 'I've been wondering who you are.'

She smiled, grateful for his friendliness. 'I'm Phaedra Chancellor,' she replied.

'American,' he said, raising an eyebrow in surprise.

'Canadian, actually.'

'Ah, Canadian.'

'Is that a bad thing?'

'No, I like Canadians, actually.'

She laughed at the languid way he dragged his vowels. 'That's lucky.'

'Hello, Tom,' interrupted Julius. The two men shook hands. 'Lovely service,' he said.

'Yes, it really was, very lovely,' Phaedra agreed. Tom didn't think he had ever seen such startlingly beautiful eyes. They were a clear grey-blue, almost turquoise, framed by thick lashes and set wide apart, giving her face a charming innocence.

'So how did you know my father?' he asked.

Phaedra glanced anxiously at Julius. 'Well . . .' she began.

Just as she was about to answer, David appeared, and her words caught in her throat. 'Ah, there you are, Tom,' said David, but his eyes fell on Phaedra and he smiled casually, as if he had chanced upon bumping into her. 'I'm David,' he said. His gaze lingered at last, drinking in her beauty as if it were ambrosia.

'Phaedra Chancellor,' she replied, putting out her hand. He took it, enjoying for an extended moment the warmth of her skin.

'Hello, David,' interrupted Julius, and reluctantly David let go of her hand. 'Where's Lady Frampton?'

'Oh, hello, Julius. I didn't see you there.'

'Well, I *am* here,' said Julius testily; he was very sensitive about being five foot seven and three-quarter inches short. 'I need to speak to her. You're tall, David. See if you can spot her from your lofty height.'

David looked down at Julius's shiny bald head and red, sweating brow, and thought how Dickensian he looked in his black suit and tie. 'She's not in here. Perhaps she's in the hall.'

'Then let's go and find her. I want her to meet Phaedra.'

Tom and David both wished Julius would go and find their mother on his own, but the portly lawyer put his arm around Phaedra's waist and escorted her out into the hall. Curious and furious, the two brothers followed after.

They finally found Antoinette in the library with her elder sister, Rosamunde. Wine glasses in hand, they were standing by George's desk, talking in low voices. 'Ah, you've found me hiding,' said Antoinette, composing herself. It was clear that she had been crying again.

'We came in here for a little peace. It's very busy out there,' Rosamunde explained in her deep, strident voice, hoping they'd take the hint and go away.

Antoinette saw the stranger in their midst and stiffened. 'Hello,' she said, dabbing her eyes. 'Have we met before?'

'No, we haven't,' Phaedra replied.

'Phaedra Chancellor,' David cut in, dazed by the force of her allure.

'Oh.' Antoinette smiled politely. 'And how . . .' She frowned, not wanting to be rude.

Julius seized the moment. 'My dear Lady Frampton, I wasn't sure that this was the right time to introduce you. But I know that Lord Frampton was very keen that you should meet. In fact, he was planning it when ... well ...' He cleared his throat. 'I know this is what he'd want.'

'I don't understand.' Antoinette looked bewildered. 'How is Miss Chancellor connected to my husband?'

Phaedra looked to Julius for guidance. He nodded discreetly. She took a breath, knowing instinctively that her answer would neither be expected, nor welcomed. But she thought of her beloved George and plunged in.

'I'm his daughter,' she said, fighting the impulse to flee. 'George was my father.'

**SIMON &
SCHUSTER**

Santa Montefiore
The Summer House

Antoinette's world has fallen apart: her husband, the man she has loved for as long as she can remember, has died tragically in an accident. He was her rock, the man she turned to for love and support, the man she knew better than she knew herself. Or at least so she thought . . .

For as she arrives at the familiar old stone church for George's funeral, she sees a woman she has never met before. And in that instant, the day she thought would close a door on the past becomes the day that everything she has ever known is turned upside down.

Phaedra loved George too, and she could not bear to stay away from his funeral. She only recently came to know him, but their bond was stronger than any she has ever felt before. As she sits before his wife, she knows that what she is about to reveal will change all their lives forever.

Sometimes it takes a tragedy to reveal the truth. But what if the truth is harder to bear than the tragedy . . . ?

**ISBN: HB 978-1-84737-927-6
EBOOK 978-1-84737-929-0**

FIND OUT MORE ABOUT
SANTA MONTEFIORE

Santa Montefiore is the author of eleven
sweeping novels. To find out more about her
and her writing, visit her website at

www.santamontefiore.co.uk

Sign up for Santa's newsletter and keep up
to date with all her news.

Or connect with her on Facebook at

http://www.facebook.com/santa.montefiore

**SIMON &
SCHUSTER**

This book and other **Simon & Schuster** titles are available
from your local bookshop or can be ordered direct
from the publisher.

978-1-84737-927-6	The Summer House	Santa Montefiore	£12.99
978-0-85720-494-3	The Shoemaker's Wife	Adriana Trigiani	£12.99
978-0-85720-341-0	The Captain's Daughter	Leah Fleming	£12.99
978-1-84983-288-5	A Gathering Storm	Rachel Hore	£7.99
978-1-84983-572-5	Left Neglected	Lisa Genova	£7.99
978-0-85720-124-9	IOU	Helen Warner	£12.99

Free post and packing within the UK
Overseas customers please add £2 per paperback
Telephone Simon & Schuster Cash Sales at Bookpost
on 01624 677237 with your credit or debit card number
or send a cheque payable to Simon & Schuster Cash Sales to
PO Box 29, Douglas Isle of Man, IM99 1BQ
Fax: 01624 670923
Email: bookshop@enterprise.net
www.bookpost.co.uk
Please allow 14 days for delivery. Prices and availability
are subject to change without notice.